D0912365

MISSING
ANGEL

BOOKS BY ROGER STELLJES

Agent Tori Hunter

Silenced Girls

The Winter Girls

The Hidden Girl

MISSING ANGEL

ROGER STELLJES

Published by Bookouture in 2022

An imprint of Storyfire Ltd.
Carmelite House
50 Victoria Embankment
London EC4Y 0DZ

www.bookouture.com

ISBN: 978-1-80314-500-6
eBook ISBN: 978-1-80314-499-3

I don't know that I have many Ukrainian fans, but the people of Ukraine have one in me. Your indomitable will to fight for your country, for your freedom, is awe-inspiring. Godspeed.

ONE

"AND SO IT BEGINS"

Isabella stuffed the blue folder and then the purple one into the back slot of her three-ring binder, then packed that into her multicolored backpack. She checked the front pocket for her cell phone, then zipped that closed as well. Her best friend, Paige, had the locker next to her and was going through the same routine check before jamming her iPad into her backpack and slinging it over her right shoulder.

"Ready?" Paige asked.

"Ready."

The two best friends walked side by side down the hallway, chit-chatting, blending in with the flow of kids heading to the middle school's front door at the end of a Wednesday afternoon.

"What time is hockey practice tonight?" Izzy asked. The two of them were on the same U12 girls' traveling team.

"Seven," Paige replied, gazing up at the sign on the wall. "We practice right after the boys' Pee Wee A team."

"That's right. I remember Carson saying they had practice before us tonight." As Izzy walked by Quinn Braddock, Peter Hayes, her older brother, Carson, and several other boys that were hanging out at their lockers, she slyly gave Quinn a shy smile, one that he returned. She wasn't quite sly enough, though.

"I *saw* that," Paige needled, leaning into her.

"What?"

"That little smile at Quinn," she accused, playfully throwing her left arm around her best friend and grinning. "That's not the first one either. I saw it at the hockey rink the other night. You think he's cute—"

"Paige—"

"Just admit it. You like him."

"Maybe ... a little."

"Have you given him your digits yet?"

"My digits?"

"You know, your cell phone number, so you can text." Paige's two older sisters always seemed to be texting boys. She talked about it incessantly.

"No," Izzy replied innocently, but then let a grin slip. "He is nice, though."

"And tall," Paige said as they walked outside and toward the bike rack. "He's a really good hockey player."

"He and Peter Hayes made Carson's hockey team this year. That's why Carson was talking to them. They all made the A traveling team a few nights ago." Carson was in seventh grade, a year older than Paige.

"How many first-year players made that team?" Paige asked. Sixth- and seventh-graders played at Pee Wee level.

"I think ... seven, but Quinn is the best first-year player."

"I bet you'll be going to some games then, won't you," Paige teased. "I'm sure just to watch your brother, of course."

"Ha ha," Izzy replied drolly as she leaned down and clicked in the numbers for the combination code for her lock. She popped it open, then coiled it up and wrapped it around the center frame post of her bike.

"Look at all the puddles. It rained a lot," Paige noted.

"The sky's still dark," Izzy warned, looking at the foreboding clouds hanging over the treeline. "It might rain more."

"We better get home quick, then. I'll see you tonight."

"See you."

Izzy climbed on her bike, crossed the street in front of the school and pedaled over to the bike path that ran along South Lakeshore Drive. Home was only a mile or so away from the middle school after the bike path cut through the county park preserve. She saw two other groups of classmates riding a few hundred yards ahead of her, also on their way home.

* * *

"Dude, are you going to go ask her?" Peter asked, glancing at their friends and teammates, Tommy and Zack, who were pedaling along beside them. Izzy Farner was riding ahead of them. All three of them, particularly Tommy, had been goading Quinn for a couple of days to do it.

"Yeah, man up," Tommy added.

"I bet I get her to come to the party, and Paige and all the rest of them from the girls' team," Quinn replied with some bravado.

"Let's see it."

"You think I won't?" he retorted.

"I think you won't."

"Wanna bet?"

Tommy always wanted to bet on stuff. His dad let him participate in his fantasy football league and football parlays, and he ran the boys' fantasy football league.

"Say five dollars?" Quinn proposed.

"I'll take that action," Tommy replied.

"Okay," Quinn said, and pedaled off ahead.

They all watched him go.

"I'd get ready to pay if I were you," Peter said to Tommy.

* * *

"Get ready," the voice in his earbud blurted.

He secured the stocking cap, stood up from the park bench and started running south, following the path.

"She'll be in the park in about a minute."

* * *

"Hey, Izzy! Wait up a sec."

Isabella looked back to see Quinn Braddock, and her heart skipped a little beat. He was super cute and now he was riding to catch up with *her*.

"Hi," he greeted when he reached her, easing back on his pedals, slowing to match her speed.

"Hi," she replied nervously. "I, um ... I saw you talking with Carson."

"Yeah, Pete and I made the team with him," Quinn replied as they started pedaling slowly, following the path along the curve of South Lakeshore Road, heading toward Isabella's neighborhood. Glancing behind, he saw that Peter, Zack and Tommy were a couple of hundred yards back.

"I like your bracelet," he said nervously. Tori had suggested that he first find something to compliment her on. "We girls like being complimented," she'd said.

"Oh, this." Izzy smiled, looking at the silver bracelet on her wrist. It had small angel and dove charms attached to it. "I got this from my Uncle George for my first communion."

"Well, it's really ... nice," he said.

"Thanks."

"Hey, um ... a week from Saturday, you know ... we have back-to-back games at the arena. Your game is at four, and ours is at five fifteen."

"Yeah, I noticed that, or my mom did last night."

"After our game, I'm having some people over to my house. I was wondering if you would, um ... like to come over too."

"Me?"

"She's got a friend riding with her now. A boy, probably from her class."

"It would be you, me, Peter, Tommy, Zack and some other guys from the team," Quinn said.

"Are you inviting any other girls?"

"Oh, yeah." He smiled. "Well, I was kind of hoping you could help with that. Would you ask the rest of the girls from our grade on your team? They're all invited. It's kind of a hockey party, your team and my team. But I wanted to make sure *you* could make it first."

"Uh ... yeah, sure," Izzy stuttered, her heart racing just a little bit. It was kind of a date. He'd just asked her over to his house, with a bunch of other people, of course, but he'd asked her. Now she had to get the other girls to come along. "We have a text string going."

"Great. My dad said we could all hang out in the basement. We'll have pizzas, maybe watch a movie, play some games, music, kind of ... hang out."

"It sounds super ... fun."

A jogger in a stocking cap and dressed in black was running in their direction on the left side of the path. They slid over to the right to make space for him.

"I suppose I'll have to ask my parents for permission."

"They know my dad well," Quinn said, smiling.

"I suppose they do. I forgot you played with Carson two years ago. I'm sure they'll say yes then."

"Cool. My house, seven till eleven, a week from Saturday." He took his phone out of his coat pocket. "If you give me your number, I can text my address."

"Oh ... okay," she said as they pulled to a stop. She guessed this qualified as giving him her digits, as Paige had said. "My number is ..." she started, and then her eyes got big. "Uh ..."

Quinn turned.

The jogger was sprinting at them, a black ski mask over his face.

"Quinn!"

"Izzy, look out!"

The man drove his right forearm into the side of Quinn's head, knocking him back into her, sending her sprawling, her backpack flying off.

"Ah ... ow ..." Quinn yelped as the man landed on top of him, crushing him between the bikes, his head slamming the ground.

I have to get away. I have to get away. Izzy scrambled up and took a step to run, but her left foot slipped, and she fell face first. The man jumped on top of her, the two of them rolling over before sliding into a muddy puddle. He picked her up and began to run with her toward the parking lot.

"*No! No!*" she screamed, kicking her legs, flailing her arms. "*No! Hel—*" The man slammed his right hand over her mouth.

Isabella wriggled against his grip, trying to break free, but his arms wrapped around her, squeezing her like a python.

* * *

Quinn was lying on his right side. Out of his left eye he caught a glimpse of Izzy kicking her legs. He tried to push the bike frames off, but he was all twisted up in them. The man threw her into the back of a panel cargo van and jumped inside after her. A second or two later, the van backed up, tires squealing, and raced out of the parking lot.

He tried to move, to take a breath, "Ah ... ah ..." Pain shot through his chest, like he was being stabbed with knives. "Ah ... oh ... ow, ow."

"Quinn!" Peter bellowed as he tossed his bike down and ran to his cousin. "Are you okay?"

"Help me," Quinn groaned weakly.

"Where's Izzy?"

"The van. The van—"

"She's in that van?" Peter turned to see it racing away in the distance.

"A man took her," Quinn replied. He wiped his face with his right hand. It came away covered in blood.

Peter turned to their friends. "Guys, chase the van. Chase the van. A man took Izzy!"

The two other boys raced away, pedaling furiously, giving chase.

"Quinn, you're bleeding," Peter yelped. "You're bleeding bad."

Quinn wiped away more blood and then reached for his phone, lying in the mud next to him. Squinting, he tapped at the screen.

"Hey, bud—"

"Dad! Dad!"

* * *

The yardage scope he playfully twirled in his right hand had told him he was 265 yards away from the cargo van. Parked along the street, his passenger window down, he had an unobstructed view northeast into the park preserve.

It had gone down just as anticipated.

The blue cargo van had just disappeared from his view, although the two brave boys were still fruitlessly giving chase.

He powered up the passenger window and pulled away from the curb, completing a U-turn and motoring away to the south. He hit the preset number on the phone. There were two rings before he answered.

"Hello."

"He's got her."

"And so it begins."

TWO

"YOU'RE NOT GETTING RID OF ME"

"It's your house too now," Braddock had said a month ago.

Those words resonated in her head as Tori peered out the double windows looking out to the long deck that fronted the house and the roiling waters of Northern Pine Lake beyond. Then she turned around to survey her interior design work.

When she sold her condo in New York City and moved back to Manchester Bay, the reality was she didn't have much to move. As nice and spacious as her condo was, she'd never spent the time making it into a home. She owned just a few pieces of decent furniture—a couch, an antique writer's desk and credenza, a deluxe wine refrigerator, and a queen-sized bed—along with three closets full of designer clothes, a collection of banker boxes she hadn't opened in twenty years and a bike she used for triathlons. That was the sum total of her possessions. It made her move into Braddock's house all the easier. They had largely been spared any uncomfortable discussions about whose furniture to keep and whose to discard. There was room for almost all of it, and to the degree she had taste in those sorts of things, it wasn't too dissimilar from Braddock's.

After a few weeks of not having her house in town to go to any longer, the one thing she realized she needed was a space that was her own that she could retreat to, but it didn't seem to her there was such a room available. Braddock had an office upstairs, but he used it a fair amount, and while he was more than willing to share it, she wanted a space that was hers. She had one idea she broached nervously.

"Can I take the guest room and make it into an office?"

"Of course. Do it," Braddock had said.

"But what if we have guests."

"Your couch is a pullout sofa, isn't it?"

"Yes."

"We'll take the spare bed out, put your couch in there, and boom, guest room on the odd chance we ever need one."

She didn't much like the color of the walls, a dated beige. "Can I ... paint it?"

Braddock laughed, "What part of 'it's your house too' don't you understand?"

"Well, I just thought—"

"I mean, you're not going to paint it pink or black or something crazy, are you?"

"No."

"Then how can I help?"

Last weekend they'd moved out the old guest bed and night-stands. Tori spent a day painting the room a light gray. Braddock removed all the old trim moldings and replaced them with new white trim that contrasted nicely with the dark wood floors he'd put in on the main level of the house two years prior. In came her couch, desk, and credenza. She'd purchased a tall, weathered bookcase at a local antique store and moved that in too. Today she'd added the final touch, an area rug.

It was perfect. A little piece of the house that was hers.

She sat in her desk chair, looking about the room, feeling ...

content. It was not a feeling she'd often had, and as she turned to look out the window and down to the lake again, she thought of that warm summer day at the end of the dock and how close she had come to possibly losing it. It was the day she and Braddock had had "the talk".

How serious was this thing between them going to be? He wanted a declarative answer.

"We've reached a point where you have to make a decision, Tori," he had said. "And it's a big one. It's a big one for you, for me and for Quinn."

"Will, please ..."

"I need to know, Tori. Are you really, truly all in?"

"Will ..."

"Before you and I go any further, I have to know."

"And if I'm not?"

He paused for a moment. "Then ... we gave it our best shot."

He'd put the question to her.

She remembered standing up out of the chair and walking to the edge of the dock, tears dripping down her checks.

The question of what happened next had been coming for some time. She'd hoped it would be one they would let slowly play out and get comfortable with. However, her own actions had forced Braddock to demand an answer here and now.

Her mind whirred in that moment, processing what he'd just put to her and what she had already been thinking about since she'd run to New York City and then returned. Was she in this for the long haul? She knew she wanted to be. But that wasn't really the question he was asking.

Could she be in it for the long haul and in Manchester Bay?

That was his question.

It was a year that had largely flown by, falling truly in love with Braddock and reconnecting with her friends. There had been good times and experiences, many of them, that had made her start to feel comfortable. Like it could be home once again. But those few weeks last summer had also showed her that all the things that had driven her away from Manchester Bay twenty years ago remained, and they weren't ever going away. While she had worked to make a certain healthy peace with the memories of her sister and father and their deaths, the fact remained that those events and reminders of them would be ever present; they were around every corner.

Can you handle that? Can you really, truly handle that?

"Tori?" he asked quietly.

"Just let me have a minute," she remembered saying in a hoarse whisper.

She recalled closing her eyes, taking a long breath, pulling air in deep through her nose, trying to calm her mind, control her trembling body and think clearly. She had to get it right.

What helped soothe her was the almost rhythmic sound of the waves as they lapped lightly against the dock and then softly on the sandy beach behind her. In the distance she could hear the warm, familiar rumble of a boat as it cruised across the lake. It was ... relaxing and beautiful and she got to wake up to it every day.

And then she asked herself: why did you go through all the therapy?

She'd needed to do it, she'd needed to get better for her own mental health. And she *was* better, all her New York friends told her so; they could see it, it was evident. But what had truly compelled her to finally do what had long needed to be done was sitting right behind her. And he was right to worry about Quinn. It was one of the things she so admired about him, how good a father he was to his son. She had wondered how she would fit into their lives. Would there be room for her? Would she be someone Quinn would like and accept and not be jealous of because she was drawing his father's attention, attention that would have otherwise been his? She had found herself caring for him, coming to love him like she did his father.

Then she'd asked herself another question: could you handle it if you walked away?

Sure, there could be some pain in staying, but how much more would there be if she left?

If she walked away, there would be no coming back. She couldn't leave for New York again like she had last summer when Braddock had asked her to stay the first time, only to then realize she had made a mistake. You only got that kind of a mulligan once. And as great as New York City was, as much as she missed it, it lacked that one thing that as she stood on the dock she didn't think she could do without.

"Tori?"

She opened her eyes and took a breath. "I'm not going anywhere."

"You're not?"

She turned to him. "I'm here and I'm staying."

"You're sure?"

"I've fought for this," she said firmly. "We've fought for this and I'm grateful for every day I've had it."

"Then why run off to New York?" Braddock asked.

"I ... panicked."

"Panicked? You?" He shook his head. "Tori Hunter doesn't panic."

"Yes, she does, just like anyone else on occasion," she said, shaking her head. "It was a big fight. We hadn't had one of those really. I was mad and I ... ran. And you're right, I had all those thoughts in New York City. I could get my job back in the city, get away from all the ... stuff that's here."

"I get it."

"So did Tracy. She saw me contemplating all that and made me face up to it. Going back there, that would have been the easy way out, and I've ... just never been someone who takes the easy way."

"That is for sure."

"I'll take that as a compliment."

"It was intended as one."

Tori smiled at that. "I'll admit, there are times I wish I'd met you in New York," she said, looking up to the sky, closing her eyes. "That we were there and not here. I miss it. When I was there, strolling around, I thought about us walking those streets together. Going to restaurants, sitting in the park, having a little condo overlooking the river. The culture, the vibe, the energy of it all. Always something new to experience."

"There is nothing I can do about that."

"I know," she replied, looking down, picking at a small divot in the wood of the dock with the edge of her sandal. She looked up and smiled. "But I don't wish that all the time or even most of the time, just ... every so often. You know, like it's a little bit of a dream. Dreaming is okay, isn't it."

"Yes."

She stepped over to him and sat down in his lap, slipping her left arm around his neck. "I'll promise you this. If you and I don't make it, it won't be because I couldn't handle being here. It'll be because of any of the number of other neuroses I suffer from."

Braddock laughed. "You're not neurotic."

"I know, I'm complicated. No, wait, you said I was ... extraordinary. Let's go with that. That sounds *way* better."

"You are," he said, and pulled her close, letting her rest her head on his shoulder. "It has to be hard at times, though, Tori, to be here. I marvel at your ability to do it."

"I can handle it," she said quietly.

"But ..."

"I can," she said, sitting back and lovingly tapping him on the nose with her finger. "Maybe this all tells me that I have some more work to do, but I'll do it. Whatever it takes. You're not getting rid of me."

Tori thought of "the talk" as she set a photo of her and Braddock in Barbados on the left corner of her credenza. Next to it she had a photo of her and Quinn after one of his hockey games last winter, the two of them arm in arm, and then a large one of the three of them sitting on the back bench seat of the boat, taken about a week after the talk. That was her life now, her and Braddock and Quinn. She didn't necessarily think of the three of them as a family, at least yet, but she loved them both.

The next question was, what about those who were her family?

The banker box sat on the corner of the desk. It was a box she hadn't looked inside of in a very long time. She'd done it once years ago in New York City, when she'd first moved into her condo and had some fleeting thoughts on decorating. She'd looked through the contents, contemplated pulling a few photos out for the built-in shelves, and then decided against it. She just couldn't bring herself to do it.

Lifting the cardboard top off the box now, she peered inside at the mishmash of framed family photos. The first one was of her mother sitting on a floral couch in the living room, holding her one-year-old identical twin daughters in each of her arms. Tori smiled, lightly running her fingers over the photo, over her mother's face. She'd died when the girls were six, at just an age where Tori's memories of her were hazy at best. Jessie and Tori favored their mother, the petite figure, the auburn hair, soft green eyes, the slightest of overbites. She set the photo on the desk.

There was a good one of her mother and father, Big Jim, the sheriff, a year before she'd passed away, he in a sharp suit, she in a summer dress, side by side at a wedding, smiling, happy, joyous. There was another of the four of them just months before their mother really started showing the signs of the cancer, Jessie and Tori in matching dresses, Jessie smiling, Tori ever serious even at six, just kind of smiling.

Under those photos was a pile of pictures of her with Jessie. In the past, those had always been the most difficult ones to look at. One in particular, taken after a soccer game a week before Jessie disappeared, had always been like a dagger. The few times she had looked at it over the years always took her back to the night of Jessie's disappearance. A feeling of being stabbed and then the knife being continuously and mercilessly twisted.

She took all four photos and arranged them on the credenza, then sat down in her desk chair and looked at them. She felt a twinge of that familiar pain, a little knot in the stomach, but it wasn't the same. That ache would always be there, but now it was more one of memories of the good times tinged with wistfulness at what might have been. As she'd learned in the last year, while you never got over it, you could learn to live with it, and displaying these photos was part of that. She had to keep going and live, because that was what they all would have wanted. She hoped they would be proud of her and happy that she was living a full life again.

As she stood up, her phone buzzed. It was Braddock, and she smiled. "Hey, you—"

"Get to the park preserve. Go now. Now! There's been an abduction."

"What? What happened?"

"Quinn was riding home from school with—"

"Not Quinn! Oh my God, not Quinn!"

"No, no, it's not Quinn, it's his friend, Isabella."

"Isabella? Isabella Farner? The girl he was going to ask to his party?"

"Yes. Quinn was there when it happened, and he's hurt. It happened in the park preserve by the parking lot. Get there *now*! I'm on my way back from Holmestrand."

"Quinn's hurt? How bad? Just tell me he's okay."

"He called me. He says he's bleeding but safe. Peter and a couple of other friends are with him. Police are on the way."

"But Isabella?"

"Taken by some guy who got into a van of some kind," Braddock answered, and she could hear his siren in the background. "That's all I know. Just get there."

"I'm going, right now."

Tori took the steps to the basement two at a time. She rushed to the gun safe in the storage room, extracted her Glock 19M and jammed in a fresh magazine, then grabbed her Kevlar vest. Back upstairs, she made sure she had her sheriff's department identification and was out the door in thirty seconds and in her silver Audi Q5. She plugged in her portable police light and siren and peeled out of the driveway. The county park preserve was less than two miles away.

The more things change, the more they stay the same, she thought as she raced down the road with flashing lights and siren.

Up until fourteen months ago, this was her regular everyday life. An FBI special agent, based in New York City, she was the one the Bureau called on missing children's cases, particularly those with some profile. At a moment's notice, she and her team could be on a chopper or an airplane, such was the urgency of her cases back then. She thrived professionally and more than a little part of her loved the ego boost from being something of a "very special" special agent of the FBI. For her fourteen years in the Bureau, finding abducted children and reuniting them with their families was her sole focus, an obsession really, until she met Braddock, solved her own sister's disappearance, and moved back to Manchester Bay, where she was now a part-time investigative consultant for Shepard County. She'd left the life in the FBI behind, but her FBI life still managed to find her on occasion.

She turned left and raced through a residential neighborhood before coming into the park preserve and turning hard right. Ahead she saw a Manchester Bay Police patrol car coming to a stop in the parking lot. She pulled into the lot behind it and got her first distant look at Quinn. He was sitting on the ground with his cousin, Peter, his face caked in streaks of blood. Other boys were standing guard around them.

Quinn saw her and a look of relief flashed across his face.

Tori felt anything but relieved as she ran over to him and knelt next to the police officer, who had a first aid kit with him. She took Quinn's face in her hands and quickly checked him over, lifting his floppy mop of hair and checking his scalp. "Are you hurt?" she asked in a voice far calmer and more clinical than she felt.

"I'm bleeding a lot."

"Yeah, buddy, you have a cut on the top of your forehead here. They tend to gush." It was a deep gash up into his hairline that would require stitches. His breathing seemed labored. "What else hurts?"

"My ..." he grimaced when he took a breath, "chest."

"Yeah, let's see." She gently pulled up his hoodie and T-shirt. When she touched the right side of his ribs, he buckled in pain.

"Can you breathe?"

He nodded. "But if I take a big breath, it ... hurts."

"How did you hurt your ribs?"

"I got pushed into Izzy and then landed on her bike and my bike landed on me."

"You got sandwiched," Tori said as she lightly ran her fingers along the side of his rib cage. She didn't feel anything protruding but saw some early signs of his skin discoloring. His ribs were probably bruised or maybe cracked, but she was hopeful that was it and he wasn't bleeding internally. There weren't any other obvious injuries to his midsection. "Does your head hurt?"

"A little."

"Look at me. Eyes open." His pupils were dilated, a sign of a possible concussion. Tori glanced to the officer, who nodded slightly, noticing the same thing. Quinn was battered but in one piece.

She stood up and walked over to his black bike, which was all twisted up with a cherry-red girl's bike. "How long ago did this happen?"

"I don't know."

"Five minutes, ten, fifteen maybe?" she calmly prodded.

"A little more than ten, I think," Peter offered. "We called Uncle Will right away."

"Tell me what happened."

"This man took Izzy in a van," Quinn replied, suddenly frantic. "He ... he was ... He took Izzy."

"Quinn," Tori said evenly, coming back to him and crouching like a catcher. "Slow down and tell me what you remember."

"I was riding on the path with her," Quinn said, grimacing. His head maybe hurt more than he was letting on. "We saw this man jogging toward us, so we moved to the right side of the path. I was talking to her and she was looking at me, I had just asked her to the party, and then ..." His voice trailed off.

"What, buddy?"

"She got distracted. I turned, and that jogger we had seen had a mask over his face. Before I could move, he tackled me into Izzy and knocked us both down. Next thing I know, he's carrying her over to the parking lot, throws her into the back of a van and takes off."

Tori heard squealing tires. Braddock had just pulled to a stop. He rushed over and took a knee next to her.

"How are we doing?"

"He's banged up but okay," Tori said, and then to Quinn, "Describe the man who took her."

"He was ... dressed in black."

"How about height? Weight? Anything like that?"

"I ... couldn't tell."

"Was he as tall as your dad?"

"No, I don't think so," Quinn replied, closing his eyes. "He wasn't a big guy, but ... not small either."

"Skinny? Chubby? Anything like that?"

Quinn shook his head slowly. "I just remember he was in all black."

"Athletic clothes?"

He took a moment. "Yeah, I think so. It looked like running stuff like you and Dad wear."

"When he was jogging, did he look normal doing it?"

He looked at her quizzically. "Normal?"

"Your dad and I were athletes. When he and I run, we look athletic. Did the man you saw seem like that? Like it was normal for him to be running?"

"Yes," Quinn said with a nod. "He looked ... like a jogger."

"How about skin color? White? Black? Hispanic?"

"White, I think. I didn't look closely at him." Quinn sounded upset, clearly feeling he'd missed something. "I'm sorry."

"Hey, hey." Tori patted his arm. "It's okay, buddy. Just do your best. How about hair color?"

"I don't ... He didn't have a beard, but ..."

"He had stubble?" Braddock offered.

Quinn nodded.

"Can you describe the van? It was a van, right? That's what you told me when you called."

"It was ... blue, I think," Quinn answered.

"Peter? Did you see it?"

"Yes, Uncle Will. Me, Tommy and Zack all saw it. It was definitely blue."

"Dark blue? Light blue?"

"Kind of a ... dirty blue," Peter said.

"Dusty blue," Zack added.

"Maybe matte," Tommy chipped in. "It wasn't shiny."

"Was it a minivan?"

"More like a repair van," Peter said. "It was boxy and had two square windows on the back doors. I saw that."

"So it was a cargo van, a panel type?"

They all nodded.

"Any markings on it?"

"No, sir," they replied in unison.

"Have any of you ever seen it before? Here in the park? Near school? Anywhere else in town?"

They all shook their heads.

"Did you boys see anything else?" Tori asked. "Was there anyone else in the van or was it just the one man."

"I don't know," Quinn said. "I only saw the one man."

"Pete?"

"I only really saw the van driving away and Quinn lying on the ground. I got off my bike to help him. Tommy and Zack chased after the van?"

"Where did it go, boys?" Braddock asked.

"It drove out of the parking lot and took the road into the neighborhood," Tommy explained, pointing northwest. "We got to the corner up there where it turns left. We could see it in the distance, and it went through the neighborhood and turned right."

"Onto County Road 44, do you think?"

"Yes, sir," Tommy said, and looked to Zack. "You think?"

"Yeah, that's where it went," Zack said. "That's when we turned and came back to Quinn."

"Good job, boys," Braddock commended. "That helps."

"And Izzy, what was she wearing?" Tori asked.

"Uh ..." Quinn stuttered. "She had a ... pink raincoat on."

"What else?"

"I don't ..."

"She had on blue jeans and a gray long-sleeved shirt and pink canvas tennis shoes," Pete offered, helping his cousin. "I saw her a few times at school today."

"And a bracelet," Quinn said. "She had a silver bracelet with angels and doves on it. She showed it to me."

Braddock's detectives, Steak and Eggleston, arrived on scene. To Steak, Braddock said, "Get an amber alert out for Isabella Farner, age eleven or twelve, I'm not sure which. She's a sixth-grader. She has black hair to her shoulders." He described what she was wearing.

"And braces, Uncle Will," Pete said. "She has braces."

"Braces, got it," Steak said.

"She was abducted by a white male, average size, dressed in all black, in a blue cargo van. Last seen going north on County Road 44 out of Manchester Bay."

Steak leaned in. "I'm glad it wasn't Quinn, man. God, I'm just glad it wasn't Quinn."

"You and me both, pal," Braddock said, and turned to Eggleston. "Take Detective Reese and get over to the Farners'. Word might have already spread, given all the kids hanging around with phones. The parents' names are Sam and Luciana. I know them. Tell them what happened and wait by the phone with them. I'll be over there as soon as I can."

His detectives briefed, he returned to Tori. "Tell me about his injuries."

"He has a cut that requires stitches." She held up Quinn's hair for him to see. "His ribs hurt a little." Then she leaned closer and whispered, "And he might have a concussion. Look at his pupils."

While he checked his son's eyes, Braddock asked, "Peter? Are *you* okay?"

"I'm fine, Uncle Will," replied a shaken Peter, his arm around Quinn's shoulders. "Quinn's the one hurt."

"I'm ... fine, Dad," Quinn said as he took a careful breath. He was a tough kid, but he was hurting.

An ambulance arrived. Braddock stood up while Tori gave the paramedics a quick rundown on what she'd observed before letting them take over.

"He'll be okay," she said as they stepped away.

"Yeah, thank God. Okay, thoughts?" Braddock switched back to cop mode. "What do you think this was, abduction or kidnapping?"

"It's so brazen, doing it here, that at first it has a whiff of just absolute crazy to it. Broad daylight in a park? But that being said ... I don't know why, but for some reason this feels more like kidnapping," Tori replied, biting her bottom lip.

"Your gut?"

"That and Quinn said the man was dressed as a jogger, didn't have a mask on and then did. She was taken here in the park, where there would almost certainly be witnesses. But at the same, he attacks right as they're at the van he has waiting.

Lucky timing or planning? The mask, the van, the specific area of attack, it looks crazy, really crazy, but ..."

"Maybe it isn't."

"Yeah. And ..." She looked around, pursing her lips. "Hmpf."

"What else?" he asked.

"Something ... something I'm seeing here that isn't registering with me yet. It flitted into my brain for a nanosecond. Now it's gone."

Braddock nodded and then walked over to check with the paramedics. They had moved Quinn to a gurney up inside the ambulance and a paramedic was flashing a small light in his eyes.

Tori peered at the bicycles lying on the ground, how they were collapsed onto one another. The glint of something caught her eye and she crouched down, using the end of her pen to lever it out of the mud. It was a small silver angel, the little loop ripped just enough for it to have fallen off Isabella's bracelet.

She looked back at the parking lot where Quinn had said the van was parked. She let her eyes follow the bike path from the middle school, the second floor of which was just visible to the southwest, then pivoted slowly to her right, turning with the path as it passed the parking lot and then headed north, where it straightened for perhaps a hundred yards before curving gradually left and disappearing into a residential neighborhood.

The county park reserve was popular with residents out looking to run, take walks or ride their bikes along the wide path. Tori had run through several times over the summer. Today there weren't many people because of the rain and the cool, damp conditions. Nevertheless, someone jogging through the park in running apparel wouldn't have garnered a second look. It would have been a completely normal sight. Other than the wide paved path, this section of the park was filled with large sections of tall native grasses and groves of trees with canopies of leaves that were approaching their peak fall hues.

She closed her eyes and processed what Quinn had told her. They were riding north along the path, the two of them talking to one another, Quinn inviting Isabella to the party. It was so sweet when he'd asked her for advice. It was just yesterday that she'd coached him on what to say. A precious little moment now ruined.

The question was why.

Braddock came back.

"How's he doing?" Tori asked.

"Vitals are fine. They're going to transport him in a few minutes to the emergency room to get his ribs and head checked out." He expelled a big sigh, but she could tell he was distracted. "What do you think?"

"Right now, I'm trying to visualize how this all went down and ..." Her eyes lit up and she started walking back toward the ambulance, the paramedic getting ready to shut the back door. "Hold on a second," she called. The paramedic held the door and Tori and Braddock climbed up inside. "Quinn, this is the path you ride home from school every day, right?"

"Yes."

"And do other kids from school ride this path each day?"

"Yes." Quinn nodded.

"How about Isabella?" Braddock said. "Did she ride it every day?"

"I don't know about every day, but I think often. She's ridden with Peter and me a few times. That's why I figured I'd ..."

"Ask her on the way home from school?" Tori finished.

"Yes."

She patted him on the hand and Braddock settled him back

down on the gurney. "You go now. We'll see you later, okay? Uncle Drew is following you to the hospital."

"Dad, are you going to find Izzy?"

"We'll do our best."

Quinn nodded and closed his eyes.

They watched as the ambulance pulled away. "He's going to be okay," Tori murmured. "Isabella, on the other hand ..." Her voice trailed off as she thought of the terror the girl would be going through, the abject fear of what was to come. "If it is a ... predator, a sex offender, we don't have much time before ..." She sighed. "We don't have much time."

She turned and walked back toward the bikes. A uniformed officer was running crime-scene tape in a wide perimeter around them.

"Quinn and Isabella are riding north along the path, talking about a party, oblivious to their surroundings," she mused. "Peter and friends are following behind, but at a distance. They're waiting for Quinn to finish asking her to the party."

"But there are other kids riding along here as well," Braddock said. "You were right earlier: pretty audacious to take someone on this path."

"Maybe our abductor times it so he can grab someone right as they get to his van."

"He just wants to abduct a kid."

"A girl," Tori said. "He attacked Quinn and Izzy and took her, so I'd say he wanted a girl. The question is whether it was just any girl, or ..."

"This specific girl."

"Right." She peered around, hands on hips. "Ballsy, doing it this way. That tells us something."

"Yeah, that he's crazy."

"Or is it a calculated risk?" she said continuing to take in the surroundings—the path, parking lot, and road. "He had the mask at the ready. Quinn said they saw him without it and then he had it on. He attacked them right at his van. I'm betting he left the door open just a crack so all he had to do was shove it open. He made sure that the only witness was Quinn. I know Peter and the other boys saw the van from a distance, but they didn't see anything else." She paused. "Is this scene, this abduction scenario ringing any bells with you at all?"

"I was going to ask you the same thing. I sure haven't seen anything like it in Manchester Bay. What are you thinking?"

"That it has a whiff of ..."

"What?"

"Experience of some kind. It's dicey to do it here. Nevertheless, this guy grabs Isabella and is out of here in like twenty seconds, and the only witnesses, at least so far, are four young boys, three of whom saw it all from a couple of hundred yards away. The only person who could identify him—Quinn, blood flowing down his face—describes him as a white male, average height with stubble, wearing black running attire and driving a blue panel van. That doesn't give us much to go on. You see crazy, and he may well be, but he was a crazy man with a plan."

Tori looked at the gathering crowd of law enforcement officers. "Nolan! Steak!"

Nolan, a new young detective in the department, jogged over, her blond ponytail swinging, Steak right behind her.

"Yeah, Tori?"

"Nolan, go back to investigations," Tori said. "We're looking for any similar abductions to this one." She gave the detective the specific items to search. "Van or truck, daylight abduction, young girl or girls. You follow?"

Nolan nodded, jotting down quick notes. "I assume we're casting a wide net."

"Five-state area for starters."

"What else?" Steak asked. "The amber alert is out there.

Any blue or remotely blue panel vans will be pulled over. We got the net out quick. He won't get that far in that van."

"Stopping vans fitting the description isn't enough. If an officer sees one in a driveway somewhere, we need to check it. If we see one in a parking lot, we inspect it. That needs to be added to what we're doing."

Steak issued orders into the radio.

Tori looked back to Nolan. "In addition to your search for similar crimes, let's run a list of blue panel van owners in the area. We don't know make and model yet, so include just about anything."

"Check."

"Go, now," Tori said, and Nolan scurried away.

Steak had finished radioing. "If there is a van visible, it will be checked," he said.

"Okay, next. The boys saw the van drive into and through that residential neighborhood," Braddock said.

"Door to door?"

"Right now. We have deputies and Manchester PD here. Let's get into the neighborhood and see if anyone saw anything between three thirty and four p.m."

"On it," Steak said, and waved over a group of officers on scene. "Hey, here's what we need to do ..."

Tori took one last look at the area. She was seeing something again. What, she couldn't quite figure yet. Something that mattered. It would come to her.

"What's next for us?" Braddock said.

"The Farners."

THREE

"THE LITTLEST THINGS OFTEN END UP BEING THE BIGGEST THINGS"

Braddock had Tori drive his Tahoe, which was odd. He always drove but insisted she leave hers behind. Thirty seconds after she pulled away, she glanced to her right and saw his hands shaking. He'd been holding it together at the park preserve, but now that he was out of view of everyone else, it was all coming out.

"Will?"

"It could have been Quinn," he said, clasping his hands then rubbing them together frantically. "If something had happened to him ..." He looked over to her, an expression of panicked horror on his face, "I'm sorry. Tori, God, I'm sorry. I didn't even think of ... Jessie. I didn't even think of what you've been through ..."

"It's okay. I know what you're feeling."

"I'm ... I'm ... Damn, I'm a mess here."

Tori pulled to the side of the road. Braddock was breathing hard, grabbing at his chest, hyperventilating. She'd never seen him so shaken.

"If I'd lost him ..."

"Look at me," she said, grabbing his thigh firmly. "*Look. At. Me!*" She locked her eyes on his.

Braddock nodded.

"Just take a minute and breathe, slowly. Do it with me."

He did as she asked, and after a few quiet minutes, he calmed, finally exhaling a long breath and wiping the sweat off his brow. "Oh, man."

"Hey, I breathed a huge sigh of relief too when I pulled up and saw him. He is going to be fine. And he's going to be there tonight when we get home."

"It's just ..."

"Hey, I know. *I know*. We got lucky," Tori said.

"Yeah," Braddock replied, breathing more normally, his wits back about him. "We got lucky, but the Farners didn't."

"Isabella isn't gone, not yet, not by a long shot. We're just getting started," Tori said determinedly, turning to drive. "Do you know the family?"

"I know Sam and Luciana a bit," a calmer Braddock answered. "Quinn played on a hockey team with their son, Carson, two years ago, and they just made the same team this year. They always seemed like nice people. They hosted a parent party."

"So that's how you know the way."

"Take the next right."

As Tori took the turn, she saw the police lights up ahead and pulled in in front of the house, a large modern two-story with the waters of Northern Pine Lake visible through a grove of trees out the back. "Are they on the lake?"

"I think this neighborhood has lake access. That big marina we cruise by from time to time is through those trees. I think they have a boat slip down there," he said.

She reached for the door handle to get out.

"Hold on one second," Braddock said. "I'm going to have you take lead on this investigation."

"But—"

"One, you're more qualified on this kind of case. Two, Quinn is a witness. And I'm messed up. Your mind is clearer, so you're lead."

"Then let's go."

As they walked up the front drive, Tori took in the house, the finely manicured lawn and bushes, the Land Rover parked out front. She could see an iron fence along the side of the house, the type you often saw surrounding a swimming pool. "What do the Farners do?"

"She's a pediatrician. He operates a financial planning and investment business in town."

"They have money, then."

"Some, I suspect. The house, as you'll see, is nice inside. They're not living check to check, that's for sure."

As Tori reached the front step, Detective Eggleston opened the door and stepped out.

"What do you know?" Braddock asked.

"I got here before the parents did, but they were hearing things on their way home from work. Their son texted them that he'd heard about it from kids who got to the scene. They tried calling her cell phone, but I told them it was found, along with her backpack, at the scene."

"Have they gotten any sort of a call?"

"No."

"Both parents are inside?"

"Yes, and Mrs. Farner's brother is here as well."

"George Santo?" Braddock said.

"Yes. He got here just a couple of minutes ago."

"And the brother is?" Tori asked.

"Local business guy," Braddock explained. "Owns a

Mexican restaurant here and one up in Crosslake, and I think has some real-estate interests."

"How are they?" Tori asked Eggleston.

"What you'd expect. Panicked, anxious, frantic. Demanding to know what we're doing," Eggs answered. "What *are* we doing?"

"Working on it," Tori said, as Braddock stepped ahead and through the front door.

"Will!" A slight woman with a black bob haircut rushed toward him. "Will, where is Izzy? *Where is she?*"

"I'm so sorry, Luciana," Braddock answered, taking her small hands in his big paws. "We don't know ... yet." Braddock shook hands with Sam Farner and then the taller man with jet black hair, George Santo.

"Will, what happened?" Luciana asked.

"Luciana, this is Tori Hunter. I'm going to let her explain," Braddock said. He gave the couple a quick rundown of her background.

"Fine." Sam Farner said brusquely. "Former Special Agent Hunter is in charge. Tell me, what the hell has happened to our daughter?"

"She was abducted in the park preserve by a man dressed in black running gear who drove her away in a blue cargo van," Tori said directly. "An amber alert has been issued. We're stopping, checking, searching any van remotely matching the description."

"And Quinn? He's alright?" Luciana asked worriedly.

"A little banged up, but okay," Braddock said as a watery-eyed Carson came around the corner. "Hey there, Carson," he greeted quietly.

"Hi, Mr. Braddock."

"Let's all sit down." Tori guided everyone through the house to the dining area. As she walked along, she took in the house's furnishings, noting the quality and the attention to detail. It looked as if each room had been designed and assembled by an interior decorator. Out the bank of windows along the back of the house, she saw the expansive pool and patio area. The place evidenced an air of success, of money.

Luciana slid an envelope across. "Those are photos of Izzy. You can use them to help get word out."

"Thank you," Tori said. "These will help."

Sam Farner cut right to the chase. "Was my daughter kidnapped for money?"

Tori took a moment. "That is one possibility." She glanced around. "You live very well. You're a pediatrician as I understand it," she said to Luciana. "And you own your own investment business, right?" she said to Sam.

"Yes."

"I'm ruling nothing out at this point. Abducting your daughter in that park, a public place, in daylight, is risky, crazy even."

"You're saying a nutjob, a predator?"

"Like I said, it looks crazy, but at the same time, something about the abduction of your daughter does not feel ... random. You look to have a certain amount of wealth, so it is at least possible that this is financially based. The man was in that park, and I think with a plan. Now does that mean Isabella was his specific target?" Tori asked rhetorically. "Not necessarily. However, she was riding with Quinn—"

"Why was she riding with him?" George Santo asked.

"Quinn was asking her to a hockey party at his house," Carson blurted. "Peter told me he was going to ask her."

"Right," Tori confirmed. "That's how we know she was taken in a blue van. Quinn saw that, as did Peter and two other boys who were riding a couple of hundred yards behind them. But my point in mentioning Quinn is that this man took Isabella despite the fact that there was someone there who could have impeded his ability to do so. Now, it could be that he came there to take a girl and she was the only one he saw on the path, or it could be that he came there to take your daughter specifically and wasn't going to let anyone get in the way. I just don't know yet, but I do find it curious that someone went to this amount of risk. That leads me to some questions I have for you. Have you noticed anyone unusual hanging around the neighborhood?"

"No," Sam Farner replied, then, looking to Luciana, "have you?"

"No."

"How about you, Carson?" Tori asked.

"No, ma'am," the boy responded in almost a whisper.

"There have been no threatening phone calls? Emails or text messages from unknown people? Nobody odd following you?"

"No," Sam said.

"Has Isabella reported to you that she noticed anyone odd, unusual, creepy, anything like that?"

"No." This time it was Luciana who replied.

"Carson?"

He shook his head.

"Do Isabella and Carson ride that path to school every day?"

"Usually," Luciana said. "Our neighborhood doesn't get school bus service. At this time of year, they cycle to school most days as we both often need to be at work early."

"And neither she nor Carson has ever had an issue before on the path?"

"No."

"Do you know anyone who owns or drives a blue cargo van? The boys said it was some sort of blue—dusty blue, a dirty blue."

Luciana, Sam and George all shared looks and shook their heads.

"Have you seen one matching that description driving through your neighborhood at all?"

They all said no.

"Our kidnapper was described as Caucasian, stubble, average height and weight, athletic-looking, wearing black running attire. Does that ring any bells at all?"

"No," Luciana said, and looked to her husband. "You?"

"No."

"And nobody has called you?"

"Like a ransom call?" George asked.

"Yes."

"No, no calls," Sam replied. "Not yet. Should we hope for one?"

"Absolutely," Tori said. "We're going to set up monitoring on your home phone line as well as your cell phones and computers. At work as well."

"Do it," Sam said. "Whatever you need, just ask."

Tori looked to Luciana. "Has anything happened at work?"

"Like what?"

"An angry parent? A diagnosis gone awry that led to a patient dying? A work relationship that soured that would cause someone to get back at you?"

"Gosh, no," Luciana responded. "We're a pediatric clinic. We haven't had anything bad happen. I mean, from time to time we have a troubling diagnosis, but that hasn't led to anyone threatening us."

"Any business problems? An employee upset with how they were treated."

"You had that billing clerk you had to fire," Sam offered. "She got angry with you."

"Yeah, but that was months ago."

"What was that about?" Tori asked.

"We had to fire a file clerk because she showed up to work inebriated. She reeked of booze and we'd been having performance issues to begin with, all of which stemmed from her drinking. She'd been warned that if it happened again, she would be terminated, so she was. As I understand it from another employee, she's now getting help. She had a problem but was an otherwise good person. I just don't see her doing something like this."

"Were you the one to terminate her?"

"Yes, me and our office manager."

"Give me the employee's name," Tori asked. She looked to Eggleston, who took the note. "Anything else?"

"No," Luciana said.

"How about you, Mr. Farner? Any issues at work with employees or customers?"

"Not that I can think of," Sam answered. "I have five employees, no issues. As for clients, we get some from time to time who aren't happy with the returns on their investments, but—"

"What about Dexter?" George Santo asked urgently. "What about him, Sam?"

"Who is Dexter?" Braddock asked.

"Walter Dexter is a former client," Sam Farner answered. "He lost a significant chunk of an inheritance. He wanted to invest the money and I recommended he do it on a diversified basis, but he got hung up on putting it all into a tech start-up he'd read about online. I told him it was risky, but he insisted on taking the plunge. I can only advise people; I can't make them do something. He lost most of the investment and sued me, claiming I didn't advise him properly. The case is ongoing. I'm not concerned I'm going to lose."

"But he's been making noise," Santo added. "This Dexter

fellow is ex-military. He's into conspiracy theories and nutty shit. He's got a bolt loose, I'm telling you."

"The lawsuit has really been more of a nuisance," Sam said. "But George isn't wrong. Dexter is a little ... angry and crazy."

"How angry and crazy?"

"He threatened to kill Sam," Santo said.

"He what!" Luciana blurted, her eyes wide in shock. "You never told me that."

Sam winced. "I didn't want to worry you."

"Well, how about now!"

"I was with Sam when he made the threat," George explained. "I'd come over to pick him up for lunch. Dexter saw him as he came out of the building and started yelling that he was going to kill him."

"To be honest," Sam said, "I didn't take the threat too seriously."

"Sam!" Luciana protested.

"I didn't, but now, well ... I don't know."

"Where do we find him?" Tori asked.

"He lives over near Cuyuna, out in the woods somewhere."

"Married?"

"No, not that I'm aware of," Sam answered.

"And describe him?"

"Mid-forties, black hair and beard, six feet tall. He was in the army, did a few tours in Afghanistan. Got out after he did his twenty and inherited some money from his mother when she passed. That's what he invested."

"How much did he lose on this investment kerfuffle?" Tori asked.

"A little over two hundred grand."

Tori's eyebrows shot up. She looked to Braddock, who glanced over at Eggleston. "Find where he lays his head."

"Right away," Eggs said and left the room.

Tori looked at Sam Farner, "Anything else about this Dexter guy?"

"He's kind of a conspiracy nut. Thinks everyone is out to get him."

"What does he do for a living?"

"I think odd jobs mostly. Carpentry. Part of his anger in that investment not paying off is he was going to have to go find a regular job. I think he was intending to basically retire, live in the woods and walk around and shoot shit."

"Do you think he's the one who's taken Izzy?" Luciana asked.

"We have to go see," Tori said as she stood up.

"Tell me the truth, Ms. Hunter," Sam Farner said. "Will you get my daughter back?"

"I can promise you I will do everything within my power to get her back."

"But no promises."

"No," Tori said directly. "But if we are going to get her back, more than anything else, you have to tell me everything and tell me the truth. I want to know anything and everything you can think of that might be important. I can't begin to tell you how many times people hold back, intentionally or unintentionally. The littlest things often end up being the biggest things."

Eggs waved to them by the front door, on her phone. Tori and Braddock joined her. "I've got the address for Dexter," she said as Steak arrived. "Do you think he's our guy?"

"He's got motive," Braddock said. "He lost two hundred grand. The Farners could probably write that in a check plus more. He fits the parameters of the description that Quinn gave us. It sounds like he has a screw loose. That might make him just crazy enough to pull something like this." He looked to Tori.

"There's only one way to find out. Let's go pay him a visit."

FOUR

"FREEZE RIGHT THERE, MISSY"

With Steak trailing behind, Braddock and Tori made their way northeast toward Cuyuna. The county roads out this way were quiet. Braddock had his flashing lights on, which was more than enough to push what little traffic there was aside.

Tori finished her call with Special Agent Zagaros of the FBI Twin Cities office.

"They'll help?"

"Yes. You were talking to Drew. How is Quinn?"

"Shook up. Six stitches in his forehead, bruised ribs and a probable concussion. Not a bad one, but in sports, we'd call it getting your bell rung. Drew is taking him back to their house for now. Mary and Roger will be over there as well."

Braddock was composed and back to driving, but she could see his angst. He wanted to be with his son.

"After we're done with this guy, you go to Quinn. I got this."

"This is the job. Thank God I still have my child. The Farners want theirs back too."

"Did you check in with Jost?" Jost Anding was the acting sheriff for Shepard County.

"I did. Filled him in."

"And?"

"He said carry on."

"He sure doesn't get in your way."

"On a case like this, I'd like him to get in the way just a little. Handle at least one part of it."

Tori grinned. "You do hate dealing with the media."

"Hate is a strong term."

"Loathe, abhor, despise, scorn, detest."

"Got any more there, Ms. Thesaurus?"

Tori grinned back.

Braddock sighed. "They have a job to do. I have a job to do. Those jobs don't work well together. And I hate gotcha questions. Only *I* get to ask the gotcha questions."

Tori laughed.

"A case like this is where I really miss Cal," Braddock said. "Have you heard from him?"

"No," Tori answered. "You?"

"Nada."

Cal Lund was now the former sheriff for Shepard County. He'd resigned following an investigation of the county attorney and sheriff's departments and their roles in the suppression of evidence in a murder trial twenty-four years earlier that had come to light last summer during one of Braddock and Tori's investigations. While the report placed more blame on the county attorney and Tori's late father, Cal also came in for sharp criticism as well. In Cal's case, the criticism had focused on the fact that he'd not come forward sooner when it was apparent there was a connection between the old case and the new. Had he done so, lives might have been saved.

Since his resignation, Cal had dropped off the grid. He didn't answer calls or texts and nobody had seen him. Tori and Braddock had stopped by his house on multiple occasions, but nobody was ever home. Tori had figured that he and his wife, Lucy, just needed to get away, but finally she was worried enough that a few weeks ago she sent a text: *Cal, proof of life!*

He finally responded: *Victoria, don't worry, I'm fine. Traveling.*

That was it. The only communication since mid August. In the meantime, the county board was going about the process of finding a new sheriff.

"Do you think Anding wants the big job?" she asked Braddock now.

He snorted. "He'd probably like the paycheck."

"I'm being serious."

"I like Jost personally—nice guy—but he's a bureaucrat. A paper-pusher of the first order. It's been forever since he did any actual policing."

"I know you have a certain distaste for those of a bureaucratic bent, but people like that have their uses."

"That's the FBI in you talking."

"I'm an operator like you," Tori said. "Yeah, bureaucrats get in the way sometimes, they're sticklers for the rules. However, need I remind you that two months ago, when you were dressing down Cal, you said that if the rules had been followed twenty-four years before, things would have turned out very differently?"

Braddock grimaced. She had him in a box. "Touché. Still, Jost is not a leader."

"Do you want it? Do you want to be sheriff? You're a leader. People look to you."

"No," Braddock replied quickly. "I hate politics. I have zero desire to run for office—campaign, beg for money, knock on doors, pound yard signs, any of it." He looked over to her, "Do *you* want me to be sheriff?"

"Not if you don't want it," she replied and slid her hand

over to his thigh. "Besides, I want more time with you, Detective Braddock; a lot more, not less."

"A lot more?"

"Yes."

"Maybe I will run then."

Tori smacked him on the arm, repeatedly.

"Okay, okay, okay," he said, laughing.

If nothing else, she'd lightened his mood.

A cool, damp, foggy darkness had descended by the time they reached the small town of Cuyuna, thirty miles northeast of Manchester Bay. Deputy Frewer was waiting for them. When he saw them coming, he pulled out in front of them and led the rest of the way.

Walter Dexter lived out in the woods another five miles east of town. Along a particularly desolate stretch of road, Frewer signaled to make a left turn onto a narrow gravel track leading into the woods. After the turn, he pulled to the right and stopped and got out. Everyone else pulled in behind and did the same.

"Do you know this guy?" Tori asked him. Frewer was like a cop walking a beat. He knew everyone in his county.

"I know of him," the deputy said. "He's something of a ... kook."

"You expect trouble?"

"Folks out this way, especially the ones living way back in the sticks, aren't always fond of us law enforcement types. If they had their choice, I think they'd prefer to live in 1822, if you know what I mean. Dexter fits into that camp. Make of that what you will."

They all proceeded to pull on their Kevlar vests. "Does this

Dexter own a blue panel van?" Braddock asked, looking to Steak.

"He owns a gray Chevy cargo van. And a pickup truck."

"Interesting."

"You think he's our guy?"

"Only one way to find out," Tori replied, and then looked to Frewer. "You know where this place is?"

"Exactly? No. What I do know is that it is way back in the woods. Barely on the grid. We'll take a right turn ahead and then drive about five miles in. His house, I think, is at the end of the road and then the end of a long driveway. Very isolated."

"Ya think?" Steak snorted, checking his gun.

"Map app doesn't necessarily show anything beyond the road."

"Terrific," Braddock moaned.

Frewer led them out along the gravel road strewn with potholes and puddles. There were few signs of life, only a sporadic mailbox to mark a driveway. It was a good five minutes before he slowed as he reached the end of the road and then turned slowly to the right.

"This isn't even on the map," Tori noted as the narrow, muddy driveway arced to the left through the dense forest, their headlights illuminating the tunnel-like approach. Given the darkness, they could only see a few feet to either side of the vehicle.

Ahead, Frewer emerged into a smallish clearing. To the right was a detached garage, the double door up. To the left, a small house with no lights on inside. Frewer parked but left his headlights on, directed at the front of the house. Braddock parked behind him. Tori got out of the Tahoe and looked back for Steak, but he wasn't there. *Where did he go?*

"It doesn't look like he's here," Frewer whispered.

Braddock stopped and snapped his right hand on the butt of

his gun. He gestured with the flashlight to the house's roof and the heavy smoke billowing out of the chimney. To the left of the front door was a vertical window; a flickering glow was visible, the glow of a fire.

"Do you leave the house with a fire going?" he said in a low voice.

Tori felt a sudden sense of unease and let her own hand rest on her gun grip in her holster. Frewer had his hand riding on his gun as well. They were in the middle of the woods, and it was pitch black. Out here, nobody would hear a sound.

Frewer turned left, cautiously walking the sidewalk running parallel to the front of the house, trying to see in the windows.

Click click!

Tori snapped her head right. That was a pump-action shotgun.

Grrrrrr!

That was a dog.

GRRRRR!

A really big dog.

A German shepherd, its ears perked high, its teeth visible, slowly emerged between Frewer's cruiser and Braddock's Tahoe, illuminated by the headlights.

Tori locked eyes with it. It was thirty feet away, staring right at her, emitting a low, continuous growl.

Oh shit.

She could feel her pulse racing as the dog took a slow step forward, and then another, its body coiled in attack mode. Twenty feet away now. *Those are big teeth, really big teeth.*

"Mr. Dexter?" Braddock called out. "We're with the Shepard County sheriff's department."

"Get off my land. Get off now!"

The voice was to their right, coming from over by the garage. Tori started slowly pivoting, her right hand now firmly on the gun grip. The dog took another step, and she carefully drew the weapon.

"Freeze right there, missy."

The dog took another step.

Grrrrrr!

"We don't want any trouble here, Mr. Dexter," Braddock continued, standing out in the open of the front yard. There was no cover between him and the garage. He was totally exposed. "All we're looking to do is ask some questions. You can see the deputy is in uniform."

"You're not."

"I'm the chief detective for the county. I wear plain clothes. I'm going to show you my badge. It's on my belt."

"Face me," the voice called out. "Move your hands real slow."

The dog took yet another step toward Tori. Then another, baring its teeth. *Grrrrrr*. It was growling loudly now, looking at her like she was a potential meal.

Tori slowly raised her right arm, while at the same time bringing her left to the grip.

Braddock pulled back his suit coat to reveal the badge on his belt. "Heel your dog!"

"Not until I get some answers. Why are you out here?"

"We need to ask you some questions."

"What about?"

"A girl who was kidnapped."

"I don't know anything about that. Now leave."

"How do we know that?" Braddock said. "Right now, you have a gun and a vicious dog on us. You seem awfully guilty of something."

"I don't have anything to say to you about some kidnapped girl," the voice yelled. "Just get off my land. You got no right to be here."

"Any day, Steak!" Braddock called out.

"Hands up, you jack wagon," Steak hollered. He was in the woods behind the garage. "You so much as twitch ... You hear what I'm saying?"

So that was where he'd gone. He'd stopped short of the clearing and snuck around the back of the garage.

"I don't know nothing about no girl being taken," Dexter protested.

"Then the conversation should be short. But you keep a gun on us any longer and you're going to get into a lot more trouble than you're already in," Braddock said. He waited a moment. "Walter? What is it going to be?"

Thump!

Dexter had dropped the shotgun.

"Attaboy," Steak called.

"The dog? *The dog!*" Tori yelled. The German shepherd was fifteen feet away, still growling, aggressive, ready to charge her.

"*Wolf! Sit!*" Dexter called out.

The animal immediately sat at attention.

Thank God, she thought as she exhaled a breath. Wolf might have sat, but his eyes didn't leave her as she inched away, careful not to turn her back.

"You alright?" Braddock asked, chuckling.

"I thought I was going to have to shoot that damn thing."

"It's just a puppy."

"I'm in the mood to shoot *something* now; don't make it be you."

"Now, Walter, you got anything else on you?" Steak asked loudly.

"Beretta on my waist."

There was a pause, then Tori heard Steak bark, "Walk."

She slowly approached, her gun in both hands but held at

waist level. Dexter came out from behind the side of his garage, his arms in the air, Steak behind him holding his own weapon, Dexter's Beretta tucked in the front of his pants and the man's shotgun in his left hand. He gave the latter to Tori.

"Was this all really necessary?" Braddock growled. "Pulling a gun on law enforcement is a good way to get yourself shot, dumbass."

"People come out this far uninvited, it's usually trouble. You all could shoot me out here and nobody would know otherwise. I have a right to defend myself."

"Well, you'd need to use something besides this then," Tori said, extracting the shells from the gun and looking to Braddock. "If I didn't know better," she said, holding up a shell with clear casing, "I'd say these are filled with rock salt."

"On the other hand," Steak said as he slid the magazine out of the Beretta, "this one was loaded for real."

"Which is not the one I had pointed at you," Dexter said.

"We're not out here to shoot you." Tori was exasperated.

"Then why are you out here?"

"Let's go inside the house and discuss it," Braddock suggested.

"Inside?"

"Yeah, Mr. Dexter. You're taking us inside."

A wary Dexter led them toward the house, calling Wolf to join them.

"He's not going to bite our hands off, is he?" Tori said.

"Not unless I tell him to."

"Then put him in the kennel. I ain't having this beast stare me down any longer."

"He's harmless."

"No," Tori growled, "he's not."

"Trust me, Walter," Steak said with a wry grin, "you don't want Tori baring her teeth at you. Nobody does."

"Wolf. Kennel," Dexter said.

The dog immediately turned obediently and went to the kennel at the side of the garage. Braddock and Steak followed closely to make sure Dexter secured the door.

Inside the house, Tori sat across from Dexter at the kitchen table. Braddock stood to her side while Frewer loitered in the open family room. A fire crackled in the fireplace, warming the boxy little house.

"Why are you on my land? You still haven't answered."

"We're here because a twelve-year-old girl named Isabella Farner was abducted today. That name ring a bell?" Tori asked. She glanced past Dexter, out the picture window to the garage, where the lights were on and Steak was poking around a panel van parked there.

"You mean Sam Farner? Did that damn swindler send you out here?"

"Did you threaten to kill him?"

"Well ..."

"That's a yes."

Dexter shook his head. "I was upset. He didn't advise me right on an investment. I lost my inheritance." He looked suspiciously over his shoulder. "Why is your man looking at my van?"

"A witness saw the kidnapper throw Isabella Farner into a dark-colored panel van and then race away," Tori said, hedging the truth a hair.

"And it was Sam Farner's daughter?"

"That's right."

Dexter sighed. "Well, shit," he said, taking off his green mesh ball cap to reveal tightly cut hair. "I'm pissed as hell at Sam, but I ain't got nothing against his little girl. I wouldn't hurt no kid."

Tori raised her eyebrows.

"I wouldn't. Not a kid. No way. No way. Uh-huh."

"Mind if we take a look around the house to be sure?" Braddock asked. Frewer had already branched out and was nosing about.

"For what?"

"You got something to hide?" Tori asked.

"I don't think I can trust you people. I should have my lawyer out here."

"You got one on speed dial who'll just show up here at the world's end at a moment's notice?"

"Well, uh ... no."

"Does this house have a basement?" Frewer asked.

"No," Dexter replied. "There's a crawl space underneath."

"How do I get there?"

"There's a door on the side of the house. You ain't going to find nothing."

Frewer took his flashlight off his belt and headed out the front door.

"What's the van for?" Braddock asked.

"That's my work van. Nothing in it but a bunch of tools and supplies."

"What do you do for work?"

"I'm a handyman, carpentry and cabinets mostly."

"You work for yourself or for someone else?"

"I don't have anything steady right now. I take work wherever I can find it these days."

"You were in the service?"

"Army. Twenty years."

"How long since you got out?"

"Five years, fifteen days," Dexter replied.

"Where were you today between three and five p.m.?" Tori asked.

"I thought I was going to be working, but the guy I was

supposed to work with didn't call me in the morning like he said he would, so I spent the afternoon at the Tick in Cuyuna drinking beers. I got home late in the afternoon, around supper time. It was still light out when I left the place, I know that."

Steak came inside the house and simply shook his head. Frewer, right behind him, said, "Nothing under the house other than some mice looking to establish a winter home."

"And people at the bar—you said it was called the Tick— can verify that you were there?"

"Sure. Denny and Char, the owners, waited on me."

Tori looked to Frewer.

"Them I know." He extracted his cell phone. "I'll check it out."

"Sorry I pulled the gun on ya. Living out here like I do, you just can't be too careful."

"You think that takes care of it?" Braddock asked, sounding dumbfounded. "That, and you threatened to kill Sam Farner."

"I wasn't serious about that. I just ... popped off when I shouldn't have."

"You got issues, Walter."

"It's why I live out here," Dexter replied honestly. "I just like to be left alone."

Frewer stepped back inside the house. "Denny says Walter was on a bar stool much of the afternoon and left well after five p.m."

Dexter wasn't their guy from this afternoon, and Tori assessed he wasn't some mastermind who'd secured an alibi while others did his bidding. He wasn't that smart. Dexter was, as Frewer said, just a kook.

"Now that you've checked on me and seen I had nothing to do with that girl disappearing, you can get off my land," Dexter demanded.

As they walked away from the house, Braddock looked over at Tori. "I really need to ..."

"Go," she said. "Take care of Quinn. Give him this." She leaned up and kissed Braddock on the cheek. "Steak can drive me back."

FIVE

"CRAZY YES, STUPID NO"

Izzy was a cutie, Tori thought as she examined one of the photos Luciana had given her earlier. She favored her mother, with her dark brown eyes and black hair that parted just left of center.

"Does that help?" Steak asked. "Looking at the photos."

"It makes her real. Keeps her fresh in my mind and ... motivates me, I guess."

He nodded and pulled into the Farners' driveway. Tori slipped the photo back into the envelope.

The second she opened the SUV door, she felt the chill. The October night had quickly turned frigid and damp, the temperature diving precipitously. It would be frosty in the morning, she thought as she jammed her hands into the pockets of her wool coat and walked up to the house. Eggleston met her on the front step.

"How are things in there?"

"Tense," Eggs replied. "About what you'd expect."

"Anything on canvass?"

"Two men in the neighborhood, a couple of blocks over,

both said they recall seeing a blue Chevy panel van parked in that same parking lot over the last few weeks."

"Did they see the driver?"

"They think so."

"Think?"

Eggs nodded. "They described him as a white male, maybe six feet tall give or take, in dark running attire. They said he had black hair, and usually wore a running hat and wraparound shades. The interesting thing is they both saw him multiple times, in both the morning and the afternoon. We're planning on hitting the park preserve first thing in the morning to see if anyone else recalls seeing him."

"Did they recall a model for the van? A license plate maybe, even a partial?"

"Nada."

Inside, Tori found the Farners in the family room, surrounded by people she assumed were friends and family there in support. She closed her eyes for a moment. For days after her sister, Jessie, disappeared, there were friends, acquaintances, people from her dad's work at the house. There was enough food to feed an army. Everyone meant well. In her case, it didn't help. Her sister was still gone. Tori knew what had happened to her now, knew that even in those days following, Jessie had already been dead. But at the time, all she could think about was what her sister was going through. What her abductor was doing to her or where he was taking her. She knew that was what was running through the Farners' minds. What was happening to Izzy? Was she still alive? Would she ever come back?

"Could I have some time with Sam and Luciana?" Tori asked, and all the guests peeled away.

"I'd like George to stay," Luciana said.

"Of course." Tori took the chair to the side of the large sectional couch where Luciana, Sam and George sat in a row.

"What of Walter Dexter?" Sam said.

"We checked on him. He's certifiable, as you suggested, but he was not involved. He has a solid alibi for the time of the abduction."

"Nobody has called us," Luciana said angrily. "I want somebody to call me."

Tori nodded. "Just because nobody has called yet doesn't mean that's not still a possibility. We're monitoring your cell and home phones now. We're going to have a police presence outside the house. It's approaching midnight. I know it feels like she's been gone a long time, but we're still less than nine hours since it happened."

"Do you think she's nearby?"

"It's possible. The amber alert was issued quickly. We had a description of the van and the abductor out within ten to fifteen minutes of the abduction. It gives us a chance."

"How? You haven't found it yet," George asserted.

"True, but that suggests to me that the man didn't stay on the road long in that van. He could have dumped it for another vehicle and slipped through our net. But he might have got off the road quick and is hunkering down somewhere, hiding, maybe waiting us out. In either event, the entire five-state area is on alert. There isn't a police officer, trooper, deputy who doesn't have their eye out for your daughter, that van, and the man who took her."

"What happens next?"

"At daylight we continue to canvass—the park preserve, neighborhood, school. We're going to talk to everyone we can talk to. I have detectives looking for like cases. We're running down known sexual offenders. We'll keep searching and searching."

"How about the FBI?" George asked. "Don't they usually handle these cases?"

"They have offered all assistance, but to be honest, when I was in the FBI, I was the person they called to handle a case like this. I know the local agent in charge for the Twin Cities Bureau office, Special Agent Zagaros. He's a very good agent and I welcome his help. I promise you we'll do everything we can."

Luciana's eyes began to water. "Izzy ... is she even still alive?"

"Honey," Sam said, putting his arm around his wife.

"Is she? Is she still alive?" she pleaded to Tori.

Tori leaned forward in her chair. "I've been in your shoes ..." she began.

"I know you have," Luciana replied, wiping tears away. "I read the stories about you last year. About your sister's case."

"Then you know I'm not going to offer you false hope. But I believe in hope. You must keep faith. I know she's only twelve, but is your daughter tough? Is she strong-minded? Stubborn? Resilient?"

"Yes," Sam said immediately. "Izzy's a fighter."

"Then you both need to be too. Be strong for her."

Luciana sighed and then nodded.

"And keep thinking about anyone who might want to hurt you," Tori instructed.

"You still think this is personal?" George asked. "Someone coming after Sam and Luciana?"

"Mr. Santo, I keep an open mind about everything until I get something solid to pull on," Tori said. "There are still multiple possibilities as to why this happened." She looked to the Farners. "If it is random, we'll find him based on evidence at the scene, a witness, or someone who sees the van, our abductor or Izzy. But it could also be personal. I need you to keep thinking on that, because if it is, you may well have the answer right here."

When they left the house, Tori got into Eggleston's Explorer and placed a call. Zagaros, voice sleepy, answered on the third ring.

"Special Agent Zagaros, I'm sorry to call so late. Hope I didn't wake Kim."

"Nah, she's on shift," he replied, waking up. "Any luck so far?"

"No, but we're gettin' after it. You offered help earlier."

"What do you need?"

"The down and dirty on Luciana and Sam Farner, the abducted girl's parents."

"You suspect them?"

"They're presenting the picture that everything is fine between them. It feels genuine. At the same time, I need to know if there is something I need to know. The Bureau is just better and quicker at that kind of thing than we are."

"We'll get on it."

* * *

Braddock slipped in the door of his brother-in-law's house. Drew greeted him and walked him back to the family room. Quinn was lying on the couch under a blanket, sleeping.

"How's he doing?"

"Tired and sore," Drew said. "He took some ibuprofen and fell asleep."

"And his head?"

"He has a little headache, but when I asked him what hurt worse, he said his ribs. That's probably a good sign."

Drew's wife, Andrea, stepped into the family room and slipped an arm around Braddock. "School is cancelled for the rest of the week," she reported. "As are all activities."

"So, for tomorrow ..."

"Mary said she'll be at your house as early as you need her," Andrea said with a smile. "I'm going to drop Peter over there too."

Braddock leaned down to Quinn. "Hey, little man."

Quinn's eyes slowly drifted open.

"Let's get you home and to bed."

Ten minutes later, he was tucking his son into bed and setting a bottle of water on the nightstand.

"Dad, have you found Izzy yet?"

"No, not yet, but we're working on it. That's why Tori's not here."

Quinn nodded and drifted quickly off to sleep again.

Braddock left the door half open and went down to the kitchen. He needed to take the edge off. He spent a moment perusing the beer selection in the beverage refrigerator. A beer didn't seem right for the moment, nor did a glass of wine from Tori's expansive assortment in the wine fridge. He went to the cabinet high above the refrigerator and took out a bottle of bourbon, then grabbed a heavy glass and sat at the table. He poured himself a drink and gulped it down.

He looked up to see bright lights beaming through the kitchen window. Tori pushed through the back door just in time to see him gulp down another drink.

"Easy there, big fella," she said as she hung her coat up and walked over to the table. She leaned down and kissed him, getting a taste of the bourbon. "How many?"

"Just two."

"Gulping them like that?"

He shrugged. It had been a day.

"How about you sip the third one with me?"

Braddock nodded as Tori grabbed a glass for herself and poured a drink. She took a sip, peering aimlessly out the window.

"What are you thinking?" Braddock asked.

"Just about Isabella. I've talked to survivors, you know. Kids we brought back." She took another drink. "She's thinking, I'm twelve, twelve ... She's twelve, Will. She's panicked, freaked out, thinking, what does this ... maniac want with me? What is he going to do to me? Is he going to keep doing this to me? Am I going to die?"

"One might wonder if it's healthy for you to do that. For you to invest in these cases like you do."

"I have to know what the victims are going through. I have to understand."

"Why?"

"Inspiration, I guess. Knowing what a child is experiencing, feeling, thinking pushes me to keep going. It helps me identify with the victim, with their family. And it also helps me to understand what Jessie went through."

"And then you found out for real."

"Yes, I did. And now Izzy might be going through that too."

Braddock nodded and took a sip of his drink. "You know, until today, I could investigate a case like this and maintain some detachment."

"Quinn."

He nodded. "I'm not detached any more. We must find that little girl. So," he poured just a small amount more into each of their glasses, "you've had nine, ten hours now, what do you make of all this?"

"I've been running it over and over. There are moments it feels random, but I really think ..."

"She was the specific target."

"Yes. Just the way it all went down."

"Like it had to go down in that park, today, at that place and time."

Tori nodded in agreement and took a slow sip of her drink. "That would explain some of the boldness of it. The rain earlier in the day meant fewer people on the trails, which reduced the risk some. Quinn's presence, on the other hand, upped it. She wasn't alone, yet he took her anyway."

"He's a twelve-year-old kid. Even if he'd realized straight away what was happening, he wouldn't have been able to put up much resistance against a six-foot adult male. Now if Peter and those other two boys had been with them, it might have been a different story." Braddock took a long drink. "He could have killed Quinn."

"He didn't," Tori said. "Crazy yes, stupid no. But still, why target Isabella Farner? Is it something about her or the parents? What do we really know about them? That's why I got Zagaros digging on them. See if the image they project is the real thing." She finished her drink. "Long days ahead. We should get some sleep when we can."

Braddock led them up the steps. Tori stopped at Quinn's door for a moment and looked in on him. He was fast asleep.

Ten minutes later, they were too.

* * *

"Sheriff, what's going on?" she demanded of her father when he came into the interrogation room. "Where's Jessie?"

"I don't know, honey."

"What do you mean, you don't know? What happened? Nobody has told me what happened."

"Your sister's car was found abandoned on County 48 with a flat tire. She wasn't with the car, and we can't find her."

"*Someone grabbed her off the side of the road, didn't they?*"

"*We don't know for sure. There was no sign of a struggle.*"

"*She's ... gone. Gone!*"

"*Tori, we don't know that for sure.*"

"*Don't you dare lie to me, Sheriff! You told us before that when girls go missing, they don't come back!*"

Tori bolted awake, breathing heavily, her heart racing.

The nightmare was familiar.

It used to come to her often. There were so many times she would be away on a case and she would wake in some hotel room, her pillow soaked in sweat, her heart racing, having just relived it all again.

While there were variations as to which point in time the nightmare would start, it was almost always the same general sequence of events. Their group of friends on the Fourth of July at the carnival in town sneaking vodka into their lemonade drinks. Her first boyfriend holding her hand, kissing her, asking if she wanted to go off, just the two of them, alone. Jessie smiling at her as they snuck away, thrilled for her twin sister and best friend. Then it always skipped ahead to the house phone ringing in the middle of the night and her father charging into the room she shared with Jessie to see that she wasn't there. There was Cal and the Minnesota Bureau of Criminal Apprehension man interviewing her, pushing her about their activities that night with their friends. And then the dagger question. When was the last time she remembered seeing Jessie?

When she started losing it in the interview, when she started to understand what had truly happened, that nobody could find her sister, that if only she'd stayed with her instead of running off, none of it would have happened, the sheriff would barge into the room, yelling that that was enough. But then she would see the vision of her father: a big, powerful man who had seemingly aged and diminished in just a matter of moments. He didn't have any answers for her either. And at the end of the nightmare, she knew Jessie would never be found and that her father would soon die of a broken heart.

It had been a long stretch now since she'd had images of that awful night in her head. Since she'd been going to therapy, it hadn't come back—until now.

She rolled to the side of the bed and rubbed her face, feeling the familiar layer of perspiration on her forehead. She needed some water to splash on her face. She stood up and started for the bathroom.

"No! No!"

She froze. Where was that from?

"No! *No!*"

Quinn.

She spun around, grabbed her robe and rushed down the hall to his room. He was sitting up in his bed, looking around, disoriented. Panicked. Breathing heavy.

"Hey," Tori said as she stepped into the room, tying her robe. "Hey, hey, hey. You're okay," she said, sitting down next to him. "You had a nightmare."

"It was ... It was ..."

"What happened today?"

He nodded, still breathing heavily and now wincing. "Ow."

"Take slow, easy breaths. Your ribs are bruised, remember?" she said softly, checking his forehead. He was warm, but not necessarily burning up.

"I saw it all again."

"Yeah, I bet you did," she said in a soothing, calm voice. "I bet you did." She put her right arm around him, patting him on the shoulder, then reached over to his nightstand and turned on the small lamp. She looked in his eyes and he grimaced, now fully awake.

"Does your head hurt?"

"Yeah, a little," he said, just as Braddock came into the room.

"What's going on?"

"Can you maybe grab a cool, damp washcloth?" Tori asked.

He was back in a flash, and she dabbed at Quinn's forehead. "Just a nightmare, I think," she said. It was 2:50 a.m. His body was sweaty, his T-shirt damp. She looked to Braddock. "Maybe get him a new T-shirt." She checked his bedding. "And a new pillowcase too."

Braddock went to the dresser. Tori helped Quinn slowly get his old T-shirt off and the new one on while his father redid his pillow.

She ran her hand gently up and down his back. "What did you see in your dream?"

Quinn took a moment. "It wasn't ... the same. It was like I remembered, just ... I don't know how to explain it ..."

"Parts of it?" Braddock offered.

"Yeah," Quinn said. "That man got Izzy, he threw her in the van, but then it wasn't ... the same." He took a drink from the bottle of water Tori offered him.

"It's not uncommon to experience something like today and then have dreams or nightmares about it," Tori said calmly. "It's pretty normal really. Nothing to be worried about. You're here with us, in your bed, in your house, safe."

Quinn nodded. They sat quietly with him for a few minutes, helping settle him. With the adrenaline from the nightmare receding, his exhaustion returned.

"You want to try and go back to sleep?" Braddock asked.

Quinn nodded, took one more sip of water, and then lay back on his pillow.

Tori stood, and Braddock stepped over and pulled the blankets back up. "Try and rest, okay?"

"Can you leave the hallway light on, Dad?"

"You bet."

They walked back to their own bedroom and got back into bed. They were now both wide awake, lying on their backs, staring at the ceiling.

"That's not going to be his last nightmare," Braddock murmured.

"You're probably right."

"Thanks, though."

"For what?"

"You know. Quinn," he said, rolling to face her. "You calmed him down, talked him through it."

"I just heard him first is all."

"You know, I see it all the time."

"What?"

"How good you are with kids." He kissed her. "I see it with Quinn, with Peter, with their buddies. I see it just when you talk to random kids. I was rattled when I got to the park today, but you were so composed. I know you were worried too, but you just had this calmness in the way you looked him over and analyzed things. You were in control. And because of that, Quinn relaxed and knew things were okay."

"I've never really thought about it. I just ... did it."

"Exactly. It was natural. You care. Kids pick up on that, gravitate to it, respect it. It's why you're so good at what you do." He kissed her gently and then rolled over to try and go back to sleep.

Tori laid her head back on her pillow and stared up as the ceiling fan slowly whirred, letting the good feeling of Braddock's compliment wash over her.

* * *

Isabella's eyes slowly fluttered open and focused on a faint light in the corner. Was that her night light? She hadn't turned that on in a long time. She opened her eyes fully.

It was not her night light. It was a small black desk lamp sitting on the floor.

Her eyes snapped wide as it all flashed back to her. The preserve, the man in the black mask charging at her and Quinn, being thrown in the van, the van pulling away and the man who had grabbed her poking her arm with a needle, and then ... She didn't remember anything after that.

How long had she been asleep?

Her head felt heavy. And her upper left arm hurt. She slid up the sleeve of her shirt to see a red mark there. She rubbed it, and then her eyes, trying to wake herself up. Then she looked over her clothes. Her pants had streaks of dry caked mud on them, as did the bottom of her shirt, and her shoes, which sat askew on the floor to the side. Even her hands still had some dried dirt on them. If she hadn't been wearing her raincoat, she'd be a full muddy mess.

Where was she?

Slowly she stood up and took a few steps around the room she was in.

It was a small, compact square. Two adjoining walls were smooth cement. The other two were sheetrock. The only interruption in the sheetrock was a wide door frame. The door was wood, but it wasn't like the six-panel door for her bedroom. This wood felt thick, sturdy, but smooth, although it wasn't painted or stained. It was raw, like it was the back of something with horizontal and vertical beams to it.

Looking up, she saw that the ceiling was unfinished, with exposed joists. There was a single light socket with a bulb in it attached to a joist running across the middle of the room. There was a light switch on one of the stud posts. She flicked it up and the light came on. Up above was a window of cloudy glass blocks. She couldn't see out, but she could tell it was dark outside. In the corner was the mattress she'd been lying on, with a single pillow and a gray wool blanket.

Ca-chunk!

She spun around, then stepped back into the middle of the room.

The door swung open. It was the back of a bookcase. A man dressed in all black, including a black face mask, stepped inside and looked her in the eye for a moment. He was carrying a tray of food, which he put down at the end of her bed. It was mac and cheese, a sandwich, and a bottle of water.

"Do you need to go to the bathroom?"

She nodded meekly.

The man grabbed her by the arm. He dragged her through a darkened area, then pulled open a door and flipped on a light. He pushed her inside and closed the door.

The bathroom was small, but somewhat modern, with a toilet and a small pedestal sink. A roll of toilet paper sat on top of the toilet tank. After she'd finished, she stepped to the sink. Looking in the mirror, she saw her face had mud on it. There was no soap, but she cleaned her hands as best she could, then splashed her face repeatedly. She saw chunks of mud in her hair too, and with wet fingers pulled it out before again splashing her face, drinking in some of the water, trying to refresh. She still had her bracelet, although she noticed one of the little silver angel charms was missing. Holding her left wrist under the water, she cleaned away the mud from the bracelet. She was going to try and wash her jeans off too when the man opened the door.

"That's enough," he growled.

He walked her back through the darkened area. The light

emanating from her room allowed her to see a couch, some sort of coffee table, and chair. A basement family room.

"What time is it?" she asked.

The man didn't respond. He pushed her through the door and pulled it closed. She heard a loud metallic *click*. She examined the door and spotted a small opening at about eye level on the right-hand side.

"Hello? Hello? Anyone?" She pounded on the wood. "Why am I here? What do you want with me?"

There was no response. The man was gone. She looked up and listened for footsteps overhead, but didn't hear any. Instead, she felt ... stillness.

The smell of the food got her attention. She sat down on the end of her bed. Realizing she was hungry, she took a mouthful of the mac and cheese and then checked the sandwich. It was peanut butter and jelly. As she bit into it, she looked around the room. Up in the far corner, attached to a ceiling joist, was a video camera, angled down and directed toward the mattress. There was an illuminated red light on top of it.

They were watching her.

* * *

She twirled her drink glass, the Scotch diluting in the water from the melting ice cube. The monitor was set next to the television. Isabella was taking bites of her mac and cheese and then of her sandwich. The girl had been out for nearly eleven hours, so it was no surprise that she was hungry. No doubt she was disoriented as well, her body clock in flux, eating a meal at 2:30 a.m. The disorientation was good. She would be less trouble this way.

Yawning, she shifted her attention to the television. It did annoy her that the cable news networks didn't provide much actual news. It was all political commentary, and at this time of night they were just rerunning earlier programming.

"Has there been anything on the news?" he asked.

"There was on the local news," she replied. "There was a little on CNN earlier, but it was brief. Will that be enough, do you think?"

He nodded, sitting down on the couch, kicking up his feet, taking a sip of his tea. "We've started things now. We just need to be patient and let things unfold. When the time is right, we'll be able to make our move."

SIX

"I'M NOT DEAD"

Tori woke at 5:15 a.m. She slipped out of bed, showered quickly, and then dressed for comfort in a dark gray pantsuit, white dress blouse, and black oxfords. As she emerged from the bathroom, Braddock came into the bedroom.

"How's Quinn?" she asked.

"Still sleeping." He stepped over to her, kissed her good morning and made for the bathroom.

It was still dark outside when she started the coffee maker and then checked her messages. Officer Reese, who was still at the Farner house, texted that it had been quiet overnight, the parents eventually going to bed late, George Santo staying in the guest room.

She poured herself a cup of coffee and went to the sliding glass door to the deck. As she peered outside, she was able to see just the slightest hint of sunrise puncturing the cloudy eastern sky over the far side of Northern Pine Lake.

Her phone buzzed. She looked to the screen and creased a smile. "Well hi there."

"I just saw a report on CNN of a child abduction in

Manchester Bay, and I said to myself, Tori has to be in on that," FBI Special Agent Tracy Sheets said on the other end.

"You would be correct." Tori gave her the rundown.

"Any leads yet?"

"Not really. There was little physical evidence at the scene. We have a general description of our attacker at best, and he had ten, maybe fifteen minutes' head start on us. That's not a ton of time, so he had to get off the road quick, but you get outside of town here, there are a lot of different directions to go and they're just about all in the woods."

"The parents haven't been contacted?"

"No. We're fifteen, sixteen hours out here, not a word."

"Sexual offender then," Tracy asserted. "It would explain the brazenness of it."

"Maybe. But why this girl? She was with Quinn, yet the guy attacked in broad daylight, in a park where people could see. Was he obsessed with her? Or just a girl that age?"

"You'll figure it out. You always do."

"What are *you* figuring out these days?"

"The Colombians."

"Colombians? That's different for you."

"Well, we have our own trafficking issues, human and drugs, here in New York City and I'm looped in with a task force with the Bureau, NYPD, Jersey State Police and the DEA. We're trying to put together the money and drug trail, and I'm researching all the players."

"Which is right in your wheelhouse."

"Yeah. I'm looking into lots of people in northern Colombia and Panama. It's interesting."

"I bet," Tori replied. Behind her, the back door opened and she turned to see Roger and Mary Hayes stepping inside. "I'd love to chat more, Trace, but ..."

"You gotta bounce. No worries. Keep in touch, sister."

"Alright, see ya." Tori clicked off the phone.

"Mornin', Tori," Roger greeted, his usual silver coffee tumbler in hand, three newspapers and a hardcover book tucked under his arm. He gave her a quick hug and peck on the cheek. "That's a sharp pantsuit. You look like a million bucks." He was ever the charmer. She really liked him.

Mary held up a white paper bag. "I brought muffins. Want one?"

"Please," Tori said as she poured a cup of coffee for Mary.

Braddock arrived in the kitchen. He shook Roger's hand and kissed Mary on the cheek before grabbing a muffin and then pouring coffee for himself. He gave them the update on Quinn and his nightmare.

"You got him calmed down, I'm sure," Mary said.

"I slept through it. By the time I came into his room, Tori had him settled."

"Oh, I see," Mary said, surprised. "That's so ... nice of you, Tori."

"No big deal," Tori said. She looked to Braddock. "We should go."

"What are our orders?" Roger asked before jamming a piece of muffin in his mouth.

"Quinn just needs to rest. No running around, riding bikes, shooting pucks, none of that today," Braddock instructed. "And keep him and Peter away from the video games. Movies are better, more calming for the mind."

"Is there any update on the missing girl?"

"Not as of now, so we've got work to do."

"Tori, work your magic," Roger said with a little wink.

"I'm working on it, Rog."

Tori and Braddock grabbed their coffees and muffins and left. Once they were on the road, Tori couldn't resist. *"That's so nice of you, Tori. God, she's back to hating me again."*

Braddock dramatically checked his watch. "I put the over–under at five minutes. It took barely one. And she doesn't hate you."

"You call that love?"

"Actually, I'd call it improvement."

Braddock's wife, Meghan, had died of cancer six years ago. She was Roger and Mary's daughter. Tori was now the serious woman in Braddock's life, living in the house full-time, bonding with Quinn and, at least from their perspective, taking Meghan's place.

Roger Hayes loved and missed his daughter, but he also loved his son-in-law and liked seeing him happy. So he was happy too. That, and he and Tori hit it off. He liked that she was this fearless badass who didn't suffer fools gladly, and told her so.

Mary's enthusiasm was more restrained. Tori knew Mary didn't hate her. In fact, they had had some good talks the last few months. The ice was melting. Nevertheless, Mary remained wary and reserved, and whether it was a slip of the tongue or not, she had a way of letting Tori know she remained that way.

"It's like I keep saying," Braddock said. "Fair or not, you gotta earn it with her. I did, and so do you."

"I know."

"I can already hear the phone call." He had a wry smile on his face. "*I hope Tori didn't think ...*"

"Yeah, yeah."

"Is Isabella alive?" he asked, turning more serious.

Tori sighed. "Yeah, I think she is."

"Is that hope, or are you basing it on anything specific?"

"Hope is not only important for the parents, but also for me, for us. If I think she's out there, I can tell myself to stay after it. I also think we had the amber alert out and the net up fast enough that our kidnapper couldn't stay on the road for long. Could he have slipped through with her? Yes, for sure. But I also think he had to know that he was seen when he took her, so realized he had to be off the road fast. That says to me that she could be close."

"It could also mean that since he had to get off the road fast, he had to do whatever it was he wanted to do and then, you know ..."

"That is not lost on me. That's where hope comes in. I hope that isn't what happened. I hope that she is the fighter her parents say she is. I hope she's not being harmed, even though I know, *I know*, that could be what's happening."

Braddock's phone buzzed. "Huh, what do you know."

"What?" Tori asked.

He answered the call, putting it on speaker. "Cal, I was starting to wonder if you were d—"

"I'm not dead, I'm in Tucson," Cal replied, a hair annoyed. "Listen, wiseass, I have a lead for you on your case."

"Do you now?"

"This requires a quick backstory. Six years ago, an eight-year-old girl named Helena Hernandez was abducted just outside Thief River Falls, Minnesota, which is around two hundred miles northwest of Manchester Bay. A man in a black ski mask grabbed her off her bike as she rode down the shoulder of a rural county road and drove her away in a white cargo van. Her younger brother was a hundred yards away and saw it happen. Does that sound familiar?"

"A little."

"Unfortunately, in the six years since, Helena has not been found. Now, I didn't recall all this myself," Cal continued. "I just got a call from Tom Gholson, an old friend of mine, now retired in Florida. He was the sheriff up in those parts when Helena was taken. When he saw the abduction on the news early this morning, he got online to read more details and then he called and told me about a man named Ian Anderson."

"And this Ian Anderson is who?"

"The suspect in the abduction of Helena Hernandez."

"*The* suspect?"

"Yes. Anderson owned a white Ford cargo van. He lived a mile west of where Helena was taken. He was also an IT employee at the local community center, a place that Helena frequented."

"And what went on at the community center?"

"Lots of kids' activities. There was an indoor jungle gym and maze, a pool, basketball courts, and rooms for other activities. Working at the community center, Anderson was around kids all day every day. Helena Hernandez and her brother were frequently there. Tom thinks that's where she came to Anderson's attention."

Cal explained that Anderson had undergone intense questioning for several days. His alibi for the time of the abduction was squishy at best. However, his van, house, and property were scoured for any evidence that he'd taken Helena, and nothing was found.

"Nothing?" Braddock said.

"Clean as a whistle," Cal confirmed. "The van had been scoured to within an inch of its life. There was no evidence to be found in it. Same at the house. His land was a mixture of woods and more open areas. It was searched literally inch by inch, but again, zip. Still, Tom was absolutely certain that Anderson was his guy. It took them two days to focus on him, and in that window of time, he thinks Anderson killed her and disposed of the body."

"He was never charged?"

"No. They never had the evidence needed. Only strong suspicion based on circumstantial evidence. There was not one piece of physical evidence that allowed them to tie her disappearance to him. They held him for as long as they could, but eventually had to release him. He left town and hasn't been seen in those parts since."

"Where is he now?"

"Tom had the good folks up in Thief do a little searching. A detective up there thinks that Ian Anderson is now Ian Pemell—his mother's maiden name—and that he now resides in—"

"You're going to tell me Manchester Bay," Tori finished.

"Not only that. Ian Pemell also has a blue Chevy cargo van registered to his name. Now, have I left you two enough to go on?"

It was just before 6:00 a.m. when Tori and Braddock sprinted into the government center.

They found Nolan sprawled out on the couch in Braddock's office. Braddock playfully waved a steaming cup of coffee under her nose. It took her ten seconds to wake up.

Her eyes fluttered open, and she grimaced. "What the fu ... Oh, uh, morning, boss."

Braddock howled with laughter.

Nolan sat up and rubbed her face. "What time is it?" she asked, before taking the coffee.

"Six," Tori said. "When I had you do a search last night for similar types of abductions in the area in recent years, did you run across one involving a Helena Hernandez?"

"Uh ... yeah, that's ringing a bell or two." Nolan stood up and walked to her cube, where she started flipping through a stack of paper. "I printed off the ones I wanted to take a longer look at," she said. "Yeah, here it is." She held up some pages. "They had a suspect named—"

"Ian Anderson," Tori said.

"Yeah, that's right. Abduction using a white panel van off the side of a county road. Only a distant witness or two. Anderson owned a van similar to the one seen by the witnesses and worked at the—"

"Community center in Thief River Falls," Braddock finished.

"What do you guys need me for?" Nolan quipped. "Or am I missing something?"

Braddock explained the call with Cal. "Cal with the big pull," Nolan, said. "Let me guess, you need me to—"

"Pull together everything you can find on Ian Anderson, now Ian Pemell. Anything you can find. Property, vehicles, employment, photos, financial. Apparently, he now lives here in River City."

"Give me a few minutes to wake up and I'll get on it."

Tori's phone rang. Zagaros. "I just emailed you a file on the Farners. We'll look for more, but this should give you an initial picture. I'll tell you up front, it's pretty benign."

"You think it's about the Farners if Ian Pemell or Anderson, or whatever his name is, is the guy?" Nolan asked.

"Don't know. We don't have anything concrete yet, so we check everything."

While Nolan started on Ian Pemell, Tori dug into what Zagaros had sent.

George and Luciana Santo originally hailed from San Mateo, New Mexico. An Internet map search showed that San Mateo was located maybe an hour northwest of Albuquerque. Sam Farner was from Santa Fe. All three were graduates of the University of New Mexico. Luciana later graduated from the University of New Mexico School of Medicine and completed her residency in Albuquerque. After that, it looked as if she and Sam moved to Manchester Bay and put down roots, joining her brother, who had moved there several years before. The

Farners had lived in Manchester Bay for twelve years and owned their home, which was valued at $790K, an amount reflective of the recent rapid increases in housing prices, as well as the fact that the house had access to and ownership of a boat slip in a nearby marina. All property taxes were current. They owned two vehicles, a Land Rover in Luciana's name and a BMW X7 in Sam's.

Sam Farner owned a financial services firm, Farner Financial and Investment, with office space in a building in downtown Manchester Bay. Luciana owned part of the practice at Manchester Bay Pediatrics. The couple also had a vacation property in Marco Island, Florida. A property search had revealed that Luciana and her brother still jointly owned ranchland outside of San Mateo, which appeared to have been inherited from their parents.

Other than the Walter Dexter lawsuit against Sam's investment firm, there was no other legal action against the Farners. Neither of them had a criminal record of any sort.

Until they had a warrant or the couple's permission, they wouldn't be able to access their detailed financial records, but Zagaros had included a summary of their tax returns for the last five years. Their joint income was on a steady upward trajectory, with a prior year reported gross income a little over $417,000. They were a successful upper-middle-class couple who appeared to still be on the way up. But while they were doing well, they were not truly wealthy, at least not yet.

Braddock returned with a carrier of large coffees from across the street and a breakfast bagel for Nolan. She took a long drink of coffee and then a satisfying bite of the bagel with egg, cheese, and sausage. "Thanks for this," she said. Then she held up a DMV photo. "This is Ian Pemell, formerly Anderson."

Tori and Braddock studied the photo. Pemell had black

curly hair, a thinnish face and what looked to be a heavy five o'clock shadow.

"The vitals are that he is six feet tall, one hundred seventy-five pounds. Black hair, brown eyes. His current house is out in the woods about a mile west of County 44 in the area south of Norway Lake. Before he moved here four years ago, he lived in Moorhead for two years, then Thief River Falls before that, moving there from Grand Forks. That's assuming this is who Cal and his retired sheriff friend are talking about."

"I can check on that," Braddock said, taking a photo of the DMV photo and stepping away to call Cal.

Nolan continued, "Pemell's current property is ten acres." She pulled up a Google Maps satellite view. "As you can see here, it's in a semi-isolated area, set back from the road in the woods from the looks of things. He also owns a piece of farm property down by Pierz, one hundred acres. He drives a 2014 Blue Chevy Express van and also has a white 2018 Honda CRV."

"Employment?"

"He is currently employed by Health Tech Administrators. The company has an address down in St. Cloud. What he does for them, I don't know yet."

"Criminal record?"

"No convictions or charges. I've started really digging in on this situation in Thief River Falls. He was never charged on that, although his name was bandied about in the press."

"What else?"

"His driving record indicates he has a lead foot: a history of speeding, a couple of them well over the limit, but otherwise cleanish."

Tori flipped through the pages that Nolan had printed off. She'd only had fifteen minutes and had come up with the basics. She needed more time.

Braddock called to Nolan from his desk. "Gholson had someone email me the investigative file on the Helena Hernandez disappearance. I'm forwarding it to you." He came back out of his office. "Everyone is gathering in the conference room."

"Hang on," Tori said. "Nolan should stay on Pemell for now. In the meantime, we should—"

"Put someone on him." Braddock nodded. "I'll get someone out there."

Tori turned to Nolan. "Keep digging. Pemell was a suspect in Thief River Falls. Now he might be here. I wonder if he hasn't hit law enforcement radar on other occasions."

"Copy that."

Braddock called the gathering to order. It included detectives Steak, Eggleston and Reese, Manchester PD uniformed officers and department deputies. Once he'd made the introductions, he turned it over to Tori, who ran through what they knew.

"The van has been described as a dirty, dusty, maybe matte-finished blue Chevy cargo van." She held up a stock photo. "According to the twelve-year-old boy who saw the suspect before he abducted the girl, the guy is around six feet tall, wearing black running clothes. Given how the abduction happened, we don't think yesterday was his first visit to the park. We have at least two people who recall seeing the van parked in that lot on multiple days and who have described the driver as medium height, wearing black running gear, ball cap, wraparound sunglasses. Was it our guy from yesterday? It sure sounds like it could be. He may well have been jogging through the park at the times Isabella would have been riding to and from school. The middle school starts classes at eight fifteen a.m. and the students are out at three thirty. Let's make sure we're talking to people in those time windows all the way from the school to the Farner house."

"Nobody gets through that area today without being questioned," Braddock added as his assistant came into the room and handed him a slip of paper. "Same thing in the neighborhood next to the park. Every door gets knocked on, even if we hit it yesterday. We need to know if anyone saw this van or the driver, or anything else related to it."

Everyone got up out of their seats and filed by Reese, who handed out information on the van and suspect. Tori noticed Braddock studying the slip of paper.

"What's that?" she asked.

"A homicide." Braddock sighed. "South of Deerwood. Some guy out in the woods, found shot dead by a friend who came to pick him up for breakfast." He waved over Steak and Eggleston. "I need to steal those two."

"You gotta at least leave me Reese and Nolan then."

"And you'll have me. I need to go out and check this out with them, but then I'll be back."

SEVEN

"A TYPICAL KICK THE STATISTICS"

Braddock took in the heavy gray overcast sky on this blustery October morning. Even after five years, the fact that the cool temperatures of fall came a month earlier in Manchester Bay than in New York City was still a mental adjustment for him. They were an unwanted reminder that the cold and snow of winter was just around the corner.

Oddly, he'd found he didn't mind, for the most part, the harsher winters of northern Minnesota. He'd picked up snowshoeing as a form of exercise, and there were seasonally themed activities, carnivals, and events throughout the winter that kept the locals busy and people coming back up to lakes country. If you dressed for it properly, they were fun. It was a three- to four-month stretch that he found manageable. Plus, it was hockey season for Quinn and that had given him another activity to attend and another social group of parents to hang with.

What did get to him were the stretches of bitter cold. Each winter there would be two or three multi-day stretches in January and February of those minus ten- or fifteen-degree days. It was a bitter, bone-numbing cold that cut through to your core no matter how many layers of clothing you wore. Those days were lurking out there, they were coming.

"Where are you, Izzy?" he muttered before taking a drink of his coffee.

This case was different; it was personal. Part of it was Quinn. The nightmare, the fright on his face, had Braddock thinking of what impact the trauma of the abduction would have on him. And then he admonished himself, because at least Quinn was home, resting and safe. Isabella wasn't. Quinn would get the chance to recover; would she?

And he knew her.

Not as well as he did Carson, but he knew her as one of Quinn's classmates. He knew her well enough to say hi to her and she to him. Her parents were friends, not necessarily close ones, but if you spend Minnesota winters traversing northern Minnesota hauling your kids to hockey games together, he found there was a unique bond that formed amongst the hockey parents, forged by huddling together at the frigid ice rinks, the pre-game gatherings and the hotels of Duluth, Moorhead, Grand Rapids, Warroad, Roseau, and Thief River Falls. Isabella had run the hallways of those hotels, swam in the swimming pools, and played knee hockey.

Where was she? Was this tip Cal had for them legit?

Those were the questions he would rather be pondering than what was awaiting him at this murder scene. He pulled up and powered down his window, Steak and Eggleston right behind him. "You again."

"Hey, I'm a ray of fucking sunshine, aren't I," Deputy Frewer replied. "Any update on Isabella Farner?"

"Nothing new to report. What do we have here?"

"Weirdness, actually," Frewer said with a headshake before looking back behind Steak and Eggleston's SUV to see Dr.

Renfrow, the medical examiner, pulling up in his van. "I'll let you and your team of seasoned professionals assess it. The decedent's name is Fred Weltz. He's been dead a while. The body is cold and gray."

"Do you know this Weltz fella?"

"A bit. He was a handyman who could custom-build just about anything involving wood. He built a hell of a wet bar for a friend of mine a couple years ago. As for the body, you'll find it in the office area of his woodshop, which is in the outbuilding to the right of the house." Frewer pivoted and gestured further west. "He was found by the guy standing at the end of the driveway down yonder there."

"And what did he have to say?"

"He and Fred always go to breakfast on Thursday mornings in Deerwood. He rolled by to pick up Fred and found what you're about to go up and see."

"Is he married?"

"Neighbor says he was a widower for many years. He has grown children. They'll need to be notified."

Braddock drove up the driveway a short distance and then pulled to the side. He and the others continued on foot to the paved area in front of the house, which was a two-story with attached garage. The woodshop was a separate building to the right that looked like a second detached garage that had a sign over the door: *Weltz Imaginative Carpentry.*

The three of them carefully stepped inside. The body was lying in the middle of the floor on an area rug. Weltz looked to be in perhaps his late fifties or early sixties, dressed in a faded shirt and worn blue jeans. His right leg was crumpled awkwardly underneath him, his arms out to the sides, his eyes looking lifelessly to the ceiling, a bullet hole in his forehead and two in the center of his chest. A broad pool of dried blood surrounded his torso.

Along the wall to the left was a mishmash of gray and lime-green filing cabinets and a mustard-yellow metal office desk. All the drawers of the desk and cabinets were yanked open and had been rifled through, with business papers strewn about. There was a monitor and keyboard on the desk, but the computer box was gone.

Dr. Renfrow made his way into the office and crouched by the body to check its temperature. He read the thermometer, then squinted for a moment, making a quick calculation.

"He's been dead at least a couple of days, Will," he said. "The body temperature is pretty much room temperature."

"And no question on cause of death," Braddock said, looking at Steak and Eggleston. "Two shots to the chest, then the shooter walks up and finishes him off with one to the forehead."

"He was basically assassinated," Steak said, his own gun out, pantomiming the act. "It looks like our killer comes in the door and does him right where he fell."

"Didn't even have time to get to his shotgun," Eggs said, gesturing to the rifle leaning against the wall between the desk and the filing cabinets. It was just five feet away from the body.

Steak stepped over and inspected the shotgun, a twelve-gauge. "It's loaded. He was ready if trouble came a-calling."

"I'm thinking our shooter might have known that," Braddock said. "He takes one step inside the door and smokes Weltz like *that*." He snapped his fingers. "Freddy here never knew what hit him."

"But why?" Eggleston said.

"That's for you two to figure out," Braddock replied.

"What a mess," Steak murmured.

"You'll have to clean it up and reconstruct all these records. Because if I'm right about our shooter knowing about the gun, one might assume he'd been here before."

"Fine, but then don't you think the killer found what they were looking for?" Eggs said, waving at all the papers lying about. "And they took the computer to boot. Going to be tough."

"That's why you two are detectives," Braddock smirked. "Detect and find another way. I'm heading back to Manchester Bay. I have a twelve-year-old girl to find."

* * *

"Why did you move to Minnesota?" Tori asked Luciana Farner. Sam and George Santo were sitting at the table as well.

"When my residency was done, we wanted to try something different from New Mexico."

"Manchester Bay is certainly different."

"It is. George had moved here, as his wife was from the area, although they met in Albuquerque. He had opened the restaurant in town, which was doing well. He said this was a growing area full of lakes and outdoor activities. We'd visited and liked it, even the winter. We thought it would be a great place to raise a family. And the local pediatric clinic had an opening for a young doctor. But, Ms. Hunter—"

"Call me Tori."

"Okay, Tori. Why does any of this background matter?"

Tori took a moment. "Your history can matter if the reason Isabella was taken has something to do with your or Sam's history, your businesses, your finances."

"What about it just being some crazy predator?" Sam asked.

"We're looking at that too. We're pursuing every angle. We're blanketing every step from the school to your house this morning and will be all day. I have detectives searching like cases to see if we have any commonalities," she said, thinking of the Pemell possibility. "The more I know about you and your family, the better. What you do, who you socialize with, any issues that you've been having. I have to ask about your marriage, too. How is it?"

"Good," Luciana said. "It's really good."

Tori looked to her with raised eyebrows.

"I'm serious. We're happy," she insisted, and then looked to Sam. "I mean, we are, aren't we?"

"Yes."

"No affairs?" Tori pressed.

"No," Sam replied with a weary smile. "We joke about it sometimes because we both know people who have had them."

"We laugh about it, because when would either of us have time for one?" Luciana said. "There's work all day and then carting the kids to hockey, to school stuff. Sam and I get to nine at night and we're fried."

"I have friends who bemoan that very fact," Tori said with a nod.

"Our lives are not overly exciting," Sam explained. "I think by any measure we're successful and live comfortably. But our life is no different than our neighbors and friends. We're nothing special. Like most people our age with families, everything revolves around our jobs and then the kids and what they're doing. Day after day it's pretty much the same. Heck, I'm forty-four. I'm figuring one day I'm going to wake up and I'll be fifty, the kids will both be driving, and I'll be wondering where my forties went. That's who we are, so I can't imagine why anyone would target us. It must be some crazy guy. He saw Izzy, fixated on her for some reason and grabbed her. That has to be it."

Reese stuck his head into the dining area and caught Tori's attention, nodding for her to follow him. "I've got a couple of people you should talk to," he whispered. "Two blocks over."

"What happened?" Sam asked. "What did you find?" His wife and brother-in-law were right behind him.

"Nothing yet," Tori said calmly. "Just something I need to go check out. I'll be back shortly."

Reese drove her two blocks before turning left into a street that ran into a cul-de-sac. The park preserve was directly behind the houses on the east side of the street. They got out and he indicated a man in blue running shoes, black running pants and a white hoodie. Another man in running attire was walking across the street to join them. "This is Ron and his neighbor, Mark. They both regularly run through the park preserve, often together. Tell Ms. Hunter what you told me."

"For the last couple of weeks, we've run the park in the morning," Ron explained. "We both work out of our houses, so we'd get up and run before work. There's been a blue van in the parking lot a number of days."

"Tell me more about the van," Tori said.

"A dusty grayish blue. Chevy. A boxy version. No windows other than on the rear doors."

"I noticed it because most of the time you see a vehicle parked in the lot, it's a car or SUV," Mark added. "But this was different. Like a repair van."

Tori nodded. "Were you running the park yesterday?"

"I did," Ron answered. "And the van was there in the morning. I saw it."

"Have you seen the driver?"

They both nodded.

"Describe him?"

"A runner, it seemed," Ron offered. "He wore running gear, always black, I think. About six foot, decent shape. Wraparound sunglasses. That sound right, Mark?"

"Yes. He had black hair, a little wavy, and usually some stubble."

"Did you only see him in the mornings?"

Mark shook his head. "Sometimes I can't run in the morning

because I'm on calls with clients on the east coast or London. On those days, I run in the afternoon. I've seen that van there then as well. It was always parked off by itself. When Detective Reese started asking questions, Ron and I compared notes and found there were days when he ran in the morning and I ran in the afternoon and the van was there both times."

Tori nodded and opened her padfolio and then one of her manila folders containing photos of blue Chevy panel vans. "Do any of these look familiar to you?"

Mark and Ron thumbed through the photos. Tori shared a look with Reese. These guys were seeing something.

"I think this one," Ron said, pulling a photo.

"Me too." Mark nodded. "This one and this one," he added. It was consistent with what Quinn and Peter had described, as well as other witnesses from last night.

Reese got a radio call and stepped away from the group.

"And the driver of the van," Tori continued. "You said he was a jogger?"

"Yes," Ron said. "I saw him a handful of times."

"Black running attire? Was he always in that?"

"Yes. Black shorts or tight running pants, black shirt, hat, shades, earphones in his ears. I don't think I ever saw him dressed differently."

Reese stepped back to Tori and pulled her away. "That was a call from a patrol officer working the park preserve closer to the middle school. She's got two people who have described the van and the driver just as these guys have. They've seen him recently running along the path that borders the school property and leads into the park preserve."

"Do they have a name?"

"No."

"Does it strike you as odd that nobody has recognized this guy?"

Reese shrugged. "Manchester Bay is a bigger town now."

"It's not *that* big and we're a provincial lot here. If you're a local, somebody would know you. We have what now? Nearly ten people with a similar description of the van and the runner. It's consistent, but nobody can give us a name."

Tori chewed on that thought for a moment. Then her phone buzzed. It was Nolan.

"What's up?"

"I got something you ought to see," Nolan said. "I just texted you a photo."

Tori went to her texts. It was a newspaper photo of a man running in dark attire with a black baseball cap and wrap-around shades. On the front of his shirt he had a racing number pinned on. She tweezed out the photo until she could read the caption: *Ian Pemell was among the locals running and sweating in the Saturday morning Manchester Bay Days Half Marathon.*

"I'll be damned," she muttered.

"I've got something else to show you as well," Nolan said.

"I'll be in shortly." Tori clicked off the call and went back to Mark and Ron. "Could the man you saw running possibly look something like this?" she asked, holding up her phone, careful not to allow the caption to show.

Ron peered at the photo. "Maybe."

Mark gave it a scan. "I can't say for sure. That picture is pretty grainy, but what he's wearing, that all-black getup, fits."

He was right, the photo was grainy, and there wasn't anything unique about the running attire, but it was something. Tori borrowed Reese's radio and called in to dispatch, who patched her through to the sheriff's deputy who was watching Pemell's place.

"I'm in my own truck, parked in a driveway on the opposite side of the road, maybe a hundred yards down."

"Is he home?"

"He has been. Right now, he's out jogging."

Tori smiled. "Get video for me."

"Come again?"

"Use your phone. Take footage of him running. Text it to me." She gave him her cell number, then placed another call.

Braddock answered on the first ring.

"Are you still out in Deerwood?"

"No, almost back to Manchester Bay. Why?"

"Meet me at the government center."

He heard the tone. "What do you have?"

"Ian Pemell. Cal might be right. He's worth a much longer look."

Tori pulled in just behind Braddock at the government center and for the second time that day they double-timed it inside. Nolan was in her cubicle. Empty coffee cups and energy drink cans littered her desk.

"Take a look at this," she said, handing over a clipped sheaf of papers. "It's a case from Grand Forks, North Dakota."

Three years before Helena Hernandez was abducted, a seven-year-old boy named Joey Martinez was reported missing from a trailer and RV park on the outskirts of Grand Forks. He was living with his mother, Juanita, and there was an on-and-off boyfriend named Mark Olson in the picture as well.

Nobody saw Joey being taken. His mother and Olson claimed that they had left him home in bed while the two of them went out to a local bar. When they came back, he was gone. The police found drug paraphernalia in the trailer and the file contained notes on a theory that Juanita's drug use had something to do with the boy's disappearance. She and Olson were detained and intensely questioned. Four people put them at the bar when the abduction was alleged to have occurred.

A man named Ian Anderson, who lived a street over, reported seeing a black pickup truck prowling around the trailer and RV park in the days before the disappearance. He hadn't seen it since the abduction, and there wasn't one in the trailer and RV park that matched the description, so the tip was viewed as credible and was the one lead vigorously pursued, but the trail quickly went cold from there. The boy was never found.

"This Anderson cat seems to show up around disappearances," Braddock muttered.

"Sure does," Tori said.

"I don't know if the Thief River investigators ever got onto this," Nolan said. "I see no mention of it in what we got from them. It seems that the investigation of Joey's disappearance was something of an uncommitted mess. Grand Forks PD said it was a county case and the county said it was the city's case. They played hot potato with it."

"This is the kind of stuff that infuriates me," Tori said angrily. "The boy went missing from a place where poor and transient people were living. It looked hopeless, so they spent their time not investigating but trying to dump it on another agency. A typical kick the statistics."

"That's my read," Nolan said. "What effort was put into it turned up very little. The only person who was helpful was Anderson, aka Pemell."

"But how helpful?" Braddock said skeptically.

"Oh, I'm sure it's just a coincidence he was involved," Tori muttered sarcastically.

They shared a familiar look. They were thinking along the same lines. Tori called Reese. "Show that photo of the runner to everyone who described the guy. Tell everyone else in the park or by the school to do the same."

"On it."

The deputy out at Pemell's house texted a video to Tori. It was of a man with black hair and heavy beard running. He was in a black ball cap turned backwards, shades, long pants and long-sleeved shirt, all black. The only thing that wasn't black was the orange flashes on his running shoes.

"What do you think?" Braddock asked.

Tori replayed the video. "It might be useful," she said as she evaluated his running stride which was a little upright with not a lot of knee bend. "You know who should see this? Quinn. In fact, let's show him a few things."

Quinn was in the family room with Peter and his grandparents, watching a movie. A fire filled the fireplace. The lights were low. Tori had the two boys come sit at the table with her and Braddock while Mary and Roger hovered nearby.

"I want you to look at these pictures and tell me if you see something that looks familiar."

Quinn looked through the van photos first. He stopped on the fifth one. He also lingered over two other photos but came back to the fifth.

"How about you, Peter?" Tori said.

Peter took his time sifting through the photos. He picked two, the fifth one and then the seventh, which was an Internet photo of a slightly different Chevy van.

"They both look like what I saw," he said as he scratched his head. "I mean, what I remember really seeing is the back of it, with those square windows on the doors that swing open."

Tori looked to Quinn. "Why this one?"

"The sliding door on the side looks right," he said. "The color is right too. Kind of a light blue."

She took out the photos of runners, one of which included

Pemell, and put them in front of him. "Do you recognize anyone?"

He sifted through the photos but eventually shook his head. "I don't know."

"Tell me what you mean by that," Tori said evenly, curious, not pressing. "What don't you know?"

"I only saw ..." He shook his head, looking a little fidgety. "I didn't get a long look at him. It was just a flash. He was running at us, but I didn't see his face. He was just some jogger coming along the path."

"That's okay. I want to show you something else." She played the video of Pemell running.

Quinn studied it, watching it through three times before shaking his head. "I just don't know. I mean, when I saw him, it was from in front. I just saw him coming and moved to the side and didn't look back until the mask was on and he was right on us." His lip started to tremble. "I'm sorry I can't remember better."

"Hey, hey, hey, that's okay," Tori said, patting him on the arm and then slipping her right arm around him. "I know it all happened really fast. And we don't know if it is this man. I just wanted to see if he registered with you at all. If he didn't, that's okay. We have to have the truth, and if you're not sure, that's okay."

"You did good, buddy. You both did," Braddock said, and then nodded to Roger, who stepped in.

"Come on, boys. Let's get back to that movie. And Grammy is ordering that pizza you wanted."

As Tori and Braddock stepped out onto the back stoop, Tori's phone rang. It was Reese. She put the call on speaker.

"We've showed the photo to the ten people who described the runner."

"And?"

"Five have said they thought it looked like the guy they saw running."

"Just *looked like*?"

"The picture's grainy," Reese explained. "The other five weren't sure. It could be him."

"But if I'm hearing you right, nobody has said it *is* the guy," Tori noted. "Nobody has definitively identified him."

"But what is also true is that nobody has said it's *not* the same guy," Braddock interjected. "The man in the photo looks like the runner our witnesses saw. He also has a blue Chevy panel van and a history of involvement in one, if not two, disappearances before yesterday. Just because nobody has said it's the same guy doesn't mean it's not. And our witnesses have looked at a grainy photo. It might be different if we could get to lineup. Circumstantially, a description has been provided that accurately describes Pemell."

"Too many points of similarity to ignore," Tori agreed. "I think it's time to take the measure of Ian Pemell."

EIGHT

"I'LL TAKE DOOR NUMBER TWO"

They were a little more than twenty-four hours post-abduction when Braddock called ahead to the deputy watching Pemell's house. "Is he still there?"

"Yes."

"Anything you can tell us about the place?"

"My visibility isn't great. I've done a drive-by or two. The woods are dense enough and there's still enough leaves left on the trees that I can't really see back there. From what I can tell from the satellite map, there is only one road onto the property. I'm watching that, and he hasn't left. I had a quick look down the driveway and could see just a bit of the house."

Tori and Braddock drove the three miles from Braddock's house and waited along the county road a half-mile from Pemell's place for backup to arrive.

"We're going to search the house as well as the property when we get there," Tori said.

"We don't have a search warrant," Braddock pointed out.

"We have exigent circumstances. We're not collecting

evidence. We're just making sure she's not in the house or on the property. In and out."

"Are you sure that holds up?"

Tori wasn't a lawyer, but she'd worked with many good ones. She knew the argument. "We have a man suspected in one abduction that bears a striking resemblance to ours, plus he was oddly involved in another one. He lives close to the location of the abduction. He owns a van that matches our description. He looks like a runner people said they've seen in the park. Plus, if we do find something, that makes our exigent circumstances argument look all the better. I can make it stick."

"And if we don't, how do we go back later?"

"By building the case for a second, more thorough look. We take him in, we question him. We keep working everything and build the case for a complete search of his house, farm, vehicles, everything." She looked to Braddock, peeved. "Dammit, you put me in charge. In my *considerable* experience—"

"Stop," he said, a smile emerging. "You had me five minutes ago."

"Then why are you arguing with me?" Tori asked, exasperated.

"Because I like getting you riled up is all."

Tori was at her best when the fire was stoked. It was just a matter of pushing her buttons a little, and he'd become proficient at that.

Reese and two patrol units had pulled up behind. "Let's go."

Braddock drove ahead and then turned into Pemell's driveway, pulling to a stop thirty feet short of the garage to the right of the house. When he got out, he waved for two of the deputies to each take a side of the house and work their way around the back.

"This place is a little like Walter Dexter's, at least from the standpoint of being set back deep into the woods," Tori said, her right hand on the grip of her gun.

"Less cluttered," Braddock said. "It doesn't have the feel of a junkyard."

He led Tori and Reese to the front door. The porch light turned on as they approached, and Reese stepped forward and knocked.

A dark-haired man of medium build opened the door, a plastic bottle of Diet Pepsi in his hand. "Can I help you?"

"Ian Anderson? Or should I say Pemell?" Tori asked a hair mockingly, looking to Braddock. "You know, I forget which it is."

"Yeah, me too. It's confusing."

"What do you want?" Pemell snapped.

Tori and Braddock flashed their identification. "We need to ask you some questions about the abduction of a child yesterday."

Pemell snorted his disgust as he stuffed his left hand in his pocket. "Every time some kid goes missing, you all show up."

Tori ignored the whining. "Where were you yesterday at three thirty p.m.?"

"I was down at my farmland."

"Would that be the place outside of Pierz?"

Pemell's eyes shifted to Braddock. "Yeah. It would."

"Can anyone verify that?"

"I don't know, probably not," he said flatly. "I was there by myself doing some work."

"So that's a no?" Tori said. She looked at Reese and another deputy and pointed to the house. "Go."

"Whoa! Hey, hey, hey. What do you think you're doing?" Pemell complained, shocked.

"Searching for Isabella Farner," she replied.

Pemell's eyes widened slightly at the girl's name. Was that recognition, or something else? Tori wondered.

"I don't see a search warrant in your hand."

"We don't need one in this case," Braddock said flatly. "As you so aptly noted, you have a history with this sort of thing."

"So in the time window of three thirty to four thirty p.m. yesterday, you're claiming you were at the farm, but nobody can verify that," Tori said. "That's what you're saying?"

"Yeah, uh ... I guess," Pemell said distractedly, looking back into the house as it was searched.

"Ian! Focus," Tori said, drawing his attention back. "When did you get home from the farm?"

"Eight, eighty thirty p.m., somewhere in there, I think."

"And you were there how long in total?"

"I got there around nine a.m. or so. I drove into St. Cloud to my employer's office for a meeting, then drove back to the farm and spent the rest of the day there."

"I see. And that would be Health Tech Administrators, correct?" She wanted him to know that they'd been digging into him already.

"Yes."

"What do you do for them?"

"IT work."

"What kind of IT work?"

Pemell snickered. "I thwart malicious intrusion attempts through preventive counter-measures."

"In English?" Braddock said.

"He's an ethical hacker." Tori looked up from her notepad. "You're certified?"

"Yes."

"As Ian Anderson or Pemell?"

Pemell glared at her with annoyance.

"You do that work from the office or at home?"

"Mostly here."

"And what were you doing at your farm all day?" Braddock asked.

"Stuff?"

He snorted. "Care to elaborate."

"I did some work on my computer from there. I do that every so often when I go check on the place."

"You a farmer too?"

"Do I look like one?" Pemell retorted. "I rent out the land to the farmer next door. I've kept the house. It was in my mom's family for years. I'll probably sell it, but I haven't gotten around to that yet."

"Why not just live there?" Braddock asked. "Rather than up here in the woods."

"I guess I just like it here."

"Wait right there," Tori said, and looked to a deputy behind her, who nodded and moved forward.

Tori and Braddock stepped into the house. To the right was the living room. Straight ahead led to the kitchen and eating area and then a den. To the left was a hallway leading back to what looked to be three bedrooms and a bathroom. Also ahead was a stairway down to the basement. A deputy was coming up the steps.

"Unfinished basement. Some storage down there, but largely empty."

Reese emerged from the back hallway. "The master bedroom is clean, neat, well organized. Second bedroom looks like a small guest room, just a twin bed, dresser and nightstand. The third bedroom is larger and serves as an office, or maybe mission control. It looks like NASA in there."

"I'm going to give the garage a look," Braddock said.

Tori stepped down the hallway and gave it all a quick scan. As Reese had described, the home office was stuffed with computer equipment, with a large bank of monitors arranged along a long desk with two office chairs. All the equipment looked expensive and high-end.

Braddock opened the door leading to the two-car garage. It was generally clean. A white Honda CRV was parked in the middle. Arranged around the perimeter walls was general yard equipment you'd typically find in a garage in northern Minnesota: an aged riding lawnmower, a less aged snowblower, a few shovels and related garden equipment that he gave an extra look but that didn't appear to have been used in some time, and a black garden hose. On the end wall was a work-bench with assorted tools and two toolboxes. The rolling garbage and recycling cans were just to the right for ease of disposal.

As he stepped back into the house, Tori and Reese were in the den looking at two bookshelves that contained an assort-ment of photos and books.

"No van in the garage, just the SUV," Braddock reported.

Tori gestured to one of the photos. It was the newspaper photo of Pemell jogging.

"Interesting he would have that."

"It is," she said, eyeing it up for another moment. "Okay, we're pushing it now, let's get out," she said. She followed Reese and Braddock out the front door.

"Are you done?" an annoyed Ian Pemell asked.

Tori ignored the attitude. "Ian, are you a runner?"

"What does that matter?"

"It's a yes or no question."

"A little."

"A little? Someone who runs a little doesn't run half marathons. I saw the photo."

"Yeah, so?"

"Just curious is all."

The two deputies who'd been searching round the back of the house came around to the front. They both shook their heads.

"Are we done?" Pemell asked. Despite his irritated tone, he didn't seem to be overly sweating the cops searching his property.

Was it old hat? *Every time someone goes missing, you people show up?* Was he used to this happening from time to time? Or was he expecting it and ready for it, playing it casual?

"Actually, Ian, we're just getting started. You need to come with us. We have more questions," Braddock said.

"And if I refuse?"

"I can arrest you, or you can agree to come. Door number one involves handcuffs."

Pemell sighed. "I'll take door number two."

NINE

"THE BURDEN IS ON YOU, ISN'T IT?"

Braddock brought Pemell into an interrogation room, then he and Tori tracked down an exhausted Nolan. She hadn't left the building in nearly two days, and had spill spots on her light blue blouse, tufts of hair sticking out from her ponytail and dark circles under her eyes.

"Nolan, you're done," Braddock said. "Above and beyond. Go home, sleep for eight hours, then come back."

"Yeah, yeah. But first, now that you've hauled him in, you might want to read this."

"Which is what?" Tori asked.

"The investigation file from Thief River Falls."

"Physical evidence?" Braddock asked.

"What there is of that is still up in Thief River," Nolan said. "They'll send it if we need it. To say they're interested in this case would be an understatement," she added as she pulled on her navy blue blazer. "Now, per your orders, I'm going to bed."

Tori took a look at Nolan's desk, which was littered with an almost comical collection of coffee cups, soda cans and bottles, energy drinks and junk and fast-food wrappers. "Okay, not sitting there." She moved to the next cube, which was Reese's, and sat down. Braddock read along over her shoulder.

Eight-year-old Helena Hernandez was abducted early on a Sunday morning. The children were supposed to limit themselves to the driveway when riding their bikes. However, like all kids do, Helena and her brother, Marco, had been venturing beyond the limitations of the driveway and out onto the road. Part of the reason they'd got away with this was because their mother was inattentive. Upon searching the Hernandez house, the police found drug paraphernalia, and Rosa Hernandez conceded that she was a heavy user.

On the morning of the abduction, Helena pedaled to the end of the driveway, then turned right and rode along the gravel shoulder of the two-lane road. Marco was well behind her. When he reached the end of the driveway, he saw his sister's bike lying on the shoulder and a man throwing her into a white panel van, which then raced away. He rode back up to the house to fetch his mother. By the time she got down to the road and called the police, it was at least ten minutes later. It took the police another five minutes to arrive. It was estimated it was at least twenty minutes and probably more before an alert was issued. Beyond saying the van was white, Marco could provide no other details.

Ian Anderson eventually became a suspect based upon the fact that he lived a little over a mile away, owned a white panel van and worked at the town's community center. According to co-workers at the center, he seemed to show an inordinate amount of interest in the children playing on the indoor mazes and jungle gyms or swimming in the community pool.

Upon questioning, Anderson claimed he was at home at the time Helena was taken, but nobody could verify that. A review of his financial information showed no credit card activity in the hours before or after the abduction until nearly noon the following day. Typically he had activity at least two or three times per day, usually for meals. There was a window of time where he fell off the grid and couldn't account for.

His house, van, and property were searched. No sign of Helena Hernandez was found, and despite several intense sessions of questioning, first without a lawyer and later with one, he never admitted to any involvement. Due to a lack of physical evidence, he was never charged. While the investigation remained open, no other suspects were ever pursued.

"They seem awfully certain he was their guy," Braddock said.

Tori flipped through the pictures of Ian Anderson's house, property, and van in the file. The house was neat, much like his current home. Orderly and minimalist. The van was clean. The property was well tended. "He doesn't appear to like living with neighbors nearby."

"Doing this, you don't want property where nosy neighbors can see."

"No," Tori said but then added, "I get that they *think* he took her, that there was some circumstantial evidence that supported that supposition, but they found nothing."

"He had a lot of time to do whatever it was he intended to do before they ever suspected him," Braddock said. "Whether on his land or at some other place."

Tori continued reading.

Ian Anderson was an only child. His parents divorced when he was two. His mother left him to be raised by his father in Bismarck, North Dakota. The father was a musician and wasn't around much. After high school, Ian attended Minot State University in North Dakota and graduated with a degree in computer science. His first job out of college was in Grand Forks before later moving east across the Red River to Minnesota and Thief River Falls.

Tori flipped the page. "Well, would you look at that."

"What?"

"Dana Bryan. He's an FBI special agent with the Behavioral Analysis Unit. He must have consulted on this."

"You know him?" Braddock asked.

"Oh yeah. I worked with him on a few cases. He's a pro."

"Did he profile Anderson?"

"These are really just his notes and impressions typed up in bullet-point form, although they read a bit like a profile," Tori replied as she scrolled the contacts in her phone and hit a number. Bryan answered right away.

"Special Agent Tori Hunter, it's been how long? At least three years?"

"Down in Wilmington, North Carolina."

"Did I hear it right that you left the Bureau a year ago, moved to ... Minnesota?"

"I did," Tori said. They spent a minute catching up, then she introduced Braddock before filling Bryan in on the purpose of their call.

"His name was Ian Anderson when you observed him," she said. "He's changed it to Pemell now, no doubt because of the Hernandez case. We were reviewing your notes from that. Do you recall your time with him?"

"It's ringing a few bells. Let me get onto my computer. Give me a second." They could hear him tapping at his keyboard. "Here we go. Oh yes, Thief River Falls. What a great name for a town, by the way."

"Their high school nickname is the Prowlers," Tori noted.

Bryan chuckled. "Seriously? That's so perfect. Okay, Ian Anderson. Yes, I remember him now."

"We're about to go and interrogate him," Tori said. "I was wondering if you had any insight to share."

"I didn't question him directly, Tori. I only observed remotely and offered suggestions."

"Remotely?"

"Watched from right here in my office over a live feed. In the end, despite the detectives there trying different approaches, he didn't break and never conceded a thing. Now, the detectives up there had a weak hand to play. No physical evidence and limited circumstantial evidence when you really broke it down."

"I agree, their case was all conjecture and supposition. The one thing they had was the van fleeing the scene; the little brother saw it and so did a man on a farm about a quarter-mile away. They were both solid on an identification that it was a van like the one Anderson owned, though no full or partial license plate. That's how they identified him as a person of interest."

"That, and he worked at the community center and was perceived to have taken something of an enhanced interest in children," Braddock added.

"That's right, Detective Braddock. The detectives really tried to hit him on that, that he was watching children, that he was eyeing them up, observing them, stalking them and Helena Hernandez was a child who was often there. He admitted he ate lunch in an area that provided him a view of the maze, jungle gym and pool areas but he said he did that to get away from his desk and the office. He said he didn't like eating in the lunchroom with other staff. He wanted some space."

"And you bought that?"

"You know, I didn't dismiss it," Bryan answered. "He had a plausible explanation for why he was there."

Tori flipped through the investigative file, perusing pictures of Anderson's home. "Dana, I'm looking at photos of Anderson's house in Thief River Falls. There are few signs of any interest in children."

"Such as?" Braddock asked.

"With a child molester, we'll often find candy, kids' food or drinks, like juice boxes, or toys, dolls, stuffed animals, games, children's movies or videos."

"Michael Jackson, Neverland Ranch-like?"

"Rarely that blatant, but yeah, that's the general idea," Tori said. "Some sign of interest."

"I didn't get the vibe he was interested in children in that way," Bryan said. "I know I wasn't in the room with him, getting a ... feel for him, but I didn't get the hit of pedophilia from him. That's not to say I don't think he abducted the girl or had some role in it, but I just didn't get that particular sense. On the flip side, my other observation, which made me think he might have done it, was that he lacked any empathy whatsoever for the missing child, her mother or brother. When he was pressed about finding the girl, about the frantic mother, the worried and traumatized little brother, about getting closure for the family, he was ... emotionless. None of that penetrated with him."

"But when it came to himself?" Braddock asked.

"Then he engaged," Bryan replied. "He defended himself. A few times it seemed like he was going to lose his cool when they pressed him on the pedophilia angle. He came off as offended, but he kept it together. And like I said, he never gave in, never admitted anything. If he'd done it, I think he understood the weakness of the evidence and knew that if he didn't give in, he could ride it out."

"Smart, then."

"He was definitely intelligent, Detective Braddock," Bryan replied. "With just a few exceptions, he was thoughtful before he answered questions, as if he was thinking about the answer and what the next question would be and how it all fit within the big picture."

"Chess player."

"Given his computer programming background, maybe gamer is a better way to think of him."

"No empathy, no emotion about the victim, so more psychopath than sociopath," Tori said.

"Yeah," Bryan replied. "I just didn't see any conscience. He didn't strike me as someone with much care for others, other than their utility to him. Toss in a dose of narcissism ..."

"Do you think he took and killed Helena Hernandez?"

He paused for a moment. "I don't know. The van, where he worked, what people said about him, his home's proximity to the abduction, they all paint a circumstantial picture of his involvement. But like I said, I didn't get the sense he was attracted to kids. I got the sense he didn't care about them—or anyone else for that matter. Given what you have now, Tori, I could be wrong. Maybe I didn't see something in him that I should have. However, even if I'd seen it ..."

"They still didn't have the evidence," Tori finished.

"No, they didn't. And he was smart, very smart, so ... one thing that I kind of recall thinking after it was all over was that he might have known exactly what we'd be looking for and had a plan for that. It's just a little note I have here. He may have played us. He's a clever one."

They were getting ready to go into the interrogation room when there was a ruckus out in the hallway.

"Oh boy," Braddock muttered.

Sam and Luciana Farner were demanding to see them, and making a show of it. Before a scene truly developed, Braddock ushered them into his office and closed the door.

"You have someone in custody, don't you? Did he take Izzy?" Luciana asked. "Did he?"

"We have brought someone in for questioning. That's all."

"Why?" Sam asked.

"This man fits the description of a man seen in the park preserve and around the school in the days leading up to Izzy's abduction," Tori explained. "He owns a van like the one seen leaving the scene after Izzy was abducted."

"And a number of years ago he was suspected in another abduction in northwest Minnesota," Braddock added. "It makes sense to question him as part of the normal course of our investigation."

"What other abduction?" Luciana pressed.

"I told you it was just some crazed lunatic pedophile," Sam asserted angrily. "I told you. *I told you!*"

Braddock stayed calm. "Again, he's just someone we need talk to."

"Did that case involve a child? Did it, Tori? *Did it?*"

"Yes," Tori replied. "But look—"

"And did they ever find that child?"

Tori took a moment before slowly shaking her head. "But Sam—"

"He's the man," Sam declared. "He took Izzy. He took our little girl and he killed her."

Luciana let out a guttural cry and Sam pulled her to him.

"At this point, what can he tell you? Where he buried the body!" he asked, his voice shaking.

"Hold on," Tori said. "Don't do this to yourselves. We don't know anything yet."

"Oh, like hell."

"We haven't questioned him," Braddock cautioned. "Nobody has identified him. I can tell you that Izzy was not at his house."

"You searched?" Luciana asked.

Tori nodded. "And she wasn't there."

"Will you go back?"

"Depends on what we learn. We have to get in there and go to work."

"What do we do?"

"I know how hard this is, *I know*," Tori replied. "But you need to go home and wait. If we learn anything, I'll call you. I promise you that."

"She's right, Sam," Braddock said. "This is hard stuff, I know. But as hard as it is, you have to let us do our job."

The Farners reluctantly relented. "It's just ..." Luciana started, wiping away tears. "I'm sorry."

"There is no need to apologize," Braddock said. "We all want Izzy back."

While Braddock tended to the Farners, helping them slip out of the building unseen, Tori stepped into the observation room to put eyes on Pemell. Waiting inside was Assistant County Attorney Anne Wilson. When Braddock returned, Tori summarized where they were at.

"And he hasn't asked for a lawyer?" Wilson asked.

Tori shook her head. "We Mirandized him."

"I assume you'll be looking to do another search at his home?"

"Yes."

Ian Pemell was sitting at the table in the interrogation room, his hands clasped in front of him, looking more annoyed than nervous.

"What's your sense of him?" Braddock asked Tori when he stepped back in. "It sounded like Dana Bryan had some doubts."

"More like conflicting information," Tori replied. "He had his senses but then there was the evidence. It wasn't enough to prosecute, but it painted a clear enough picture. And now his name pops up a third time?" She said with a raised eyebrow. "I mean ... come on."

"What do you make of the fact he hasn't asked for a lawyer?"

"That we better get in there before he does."

"How do you want to go at him?" Braddock asked.

"We don't have time for anything other than head on."

When Tori and Braddock interrogated together, they often played against type. Braddock was a tall man with dark features who towered over people. At times, he didn't need to even speak. With his height and commanding presence, he could intimidate with a cocked eyebrow and narrowed eyes, particularly with his fall beard thickening. And if he needed, he could let loose an aggressive in-your-face torrent of his New Yawker accent, which could throw any northern Minnesotan for a loop.

Tori was a good foot shorter, petite, with longish auburn hair, soft features, deep green eyes, and a warm, attractive smile. She was more alluring than intimidating and lacked a visible hard edge. As a result, most suspects assumed Braddock would be the tough guy and Tori would be the softer touch, the friend in the room, and there were times they would take that approach.

Not today.

If Braddock could release his New Yawker on occasion, Tori had an angry Bawston in her arsenal that she'd mastered in college. It was really more of a drunk Southie as it was perfected while playing drinking games. She'd not used it in some time, but today was a day to pull out all the stops.

"I've been waiting," Pemell said when they stepped into the room, before casually checking his watch and then taking another drink from his coffee cup.

Braddock sat down across the table, opening his notebook

and clicking his pen. Tori leaned against the wall behind him, her arms folded casually.

"Sorry about the wait, but as I'm sure you know, these investigations move at their own pace," Braddock said reasonably. "There are i's to be dotted and t's to be crossed. We have some questions. There's a missing girl we're trying to find."

"I watch the news. But I don't know anything about that."

"Helena Hernandez might like a word," Tori mused.

Pemell snorted and shook his head. "You know, every time—"

"Yeah, yeah, yeah. Some child goes missin' and everyone looks at poor little Ian," Tori replied before leaning in, going Southie. "You know, I could give a shit about how butt-hurt you are about that."

Pemell's eyebrows shot up, as did Braddock's. This was new to him too.

"She gets feisty about missing children," he said evenly, stifling his surprise. "Particularly little girls."

"And boys," Tori chided, and then let an evil grin emerge. "Like Joey Martinez."

Pemell smirked. "I told the police about the guy who might have taken that kid."

"Might have?"

"I didn't see it happen, but I saw him cruising around the trailer park."

"Oh, I just bet you did," Tori said, walking around behind him. "I'm sure it's just a big giant fuckin' coincidence that yahr name came up in that case, Helena Hernandez's disappearance, and now this one." She leaned down and whispered in his ear, "I mean, the odds are almost unfathomable ... that you're not involved."

Braddock sat back and crossed his left leg over his right,

clasping his hands around his knee. "Come on, Ian. Coincidences don't happen. Not in cases like this."

"In gambling terms, to continue the Vegas analogy, this is what we call a fahkin' trend," Tori said, now leaning against the wall behind Pemell.

"I had nothing to do with Helena Hernandez disappearing, but it follows me everywhere I go. I had to change—"

"Your name," Braddock finished. "Yeah, I can understand that."

"Boo frickin hoo," Tori barked.

"I can never get away from it."

"Maybe you shouldn't," Braddock said flatly. "Kids are missing. Your name keeps popping up."

"In other words, you are kind of a gaping asshole," Tori muttered. "Who thus far has gotten away with it."

Pemell rolled his eyes.

"Speaking of getting away, Ian, you're a runnah, aren't you?" Tori asked. "How often do you take one?"

"Almost daily, depending on my schedule."

"Where?"

"I often run along the road I live on. I jog the paths through Manchester Bay. I run the trails around the high school and middle school area."

"Do you run in the pahk preserve?" Tori asked.

"I have."

"Not a shock, I suppose. Lots of kids going through there for you to take an interest in."

"I didn't—"

"Izzy Farner frequently rode through there on the way to and from school. She was riding through there yesterday when she was abducted by a man in black running clothes, driving a blue Chevy cargo van, who looked exactly like you."

"That wasn't me!"

"Were you running there yesterday?"

"No!" Pemell replied angrily. "I told you earlier. I went to my farm yesterday."

"Let's talk about that," Tori said as she started to pace around the room. "Tell us about your day. I want everything from the time you got up in the morning until we came out to your house today."

"I got up early. I went for a run."

"Where?"

Pemell sighed. "A loop from my house along the county road to the dirt road at the southern end of Norway Lake and then back. It's four-point-two miles. I run it often. You know where it wasn't? The park preserve."

"After that?" Braddock asked.

"I drove down to the farm."

"Which vehicle?"

"My CRV."

"Now that's not the only vehicle you own, is it?"

"No. I own a van."

"A Chevy cargo van," Tori said. "Blue. To be specific."

Pemell nodded. "It's not illegal."

"No, but it certainly is interesting. Especially after all the trouble ownership of a van caused you in Thief River Falls."

"And where do you keep it?" Braddock continued.

"At the farm. It stays there most of the time. It doesn't fit in my garage."

"Why do you have it?"

"In case I need things for the farm."

"Odd choice, don't you think? Most people on farms own pickup trucks."

Pemell shrugged indifference.

"What route did you take down there?"

Pemell described his drive down, taking Highway 25 and

arriving at the farmhouse at 9:15. He said he immediately jumped into the van and drove down to St. Cloud. "The meeting lasted an hour, and then I left and drove back to the farm."

"Why switch to the van?"

"It's not good to leave it without starting it up and driving it every so often. And it was a bit dirty, so I had it washed."

"Where?"

"In St. Cloud. Then I drove it back to the farm. I did some work from there and around the barn before I decided to head home."

"What time was that?"

"I think it was just after eight p.m."

"And when you drove home, which route did you take?"

"Same way I went. County 25."

Tori and Braddock both knew that on County 25 there was nothing but farmland and woods from Pierz north to Manchester Bay. No chance of a traffic cam catching a glimpse to confirm.

She sat down on the table to Pemell's left, looking down at him and slipping back into her Bostonian accent. "So, Ian, what you're telling us is that nobody can account for you basically from noon yesterday on."

"Look—"

"So, fah example," she continued, "if someone said they saw a dusty blue Chevy panel van like the one you own in the park preserve between three thirty p.m. and four p.m., you can't dispute that?"

"I wasn't there."

"Can anyone verify that?"

He sighed. "No."

"And with that blue Chevy panel van, we have witnesses describing a man six feet tall, black hair, black running pants, shirt, stahking cap running in the park preserve between 3:30 and 4:00 p.m. yesterday."

"Again, it wasn't me."

"Oh come on, Ian! They are describing you! *You!*" Tori slapped the newspaper photo down in front of him. "That's you, is it not?"

"Yeah, that's me," he replied. "Yesterday was not me."

Tori leaned in. "Both are you. That is the description of the man who abducted Isabella Farner, racing out of the park preserve in a blue Chevy panel van in the direction of your house. They're all fahking describing you, Ian."

"No—"

"Where is she? Where is Izzy?"

"I don't know. I've never seen that girl before."

"Really? I mean, really? That's what you're going with?" Tori asked sarcastically before sitting down next to him. "This won't end well, you know," she said more evenly. "It can end better if you tell me where Izzy is. Where is that sweet little girl? What happened to her?"

"I have no idea."

"Bullshit," she growled, slamming the table. "Now you've made me angry. Now I'm comin' for ya. The federal prison system is littered with guys who will tell you that is not something you want. And I ain't coming for you just for Izzy Farner. I'm coming after you for Helena, for Joey Martinez and for anyone else you hahmed. I am going to make it my mission in life to put it all on you."

"I'd listen if I were you, Ian," Braddock said with a wry grin. "I know from experience she won't stop."

"I've taken down way better, tougher, smahter ones than you, Ian. Yahr nothin'."

"All the evidence points to you," Braddock murmured.

"If you got all that evidence, Detective, then arrest and charge me."

"You think we won't get it?" Tori said, knowing it was both a threat and an admission.

"I'm telling you, it wasn't me," Pemell insisted, folding his arms. "You're barking up the wrong tree. The both of you are."

"Prove it," Braddock said flatly. "Prove to us it wasn't you."

"Prove it *was* me, Detective Braddock. The burden is on you, isn't it?" Pemell turned back to Tori. "And with that, I got nothing else to fahkin' say to you."

Out in the hallway, Wilson joined them, a little smirk on her face. "I didn't know you were a Masshole, Tori."

"I still got a bit of it in me," Tori said with a wry smile. "Just trying to mess with him a little, throw him off. Not that it really worked. He's not wrong, the burden is on us. And right now, we don't have it."

"You've got the search warrants at least," Wilson said. "I'll have them for you within the hour. You can start turning this guy's life inside out," she added as she put her cell phone to her ear.

"I want you to do something for me," Braddock said when Wilson was out of earshot.

"Name it."

He leaned in. "Talk a little dirty to me that way the next time we're fooling around."

Tori smiled and whispered, "Sah thing, hun."

TEN

"IT COULD SUCK THE VARNISH OFF A TABLE"

They served the search warrants on Pemell and then drove him back to his house while he read them.

"I suppose I should contact my lawyer."

"That's up to you," Tori said, now back to speaking like a Minnesotan. "But it won't stop the search. Now, we can break the door down at the farmhouse or ..."

Pemell shook his head while sliding a key off his key ring. "Knock yourselves out."

They left him with deputies and two forensic scientists from the BCA and made a speed run down to Pierz. The farmhouse was set back a distance from the county road in a grove of mature trees that shielded it from view.

When they got out of Braddock's Tahoe, puffs of their breath floated in the crisp, clear evening air, a full moon providing illumination along with all the portable lights.

"Pew," Tori moaned as she stepped outside. "That smell."

"Ah yes," Braddock said with a grin. "The lovely scented aroma of fresh Minnesota manure. You're in farm country now. Don't tell me you never experienced this as a kid?"

"It's been a stretch," she replied, her eyes watering. "Oof, that's bad."

"Breathe through your mouth."

"Like that helps." The breeze out of the northwest was pushing the pungent odor in.

"You'll get used to it," he said, and then looked back down the long driveway to the road. "No media."

"Give them time," Tori replied. "My guess is that by now they're camped on the road outside Pemell's house back in Manchester Bay."

The Morrison County sheriff greeted them. A big car hauler was already on scene and forensic scientist Ann Jennison from the BCA was overseeing the operation. The hauler driver was hooking up the cables underneath the bumper of the panel van, which had been pulled out of the barn.

"That van looks really clean," Braddock observed as the sheen of the exterior glinted in the light.

"I'd say almost pristine," the sheriff said with raised eyebrows. "Hardly a speck of dirt on her."

"Was the barn door closed when you arrived, Sheriff?"

"Yes, ma'am. It had a deadbolt on it." Tori looked over to see a squared lock hanging loosely on the door handle, a victim of bolt cutters.

While Jennison worked with the van, Braddock and Tori stepped over to the old farmhouse, a smallish white two-story with a front porch. They quickly searched their way through the boxy house. It was clean and orderly, and fully furnished down to a kitchen full of plates and silverware and a shower with shampoo and soap.

"Odd that he uses this place," Tori mused, as they stepped back outside and peered around. "I mean, this is the middle of nowhere."

"Quiet and private."

"True. Nobody would hear or see a thing out here. Not even the cows."

"I get the economic case for keeping it," Braddock said. "If he's renting out the land and getting paid on it, he may come down from time to time to make sure it's being farmed properly. I would if that land was supposed to be generating income for me. And I bet on occasion he rents the house out, perhaps to farm hands. Plus, other than paying taxes, he owns it free and clear. If the land is making him money, why get rid of it?"

The white barn with green trim was chipped and faded and in need of a coat of paint, although it remained an otherwise sturdy structure. Besides space for the van inside it, there were hay bales, shovels and rakes, and penned areas once used for animals. Overhead, there was a loft filled with more hay.

They stepped back outside to see that the van was now up on the hauler bed and ready to be driven away.

"Ann, that van is top priority," Tori said.

"I'll start processing when I get back. I'll work it overnight."

Jennison left. Other BCA agents were now working inside the house.

"There's nothing left to do here." Tori headed for the car.

Their next stop was Health Tech Administrators in St. Cloud. Phyllis Simpson, the owner, let them inside the one-story blue glass and cement office building in an industrial park of like buildings. The IT director, Jim Wolfson, was there as well. Simpson quickly explained that the company administered health and pension plans for employers. Pemell was employed as part of the IT group, tasked with maintaining the security of their clients' business and employee data.

"What has Ian gotten himself into?" Simpson asked. "You suspect him in this abduction in Manchester Bay? Have I been employing some sort of a pedophile? My gosh."

"We don't know that. His name has come up as part of our

investigation," Braddock answered. "That's all I can say at this point."

"He's an ethical hacker for you?" Tori asked, getting right to it.

"He's quite good."

"What makes him good?"

Simpson thought for a moment. "For starters, he has great technical skill and knowledge, and is innovative."

"You have to have a criminal mindset, right?" Tori asked. "Think like the people trying to get into your system and access the data."

"Yes," Wolfson answered, nodding. "He's extremely patient and persistent. To do the job you have to methodically pick away at things, hunting for vulnerabilities. But when he does find a way in, he then seems capable of helping me solve any problems we have."

"That seems to check all the boxes," Braddock said.

"And he's cool under pressure too," Simpson said. "I mean, almost flatline. We're all frantic when someone is attempting to hack us, but I listen to him on the phone and wonder if he even has a pulse."

"He works remotely, then?" Tori asked.

Simpson nodded. "Mostly. We're responsible for a lot of personal and financial data, so he hacks around our system trying to find our vulnerabilities. When he does, he gets on the phone with Jim, and they figure out how to close the hole."

"How long has he worked here?"

Simpson reviewed the personnel file. "I hired him a little over four years ago."

"Ever have any performance or disciplinary issues with him?"

"No," she replied, and looked to Wolfson, who shook his head. "He gets his work done. He's a reliable employee."

"Why not have him work here in the office?"

"He prefers not to, and I'm ... good with that," Simpson replied.

Braddock caught the hesitation. "Why?"

Simpson looked to Wolfson again. "Ian is not the most ... social person. I mean, he's an odd duck. He is very smart but doesn't have a lot of tact. He has no problem slamming people if they're not keeping up with him."

"You're saying he's kind of a dick."

Wolfson nodded. "I don't think he gets that he's being that way. He seems to lack that ability to pick up on those kinds of social cues. So the less time he spends in the office, and around our other people, probably the better."

"But he did come into the office yesterday, around eleven a.m.?"

Wolfson nodded. "He comes in when we have our department meetings. It lasted an hour or so, then he and I discussed a matter for another ten minutes and he left."

"When he got here, was he driving his Honda CRV or his van?"

"Uh, I don't know, but we could check. I have security cameras that monitor the parking lot."

Simpson led them to her office, where she pulled up footage on a computer screen. At 10:55 a.m., a blue Chevy panel van pulled into the parking lot. Ian got out of it and walked into the building. Simpson fast-forwarded through the video, and they watched him leave at 12:10.

"Did he say what he was doing for the rest of the day?"

She nodded. "He said something about working from his farm. I know he has some land north of here."

"Email a copy of that video footage to me if you would," Braddock asked, handing her his card.

. . .

Their next stop was the car wash. It had closed several hours ago, and the manager was sitting outside in his car, the window down, smoking a cigar, awaiting their arrival.

"Thanks for coming in at this late hour," Tori said.

He nodded. "Not a problem. I went and had a few beers down the road and rolled back."

"Still."

"Hey, gotta do it, you know, especially if it involves a missing girl. I got a daughter of my own, though she's twenty now. What time are we looking at here?"

"Between twelve ten and three p.m.," Tori replied.

The manager took them into his office and sat down at his desk, where he went through the surveillance footage for that time window. "Here you go."

At 12:22 p.m., the van pulled up into the opening for the car wash. Once it was set in the track, Pemell got out and went inside. After the exterior wash was completed, an attendant pulled the vehicle forward. One man wiped down the exterior while the other vacuumed out the inside.

"Is that vacuum powerful?" Tori asked.

"It could suck the varnish off a table."

Braddock hung up his call with Mary.

"How's Quinn doing?" Tori asked.

"Sounds like pretty good," Braddock said, his wrist draped over the steering wheel as they drove north back to Manchester Bay. "Roger and Mary took him to their house for the night. He's staying there."

"How was he feeling?"

"Better. They played a few board games tonight and he was into it, lively, obnoxious, normal, at least for a while, until he lost some steam."

"That's a good sign." The three of them often played board games, and Quinn was ever the competitor, and an enthusiastic over-the-top celebrator when he won.

"Mary thinks he'll be good to go back to school by Monday."

"Kids heal fast."

Braddock nodded. "I'm most happy about his head. Concussions are worrying, especially at his age. If that's resolving, it's good."

It was midnight when they made it back to Pemell's house outside Manchester Bay. Reese was on scene, standing in the front yard drinking a gas station coffee.

"The BCA is still inside," he reported when they arrived. "I went through the place with Nolan. She's still poking around."

"Nolan?" Braddock asked. "She's supposed to be sleeping."

"Maybe she's sleepwalking then."

"Did you find anything of interest?" Tori asked.

"Nothing that jumps out. Nothing that said Isabella Farner had been here, that Pemell's been observing her, that she was at all on his mind. Maybe the forensic scientists will find something that says otherwise."

"How about something that didn't jump out?"

"His clothing piqued my interest on my second time through his closet."

"How so?" Braddock asked.

"He's not much of a dresser shall we say. Lots of jeans, T-shirts and sweatshirts, very casual. He might own two collared long-sleeve shirts. If he had to go to a wedding, he'd have to rent or buy something. What he does own is all hues of black, dark blue and gray. Not a bold color to be found, and that includes his running clothes. He likes black especially. Very monochromatic."

"I suppose that tells us something," Tori said. "People who described our runner and van owner said he was in black running clothes."

"It's a piece," Braddock agreed. "A small one. Find enough small ones and all the sudden you got something."

"Maybe the computers will tell a different story," Nolan remarked as she approached. "We'll need someone to scrub those."

"I thought I told you to get some rest," Braddock said, scowling.

"I got four hours, I'm good," Nolan replied before offering a sarcastic grin. "There's a little girl missing and you're searching houses and farms? I ain't missing out on that. I'll sleep when it's over."

Now that was natural police talk there, Tori thought. Nolan could be on her team any day.

Tori and Braddock stepped inside, and this time Tori took a tour around with a more discerning eye as to Pemell and how he lived. Like the farmhouse, his home was orderly and neat. It contained minimal furnishings. As she checked out the kitchen, she noted empty cupboards or ones with few items inside. The living room had a bland sofa, a squared black coffee table, and one chair. The den in the back of the house was much the same: a couch, a recliner, and a flat screen that sat on a small entertainment cabinet. Inside the cabinet was an old stereo system with CDs and a few movie DVDs.

Pemell's bedroom had a queen-sized bed, a nightstand, and a dresser that held clothing basics: T-shirts, socks, underwear. The closet was as Reese had described. The man owned one pair of black dress shoes and two pairs of black casual loafers. There were several pairs of running shoes of various brands.

If he'd had Isabella at the house, she probably would have

been in the basement. Tori found Braddock down there, peering around at the mostly empty space.

"He doesn't own much," he remarked. Six boxes of junk sat on the shelves. "The guy lives like a monk."

Tori nodded as she slowly walked the area. In another corner was the furnace, water heater and water softener. There was barely a speck of dust on the floor. "And cleanly."

"It's late and we're accomplishing nothing here," Braddock noted. It was after 1:00 a.m. "It's been a long one. Let's finish things up and get back at it first thing."

"We haven't found Izzy yet. She's out there somewhere."

"Is she?"

"Ye—" Tori stopped herself and closed her eyes. "I don't know."

"That's right, we don't know. Look, if she's dead, our sleeping won't matter," Braddock said matter-of-factly. "If she's still alive, you're not going to find her if you can't think straight. For now, we rest."

An hour later, the two of them were lying in bed, Tori's eyes hypnotically following the arms of the ceiling fan around in a circle. She was tired, but sleep was elusive. Braddock seemed to have drifted off.

Or not.

"Penny for your thoughts?" he asked.

"That's all they're worth?"

"I need a sample of the merchandise before I agree to pay more," he said, although his eyes remained closed.

Tori smirked. "Right now, I'm thinking about Isabella and where she could be, and then I'm thinking about Pemell and him having the van washed before the abduction."

"I've been thinking along those lines as well," he said. "We won't find anything. But you already know that. You're looking for the deeper meaning of it."

"Did he do that just by happenstance, or did he do it so that when we had the BCA process the van, he could say, of course you didn't find anything. I had just had it washed yesterday."

"In other words, he uses the van in the abduction, does whatever he did with Isabella, and then takes it back to the farm and washes and vacuums it again, but he's already covered why there would be no evidence because he had it ..."

"Washed and detailed the morning of the abduction," Tori finished. She sighed in frustration.

Braddock rolled to face her. "Ian Pemell feels a whole lotta right, and then ..."

"He doesn't." She looked at him. "You see it too."

"I do."

"I'm thinking about all this, it's running around in my mind. And I've seen something, noticed something important. I saw it yesterday, something in the park preserve, but I just can't work it out."

He rolled onto his back and pulled her to him, letting her rest her head comfortably on his chest, lightly running his fingers through her hair. "Let it go for now. It'll all be there in the morning."

"I'm not wired like that. It just stays with me."

"I know," he said as he gently kissed the top of her head before pulling her closer, wrapping her in his long arms. "Is that a little better?"

"Much," Tori said, her eyes closed, her body warm against his. A few minutes later, she drifted off to sleep.

* * *

Ca-chunk!

Izzy burst awake and sat up as the door opened and light poured inside. The masked man dressed all in black stepped into the room. He held a newspaper and a cell phone.

"What time is it?" she asked, trying to regulate her eyes to the bright light.

"Sit here," he ordered, pointing to the end of the mattress and ignoring her question.

She pushed off the musty wool blanket and sleepily slid to the end and put both feet on the floor.

The man handed her the newspaper. The headline read: *Isabella Farner Still Missing*. "Hold the front of the paper toward me."

Izzy did as she was told, but let her eyes drift right out the door. Whenever she'd been led to the bathroom, the lights were always turned off and she couldn't see anything. With the lights now on in the room, she could see across to an open door and then a stairway up.

"Hold the paper up and look up at the phone."

She held still while he took several pictures, changing his angle a few times. Then he snatched the newspaper from her and started for the door.

"I need to go to the bathroom," she said.

He sighed. "Okay." He stuffed the phone into his back pocket and walked her there with his hand on her back.

After she flushed the toilet, she stepped to the sink and washed her hands, then reached to the small towel to dry off. Her arm in motion to knock on the door, she glanced left and noticed the water wasn't draining from the sink. The stopper was plugging it. She reached for the lift rod behind the faucet handles and pulled up, but the stopper didn't move.

"Hmpf," she murmured as she reached down into the water and pulled the stopper loose. It wasn't attached. She pulled it all the way out and watched as the water quickly drained.

Thump! Thump! Thump!

"Just a second," she said as she examined the stopper for a moment before stuffing it back in the drain and then wiping her hands on the towel again. "Okay."

The man opened the door and led her back to her prison. Leaving her in the middle of the room, he pulled the door back into place.

Ca-chunk!

Izzy lay back with her head on the pillow. The room was cold, and she pulled the blanket up to her chin and thought about the sink stopper in the bathroom. Her eyes drifted up to the camera, the small red light illuminated.

* * *

Rust climbed the steps and closed the door behind him, then went to the dining room to find Vaughn and Cain sitting at the table. They reviewed the pictures he'd taken, whittling them down to the one they wanted.

"You know where to go," Cain said.

An hour later, his dashboard clock reading 4:07 a.m., he turned the corner and switched off his headlights. He drove carefully along the street, seeing the path and then pulling over to the right, parking underneath the broad canopy of a massive oak tree. He sat for two minutes, the engine off, surveying the neighborhood. The houses within his field of view all remained dark. He pulled his black stocking cap low on his forehead and reached for his coffee tumbler.

He walked around the back of his truck and then up onto the sidewalk, passing one house before he turned left down a paved path, the night air still, puffs of his breath lingering in the air as he hurried along in his black running shoes, nylon sweatpants and layered black coat.

The path weaved its way through a dense tree and slew-like wetland mix until it emerged between two houses and onto another leafy street. He turned right along the sidewalk, eyeing up the row of four mailboxes and newspaper slots mounted on the thick brown-stained wooden post. Taking one last glance around the darkened neighborhood, he pulled open the third mailbox and stuffed the small package well inside, then kept right on walking.

ELEVEN

"WE'VE BEEN EUCHRED"

Whoosh!

Tori's eyes slowly fluttered open at the gust of wind and the little thump made by one of the bedroom window panes. She turned her head to the right: the clock on the nightstand said it was 5:48 a.m. She knew her alarm was set to go off at 6:15. Did she sleep a little more or get up. She slowly lifted the comforter and slipped out of bed.

Inside the small walk-in closet, she allowed herself a brief smile. Everything here was hers.

If moving her furniture in hadn't proved a challenge, moving her clothes in had. Some groundwork had been laid. Over the last year, she had slowly but steadily commandeered nearly half of the small walk-in closet. She and Braddock had joked about it often, her clothes slowly multiplying like an invasive species. However, when she made the full move, it became readily apparent that the closet wasn't remotely close to having the requisite capacity.

"You can't possibly wear all of these," Braddock had

remarked in wonder at the stacks upon stacks of garments on the bed.

"Oh yes I can," she said with a big smile. She put some of them in the guest room closet, but she still needed more space. "This is a real problem," she noted over dinner one night early on. "We're stumbling over everything. The clothing rod in the closet is going to collapse under the weight. I have to be careful every time I try to pull out an outfit."

Braddock solved the problem the next day by buying a large armoire and moving all his clothes into it, leaving her the closet.

"Well now I really know you're committed to this relationship," Tori said before kissing him. "It must be love."

"This is a temporary solution, though," he'd said. "The armoire eats up a lot of space in here." He looked out the back window to the small gap between the house and the detached garage. "But there is one thing I've been thinking of doing."

"What's that?"

"Adding on."

"Adding on? To the house?"

"Yeah. Tie the house into the garage. Why not?"

"Because it would cost a lot of money."

"Everything costs money," he said with a mocking wave. "I've got the money. I own the house free and clear."

"Wait? You don't have a mortgage?"

"No," Braddock said. "The house was a gift to Meghan and me from Roger and Mary. It was going to be our summer house so we would come back and visit. When I moved here with Quinn, Roger gave me the keys and said it was mine. I just pay the taxes."

"So you could do—"

"Whatever I want. You have any ideas?"

"I don't know. I mean, it's your house."

"No," he said. "It's *our* house. If you have any ideas, any wants and desires, I'd like to hear them."

"Gosh," she mused, looking about the master bed and bathroom. "More space in here, in the closet and bathroom, would be nice. Make it a real master suite."

"Okay then. That's a start."

Braddock was serious. He had an appointment scheduled with an architect the following week to discuss a larger master suite, along with an expansion of Quinn's bedroom. And he was also thinking about remodeling some other parts of the house, "To really update and modernize it for us."

For us.

That was something she was still getting accustomed too, the concept of *us*.

She put on some exercise clothes, tiptoed out of the bedroom, and made her way down to the basement and the exercise bike. A former triathlete, Tori had thought the last thing she needed was some manic instructor on a video screen urging her to keep going to be her best self. *I am motivated.* Braddock suggested she give it a try one morning when there was a biblical deluge outside preventing her from her normal run. He looked up the scheduled classes on his phone. "Lookie here. There's a live one in ten minutes. Sixty-minute high-intensity interval bike ride. High-intensity, *perfect* for you," he mocked.

"Ha ha."

"Give it a shot."

"I don't know ..."

"You said you've been feeling the running in your joints a little," he said. "Maybe this would be better for them. I mean, what do you have to lose? You'll get a good workout. You will sweat—profusely."

"Okay, okay. Show me how this works."

He set up her profile, showed her how to find the class, and then left.

She got on the bike, and fifteen minutes in, a good sweat building, she found herself warming to it, the pace, the music, the energy. Not so much from the instructor, who was ridiculously enthusiastic and overly caffeinated. Nobody could be that up all the time, could they? Rather, it was seeing the others in the studio also working out, and their statistics on the side of the monitor, and the fact that there were standings. *Standings?* She saw her name well down from the top. That was when competitive Tori kicked in.

Sixty minutes later, her body glistening with sweat, her water bottle completely drained, she emerged from the basement to find Braddock in his workout clothes, ready to head down for his turn. He took one look at her and smiled. "So?"

"It was fine."

He laughed. She said *fine* when she couldn't bring herself to admit he was right, another competitive trait.

Her actions in the weeks following answered his question anyway. She was on the bike more and more. In passing, she'd even mentioned getting the companion running treadmill.

"That would be ... fine," he said with big toothy smile.

"Okay, okay, you were right. I like it. Dammit, I hate it when you're right."

Now she got on the bike and joined the half-hour class that started at 6:00 a.m. Exercise was also when she processed what was on her mind and worked through problems. And as she'd said to Braddock last night, something was gnawing at her about the case. It was something about the park preserve, about that spot, about how the abduction had occurred. It had popped into her mind when she'd first arrived on scene, but then she'd lost it in the scramble around Quinn and assessing his condition. She needed to go back to the park.

The cycling class completed, she got off the bike and made her way upstairs. Braddock was up, dressed in his workout clothes. "I'm going to just do a quick half-hour one."

"Will you be selecting the class with the perky blonde or the steamy redhead?" Tori asked.

"Duh, the steamy redhead."

She laughed and snapped him with her towel.

Braddock had made coffee. She poured herself a cup and went back upstairs thinking about the case, the park preserve, Ian Pemell, Isabella, all of it, on an endless loop in her head.

She took a shower, letting the warm water and steam work her muscles before she finally dressed and made her way to the kitchen and a coffee refresh. As she sat down at the table, her phone buzzed. She didn't recognize the number other than that it was a local exchange. "Hello?"

"Tori?"

"Yes."

"This is Luciana. Is it okay that I called?"

"Of course." Tori could tell she'd been crying.

"All I can think about is Izzy."

"If it's any consolation, me too," Tori said.

"On the news they're reporting that you searched a house here and then some farm further south. Is that true?"

"Yes."

"Are they owned by the man you brought in yesterday?"

"Yes."

"Have you found anything?"

"That is all still in process."

"Did he take her?"

Tori hesitated. "We don't know. He hasn't admitted to it, he's denied involvement. Based on our interview of him and what we've learned, we had enough for search warrants. I'll know soon if we've found anything."

"They said he was a suspect in a case like this in Thief River Falls."

"He was a person of interest in a disappearance up there," Tori answered. "It was a similar kind of case, a similar method of abduction, which is how he came to our attention."

"He wasn't arrested then. They said there wasn't enough evidence to charge him," Luciana said, her voice quivering now. "Is that going to happen again?"

Tori took a breath. "We don't know for certain that he took Isabella."

"But he's done it before."

Tori didn't necessarily disagree with her thoughts on that point. "The investigators in Thief River Falls couldn't prove—"

"They never found the missing girl, Tori! He got away with it. And you're not going to find Izzy either."

She was getting spun up and upset. Tori's educated guess was that she'd spent the whole night doing this. "Luciana," she said calmly.

"He's going to get away with it again," she said, sobbing. "He is."

Braddock came into the kitchen and mouthed: *Luciana?*

Tori nodded. "We don't know yet that this is the man who took Izzy. We don't know that."

"But, Tori—"

"His name came up. There was reason to take a longer look at him given the history, so that's what we're doing."

"The news said he may own a vehicle like the one involved in the abduction."

The newsies were on the story good, Tori thought. "As we told you, witnesses described a blue cargo van racing away from the scene."

"And this man owns one."

"Yes."

"But you haven't found any sign of Izzy yet."

"No, but—"

"She's been missing for so long now. It's been forty hours, Tori!"

"That clock is running in my head too."

"If it's not this man, do you have any other suspects?"

Tori closed her eyes and shook her head. It was another thing bothering her. Ian Pemell was all they had, and they were, as Luciana had pointed out, forty hours in. "No," she answered truthfully. "But in my experience, that can change quickly. What's important is—"

"Dammit, don't manage me, Tori! I manage people through crisis all the time. I know the technique. I know the tone. I know the vocabulary."

"I'm not," Tori said. "I won't do that. You and your husband are Will's friends. Isabella is Quinn's friend. I'm just speaking from having been through this a lot of times."

"How many of these cases have you handled?"

"Too many."

"In your experience, do the children always come back?"

"Always?" Tori replied before pausing. "No."

"At least you're honest."

"What's also true is that just because time is ticking and we're this many hours in, it doesn't mean she *won't* come back. You have to hold on to that. It's all you can do. Don't give up. I'm not, so you can't either."

* * *

George Santo looked out the window beside the front door and then stepped out onto the stoop with his cup of coffee in hand. He headed down his driveway to the street, then walked to the bank of mailboxes a house to the south. Margie Nelson, one of his neighbors, was there with her elderly black Lab, Otis. Margie served as something of a neighborhood social director.

"Morning, Margie," George greeted, and then leaned down to scratch Otis gently behind his ears.

"Oh, George," Margie said sympathetically. "Is there any word, any word at all, on your niece?"

"No, not yet," he said as he pulled out his *Star Tribune* from the newspaper slot.

"How are Luciana and Sam holding up?"

"Not well. They're petrified, and so far the police don't seem to have any answers, although we heard on the news that they might have a suspect. They did some searches, but they haven't told Sam and Luciana anything about it yet. But if they're doing that, my worry is ..." He caught his breath. "Well, if they're searching, I'm not sure it's good. I'm not sure that means they're going to find her alive." He sighed hard. "It's tough. Luciana and Sam are just wrecks right now."

"And I can tell you are too," Margie said, patting him on the arm. "I know what that little girl means to you. Please know we're all thinking of you."

"Thank you, Margie. You're very kind."

"Let Luciana and Sam know they're in our prayers. They're all in our prayers. If there is anything we can do—food, errands, searches, gosh, anything—you just let us all know. We don't want to intrude, but we want to help."

"Thanks, Margie. People are just so kind here."

"It's Minnesota. It's what we do for our friends and neighbors. You have my cell; call any time and I'll rally the troops." Margie turned and walked away with her newspaper and mail.

George slipped out his newspaper and then opened his mailbox. Yesterday's mail was still inside. He removed it and then looked inside again. What was that?

* * *

"That had to be a tough call," Braddock said as he turned onto Lake Drive, heading toward town. "She sounded like she was ..."

"Desperate," Tori said, finishing the thought. "She feels her daughter slipping away. She's starting to have those thoughts that she'll never see her again. I know what that's like."

As Braddock turned the corner and entered the parking lot for the government center, they both saw the assembled media. Trucks from all the Twin Cities television stations were visible, as was a van for the regional television station based in Manchester Bay.

"Terrific," he said sarcastically.

"You had to know this was coming," Tori muttered as he pulled into a parking space.

The reporters had already identified Braddock's Tahoe and quickly descended on them en masse.

"You have anything you want to say?" Tori asked.

"You're the lead."

"You're chief detective."

"And I delegated."

"We don't have anything that is ... updative."

"Is that a word?"

"It is now."

They made their way to the entrance, walking the gauntlet. Reporters hovered around them like an amoeba, following them along the sidewalk, hurling questions about the searches, and whether there were any leads on the whereabouts of Isabella Farner.

Braddock issued a string of "no comments" as they battled through the crowd.

"Special Agent Hunter," a reporter hollered. "In your experience—"

"I have no comment either."

"But aren't you concerned about how many hours it's been since—"

"No comment."

"Is Ian Pemell a suspect? Will you be charging him?" another reporter asked, stepping in front of her, forcing her to stop.

Tori locked eyes with him. He'd specifically named someone who was not yet charged or in police custody. Regardless of whether Pemell's name was or was not already out there, that was something responsible news organizations did not do.

"What part of no comment didn't you understand?" she said as she glared at the man. She might have been much smaller in stature, but the flash of displeasure in her eyes quickly backed him off.

Braddock stopped. "I understand you all have questions and are looking for information. All I can tell you right now is that our investigation is ongoing. At this point I have nothing for you on the two properties that were searched. When we do have something to report, we'll report it."

"Well, that was fun," he said once they were inside the building.

"That reporter blurted out our suspect's name for everyone to hear."

"It's not like they don't all know who he is at this point. It's out there. An address search gives them his name. They know about the old Thief River Falls case."

"Sure," Tori replied. "But he hasn't been charged with anything. And if we don't charge him, it'll just be a mess."

"I don't disagree," Braddock said. "By the way, where did

you learn to stare daggers like that? I think that reporter thought you were going to kill him with X-ray vision or something."

"I have absolutely no idea what you're talking about."

"I hope you never give me that look."

She turned and smiled seductively. "I'll save it for when I get the chance to use my Boston accent in the way you asked me to yesterday."

"Hmm. That could be hot."

When they stepped inside the investigations unit, Nolan was back in her cubicle. Her desktop had been cleared, but her garbage and recycling cans were overflowing. It looked like a landfill.

"Tell me something," Tori said.

"I've been through Pemell's phone records. Very little activity. Many of the calls are to three co-workers, I presume discussing work-related things."

"For a techie he sure doesn't spend much time on his phone?" Tori asked.

Nolan put her hand on top of a stack of papers. "His financials look pretty ... mundane. Health Tech Administrators provides a steady paycheck, certainly more than I make." She looked up. "Maybe I should have gone into IT."

"They don't let you carry a gun. You'd be bored shitless."

"True, although more money would be nice. What do you say, boss?"

"The only money I'm interested in right now is Pemell's finances," Braddock said.

"Finances. Right. He's getting rent payments for the farmland in Pierz. He has some money in the bank, checking and savings, that gives him a cushion. His pay stubs show that he puts money into a 401k, although I wouldn't call it a robust balance. He has normal bill activity: a mortgage, plus a monthly payment on his Honda, utilities, insurance on the SUV and van. He buys his running gear through Amazon or from other online retailers. He also orders in food a lot. He particularly likes Mexican. There are a ton of charges to the Taco Truck."

"The little Mexican food place on the street?" Tori said.

"Yes. Three to four days a week he has charges there. He's not much for cooking his own meals, apparently."

"What about his computers?"

"The BCA has techies going through them, but I've heard nothing yet. He'd have to know we'd scrub them, so I'm not holding my breath."

They left Nolan to continue her work and went to Braddock's office, where Steak and Eggleston were waiting.

"Where are you two at on your homicide?" Braddock inquired as he took a seat behind his desk. "I could use some good news for a change."

"We don't have any really," Steak said. "We're working it. The shop was dusted for prints, but apart from Weltz's, there was only one other set, and those were on one of the saws in the back, nowhere near the office area. Those prints are being run, but I tend to think they're not going to tell us anything."

"The friend who found him hadn't heard from him in a few days but said that wasn't unusual. He couldn't think of any enemies Weltz would have had," Eggleston reported, flipping through her notes. "He was by all accounts a pleasant fellow, a whiz at building custom shelving, doors, bars, tables, things of that nature. We found a pitch book of things he'd made," she added, handing it over to Tori, who quickly flipped through the photos.

"Wow," she said. "Look at that bar."

"The black wood one that looks like an Irish pub?" Steak said.

"Yeah."

"That's way cool."

"Something like that would look good in your basement," Tori said to Braddock.

"You mean our basement?"

She smiled. "Yes, our basement."

Braddock looked at the photo. "It would at that."

"You two, living together," Steak needled. "It's so cute."

"Shut up," Tori retorted.

"Weltz's business records looked like they were rifled through," Braddock said, getting them back on track. "That says to me that the answer lies there."

"Sure, except for the fact that these guys probably found what they were looking for and took it."

"Then figure out what's missing," Tori suggested.

"How about you work your case and I'll work mine," Steak retorted, playfully whacking her in the shoulder with his notebook.

"All kidding aside, though, that's what you need to do," Braddock said. "He had family, didn't he?"

"Two adult children. We're meeting with them here shortly, but neither lives locally or had daily interaction with him. His son lives in Minneapolis and his daughter in Sioux Falls, South Dakota. They probably won't be able to tell us much."

"Did he have anyone who worked with him?" Tori asked, still holding the portfolio of projects. "I would think he must have had some help building and installing some of these things. They're big jobs."

"Not to mention the fingerprints on the saw," Braddock noted. "Those could have been from the helper."

Steak looked to Eggs. "What do you think?"

"We organized the business records, so we need to go through them. It's a big stack—heck, a couple of stacks. And we need to look at his finances and bookkeeping. If we go through all that, we should figure out if he was paying someone."

"Where are you at on Isabella Farner?" Steak asked Tori.

Tori's phone started buzzing. She looked at the screen. "I think we're about to find out."

"The van is clean as can be, outside and in," Jennison said as she walked them around the vehicle.

"Nothing?" Tori asked, eyebrows raised. "Seriously?"

"Nada," Jennison replied with a shake of the head. "Hardly a speck of dirt. I mean, you could eat off the floor."

"He had it cleaned Wednesday. We have the footage from the car wash," Braddock noted. "They said it was a powerful vacuum."

"They weren't lying," Jennison said. "I mean, we didn't even find one hair back there. Not a one."

Tori leaned into the back of the van. "Does he keep it clean like this all the time?"

"I wondered about that too." Jennison crooked her finger for them to follow her to her computer. "This is the surveillance video from the car wash." She moved the mouse and fast-forwarded to when the van emerged from the washer, then froze the picture. "Look inside the back. This was before they vacuumed it."

"Pretty clean," Braddock said. He turned and walked back to the vehicle.

"I thought so too." She clicked to a different camera angle. "The front cab was clean as well."

"Which fits in a way," Tori noted. "His house was neat and orderly. The farmhouse as well. No reason his vehicle would be any different. Has your team found anything at either house?"

"Not so far. Both places have been processed, but I've seen

nothing that suggests that Isabella Farner was in either. And I have found no evidence that she was ever in that van."

Tori and Jennison went back to the van to join Braddock. Tori looked in the back again. The floor was covered with black rubber. There were brackets running horizontally on either side that could be used to secure cargo. There were also slots for a second-row bench seat.

"Before you ask," Jennison said, "the bench seat is over there." She gestured. "We found it under a tarp in his barn and processed it. It's clean as well. I don't think it has been used much, probably not for years."

Tori walked around the van. She noticed a small amount of dirt on the tires, but not an excessive amount. "There's some dirt here under the wheel wells."

"I noticed that as well," Jennison answered. "We took a sample for testing, the results of which I'm awaiting, but I'd wager a hundred dollars it'll match the soil on his driveway. That's what my eyes are telling me anyway."

"The barn floor is soil as well," Tori noted. "Is there any possibility that he had it washed in St. Cloud, drove it back to the farm, used it for the abduction, and then washed and vacuumed it again? I mean, he had time to do that. We didn't start looking at him until ... seventeen, eighteen hours after the abduction."

Jennison crinkled her nose. "I didn't see anything out at the farm that evidenced that. No buckets, cloths, or car wash soap. I could go back and take another look."

"Don't bother," Braddock said.

Tori swiveled to him. "Why not?"

"Because I don't think he could have done it, at least not with *this* van." He was tapping on his phone, using the calculator.

"How come?"

He gestured to the sticker on the side door. "He had the oil changed eight days ago, in Little Falls. The mileage sticker says the van's mileage at the time of the change was 82,457. It's ten miles from Little Falls to his farmhouse. It's thirty-three miles to Health Tech Administrators and then thirty-three miles back, so sixty-six on a round trip. That would be a total of seventy-six miles. The odometer currently reads 82,533. That's seventy-six miles on the dot post oil change."

"You can manipulate an odometer, can't you?" Tori asked, and looked to Jennison, who was pulling on rubber gloves.

"It's not super easy to do, but our suspect is an IT guy. Let's look."

In the meantime, Tori called Nolan. "Look at his financials. Did he have a credit card charge last week in Little Falls at ... Falls Service? Uh-huh ... What day? ... Okay." She shook her head. "He had the oil changed eight days ago."

It took Jennison nearly an hour, with the help of another tech, videotaping and snapping photos along the way as they worked to get to the circuit board behind the dashboard. Once they accessed it, she looked it over carefully and checked for fingerprints.

"No prints," she said.

"He could have wiped it down," Tori replied.

"I don't think so. I mean, look at what we just had to do. We had to disassemble the dashboard. He would have had to do the same, and I see no evidence that that has been done within the last two days. If you look closely, there is just the slightest film of dust on the board. A natural kind of accumulation over time. If it had been disturbed, we'd be able to see it."

"And the mileage adds up perfectly," Braddock said. "I mean, on the nuts."

"Damn." Tori grimaced. "This wasn't the van our witnesses saw in the park preserve."

"I have to say, I was dubious he would have used his own van," Jennison said. "I mean, pardon my French, but if you're smart, you just don't shit where you eat."

Tori closed her eyes and smiled. It all suddenly clicked.

Braddock saw it. "What?"

"I know what's been bothering me," she said. "I know what I saw now. We need to go to the park preserve."

"I saw it just after I got here and checked on Quinn," Tori said as Braddock pulled to a stop, the yellow crime-scene tape still fluttering in the afternoon wind. "It just didn't register fully with me at the time, but now it does."

"Why?"

"Think about what Jennison said. You know, you don't sh—"

"Yeah, yeah," Braddock finished. "I get that. But he still hasn't accounted for his whereabouts during the abduction."

"Except the whole premise of that assumes he was using his van. We've conclusively proved that he didn't. That was not the van used on Wednesday."

"Are you suggesting he used a van that looks like the one he owns? You think he went that far?"

"No, I don't think he used one at all," Tori said, shaking her head. "Think about what we know about Ian. He's an ethical hacker. His employer describes him as smart, organized, intelligent, and cool under pressure. The police in Thief River Falls never cracked him, he never gave them anything. You and I went after him, and he didn't so much as flinch. He got a little flustered here and there, but overall, he parried us pretty good. Meaning ..."

"He planned it so well we can't possibly prove it, or more likely," Braddock grimaced, "he didn't do it and knew from experience that once the process had played out, we'd walk away from him."

"What did Dana Bryan say? He was more psychopath than any sort of sociopath. No empathy."

"Right."

"He's this cold and calculating type. So would a cold, calculating psychopath use his own vehicle for the abduction? And would he use it to abduct someone where there were as many potential witnesses as there are here in the park? Would he do it in a place where he runs on occasion, and while wearing his usual running attire, so that people could recognize him?"

Braddock was following now. "Nor would he have fled the park preserve through a residential neighborhood where more people could see him when if he turned left instead of right out of the parking lot, in a quarter-mile he's on the county road where it's far less likely he'll be spotted."

"Nor would he drive the direction that takes him near his home, because if he did that, he would draw people there."

"What was it he said? The burden isn't on me, it's on you," Braddock said. "Still ..." his voice drifted off, "there is something about him that isn't sitting right with me."

"Me neither." Tori nodded in agreement. "I read the Helena Hernandez investigative file. I see why the police up there focused on him. I think he did that one. The facts are a lot like this case. He owned the same kind of van. He lived nearby."

"All facts that you could find on an Internet search," Braddock said. "And if you knew Ian Anderson was now Ian Pemell and lived here ..."

"He would be an obvious suspect once we ran across his name, and we would spend time, a lot of time, looking at him."

Tori took a long look around the park preserve, the area of the abduction, the escape routes. "We've been euchred."

"He didn't do this."

"But damn if someone didn't want us to think he did." She scanned the area again, visualizing in her mind how it had gone down. Closing her eyes, replaying what Quinn had told her. "Was this a one-man job?"

Braddock contemplated the question. "He gets Izzy in the van and races away immediately. I mean, that's what Quinn said. But I know what you're inferring. Could he have done it by himself? Or was there a second man?"

Tori nodded. "Someone in the van to control Izzy, who is twelve, a hockey player, someone who would have some fight in her. She might not just sit idly in the corner while this man takes her. She would struggle."

"Unless she couldn't."

"I want to talk to Pemell again."

A sheriff's deputy was parked at the end of the long driveway to Pemell's house and moved to allow them to drive in. Pemell let them inside. Oddly, he had not yet retained a lawyer. They took seats in the den in the back of the house.

"Did you get an oil change on your van a week last Thursday?"

Pemell's eyes brightened. "I did. In Little Falls. Falls Service. That was the last time I drove the van before Wednesday, when I got it washed. The mileage should—"

"We know," Tori said. "Hypothetically, if it wasn't you in the park preserve, if that wasn't your van, then why would someone go to such lengths to put you there?"

"I told you it wasn't me."

"That wasn't my question, Ian."

He shook his head. "I'm not naïve. I'm forever screwed by what happened in Thief River Falls."

"Ian—"

"I know, not your question, but don't I have a right to defend myself?"

Tori stared him down.

"Okay, fine. It's been six years since Thief River Falls which I didn't do."

"Ian!"

"Fine, you don't believe me, but that wasn't me then and this isn't me now. People up in Thief had it in for me, which is why I left. I couldn't stay. But I've had no issues with anyone since I've been here. I can't fathom why anyone around here would have something against me. I changed my last name. I don't venture out much other than to take a run or grab something to eat. I keep my head down and work out of my house for a company an hour away, or at least I did. I'm probably going to be fired now."

"Yet a van just like yours was used," Braddock retorted. "Witness descriptions describe someone who looks an awful lot like you, all the way down to your black monochromatic running attire."

"I wear black because I'm color blind."

"Fine, interesting side note."

"Detective Braddock, Agent Hunter, has anyone identified me? Has anyone said it was me?" Pemell asked. "Answer me that question."

"No," Braddock conceded.

"There you go," Pemell asserted. "I don't know who has it in for me. Maybe nobody does other than the fact that I live here, and I have this ... history. And now you've spent all this time on me, and that poor kid is out there somewhere. Go find her."

Tori ignored his insincere show of sympathy. "Has your house been broken into recently?"

"No."

"I noticed you have a security system. Do you activate it when you leave?"

"Always. The equipment in my home office is valuable."

"Have you noticed anyone paying particular attention to you. Observing you when you've been running? Following you around town? Tailing you?"

"No, I don't think so," Pemell replied. "Like I've told you, repeatedly, I don't get out much. I keep to myself."

"Come on, Ian," Tori said impatiently. "You're arguing it wasn't you and that you've been set up. To get all this right, someone must have been paying you some attention. Look at where you live. How did you not notice them?"

"Don't you want to get back at who did it?" Braddock said.

"Yeah, if I knew who."

"You're sure you haven't seen anyone watching you? Following you?" Braddock pressed.

"If I had, I'd have told you. I'd have told you right away to avoid all this." Pemell rubbed his face. "Fuck! I don't want this, any of this. It's a nightmare."

Braddock looked to Tori and tilted his head for them to leave. The two of them slowly pushed themselves up out of their chairs.

As they got to the front door, Tori turned back. "Interesting timing, though."

"Timing?"

"That you just happened to pick Wednesday to drive down to the farm and get the van washed inside and out," she said. "I guess that was lucky, wasn't it?"

Pemell snorted a laugh. "Oh, I'm lucky? After the last two days? Right."

"Just noting the convenient timing. Funny how it all worked out."

"Whatever," he replied with a dismissive wave. "It's when I had my meeting at work."

"And for the record, Ian," she added, "I've read the investigative files from Thief River Falls and Grand Forks. Don't for a minute think that this means I don't think you took Helena Hernandez or Joey Martinez."

When they got into Braddock's Tahoe, he chuckled.

"What?"

"You *really* hate that guy."

"He might not have done this, but he's not a good guy."

"You're going to take a look at those other cases when this is over, aren't you?" he said with a smile.

"Everybody needs a hobby."

"Even if it's a morbid one."

"Find me a retired detective who doesn't work a cold case that haunts them now and then. I've got a couple that stick with me. I bet you do too."

He nodded. "There's one in particular that I think about from time to time."

"Just my point. I want to know what happened to those kids."

Braddock turned left, heading back toward Manchester Bay. "He's right about one thing. We've wasted a good twenty-four hours on him."

"Yes, and maybe ... no. In a way, this is good news."

"What do you mean?"

"If someone went to these lengths to frame him, they did it for a reason, and I don't think it was to bury Isabella in the ground six hours later," Tori said. "She's still alive."

TWELVE

"IT WAS MORE LIKE SOMEONE GAVE THEM AN AMBIEN"

It was dark when George pulled past the Manchester Bay squad car at the end of the driveway. He circled the end of the cul-de-sac and parked, then closed his eyes for a moment, took a long breath and blew it out before getting out of his car. Stuffing the newspaper under his arm, he nodded to the now familiar patrol officer as he walked by and made his way up the driveway.

Detective Reese from the sheriff's department was standing out on the front steps of the house, chatting with another uniformed officer, as he approached.

"Detective Reese," George greeted.

"Mr. Santo."

"Have there been any developments?"

Reese shook his head disappointedly. "Sorry."

"Nothing on that man they questioned yesterday?"

"No, sir."

George went inside and closed the front door, sighing in relief. He seemed to have got by Reese without notice. He felt his heart racing as he walked to the back of the house and found Luciana and Sam sitting in the family room, both staring vacantly out the picture window into the darkness. Sam turned and nodded to him.

"Where's Carson?"

"Downstairs with a couple of friends, hanging out. Trying to have a ... normal night," Sam said, and then noticed the anxious look on his face. "George, what is it?"

That caught Luciana's attention, and she stood up out of her chair and walked quickly to her brother. "Are you okay?"

George looked back to the front door. Reese was partially visible out the narrow side window. "We need to go upstairs," he said as he started toward the steps.

Luciana grabbed his arm. "Wait? Why?" she asked, peering into his eyes.

"Just ... come on," he whispered. "I have to show you something."

In the upstairs master bedroom, he closed the door behind them.

"What?" Sam demanded.

"I found this in my mailbox today." George showed them a cell phone, then swiped the screen to display a photo.

"Izzy! Oh my God," Luciana blurted loudly.

"Shh," George cautioned, putting his hand to her mouth. "Quiet."

The photo was of Isabella holding up a *Star Tribune*. George held his own newspaper up. It was the same edition. "It's today's paper. She's alive."

Sam and Luciana took in the photo. It was the first glimmer of hope in two days.

"They called me," George said, gesturing to the phone. "This isn't my phone. The kidnappers left it in my mailbox this morning in a leather case. A few hours after I found it, it rang. That's when the photo was sent."

"What?" Sam said. "Who are these people?"

"I don't know."

"Why did they contact you?"

"I have no idea," George answered.

"Because they can't contact us," Luciana said.

Sam closed his eyes and nodded. "The police are monitoring our phones, emails, texts, everything. They're not monitoring George."

"We need to tell Will and Tori Hunter," Luciana said. "This is what Tori specializes in. I mean, last year she and Will found those twin girls—"

"No, hold on, I don't think you can do that," George cautioned.

"But they could maybe trace this call. Track down the phone. Find these people and Izzy."

"Sis, they might be able to do all that, or they might not. The caller was clear: no police. They said they're watching."

Sam and Luciana's eyes both widened.

"If they see us cooperating, if they even get a whiff of it, they'll kill her and walk away."

"But—"

"Don't think for a second these guys care about Izzy. She's nothing more than a means to an end for them."

"A means to what end?" Sam asked. "What do they want?"

"Money," George said.

"How much?"

"Two million."

"In cash?"

"No," George said. "Crypto."

"Really?" Sam furrowed his brow. "Bitcoin? Ethereum?"

"Yes."

"That's so weird," Luciana said, shaking her head. "Crypto's not even real, is it?"

"It's real," Sam responded. "I have people asking me about it all the time, wanting to invest in it. I'm managing some investments for my clients along those lines. I've gotten into it a little bit myself to kind of check it out, learn it."

"But you can't spend it or use it to pay for things."

"Yes, you can. It's becoming more common," he said, pacing again, his mind working.

"And I suppose when you think about it, we don't have to make a money drop with trackers and dye packs for the police to trace or monitor," George reasoned. "Even if you didn't tell Tori and Braddock, with cash you'd have to deliver it. The police would follow."

Sam nodded in agreement, seeing the logic. "This way, there's way less risk of that."

"Crypto has been used to pay off ransomware attacks," George added. "I guess I can see the application here."

"You click enter and it's gone," Sam said. "And there are ways to convert or exchange it for cash." He thought for a moment. "But I don't have remotely close to what they're asking for. And it takes time to acquire more of it, and I'm not that adept at it yet. I'd have to convert a bunch of cash, and that would get noticed." He took out his phone, "I should check how much I have."

"Don't," George said, reaching for his arm. "The police are monitoring your phone. If they see you checking your accounts, they might get suspicious."

"Then what do we do?" Sam said. "Or are they expecting me to raid my clients' accounts? I guess if that's what it takes—"

"No," George said. "No, no, no. We're not going to make this any worse. I'll pay it. I have most of it."

"You do?" Sam said.

"Georgie?" Luciana gasped. "No."

"We've discussed crypto, but I didn't realize you'd gone in so big on it," Sam said. "You haven't been like some of my foolish clients, who want to put all their money there? I've been talking people off that ledge a lot lately."

"No. Not ... all of it," George said, shaking his head. "I'm not crazy, but business has been really good the last few years, so I was able to try a bigger bet there the last year or two and it's paid off. I'm close to the two million. Given current values, I'm about two hundred grand short of the mark."

"Really?" Sam asked. "That's a lot more than I thought you had."

"If it's good enough for a bunch of billionaires, I figured it's good enough for me. Two months ago, I wouldn't have had what they're asking for. But right now, it's been increasing like crazy."

"But why us?" Luciana asked. "Why Izzy? I mean, who are we?"

"A doctor who owns part of a medical practice. A savvy investment planner with a thriving business. You live very comfortably, so you would seem to have the money."

"But two million dollars?" She looked to Sam. "I mean, where do they get that number? Forget this cryptocurrency stuff, do we even have that much?"

"Um ..." He started doing the mental calculation. "If we took ourselves down to the financial studs, we probably do. I'd have to liquidate everything, sell the house, the place in Marco Island, the works. Do that, and we maybe have it."

"They have to know that, don't they?"

"Yeah, you would think so. If they did their homework on us. Or on ... George," Sam said, his jaw dropping. "Did they do it on you?"

"What do you mean, Sam?"

"The break-in—"

"Oh man," George said, his eyes bulging.

"Two months ago. They stole your—"

"Laptop computer."

"Georgie," Luciana said.

"You're not the target ... I am. That's how the kidnappers know this. Know I have this," George muttered. "That's why they're coming to *me* with this."

"What? Why?"

"My screen saver on that computer. It was a picture of me and Izzy. I mean, if you're in my house, you see all kinds of pictures of Izzy and Carson. You'd think they were my kids. Oh my God, Sam, sis, I ... I ..."

"No. No, this is not your fault," Luciana said. "Don't even think that way."

"I can't ... I can't ..." He started hyperventilating.

Luciana went to him and eased him down onto the bed. "George? George!" she said, cupping his face in her hands. "Breathe." She reached for his neck, checking his pulse.

"Is he okay?" Sam asked, stepping to him as well. "Easy, brother."

"I think he's just upset."

Sam ducked into the bathroom and came back with a glass of water.

"I just ... I'm sorry." George took a moment, catching his breath, then drank some water while Luciana retrieved her medical kit and took out her stethoscope. She had him sit still and checked his heart rate. It was running a little hot, but she didn't think it was anything to worry about.

The three of them were quiet for a few minutes while George calmed himself, regulating his breathing. Luciana sat with him while Sam stood over at the bedroom window, his back to them, looking out, arms folded, deep in thought.

"I'm okay, sis," George said, taking another drink of water. "I'm so sorry, though."

Luciana looked to her husband. "What do we do? How do we get her back?"

"We have two options. We figure out how to pay, or we go to Will Braddock and Tori Hunter with it and take our chances they can get her back."

"No," George said. "They were clear. If you go to the police, they'll kill her. I got this."

"George, no—"

"I got this, sis. It's my fault."

"It's not your fault!"

"It is. They came at me because I can cover it. They took my niece. I know she's your daughter, but Izzy and Carson are my kids too. I love them. Let me do it. Let me handle it."

Luciana looked to Sam and then closed her eyes, shaking her head.

Sam nodded and turned to George. "I can and will pay you back. It'll just take some time, when I don't have someone watching my every move. I'll write it up tonight, the commitment. But, Georgie, you're sure you can handle it for now?"

"We have to get her back," George said, looking to Luciana. "Sis, I'll do whatever it takes. Whatever we have to do."

Luciana hugged him, the two of them embracing tightly.

After a minute, Sam spoke, "What's next?"

"I'm supposed to go home now. They're going to call and tell me what to do. I'll have to pull this all together." George looked at him. "I'll need what you have, so we'll have to figure out how to do that. A wallet-to-wallet transfer of some kind."

Sam nodded. "In the meantime, we have to just try and act normal."

A car door slammed outside. Sam went over to the window to look out. "Great timing."

"What?" Luciana said.

"It's Will and Tori Hunter."

"We wanted to give you an update," Braddock said as he and Tori sat down at the kitchen table with Sam, Luciana and George.

"You have news?" Sam asked.

Tori exhaled a breath. "I wanted to follow up on the man we brought in for questioning. Based on what we've found and haven't found, we're pretty certain he is not the man who took Isabella."

"Pretty certain?" George said.

They spent several minutes explaining how they'd reached that conclusion while Sam, Luciana and George listened intently but without asking questions.

"His van was not the van used in the abduction. It's a physical impossibility based on the mileage," Braddock said. "We think it was made to look like he took Isabella."

"You think he was set up?" Luciana asked.

"It has that look to it," Tori replied. "As for the other abduction, or maybe two, he may have been involved with, I reserve judgment. I think there is something to all that but for your daughter, we just don't see how he could have done it."

"But someone went to great effort to push us in that direction," Braddock added.

"I see," Luciana said, nodding.

"Now, here is what I view as the good news," Tori said hopefully. "If someone went to those lengths to make it look like someone else was responsible, we think that means Isabella is still alive. If she is, we also think they may reach out to you."

"Does that mean you'll be keeping people here at the house?" Luciana said.

"Yes, of course. This is a setback, but at the same time, like I said, I think it gives us reason for hope."

"Besides waiting for a call, what do you do next?" Sam said.

"We hunt. Unfortunately," Braddock said with a small headshake, "since we spent the last twenty-four-plus hours really digging deep on this suspect, because he looked good for it, we lost some momentum in investigating others who might have some motive to harm you."

"I can't think of any other reason why someone would go to this effort to take your daughter unless *you* were their target for some reason," Tori posited. "Our next step, and we've already started, is to re-engage in your personal and business records. Maybe within those we will find someone with motive."

"I know we've already asked, but have either of you been able to think of anyone who has a reason to come after you this way?" Braddock said. "Anything that can explain what is going on here? Someone took your child. We're trying to figure out why."

"Based on what we've found so far, they would be pretty intelligent, capable of planning this, and have some resources." Tori looked at Sam. "Did you have something go wrong with a high-net-worth client, perhaps? Not a Walter Dexter type, but someone with some real money?"

"No. I can't think of anyone like that," Sam answered flatly. "Nobody has lost a bundle the last ten years unless they were an idiot. It's why business has been good. People have been making money. You keep them on course, they can't help but improve their situation."

"But, Sam," George said, "it has to be someone. They should look through all of that again, don't you think? Just because you don't see it doesn't mean they won't. I mean, you're good, but not everyone is happy with how things go."

"Uh ... yeah, I suppose." Sam nodded, his arms folded. "Whatever you need," he said quietly.

"Same thing with you, Luciana," Braddock said. "A malpractice claim, maybe? A condition that wasn't diagnosed properly? It wouldn't have to be recent. It could be something from years ago. People carry grudges, grievances for years, letting them fester. Maybe it's not even you, but another doctor at the clinic who had an issue."

"I just can't think of anything," she said. "But ... maybe it does have something to do with another doctor. I hadn't thought of that possibility. My partners have said you can have whatever you need, as long as we protect our patients' privacy."

"And nothing personal has happened?" Tori pressed. "With the two of you? If there is something, now is the time to tell us."

"No," Luciana said calmly, shaking her head. "You can look at anything you need of ours. Phones, email, texts, whatever you need ... go ahead."

Tori looked to Braddock, who furrowed his brow momentarily before turning back to the Farners. "Okay then. We need to get back at it."

As they walked down the front sidewalk, Braddock took a quick call from Steak. "We'll be there in twenty minutes. We'll stop and get some takeout." He hung up and looked to Tori. "Steak and Eggleston want to check in. Said they had an interesting development in their case."

"Let's get Reese and Nolan in there too."

"Done," Braddock said as he sent a quick text.

When they were in the Tahoe and pulling away, he said, "They took that ... quietly. You told them there was reason for hope, and ..."

"Nothing. They hardly perked up."

"It almost feels like we've already lost them. That they're resigned to the outcome."

"Maybe," Tori said.

It was just after 8:00 p.m. when Tori and Braddock came in carrying boxes of Chinese food. "You two figure out the Weltz case yet?" Braddock asked Eggleston as he passed the sweet and sour chicken to Tori.

"Working on it," Eggleston replied, scooping Pad Thai noodles onto a paper plate. "I love this stuff." She passed the box to Steak and stuffed a gob of noodles into her mouth. "We talked to his kids today. They didn't know much about his business or who he had done work for. But ..." She took another mouthful and looked to Steak.

"But," Steak picked up the thought as he loaded his plate, "later in the day, Weltz's son called me back and said he remembered meeting a guy one time about a year ago who his dad said helped him from time to time. He couldn't remember the man's name, but he described him as kind of twitchy and squirrelly, slim, maybe six feet tall, and might have been in the military the way he stood ramrod straight. He wore a flannel shirt and mesh ball cap and had a panel van full of tools and wood. Now who does that sound like?"

Braddock chuckled. "No way."

"Walter Dexter," Steak said with a smile before shoving a forkful of food in his mouth. "We drove back out there early tonight. I called ahead of time so we didn't have another ... incident."

"He's not your suspect, though?"

"No. He alibis out."

"Although he is a really paranoid guy," Eggleston said as she evaluated the contents of the beef and peppers carton. "The world is out to get him, let me tell you."

"After we got past his dense layers of paranoia, he confirmed he did work for Weltz here and there for cash. He was a little leery of admitting the cash part, because ..."

"We're all government and we might drop dime on him to the IRS."

"Of course he was," Tori said with a laugh as she used chopsticks to load noodles onto her paper plate.

"Dexter thought he and Weltz were going to do an install a couple of days ago, but Fred never called him. That's why he was riding the barstool all day at the bar in Cuyuna."

"He said he'd come in and take a look at the business records and see if he could tell what was missing," Eggleston said. "We're meeting him tomorrow."

Nolan and Reese rolled in and eagerly made up plates of food. "I've hardly eaten all day," Reese muttered.

"Consider yourself lucky. All I've done is empty the vending machine," Nolan quipped. "All that sugar, my dentist is going to pop a gasket when she sees me next week. This," she added, a copious scoop of spicy beef overflowing her spoon, "is a godsend."

"We need you to get started ..."

"On the Farners finances? Yes. I'd done a little before we got onto Pemell. I've had a few calls with Zagaros, plus we've had access today to their tax and financial records. I've been through their bank accounts, retirement plans, tax returns, financial disclosure documents, things like that."

"How wealthy are they really?" Tori asked.

"They're in a tax bracket we all aspire to," Nolan replied. "Between the two of them they're pulling down pretty good coin, just over $417,000 in gross income last year, which Zagaros told you about. It's been on an upward trajectory, as five years ago they brought in a little under $250,000, which is still pretty damn good. In general, he earns a little more than she does. They both have retirement accounts. He must find ways to jam more money into his, because it's nearly double hers. They make good money and aren't shy about spending it."

"Debt?"

"They have two mortgages, which are beefy, here and Marco Island, plus monthly payments for high-end vehicles, and then Luciana's medical school debt is still a healthy monthly payment. They have some money in the bank, although it wouldn't blow you away. So, while it's a comfortable financial picture, it doesn't scream excessive wealth. Not yet, anyway."

"What's their number?" Braddock asked. "If they liquidated everything, what might they have?"

Nolan did a quick mental calculation. "Maybe $1.8 to $2 million, but other than the checking and savings accounts, it's all tied up in property and investments. Ten years from now, that figure will be a great deal higher given their financial trajectory, though again, they're on the way to a nice comfortable amount but nothing crazy. To me, that's why someone like Ian Pemell made sense."

They discussed Pemell and the fact that he might have been set up, and how that he was meant Isabella might still be alive. Nolan also confirmed that checks on registered sex offenders in the area hadn't turned up any good possibilities. "Doesn't mean there isn't some other crazy we don't know about out there, but the ones we do have been cleared."

"This just doesn't strike me as that kind of deal," Tori said.

"Cargo van?" Reese said. "That screams weirdo."

Braddock nodded. "But nothing else does. The planning, the set-up of Pemell suggests someone with motive and resources. Like they're after something. Which is why I think it's someone who has it in for the Farners for some reason. Business and patient records need to be scoured again. Nolan, check for complaints against either of their businesses. Lawsuits, filings with the state Better Business Bureau, you know the drill. If it isn't financial, based on what we're seeing, there could be a non-financial reason."

"For someone to plan this, they would have had to be watching both Pemell and Isabella," Tori said, looking over at Reese. "We need to see if there is any footage anywhere that we can use to identify these guys. Check from school to her house. Isabella was also heavily into hockey, so we should see if anyone was watching her there. And same for Pemell. We could ask him some more questions about where he's spent his last two to three weeks and see if anything pops."

"That's a needle-in-a-haystack search if there ever was one," Reese said. "I may need some help."

"We'll get it for you." Tori looked to Braddock. "Won't we?"

Braddock nodded. "Let me know what you need and I'll make it happen. Also, Sam and Luciana say their marriage is good. I think it is, I get the sense it is, but make some discreet inquiries."

"On it."

The six of them ate for a half-hour, discussing their cases, throwing out speculations and theories. Nolan departed first. She too said she might need assistance, which Braddock approved. Reese was already coordinating his plan for first thing in the morning.

"Solve the Weltz thing, would you?" Braddock said to Steak and Eggleston as they stood up to leave. "We could use you on our case."

"We'll see what Dexter gives us tomorrow," Eggleston said. "You could pull one of us off that and let the other work it. I think you're right, the answer is in the business records. If we can find what's missing, then we'd have something. Witnesses and forensics aren't going to get us home on that one."

Braddock nodded and the two of them headed out the door. Steak stopped and stuck his head back inside. "If Isabella is still alive, *why* is she still alive? There hasn't been any contact with the parents, right?"

"No."

He looked perplexed. "If she's alive, isn't the play to the parents still on? And if so, why has it taken so long?"

"The abductor needs time for some reason," Braddock suggested. "It's only been two days. I'm thinking they're trying to put some space between Manchester Bay and wherever they have her. Or maybe they're waiting us out a bit before they make contact."

"I suppose," Steak replied. "Good night."

"Or do the Farners need more time?" Tori murmured under her breath after he'd left.

Braddock knew the tone and sat back in his chair.

"When we told them Pemell didn't do it, what did you expect for a reaction?"

"Based on the phone call you got from Luciana or yesterday out in the hallway here, I expected them to be upset, distressed, distraught, frustrated," he replied. "I expected they would be angry with you and particularly irritated with me because they know me. I thought when you suggested there was a possibility that Isabella was still alive, they would have renewed hope. Instead, they took it all in stride."

"It was more like someone gave them an Ambien," Tori replied. "I kind of took it initially as resignation, just like you did. The comatose haze I've seen parents drift into, as if they can't believe this has happened to them. That reaction has been there at times. That's what I thought I was seeing. It might be what I was seeing."

"Then Steak asks his question."

"And that has me re-evaluating. As I rerun it, their reaction was more like ... they were distracted." She stood up and started pacing around the small conference table. "I've got an uneasy feeling all the sudden."

"Me too," Braddock agreed. "What do you want to do?"

Tori slipped on her coat. "Think and observe."

THIRTEEN

"YOU COULDN'T BE CLOSER THAN WE WERE"

They dropped Braddock's Tahoe at the house, changed clothes and threw on dark baseball hats, then made quick tumblers of hot chocolate and drove Tori's Audi back to the Farners' neighborhood, parking in the opposite cul-de-sac so they had a direct view of the front of the house.

Tori settled in her seat and took a drink of cocoa while Braddock radioed to the deputy parked out front that they were down the street just taking a look at things and not to alert anyone else to their presence.

"So is the plan literally to sit here, think and observe?" he asked, binoculars up to his eyes.

"For now," Tori said, contemplating whether she wanted to go back and talk to the Farners again, running the pros and cons through her mind.

In the meantime, Braddock called Quinn, who was staying over at his cousin's house for the night.

"You sound better."

"I'm fine, Dad," Quinn said. "The ribs still hurt some, but not my head."

"Sorry I've been away." Braddock looked over to Tori. "Sorry *we've* been away."

"It's okay," Quinn said. "Dad, can I go to a friend's house tomorrow night to watch movies? Peter is going, and a few other guys from the team will be there too."

"Which friend?"

"Ryan Grant. He's a seventh-grader on the hockey team. They live by the university."

"You're sure you're up for it?"

"Yeeeessss. Come on, Dad."

"Okay. We'll figure out a way to get you over there then."

"Thanks."

They talked for a few more minutes before Quinn hung up for the night.

"He manipulated you to yes pretty easily," Tori said, grinning, the binoculars up to her eyes. "His head is fine I think."

"He did. But don't sit there too high and mighty. I've seen him work his charms on you, and you can't get your credit card out fast enough for him. You're spoiling him."

"That's because he's so cute."

They sat in silence for several minutes, the engine running, the heater pushing out warmth, before Braddock blurted, "You know, we could always just make out." He reached over and ran his hand along her inner thigh.

"So typical," Tori replied with a good-natured eye roll. "One-track mind."

"I'm a guy with a hot girlfriend," he said as he leaned in and nibbled her earlobe. "What other track is there?"

"I'm hot, huh?"

"I sure think so," he said, kissing her neck.

"Okay, okay, down, boy." She laughed, pushing him away playfully. Braddock had many layers to him, but he had an innate ability to make her giggle like a schoolgirl. She rather liked being the object of his frequent desire.

She turned her attention back to the Farner house. Braddock observed the intensity of her stare as she chewed on her bottom lip, deep in thought.

"I know that look."

"What look?"

"The something-doesn't-add-up look," he said quietly.

"The more I replay the last time we were in that house, the more I feel like there was something we didn't pick up on. We were expecting one thing, and because of that, we didn't necessarily see what we should have seen."

"You think they're holding back?"

"They're your friends. You tell me."

"I know them, but I don't know them well enough to know when they're not being fully honest," he said. "I think they're loving parents who would do anything for their kids."

"Does anything not include telling us everything?"

"Why wouldn't they tell us everything?"

"I don't know. Maybe they have." She wanted to take another run at the Farners, although given the late hour, maybe not tonight. She turned to Braddock. "I think we pay them a visit tomorrow—"

"Hang on."

He raised the binoculars to his eyes and Tori turned back to the house.

George Santo had exited the front door and was slowly walking down the driveway to his parked BMW.

"George seems very close to Sam and Luciana, doesn't he?"

"You can tell George and Luciana are close," she said.

"Like you and Jessie?"

"You couldn't be closer than we were."

"So if Jessie were alive today, she would be involved in your life, aware of everything going on. She would be there for you if you were in crisis."

"I know she would. And I'd have been there for her."

"Kind of like how George is there for Luciana?"

"I like to think so." Tori thought for a quick moment and then looked to Braddock, catching his drift. "So much so that if someone wanted to communicate with me but they couldn't because I was under twenty-four-seven police watch and protection, my phones, computer, texts, emails all monitored, they could ..."

"Just contact Jessie instead?"

She froze for a moment. "Huh."

"I'm not saying that's what's going on here," Braddock said. "But going back to Steak's point earlier, if this is a kidnapping and they want something from the Farners, they would have to communicate that to them somehow, in a method that we're not able to track."

"These guys weren't watching just Isabella. They were watching the whole family. And if they were doing that, what they would have seen was that George Santo is around a lot."

Tori looked back ahead to see Santo's BMW turning left out of the cul-de-sac. When he disappeared from view, she hit the gas and followed him as he drove back to his house just a few miles away, in a more established neighborhood of classic older homes in the heart of Manchester Bay. She pulled to a stop a block north, watching the garage door come down and then the interior house lights turn on.

"This morning Luciana is on the phone with me. She's emotional, angry, sad," she said. "Same with her and Sam at the government center yesterday. Tonight, they're calm, sedate, accepting, if not checked out."

"If the call came," Braddock said, "it came today. What I can't figure is the why and the what. Nolan did the math. The

Farners are solidly upper middle class. Successful, living comfortably, well on their way to living more comfortably, but they're not rich. They don't have enough to justify life in prison for kidnapping."

Tori nodded and thought about what he was implying. "Let's say you're right. Maybe they're not after ransom, or the ransom could be something other than money."

"Like?"

"Remember my case down in Des Moines? The little girl was kidnapped so that her father would drop all the electronic security to the company's computer systems. They made a ransom demand, but it was really about something else entirely."

Vaughn took a drink of her coffee, sitting in the passenger seat of the Suburban as Cain followed Hunter's Audi. Cain had warned her about Braddock and Hunter two months ago. And that was before the unfortunate happenstance that Braddock's son was riding with Isabella Farner through the park when they grabbed her.

"I've done the research on law enforcement here. You're not dealing with your standard county sheriff's detectives," he'd said. He'd provided a report and then photos of Will Braddock.

"He's ... handsome," Vaughn had remarked, admiring a photo of the detective on a dock, in swim trunks, T-shirt and sunglasses, hair wind-blown. "Were this another time, another place ..."

"You don't get to bed him. You need to look past the tall, dark and handsome shit, and start developing a healthy respect for his abilities if we're going down this path. Braddock will lead the investigation and no doubt will bring in Hunter. They're not to be underestimated. He was NYPD for years, a detective first grade. He worked on the Joint Terrorism Task Force. He's a serious and smart guy."

"What's he doing here?"

"Family reasons," Cain said, reciting the history. "As good as he is, you also have the woman. She's dangerous."

"The little doll?"

That had been her first reaction when she'd seen the photo of retired FBI Special Agent Tori Hunter getting off a boat at a bar on the lake. She had her hair pulled back in a bouncy pony-tail, and was wearing flip-flops, white cut-off shorts, a red bikini top and sunglasses, carrying a can of seltzer, looking the part of your typical weekend party girl. The photos showed that she was obviously fit, toned arms and legs, and not an ounce of fat on her. Vaughn could certainly understand Braddock's attrac-tion to her, and hers to him.

But fear?

She didn't see it. Hunter was small and physically unimposing.

Cain openly laughed at her initial reaction. "Sometimes big things come in small packages," he said, handing over a sheaf of papers.

Vaughn read the summary of Hunter's record, including her many awards and commendations, and studied her Bureau identification photo: dark business suit, hair in a neat shoulder-length bob, a reserved, professional smile. She flicked through the newspaper clippings Cain had assembled. "Impressive," she acknowledged.

"To say the least. There is no avoiding her if we do this here. She will be hunting us. You need to know that. They both will be. And you'll be on their turf. Not down in Albuquerque where you could ... influence things more."

"Then we need to give these two something else to look at and focus on while we do this."

That something had been Ian Pemell. Hunter and Braddock had taken the bait, but not for as long as they'd planned and hoped for. And now what Cain had warned of might be coming to pass. Their interest in Santo was disconcerting.

The Audi signaled a right turn. Cain followed at a distance, killing his headlights. Giving them two minutes, he slowly drove by the house they knew belonged to Braddock. They saw the Audi SUV parked next to the unmarked sheriff's department Tahoe. Through a rear window into what looked to be the kitchen, they saw the two of them talking and Braddock taking a drink out of a beer bottle.

"They're done for the night," Vaughn observed. "Keep driving."

"What am I looking for?"

"Just get familiar with the road along here. It's my understanding that the two of them drive it often. Braddock has family down this way."

FOURTEEN

"WHY IS THE MONITOR ALL BLACK?"

The only thing they'd left with her to pass the time was a coloring book and crayons. It beat doing nothing.

Isabella sat on the mattress, the blanket over her legs, wearing her raincoat, and colored her third picture since she'd been served dinner—or at least she assumed it was dinner. The only natural light in the room came from the narrow glass-block window. She couldn't see out, but it did give her a sense of time. After her lunch earlier, which had been another peanut butter and jelly sandwich, she'd made a point of taking a long nap. The man in the black mask had brought her a lukewarm kid's meal with a cheeseburger, fries and soda just after it had turned dark outside, which at this time of year was usually around 6:00 p.m.

She'd counted to sixty sixty times in her head while she colored the first picture in the book. While she didn't count for the next two pictures, she thought they took about the same length of time to color, so she figured it was around 9:30 when she heard the now familiar sound.

Ca-chunk.

She looked up from the coloring book.

The man stepped inside. "Why do you have your raincoat on?"

"I'm cold."

"If you want to go to the bathroom, you need to go now."

She nodded and set aside the crayon box and coloring book. As she got up from the bed, she noticed the hands on the watch on the man's left wrist. They were upside down, but she could tell it was 9:50 p.m. Her sense of time was in the ballpark. He led her across the darkened room to the bathroom, turned on the light and closed the door behind her.

When she'd finished, she flushed the toilet and turned on the faucet to wash her hands. Under cover of the combined sound of the toilet and the running water, she slipped out the sink's stopper. There was a zip-up pocket on the inside of her raincoat. She stuffed the stopper in there and zipped it closed. Then she washed and dried her hands and knocked on the door. The man let her out.

"Wait here."

Her heart skipped a beat and she held her breath as he stepped back inside the bathroom. He reached for the hand towel and felt it for dampness. She was certain he would notice the missing sink stopper when he checked the faucet handles, making sure they were both turned all the way off. But he just took the hand towel off its hook, flipped down the light switch and closed the door.

"Go on," he said, placing his hand on her upper back, guiding her toward the light of her room.

He pulled the door closed behind her and she heard the latch click. She sat back down on the bed, and as she carried on with the page she had started in the coloring book, she began to count in her head again. *One, two, three ...*

.   .   .

Her first two nights imprisoned in the small room, she'd slept with the small lamp on. Tonight, she'd made a point, after a couple of hours of tossing and turning, of getting up and turning it off.

She pulled the covers up over her and closed her eyes.

One, two, three ...

She found a good cadence to breathe and count.

Fifty-eight ... breathe ... *fifty-nine* ... breathe ... *sixty*. One hour.

She stayed still and started again.

Fifty-nine ... breathe ... *sixty*. Two hours.

Very slowly, she slid her pillow under the blankets. Then she slithered along the wall to the end of the mattress and stood up. Picking up her raincoat, she unzipped the interior pocket and took out the stopper. She set it on the floor but held on to the coat.

Her eyes were adjusted to the dark. It helped that there was just the slightest glow coming from the glass-block window. It gave her a sense of the room, the space, and allowed her to make out the outline of the camera up high.

Keeping her back to the wall, she moved slowly forward and then turned left. Three more steps and she was underneath the little red light. Clutching the coat in both hands, she took a step out from the wall and turned to look up at the camera. She rocked her hands up and down, then tossed it up, but not far enough. She tried again, the same rocking motion before throwing it. This time the coat caught on the camera for a second before falling back down.

She froze.

There was a creak in the floor right above. And then another one.

Was he coming?

She stood still, her back against the wall, directly underneath the camera, listening, sensing for the vibration of the man coming, fearing the door would push open any second.

He didn't come.

The house was quiet and still. The only thing she heard was the hum of air circulating through the air ducts above her.

She closed her eyes and let her breathing ease. Pushing away from the wall, she turned and gripped the coat in her hands again. This time she bent her knees and jumped before releasing it, watching as it sailed up and over the front of the camera. The red light disappeared.

She held her hands ready, expecting the coat to fall.

It didn't. It held.

She stepped over and turned on the small lamp. The raincoat's hood was fully over the camera, as if it were hanging perfectly upon a hook.

Isabella picked up the sink stopper and examined the door, the small metal plate on the back of the latch. If she could chip her way through the wood around the edge of the plate and create a gap, she might be able to use the stopper to lever the latch open.

She started working away at the wood.

* * *

When she was engaged in a case, Tori often had trouble sleeping for any stretch of time. Her mind was too restless.

Braddock, on the other hand, had this innate ability to just kind of shut things out and then come back to them.

Maybe that was just attributable to the differences between men and women. Yin and yang. Something.

He was still fast asleep at 5:30 a.m. when Tori slipped out

of bed and made her way down to the kitchen. She brewed a cup of coffee, then sat down at the table and started reading through her investigative notes. She texted Nolan: *Are you up?*

Nolan texted back a minute later: *I am now*.

Tori made the call.

"Yeah?"

She explained what they had speculated about Santo. "We haven't looked at him yet. We need to, and fast. Can you do it?"

"It's Saturday," Nolan replied. "The Farners are giving us access to everything, but will Santo?"

"Probably not. If we ask him ..."

"We alert him," Nolan said. "I can find publicly available information, but that might not tell you what you need to know. It's a matter of resource access."

Tori thought for a moment. "Okay. Let me make another call." She swiped into her contacts.

A sleepy Special Agent Zagaros answered on the third ring. "I should pay attention to the *former* in former Special Agent Hunter when you call at this hour."

"Sorry."

"I guess sleeping in this morning is not an option."

"No, but you're doing me a serious solid by not." Tori quickly recapped where they were at and what they were thinking. "We don't know if there is anything to this or not, but we need to know what Santo is about."

"Okay," he said with a yawn. "I'll get someone on it."

Tori hung up and called Nolan back. "Okay, the FBI is going to work on compiling a brief on Santo," she said as she took a drink of coffee, watching the sun rising over the eastern horizon. "In the meantime, here's what I need you to do ..."

* * *

Come on. Come on.

Isabella wiped away a tear. She'd been prying at the wood around the latch for hours, but couldn't get the flat edge of the stopper in far enough to lever it open. Turning around, she looked up at the window, and there was light; the sun was coming up.

She turned back and jammed the stopper in again, chipping at the wood. It went in deeper. She yanked it out and pushed it in harder, working it into the opening.

Clunk! At last it hit metal.

She was breathing hard and sweating as she gripped the round top of the stopper and started pushing it to the right, trying to lever the latch back. She could feel it moving as she heaved against the stopper.

Ca-chunk!

The door popped loose toward her. She cautiously pulled it back and listened. Silence. Gingerly she stepped out of the room. With light seeping through the window just past the bathroom, she hurried over to the door that led to the stairway.

Tiptoeing up the carpeted steps, she crept her way to another door, which was open a crack. She peered around the edge and could see into a kitchen. Beyond that was what looked like a living room. A man was lying on his back on a couch, his right arm hanging limply toward the floor. She could hear him snoring.

She slithered through the gap, careful not to make a sound. To her left was a door leading outside. She gently turned the deadlock, then twisted the knob and pulled the door, it was a bit stuck, and she had to give it an extra cautious pull to open it. She pushed at the screen door and stepped out onto the back stoop, then turned to close the inside door. She gave it an extra yank to close it but as she did so, her hand slipped off the door-knob and her elbow flew back into the screen door.

* * *

Bang!

Lowe snapped awake on the couch. *What was that?* He looked back into the kitchen.

"Did you hear that?" Rust asked, rushing in rubbing his eyes.

"Yeah." Lowe looked to the monitor, but it was dark.

Cain came down from upstairs. "Why is the monitor all black?"

"She's sleeping."

"There's a window in there. Light shows in and the sun's coming up," Cain said. "Do you see any light there?"

Rust rushed down the steps to the bedroom and found the door open. "She's out! She's out!"

"Dammit," Cain growled. Stepping to the window, he caught a flash of movement to the left where the driveway carved through the dense trees.

* * *

Isabella pumped her arms. There was open daylight ahead as the driveway turned to the right. She emerged from the cover of the trees and there was a paved road ahead. A vehicle was coming from the left, a delivery truck.

"Help! Help! Stop! Stop!"

She waved her arms, sprinting for the road.

"Help! Help me!"

The truck pulled to the shoulder and skidded to a hard stop. A woman in a gray uniform jumped out and ran around to the back. It was as if she had suddenly recognized who was flagging her down.

"Please help me!"

"Come on, kid!" the woman said, reaching for Isabella's hand.

Boom! Boom! Boom!

The driver's eyes went wide and she collapsed backwards to the ground, the chest of her gray delivery uniform rapidly turning red.

Isabella spun around. Two men were heading for her.

Run! She sprinted past the delivery truck and along the shoulder.

Boom!

She looked back. One man had stopped, but the other one was still chasing her. *Run. Run.*

She could hear his footsteps thundering behind her. He was closing in fast.

No, no, no. Gotta get away, gotta get away.

She heard an engine roaring and looked back over her left shoulder. A black SUV was speeding after them.

"Get her! Get her!" called a voice.

The man was only ten feet behind her now.

To her right, across a narrow ditch, was a barbed-wire fence. If she could just get through that and into the woods …

She veered hard right and jumped.

The man turned as well, tumbling down into the ditch behind her and rolling into the back of her right leg. She fell face first into the long grass.

"Oof," she grunted.

Get up! Get up!

She scrambled to her feet and clambered up the far side of the ditch. The fence was only five feet away. *Scoot under the wire and run for the woods.* She dove for the gap at the bottom.

No!

His grip around her left ankle stopped her in her tracks. She rolled around and kicked at his hand. "No! No!"

He grabbed her leg with both hands and yanked her back.

"Let me go! Let me go!"

The SUV skidded to a stop. "Get her in here, now, before somebody sees!"

The man wrapped his arms around her and heaved her up out of the ditch.

Isabella kicked her legs frantically. "No! No! Let me go!"

He clamped his hand over her mouth.

Two people were in the truck. She recognized the person in the front passenger seat.

"Get her in here!" the driver barked.

The man opened the back passenger door and threw her inside, then jumped in on top of her. "Go! Go, go, go!"

The SUV violently U-turned, then seconds later turned hard left. They were taking her back to her prison. After a minute or two, it skidded to a stop, and she rolled into the back of the seat. "Ow."

"Get her inside! Now!" barked the woman she recognized. "And make damn sure she can't get out again."

The man descended the steps rapidly. Back in her room, he put her in the far corner.

"Don't move!"

Isabella sat on the floor, pulling her knees to her chest. The man had short black hair, a beard, and muscular arms. She thought he was the one who'd been coming into the room to check on her.

He leaned down and picked up the sink stopper, then examined the back of the door and shook his head. Stuffing the stopper in his pocket, he took the raincoat off the camera, then grabbed the blanket off the bed and shook it, before checking the mattress and pillow. Once he was satisfied she wasn't hiding anything else, he threw it all down, then grabbed the small lamp before reaching up and removing the overhead light bulb.

"Why are you doing this to me? Why am I here?"

"You shouldn't have done that," the man said. "You really, *really* shouldn't have done that."

Lowe came out of the basement to find Vaughn looking out of the window. He did the same, not saying a word to the woman paying the bills. He gave his coat pocket a light pat for his gun while keeping a wary eye on her. All seemed quiet, and a few minutes later, Cain came walking briskly up the road and made his way back inside the house.

"I think we're good. No sign of anyone out there. I saw one vehicle pass in the ten minutes I stood at the edge of the woods." He looked at Lowe. "How in the hell did she get out without us seeing?" he demanded.

Lowe held up the sink stopper. "Jimmied the door open. She'd hung her raincoat over the camera." He handed Cain the stopper. "She won't get out again. I put two clamps on that door."

"Clever girl, maybe too clever," Cain said. He handed Lowe a key fob. "First wash that bloodstain off the road out there with a bucket of water. Then go pick up Rust and get both your asses back here. We got some work to do."

Lowe nodded and left the house, pulling out his cell phone as he did.

"We're damn lucky nobody else was out on that road," Cain said as he looked to Vaughn.

"What about the gunfire."

"I don't think that will be a problem. It's early. Around here, if anyone heard it, they'll just think it was someone out hunting. It's bird season of some kind around here. I bet I heard gunfire twenty times when I was down at the end of the driveway so I don't think that will be the problem. We're just lucky nobody else came driving down that road."

Vaughn nodded and turned to observe the monitor. Isabella was still curled up in a ball in the corner, a blanket pulled up tight, crying. "It's one thing that she saw your face, or Lowe's. But she saw mine, and that's a problem."

"And it's not our only one with Santo being watched."

"That's why we're going to need to make the move we talked about," Vaughn said. "And this time, you're handling it."

FIFTEEN

"I KEPT POKING THE BEAR"

Steak and Eggleston were waiting when Walter Dexter arrived in his panel van. The quirky handyman was dressed in his standard flannel shirt and mesh ball cap, and was holding a soda can into which he could spit his chew.

"You're going to have to leave that out here, Walter."

"Why?"

Eggleston shook her head. "Because it's a crime scene."

Dexter looked to Steak. "You like a chew, I can tell."

"If we could chew at crime scenes, I would. No dice. Leave it here."

Walter sighed. "I like a chew when I'm nervous."

"Nothing to be nervous about here."

"Youze guys are cops. I'm always nervous around cops."

"We like it that way," Eggleston said with a little smile.

Dexter set his can down, swiped out his chew and tossed it away. Steak lifted the crime-scene tape for them to all step under and then unlocked the door to Fred Weltz's office.

The two detectives spent several minutes laying the records of Weltz's carpentry projects out on the desk. Usually this was something they would have done at the government center, but Dexter had said he would have better recall at the woodshop because that was where they would look familiar to him.

For the next hour, he looked through the records, remembering the jobs, telling stories about each one, the unique customer requests and the difficulty at times with installation. "But it is interesting to go into all these fancy-schmancy places that would hire him to do this stuff. There are some folks in these parts who own these lake places who really have some money."

"That they do."

"Crooks, every one of them," he continued. "They're all ripping someone off, I'll guarantee you that." The tin-foil hat had been reactivated. "It can't all be legit. No way."

"Okay, sure, Walter," Steak said as he organized the stacks.

"I'm just saying. Lot of crooked folks out there taking advantage of people. The media, the corporations, the colleges, and the politicians, and don't even get me started—"

"Then don't get started," Eggleston said. "Did Weltz ever get stumped on a project? Did he ever have one he couldn't figure out?"

"Not that I saw. Now, there were times things took a little longer, but he always got it together in the end."

"And he never had any issues with anyone? Nobody that was dissatisfied with his work?"

"Not that I knew of. Fred always said he'd work on it until the customer was happy. That was the most important thing. He wanted to make a buck, but I think he got a bigger boost from someone being pleased with whatever it was he'd built." He held up a receipt. "This staircase was really nice. A grand one that wrapped around the foyer. It was a challenge to install, though."

"You would help on the installs?"

"Sure, sometimes. Most times actually." Walter had reached the end of the stacks of files. He frowned. "There's one missing. It should be here."

"What was it?"

"We did this bookcase recently. I mean, I think we finished it up two, maybe three weeks ago."

"What kind of bookcase?"

"Three pieces. The trick was that the middle section was a door that swung in."

"Like for a hidden room or something?" Eggleston asked.

"Yeah, I suppose. It was cool. I helped Fred build it."

"Did you help install it."

Dexter shook his head. "You know, I didn't. I was surprised he didn't ask me to. It definitely would have needed someone else. Maybe the homeowner assisted. Odd that there's no record of it here. It was a big project."

"Do you remember anything about the people who ordered it?"

"No. I never met them. Fred needed my help on the cutting and assembling. Then, I don't know, maybe a week, ten days ago, I came here one day and it was gone. I asked him where it was, and he said he'd installed it, and that was that."

"Did he ever say *where* he installed it?"

"Not that I recall."

"Walter, is that the only one that seems to be missing?"

"I think so. At least of the recent work we'd done."

Steak looked at Eggleston. "That could be what we're looking for."

"Maybe, but without a name ..."

"You might try talking to some of the people he recently did work for," Dexter suggested. "His business was all referrals. Maybe they'd know who that project was for because they referred the customer to him."

"What was his usual backlog on a project?"

"He would be booked out two, maybe three months usually."

"So that's how far we go back," Eggleston said. "Let's start making calls."

* * *

"I'm going to my office," George said almost in a whisper. "I can pull everything together there. I should have what I need by the end of the day." The three of them were huddled together in the master bedroom.

"And then what?" Luciana asked.

"I wait for the call. And then, sis, we get Izzy back. We get her back. I promise."

"How?"

"I don't know yet. They called again and told me I'm supposed to be ready sometime tonight. That's my deadline. Sam, can you make your transfer to me?"

"I'll need to go to my office to do it," Sam answered. "That might raise an eyebrow or two."

"If anyone asks, you needed to get out of the house for some air, so where else would you go? Make sure you use someone else's computer to make the transfer. I'll keep an eye out for it. Once you send it, we should have all we need. Then we wait for the call. I do whatever it is they ask, and then they'll release her."

"How? Where?"

"I don't know. My hope is that I'll be told where to go to pick her up. I'll never see who these people are. That's why they want the ransom in crypto."

"But even if you transfer them all this ... money, what guarantee do we have?" Luciana asked. "What says they don't just take the money and run?"

"We don't have any guarantee," George said worriedly. "We don't."

Luciana looked to Sam. "We should let Tori and Will know about this. They could help us. Can't we do both things here?"

Sam shook his head. "I haven't seen much out of them other than telling us what they haven't found."

"Have they given you any indication that they're onto these kidnappers?" George asked. "Anything at all."

"Well, no," Luciana answered. "No, they haven't."

"I don't think we know anything for certain either," he said. "They've reached out and sent us a picture of Izzy. We know she's alive and they've told us what they want. If we pay, I think we'll get her back, as long as we don't screw it up."

"But you said there's no guarantee."

"No, but think of it this way, sis. This is like those ransomware attacks we talked about. If a company pays and then the attackers don't remove the ransomware, then other victims will know not to pay up, right?"

"Yeah ..." Luciana slowly nodded. "I suppose."

"It's just a transaction to these guys. Izzy is nothing more than a means to an end. They get what they want and move on and do it again to someone else."

Luciana looked to Sam again.

"We do what we have to do to get Izzy back," he said.

"But, George, even if we get her back, you're out all this money, and while we can pay you back, it'll take time."

"It'll hurt, but I can handle it," George said. "You do what you must for family. Whatever it takes to make things right."

"We will pay you back," Sam said. "We'll cover it somehow."

"How about the ranch?" Luciana suggested. "I could do

that."

"There's a thought," Sam said. "That's what we should do."

"Uh ... you sure, sis?" George said.

Luciana nodded. "I know it's not real valuable, but it's a start on paying you back."

He nodded reluctantly. "Okay, we put that in the hopper."

"I know that's still nowhere near enough but still ... it's something."

As they left the bedroom, they saw that Carson's bedroom door was closed.

"How's he doing?" George asked as they walked down the steps.

"Pretty quiet," Sam said. "He's spending most of his time in the basement. He wanted to go over to a friend's house tonight. That was a no-go."

"I'm not letting him out of my sight," Luciana agreed.

* * *

"I'll get you and Peter picked up tonight. I can do that," Braddock said to Quinn, the call on speaker. "I'll probably have you stay at Roger and Mary's, though, as we might be working late."

"When do you think the case will be over?"

"Don't know, buddy. We go like this as long as there's hope. I was going to ask, have you talked to Carson at all?"

"Just some texts. He was invited to Ryan's house tonight, but his parents said no. I don't think they're letting him go anywhere right now."

"I'm not surprised," Tori said.

"He did say they let him stay up late and watch whatever he wants. He's been watching movies and playing games in the basement. He even slept down there, as he figured his parents didn't want him to hear what they and his uncle have been talking about."

Braddock raised an eyebrow. "Why is that?"

"I don't know, Dad. He said they all talk in his parents' bedroom. Carson's room is right next door." Quinn dropped off the line for a minute and they heard voices in the background. "Hey, Dad, I'm leaving for practice."

"Just watching, right?"

"Yes, Dad."

"How are your ribs?" Tori asked.

"It doesn't hurt when I breathe anymore."

"Not at all?"

"Well ..."

"Yeah, that's what I thought."

They talked for another minute before Braddock hung up. "What do you make of what Quinn said about Carson?" he asked Tori.

"Not sure."

"You want to go talk with them?"

"Let's get coffees first, and then let them know we're coming over."

* * *

A half-hour later, Luciana let them in and led them to the kitchen, where Sam was waiting, sitting at the table with a cup of coffee. Tori took a chair and eyed them both up. Braddock took a seat at the near end and did much the same, assessing.

Tori waited a moment, allowing for some awkward silence before asking Luciana, "Where's George?"

"He went to his office. The restaurant business doesn't stop."

"I'm sure weekends are big for him."

"They are."

"Do you have anything new to report?" Sam asked.

"No developments overnight," Tori replied, and then ticked off on her fingers what they were doing, a defensiveness in her tone. "We're still out knocking on doors. All law enforcement has a description of Isabella. We're using the news media to get the message out. We're monitoring your phones and computers. We have officers out questioning ... people who need to be questioned," she added, not wanting to explain that she meant known sex offenders. "We're digging into all of that. And we're continuing to evaluate customer lists, patient lists, running criminal backgrounds and histories. Detective Braddock and I are involved in all of that."

"That doesn't sound like anything different from last night," Sam said.

"It isn't. Unless ... you had anything to update *us* on," Tori replied, prodding.

"We've just been here ... waiting," Luciana answered.

Tori felt like saying: for what? But thought better of it for now.

Braddock eased them back. "How are you holding up?"

"We're fine," Sam answered.

"Well, we know you're really not," Tori said, looking Luciana straight on. She let her statement hang in the air for a moment, but neither Luciana nor Sam responded, instead sharing a quick sideways glance. "You two seem ... distracted."

Sam shrugged. "We're handling it."

"Handling it how?" Braddock asked directly.

"We're ... coping."

Luciana stared blankly ahead. Tori asked her, "Are you sleeping?"

"Not really."

Tori nodded. "It's keeping me up at night as well, in part

because I keep thinking about Izzy and what she's going through, and in part because it's such an odd case."

"How's that?" Luciana asked, her gaze drifting away. There had been tears most of the times Tori had spoken with her, but this morning her eyes were dry. Was she cried out? Was she resigned? Where was the fight that had been there twenty-four hours ago?

"Well, like we said before, the planning and execution means it doesn't appear to be a random, spur-of-the moment kind of thing. This has all the hallmarks of a well-thought-out attack. Your daughter was targeted. Why?"

"We don't know," Sam said.

"You said targeted," Braddock said, leading Tori. "You've seen this before?"

"Well-planned and executed abductions, sure," Tori said. "Sadly, I've seen many. Most recently was just last winter up in Crosslake. Savannah Devenish. You all know the case, right?"

"It was hard to miss," Sam noted.

"Interesting investigation," Tori said. "I can say that now, because while it took a few days, we got the girls back. That abduction, like so many, involved family members. A parent abducting their child usually. In some cases, like last year, trying to leave the country with them. In other cases, it's almost irrational. No real plan other than to flee and attempt to hide, and eventually they'll be found. Here, though, it's different. This has the feel of a very well-planned abduction, but there seems to be something missing."

"What's that?"

"This kind of crime requires a why," Tori replied, looking Luciana and then Sam in the eye. "I can't find the motive for it. We've been through your client lists and patient lists, and yes, we're talking to people and maybe something will yet emerge, but there sure isn't anything in there jumping out at us. Part of that is because neither of you can really point to anyone. You're a good doctor, Luciana, I know this to be the case."

Luciana nodded slightly, but looked down.

"And, Sam, your business is doing very well, which tells me you do right by your clients."

"I do."

"So it doesn't seem like there's anyone who would want to come after either of you," Braddock said.

"What are you getting at?" Sam asked.

"That really leaves only one other option. Ransom. But that doesn't make sense to us either."

"Why not?" Sam furrowed his brow.

Braddock looked to Tori, who stood up and started pacing about the room, stopping to look at photos on the built-in bookshelves. "Well, assuming you've disclosed everything to us about your financial picture, you don't seem wealthy enough."

"Excuse me?" Sam said testily. "Now hold—"

"Don't get me wrong, you're both doing well. You're in your early forties. You have a beautiful house, nice vehicles, I'm sure a terrific boat. Thriving businesses. It's obvious you're climbing the income ladder. You're successful and intelligent people."

"Tori," Luciana started, "I'm not—"

Tori kept pacing. "It's a simple risk–reward equation. The sentence for kidnapping at the state level is twenty years. If we charged federally, it could be life, so if you were going to kidnap for ransom, logically the risk has to be worth the reward. I just wonder if there is enough reward here."

"My daughter—"

"Is our sole focus, just as she is yours," Tori kept on, now making a show of examining a collection of books arranged on a shelf. "We're just trying to make sense of it all. And right now, it doesn't make sense."

"Does it have to?" Luciana asked.

"Yes," Tori replied, turning and walking back toward them. "People talk about senseless crimes, and some can be, but not this one. This one was done with a purpose. What was that purpose?"

"I wish we knew," Sam said calmly. "I wish we knew."

"Me too," Tori said dejectedly.

She looked to Braddock, who nodded for them to leave. They had done what they'd come to do.

Sam and Luciana walked them to the front door. Braddock stepped out first, and Tori followed, but then stopped on the stoop and turned to Luciana.

"You know, I talked earlier about that case last winter. We were lucky to get those girls back. We could have gotten them back sooner, though."

"Why didn't you?"

"The father of the abducted girl didn't tell us everything. He didn't tell us about an affair he was having, even though we asked. As I said, we could have gotten her back sooner, and what's worse, some people died who didn't have to."

* * *

"That was fucking offensive," Sam growled angrily.

"They're suspicious," Luciana said as she peered through a gap in the curtains, watching Braddock pull away. "Of us."

"Let them think what they want."

"I know what George said, but maybe we should tell them."

"If they actually had anything that told me they knew who we were dealing with, if they had more than George—hell if they had half as much—then I might think different. They've got nothing."

"They don't have nothing. They were just here telling us that. They're going to keep watching us."

"Let them."

* * *

Tori waited until Braddock had driven them all the way back to the government center. "I kept poking the bear."

"You were borderline insulting," Braddock agreed as they walked up the steps to the building. "You were provoking them. I mean, the one time you got a rise out of Sam was when you said that ransom didn't make sense because they weren't wealthy enough."

"You notice he didn't say they hadn't been called. He said ..."

"Why not," Braddock said. "Hmpf."

"They should have come off the top rope after me. I was hoping they would. It would have opened the door. But they didn't."

"Okay, but while we suspect there has been contact, we don't have any proof. For the moment, let's assume something is happening here." They stepped through the door. "If it is, they don't trust us enough to tell us what it is."

"Or they trust somebody else more. They're parents. They want Isabella back, and right now they think the way to get her back is to not let us in."

"What do you want to do?"

"Give them space," Tori replied. "And watch them like hawks. Santo too."

"Tori?" A uniformed deputy called to her from reception. "There's someone here to see you."

Tori walked down the hall. A woman in nursing scrubs was sitting in the waiting area.

"I'm Tori Hunter. You asked to see me?"

The woman stood up and stuck out her hand. "Hi. My

name is Rosa Hernandez. My daughter is ... was Helena Hernandez."

"Uh ... hello," Tori replied, momentarily taken aback, before shaking Rosa's hand.

She led the woman back to a small conference room, then stepped out and poured a cup of coffee for Rosa and grabbed a bottle of water for herself. When she returned to the room, Rosa looked at her quizzically.

"What?" Tori asked.

"You know, I just thought you would be ..."

"Taller?"

"Yeah. I just figured that because you were an FBI agent who had done all these things, you would be bigger. I see all these police in the emergency room, and they're usually stocky or tall."

Tori offered a small smile. It wasn't the first time she'd heard that. "Maybe I broke the mold."

"I'm sorry I didn't call ahead, but I was afraid you wouldn't see me," Rosa said. "I hope it's okay I came here."

"Of course. How can I help you?"

"I saw the reports on the news about the abduction of that twelve-year-old girl, Isabella. And I saw that Ian Anderson was a suspect—or at least I assume it was him. He took my daughter. He took Helena."

"Well, Rosa—"

"Have you looked at Helena's case?"

"I have."

"What do you think? Did Ian Anderson do it?"

"I understand why he was a suspect. It's part of what made him one here as well."

"I know they couldn't prove it," Rosa continued, nodding. "I know the attorneys said they needed proof, but it was him. The detectives in Thief River thought he did it." She recited the facts of the investigation as she knew them, which was consistent with what Tori had learned in reviewing the investigative file. "He had that van. He was at the community center. I saw him driving by the house. If I hadn't been so ... out of it ..." Her voice trailed away, and she wiped away a tear from her cheek. "I was hoping that now this man is a suspect again, you could get him to tell you what happened to my Helena."

"I'm sorry, Rosa. He's no longer a suspect. We've determined that he couldn't have abducted Isabella Farner."

"You're sure?"

"Yes," Tori replied. "We are. In this case, we are."

Rosa looked crushed.

"I'm sorry. And I'm so sorry about your daughter."

"I was hoping this might be a chance to find out what happened to her."

"I understand."

"And then I saw that you were investigating," Rosa added. "I read some stories about you. About cases you've worked on. It gave me some hope."

Tori nodded. "I see you're in scrubs. You're a nurse now?"

"Yes." Rosa nodded proudly. "I'm an emergency room nurse in Fargo. I drove over here after I finished my shift this morning."

"How long have you been nursing?"

"Almost three years," Rosa said. "After Helena was taken, I ... I knew I had to be there for my son. I had to get clean. While I was doing that, my counselor referred me to a nursing program."

"Good for you," Tori said. "I'm sorry. I wish I had better news for you."

Rosa nodded, looking down.

"I just want to know what happened to Helena. I just want to know."

SIXTEEN

"AND THIS INVOLVES YOU WHY?"

"Too bad Fred was murdered," Steak said. "The man had it going on business-wise."

Steak and Eggleston had spent the morning driving around Manchester Bay and the nearby lakes interviewing Weltz's customers—at least those that were available. What the calls and stops showed was that Weltz had himself a long list of upscale clients. People who could and would pay for the kind of high-end carpentry work that was his calling card. Some of the projects were for people who had closed their summer places up for the year. In those cases, driving between homes Eggleston made calls, tracking the homeowners down. The praise for his abilities was universal, not an unhappy customer among them.

After they stopped for a quick lunch, they made their way to the Stearns' house at the north end of Northern Pine Lake.

"It's really nice," Steak said as he evaluated the dark wood of the massive bar in the walkout basement of the house. It looked like it was right out of an Irish pub; in fact the whole room did, from the entrance to the built-in shelves and furniture pieces the Stearns had added.

"We told him what we were looking to build, gave him some design thoughts and pictures, and he came back with plans for this," Mr. Stearn said. "I'm so sad to hear that he was killed."

"He did this project for you when?" Eggleston asked.

"He finished it the last week of July," Stearn said. "Install took him about a month, maybe a hair more. That allowed time for the plumber, electrician, and painter to come in and do their parts too. So he was back and forth, I'm sure working on other projects as well."

"When he was here, did he ever tell you about any of those other projects he might have been working on?"

"Oh, sure," Stearn replied with a big smile. "He was a talker, that guy. He could be measuring, installing, leveling, whatever it was, and if you happened to be there, he was talking. Yak, yak, yak, yak, yak."

"About other projects."

"Sure. I know he was working on a large customized bookcase and desk arrangement for friends of ours named the Goldmans. Their house is on the east side of the lake, just north of town. They wanted matching bookcases with a few extras on either side of their old fireplace. We referred Fred down there and I know he finished that project for them like in a week."

"That quickly?"

"Yeah," Mr. Stearn said. "It was a pretty simple project, although on one side they wanted a built-in case with a door to hide their flat-screen television. They were having a big party and wanted it ready before they hosted, and knowing them, they were willing to pay to see that it was done. Evelyn Goldman was so pleased with it. She knows everybody in town, so I'll guarantee you she referred Fred to others. You should go talk to her. She'll be a fountain of information."

"Evelyn Goldman," Eggleston said, jotting down the name in her notepad. "Do you have a phone number?"

* * *

"It was a short trip, an hour then back home," the deputy monitoring the Farner house reported to Tori.

"Did he meet with anyone?"

"Not that I saw. There were no other vehicles in the parking lot. Nobody else went in or out. He was in there for a half-hour give or take, and then he was out and back here."

"Was he carrying anything?"

"He had a shoulder bag when he went in and had the same bag when he came back out. That's the update."

Tori hung up and dug another Kettle potato chip out of the bag on the conference room table. She and Braddock had briefly debated watching the Farner house, but other than Sam's brief trip to his office, the couple were sitting tight, and there wasn't anything to be gained by waiting there doing nothing. As for Santo, Reese reported he'd been at his office above his restaurant for much of the day.

It felt like something was percolating. Izzy was not far away. If there was movement, they would have to move with it.

In the meantime, she was going through the interview summaries from the officers who had conducted witness interviews at the scene and in the Farners' neighborhood. All that did was push her back to Ian Pemell. By the time Braddock reappeared in the conference room, she had moved on to rereading the Helena Hernandez and Joey Martinez disappearance files again.

"You must be bored," Braddock said when he sat down.

"And frustrated and ... confused."

"And then there's Rose Hernandez visiting you."

Tori sighed. "Yeah, and then there is that."

"Care to talk about it?"

"Not much to say." She took a drink of her soda. "I couldn't give her anything. I had to tell her that I don't think anything we have here can give her hope of finding out what happened to her daughter. She asked about Pemell, and I had to tell her that the man thought responsible for her daughter's disappearance was not responsible for the one here."

"That's not your fault."

"I know, but still, she drove all the way here from Fargo and I had to send her on her way with that disappointment."

"It's a downer."

Tori nodded and leaned back, closing her eyes for a minute, rubbing her temples.

"Did I see that she was in nursing scrubs?"

"Yes. That's what makes it doubly brutal. She's completely turned her life around, but it took her daughter's abduction to motivate her to get straightened out. She carries that guilt with her every day. I feel for her. I wish I could help her." Tori held up the Thief River investigative file. "Because she's right, I think Pemell did take her daughter."

"You reckon it's him?"

"I see what they saw. They had the circumstantial, but no specific hard evidence. They needed just one good piece, one little speck of physical evidence that Helena was in his vehicle, at his house or on the property; that's all it would have taken."

"It's all about the time interval, if you ask me," Braddock said as he plopped down into a chair. "There was a window for him to do whatever it was he did before the police identified him as a suspect. He had time to kill her and clean it up. It was over before they ever started on him. His head start was too big to overcome."

"That might explain it." She shook her head. "Pemell did it, or he did … something."

"Something?"

"Yeah, something." She tossed the file onto the table. "He's a good neighbor in the trailer park for the Joey Martinez disappearance. Then Helena Hernandez. As we like to say, there are no such things as coincidences, but there are patterns."

"Which is what made him a suspect here." Braddock took a long swig of his soda. "It takes three like murders to make it a serial. This is the third."

"He didn't do this, or if he did, he set it up so well we just can't get at him. But there is one thing that kind of bugs me about him as a suspect for the Thief River and Grand Forks cases. Or even here, for that matter."

"What's that?"

"After interviewing him here and at his house, I'm kind of with Dana Bryan. I didn't get the pedophilia feels from him."

"He lacked the requisite aroma?"

"Yeah. I reread Dana's notes, where he says he didn't think he had that kind of urge for children. I'm not a psychologist, but I've been around, seen enough of those types, and Ian didn't give me those creepy-crawlies. I don't think he's into kids."

"I thought you said he did it?"

"I think he did. My question would be why. For what end if it wasn't sexual. If he isn't interested in kids that way, why do this? There is something about him that … interests me. Some evil lurks there. Ethical hacker? Pfft. My ass. He's an operator. If I were his employer, I'd be double- and triple-checking everything he's done for them. I wouldn't trust him as far as I could throw him."

"They probably won't after our visit."

"At least something good might come of this then."

Braddock burped a laugh. "Why do I have a feeling you have a new hobby?"

"Ruining his life and proving him guilty?" Tori replied with a wan smile.

"Yeah?"

"Consider it a public service."

Braddock's cell phone buzzed. "Yeah ... Uh-huh ... Yeah, that is odd ... Where did you find the truck? ... Alright." He checked his watch. "No, I'll come down and take a look."

"What is it?"

"That was the police chief down in Little Falls. His men found an abandoned delivery truck with the driver stuffed in the back with three gunshots in her."

"And this involves you why?"

"Because her last delivery was down along the southern end of Shepard County. I'd send Steak or Eggs, but they're working their case, and all our other people are on the Farner deal. It's a half-hour down there. I can be back if anything pops."

"You want me to come with?"

Braddock smiled. "I need you here." He pecked her softly on the lips. "If anything does happen, call me. I'll haul ass back."

"Okay," Tori said, before pulling him down for another kiss, one that she held for an extra second.

"Hmm. Hasn't been much time for you and me the last couple of days."

"We don't need all that much time," she replied with a seductive smile, flicking her eyebrows. "Your office door has a lock, and a reasonably sized couch."

"I like where your mind is at," he said. He kissed her one more time, then looked to his watch. "Oh dang it."

"What?"

"Quinn. He and Peter have to be picked up at ten. I said I could do it. If I'm down in Little Falls ..."

"I'll take care of it."

* * *

"It's just a tragedy what happened to Fred," Evelyn Goldman said as she stood with Steak and Eggleston in the foyer of her grand home. "He seemed like a very nice fella," she added. She led them into a large family room area and gestured to a wall with a tan-bricked fireplace. "That's what he built right there, the white cabinetry around the fireplace."

"It looks very nice," Eggleston said, stepping closer to inspect it. There was deft craftsmanship in the work, layered ornate moldings cut to fit seamlessly against the rough edges of the stone. Goldman had filled the shelves with local decor and artifacts, photographs, and hardcover books. It looked natural, as if it had been in the room for years.

"I couldn't believe how good it turned out and how fast he did it," she said. "And many of the people at the party noted it."

"Did he ever talk to you about any work he did for other clients?"

"Oh yes," she said, chewing on her bottom lip. "He talked about this project or that. I do know that three people at the party asked me for his number, and I think they all hired him to do something for them."

"Who were those people?"

"Jim and Jennifer Sax—you've probably heard of them, they own the jewelry store in town."

"We actually talked to them earlier," Steak said, gesturing to the list Eggleston was holding.

"Then there were the Hofners next door."

"We were going to stop over there next."

"They're on a trip in Europe right now, have been for a few weeks," Evelyn said. "I know he was going to build them a bar in their basement as part of a remodel."

"You said three people," Eggleston said.

"Oh yes. I also gave the number to Georgie."

"Georgie?"

"George Santo."

Eggleston looked up and then glanced to Steak. "The third person was George Santo?"

"Yes. He said he had a project for Fred."

"And do you know if he hired him?"

"I know he talked to him, because Fred chatted with me in the driveway like a week later when he met with the Hofners. He said he and George had met."

* * *

"Do you have it?"

"I'm close."

"Close isn't having it."

"I will have it. The question is whether I can shake free of my shadow once I do."

"You worry about your end of the deal, and I'll take care of mine."

SEVENTEEN

"WHY DID SHE GET OUT OF THE TRUCK?"

Little Falls was literally the geographic center of Minnesota. It was perhaps best known as the boyhood home of aviator Charles Lindbergh, hence the reason the local high school nickname was the Flyers. The town took its name from the small falls on the Mississippi River upon which it was settled in 1848. With a population of just over 8,000, it was located halfway between St. Cloud to the south and Manchester Bay to the north.

Braddock approached, his police lights flashing. An officer waved him ahead and he parked just short of the yellow police tape that was strung across the narrow driveway leading around to the back of a machine shop located on the northeastern edge of the town.

When he got out of the Tahoe, he felt the cool piercing chill of the evening. He zipped his black North Face coat up fully. The rain earlier in the week had preceded the cold front behind it. It was after 8:00 p.m. now, and with the crisp air and clear skies, he was betting there would be a heavy frost and maybe some patchy fog in the morning. He reached into the car for a pair of gloves and a black stocking cap, which he stuffed in the pocket of his coat.

He showed his identification to an officer, who then lifted the tape for him. "Chief Glyndon and Agent Poston are around the back."

Behind the one-story cinder block building, he found a hive of activity around a Courier Connect delivery truck. The truck had been reversed into a nook so that it would have only been visible if someone drove around to the back of the building. The rear door had been lifted. BCA Agent Curt Poston was standing behind the truck, a baseball cap warming his shaved head. Next to him was a man in a camouflage hunting coat and ball cap.

Poston saw Braddock and waved him over. "Will, this is Little Falls police chief Frank Glyndon."

"Chief," Braddock greeted, shaking his hand. "Turkey hunting?"

"That's right."

"Get anything?"

"A couple this morning. We were out at my family's property when I got the call."

"What do we have here?" Braddock asked as he took a step forward and peered into the back of the truck.

"The victim is the truck's driver, Penny Teague, of St. Cloud," Chief Glyndon said. "She clocked in at six this morning and took the truck on her scheduled route through Morrison County up into southern Shepard. She made her first four deliveries in Shepard County, going east along County Road 56 here." He gestured to a map on his cell phone. "Her last confirmed delivery was at this address right here on County 56 before turning south. The next delivery was just over five miles away, down here on the north side of Platte Lake."

"Which is still Shepard County," Braddock murmured.

"Right. From there she was to drive south into Morrison County and make a delivery on the south side of Sullivan Lake, and several more from there. I think there is a decent chance she was killed in your county."

Braddock crinkled his nose and nodded in agreement.

"I know you have a few things going already," the chief added.

Braddock chuckled ruefully. "You could say that."

"Sorry to pile on."

"What do we know about Ms. Teague?"

"Twenty-eight years old. Single. No children. Lives in an apartment in St. Cloud. No criminal record," Poston reported. "Company says she's been employed just over a year. A good, solid, reliable employee was how her manager described her to me."

"How was she killed?"

"Shot, three times," Poston said as they both stepped up onto the truck's back wide bumper. "You can see the two to the chest and then one dead center in the forehead."

"Execution?"

"The one to the head looks like it; you can see that one was close range. The other two are more ... spread."

"Suggesting some distance," Braddock said, observing one wound to Teague's upper left shoulder and the other to her lower abdomen. "Get her from distance and then finish off the job." Braddock looked to the medical examiner, who was now approaching with a gurney. "Doc, do you have a time of death?"

"I'd say somewhere between seven and eight this morning."

"Twelve to thirteen hours then, at this point," Braddock said. He looked to Poston and Glyndon. "Why? What did she do?"

"We don't know—yet," Poston said.

"Could it have been something she was carrying?" Braddock suggested. "A package someone desperately wanted. A package someone couldn't allow to be delivered?"

"That's what I figured," Glyndon said.

"It seems the most likely scenario," Poston agreed. "Our killer was following her; he saw his chance out in the countryside and made his move."

Did that sound right? Braddock took out his small flashlight and shone the beam around the back of the truck. "She wasn't shot inside here. Not enough blood."

The medical examiner nodded. "Her body was placed in here after she was shot."

Braddock walked around to the front compartment. "No blood in there. She was shot outside of the truck."

"What are you getting at?" Poston said.

"The question is not only where did she stop, but why did she stop. Why did she get out of the truck? Was she shot while making the last delivery, perhaps?"

"We wondered about that," Poston said. "I called the recipients. They'd been anxiously awaiting the delivery. It was a birthday gift for their granddaughter. A face-to-face is necessary with them, but my quick impression off the phone call was they didn't sound like the types to be receiving a package that was problematic."

"Hmpf," Braddock snorted. "Then why the heck does she stop? That's what I don't get. But she must have." He took a quick look around. "I assume this business wasn't open today?"

"No."

"Nobody would see the truck then unless they came back here for some reason. Who found it?"

"One of my guys," Glyndon said. "The company noticed when the truck didn't return from the route. It should have been back by three p.m. When it got to about four, they went to their GPS system and saw it sitting here. This location wasn't on the delivery route. They tried reaching the driver, but there was no response. They contacted our department to check, and now here we are."

"We have to find where she was shot and then maybe we can get some answers," Poston said. "Which leads to a question."

"Jurisdiction," Braddock said.

"I think it's likely she was murdered in your county, but we can't be certain. I know you have your hands full right now. Do you want the BCA to take lead on this one?"

"If you're offering?"

"We can take it," Poston said. "I'll keep you looped in."

* * *

"It's all together?" Sam asked after he closed the master bedroom door.

"Yes. Now I wait," George said, patting his pant pocket.

"We have something for you," Luciana said, looking to Sam.

"This is my promise to repay you every cent," Sam said, handing over a thick binder clipped document.

George slipped on his reading glasses. It wasn't a contract in its phrasing and structure. It was more a narrative of how Sam and Luciana would make him whole. He turned from the first page and stopped on a paragraph that started with the heading *Down Payment*. He read that and then flipped to the back of the document. Attached was a second document, one he'd had drafted himself a few years ago. It was a purchase agreement for him to buy Luciana's half of their family ranch just outside of San Mateo in New Mexico. She and Sam had removed the price, replacing $250,000 with a zero. He looked up.

"It doesn't near cover all this, but it's at least a start," Luciana said quietly. "You're the real estate guy. I'm sure you'll figure out what to do with it."

"You're sure? You're absolutely sure?"

"Yes," Luciana replied, hugging her brother.

George nodded, then took a pen from Sam and signed the back page of the document.

"We'll need to get the ranch valued," Luciana said. "It's not worth that much."

"Let's just get Izzy back. We can worry about all that later."

Exhausted from her escape and chase, Izzy fell asleep for what she thought was several hours. When she woke, the sun had set, and it was dark outside and inside her room. She sat cross-legged on the mattress. Her clothes were filthy. She'd had to pick mud from her hair and try and wipe away the dirt she felt on her left cheek. As she sat there, she wondered about one thing in particular.

Why had she seen her uncle George's friend in the SUV?

She took her mud-caked bracelet off, wiping the dirt from the charms. It had been hours now. No trips to the bathroom. Nothing to eat or drink. There had been no contact since she'd been brought back to the room.

What was the woman's name?

It was a few years ago that she'd come to dinner at their house with Uncle George. She'd worn a showy dress, a fur coat, flashy jewelry, her hair all done up.

Why was she there? wondered Izzy. And why didn't she help me?

It occurred to her that this was why the man had said she

shouldn't have tried to escape. She wasn't supposed to have seen the woman, or any of them for that matter.

But why would she want me? Is it to get back at my uncle?

An engine started up outside. Another one had started a few minutes ago, and the headlights had briefly flooded the room with light through the glass-block window before the vehicle had pulled away. A door closed above her, and then a few seconds later car doors slammed and another vehicle drove away.

Sitting motionless on the bed for a moment, the only thing she felt was her heart beating and the air through her nose. A stillness had settled in as if the house was at rest.

She looked up to the camera. The red light was out. It had never been out before. It was off. Nobody was watching her.

Something was happening.

This wasn't good.

I need to try and get out of here.

She crawled off the mattress towards the door. In the darkness, she couldn't see the latch or the hole she'd chiseled with the sink stopper. She felt for the gap. Her right index finger was too big to fit into that little hole. She tried with her other fingers but couldn't jam even her pinky finger in there. Squinting, she picked at the wood with her right index finger.

"Ow!" A splinter. "Ow, ow, ow." It stung. She wiped her finger on a non-soiled section of her jeans, and then sucked on the end of it. She couldn't even see the little hole. She felt for it again, with her left index finger this time, but it was just too small. It had to be made bigger. A lot bigger to get her finger in there.

She hunted around the room for anything sharp that she could use, but there was nothing. They'd taken everything away. All she had was a pillow and blanket, the crayons and coloring book, and her bracelet. *The bracelet ...*

She yanked off one of the small silver angels, then found the gap again and used the charm to pick at the wood around it. But the angel was small and brittle. It couldn't penetrate the wood, instead bending and then snapping in two. She pulled off one of the dove charms, hoping that the bird's sharp tail would dig in, but after a few minutes of chipping and jabbing, the tip broke off.

This wasn't working.

In desperation, she grabbed the pack of crayons. Pulling one out, she carefully felt for the gap with the tip, then tried slowly pushing it into the hole, seeing if she could wedge it in there to act as a lever.

Crack!

She reached for another crayon and tried again.

Crack!

"Come on! Come on!"

She jammed crayon after crayon into the gap, but it was useless. They all crumbled when she applied any pressure. She tried with her fingers again, picking at the wood, but all she did was give herself more splinters.

This wasn't working either.

Sweating, she mopped her brow. Her hand was throbbing, and she could feel blood trickling down her finger. She wiped it on her pants.

My coat. They had left the raincoat in the room. She turned a pocket inside out and yanked at it repeatedly until she ripped it away.

Yes.

She wrapped the nylon fabric around her right index finger and again tried jamming it in the hole, scraping, prying at the hard wood, but even with her finger covered, she just couldn't break it down and make the hole bigger.

"Come on. Please, please, *pleeeeaaase!*"

She crumpled to her knees, sitting back, staring at the door.

There was no way out of the room.

Exhausted, tears pouring down her cheeks, she picked up what was left of her bracelet, then crawled back over to the mattress and curled up under the blanket.

EIGHTEEN

"INTERESTING YOU'RE NOW SUDDENLY MOVING"

Braddock checked his watch before he got into the Tahoe. It was 9:33 p.m.

As he pulled away, he reflexively flipped up his right turn signal to go west over to the H-4 and back to Manchester Bay.

Wait.

He held at the corner for a moment, then reached for his notepad sitting on the passenger seat and flipped it open. He found the address and tapped it into the GPS system. *Let's go check it out.*

For twenty minutes he left-and-righted his way along the dark county roads through the flat farmlands of Morrison County. He didn't know the southeast corner of Shepard County well. There were few calls down this direction that ever required him to respond. It was rural and lightly populated save some areas around a grouping of small lakes that were surrounded by cabins.

The BCA was taking lead on the investigation, but he was curious as to why the driver had got out of her truck. As he drove to the address of her last delivery, he contemplated possibilities.

There were two that came immediately to mind. One was that she was somehow forced to stop. The second was that she stopped voluntarily.

The problem with the first one was that if she'd been forced to stop, would she have gotten out of the truck? Wouldn't she have tried to radio or call for help? The truck had a radio. She had a cell phone. No call was made.

The second possibility made more sense to him. She stopped and got out of the truck voluntarily. But what would make her do that? The most obvious answer was she pulled over to help someone. Another vehicle stopped at the side of the road perhaps.

He reached the address of the last delivery she'd made and began the drive to the next, which was a shade over five miles away. She could have taken two routes, although only one was likely, the one that didn't involve traversing a winding gravel road. He turned on his police lights and took his time. The route first took him south for two miles before a turn left sent him due east toward a cluster of lakes and thick forested areas. For the first four miles, he drove through what looked to be a mixture of small farm fields and groves of dense trees and underbrush. There were few driveways.

At his slow pace, it took him twenty minutes to cover the distance. In that time, he saw only one other vehicle.

There is nobody out here.

When he reached the next delivery destination, he was only a half-mile from the southern border of the county. He pulled to the shoulder. Five miles, no obvious sign of anything. He wasn't sure what he'd expected to find. However, he was reasonably certain the murder had occurred somewhere in that five-mile stretch.

Did Teague drive the other route, the gravel road? In the unlikely event she did, he took the loop, but it ran him through farm fields, and he passed only three marked driveways. Again he saw nothing that gave him pause. But then what would you expect to see in the dark of the night?

To even get an idea of where the shooting might have happened would have to wait for daylight and someone driving the route very slowly, if not walking it. Any evidence that might have existed could have been wiped away by the killers by now, given that the murder likely happened at least fourteen hours ago. And that assumed it had happened along this route to begin with. There could be any number of other explanations; he was only dealing with the most likely or logical of them.

"Besides, buddy, it's not your case."

He turned off his police lights, sat back in his seat and drove north.

* * *

"Both vehicles have been gone a good ninety minutes now," he said, dropping the binoculars from his eyes. "I don't see anyone else. The lights are off. I think we're good. It should take no more than five minutes, in and out."

"It's now or never."

* * *

Cain pulled his gloves tight and secured his face mask on his head, ready to pull it down, then slid out the magazine, checked it, and slid it back in.

Lowe called Vaughn. "We're moving. Make the call."

* * *

"Do you have it?"

"Yes."

"Everything?" Vaughn asked.

"Everything."

"Sit tight. Instructions are coming. We have something to take care of first."

* * *

Tori pulled up in front of the Grant house. Quinn and Peter were saying goodbye to their friends at the front door. Her phone pinged. A text from Zagaros: *I'll call you in an hour.*

The passenger door of the Audi opened.

"Hey, you two," she greeted as Quinn got into the front passenger seat and Peter into the back right behind him. Quinn fist-bumped her. "Did you have fun?"

"Sure did. We watched *No Time to Die* and then we played NHL 21 for a couple of hours."

"Bond flick. Your dad loves those movies. He talked about us renting it. Was it good?"

"Yeah," Quinn said as Tori drove down the hill toward town. "Lots of action. That woman double-O, she was kind of ... badass."

"Badass, huh?" Tori asked with a wry smile and raised eyebrow, and then looked in the rearview mirror. "How about you, Pete?"

"It was okay."

"You don't sound so impressed."

"It was good, although it amazes me how Bond rarely misses, yet everyone misses him."

"Funny how that works," Tori said as she drove through town and turned right onto County Road 44 heading north-west, the bright lights of Manchester Bay drifting behind. Her phone, resting in its holder mounted to the dashboard, buzzed. Braddock was calling. She tapped the screen to answer.

"I have the boys. We're on our way to drop Peter off at home."

"Hiya, boys," Braddock greeted cheerily.

"They watched the new James Bond movie," she reported, watching attentively for deer along the dark road. Braddock almost took one out about a week ago when they were coming home from dinner.

"I've wanted to see that. How was it?"

"Pretty good," Quinn answered. "You'll like it."

"Apparently there's a woman double O who is a total badass. At least that's what Quinn says." Tori looked up at a flash of light in the rearview mirror. A set of headlights coming up on them.

"Badass, huh? I guess we'll have to rent it."

"I guess we ..." she began, but the glare in the rear-view was blinding. The headlights were right behind them, the engine roaring. She looked in the mirror again and the headlights suddenly turned off.

Not good.

She turned to her left and first felt it, then saw the black SUV coming up on her side. "Boys, buckle up. Buckle up now!"

"Tori?" Braddock called.

She accelerated, but a hair too late. The SUV turned hard into her.

"Whoa!" Quinn yelped. "*Whoa!*"

"*Tori!*"

The SUV rammed her, her right-side tires skidding on the gravel of the shoulder. She turned the wheel hard left. "*Hang on! Hang on!*"

"What's going on!" Braddock bellowed over the phone. "Tori? *Tori?*"

"We're being run off the road!" she yelled, fighting the steering wheel, feeling her right front tire climb back onto the asphalt. She yanked hard left into the SUV. The collision created separation, and she sped ahead, but the SUV was still right on her.

"Dad, we're on 44!" Quinn yelled. "We're on 44!"

The steering wheel shaking, holding on tight, Tori checked left. The passenger-side window on the SUV was down. An arm reached out.

"Heads down! Cover up! *Cover up!*"

Boom! Boom! Boom! Boom!

Glass shattered all along the driver's side. She ducked but kept her eyes ahead. Headlights. A vehicle was coming. She veered right, her right-side tires dropping hard onto the gravel shoulder. The oncoming vehicle passed between the Audi and the SUV, honking.

"*Tori! Tori!*" Braddock's voice called.

She pulled hard left onto the road again, the Audi's engine powering them ahead, but the SUV was right there on top of them. "Here it comes again, boys!"

The big SUV rammed into her left front fender, rattling the whole compartment.

Boom! Boom! Boom!

One shot went over her right shoulder, shattering the dashboard screen. Another went through the windshield. She glanced right and glimpsed Quinn's terrified face.

A left curve was coming. The big SUV rammed into the driver's-side door, jostling her hard, her left hand slipping off the steering wheel. "No, no, no." She got her hand back on the wheel just as the SUV banged into her again, behind her door.

They hit the curve. There were dense woods that pinched in tight on the right. If they forced her off there …

Don't let him get ahead. Don't let him get ahead.

She turned her wheel left, accelerating, initiating contact, then yanked it right before turning hard back left, crashing into the SUV again. They were running side by side, her right-side tires alternately off and on the gravel shoulder as she struggled to hold the road around the curve. She leaned left, gripping the wheel.

They passed the trees.

Ahead, another set of headlights was coming. She caught the glint of the street sign. The right turn.

She hit the brake.

The tires grabbed the pavement and squealed. The Audi skidded.

The SUV surged by.

She whipped the steering wheel right, turning onto the gravel road, fishtailing, clipping a tree with her back left side. The collision straightened them out and she zoomed ahead before turning hard left.

Roger and Mary's house was the third one on the right. She veered into their driveway and jammed to a stop.

"Get out! Get out! *Go! Go! Go!*" she urged, pushing Quinn out the passenger-side door. Peter followed him out. "Get in the house, boys! Get in the house!"

"What's all the ruckus?" Roger Hayes called from the steps, Mary behind him in the doorway. That was when he noticed Tori's car, steaming and battered. "What the hell?"

"Rog, get them inside! *Now!*" Tori ordered, her gun out. She took cover behind the Audi.

"Come on! Come on, boys!" He ushered them into the house.

"Tori!" Braddock's voice called. "Tori, are you there? *Tori!*"

She quickly reached into the Audi and picked up her phone, which miraculously was still in its holder. "The boys are okay. I'm at Roger and Mary's. We need backup."

Braddock dropped off the line for a moment. She set the phone on the car roof and scanned the immediate area.

Click, click.

She glanced back. Roger was behind her, shotgun in hand. Another one leaning against the house.

"Rog, get the hell inside."

"Not a chance, girl. The boys told me what went on out there. I got you. I'm pretty fair with one of these." He hunted and shot clay and skeet competitively.

"Well then, get down behind the car so you have cover. You're a sitting duck there."

Her phone buzzed again. Braddock. She tapped to answer.

"What the hell happened?"

"A dark-colored SUV. A big one, Suburban, Expedition, Navigator, something like that. Tried to shoot us and run us off the road. Last seen northbound on County 44. The passenger side will be all scraped up from dodgem cars."

* * *

Vaughn secured her leather gloves and gripped the steering wheel, then exhaled a long breath. It wasn't often she got into the midst of it. That was what Cain and his boys were for. But this gambit required a fourth person, and this part was the easiest.

"You sure you're ready to do this?" Rust asked, pulling his own gloves tight, his gun, suppressor screwed on, resting on his lap.

"All I'm doing is driving."

"Keep your speed steady. We get one shot at this. Don't get excited and speed past. You understand what I'm saying? It's easy to do; the adrenaline goes, and your foot gets excited and heavy." He was speaking from experience. "Just look straight ahead, stay cool, and I'll take care of the rest."

Vaughn nodded. They both looked a block ahead at the detective parked on the right side of the street in his pickup truck. He'd been settled in that position for the better part of three hours.

* * *

Nolan parked and put her binoculars up to her eyes. Santo's back was to her. He was sitting down, having a drink while watching college football highlights.

The radio exploded in chatter; a report of shots fired on Tori on County 44.

"My God," Nolan muttered, and reached for her radio. "Reese? Did you hear that."

"Yeah. What the hell?"

"Go. Go now! I got this. I got eyes on Santo."

Ten seconds later, she saw Reese zoom between the houses a block over and then across in front of her a block ahead, a flashing light on his dashboard.

* * *

"Okay, let's go," Rust said quietly, powering down his passenger window and picking up his gun, setting it in both hands. "Again, calm, easy speed."

"Right." Vaughn felt her pulse racing as she checked the side mirror again and then the rear-view. *Remember, steady*, she told herself as she dropped the gear shift and started pulling forward.

"Hold on!" Rust said. "Stop. *Stop!*"

The detective pulled away speedily.

"Don't chase him."

A moment later, they saw a flashing light start up on his dashboard.

"Hmm. That's gotta be Cain," Rust said. "They're calling all cars."

The television talking head was reviewing college football highlights, but he wasn't watching. He set the framed photo of him and Luciana to the side and picked up the one of him and Isabella taken a year ago on her eleventh birthday. He allowed himself a small grin, the two of them holding up the birthday cake for the photo. She was such a beautiful little girl, the spitting image of her mother: lustrous skin, pretty eyes, long black hair.

He heard an engine roar by outside as he raised his glass of Scotch to his lips and took a drink. A siren suddenly blared, and he snapped his head around. The sound was behind him but was going away.

The cell phone on the coffee table buzzed.

"Yeah?"

"You're clear. Leave now. Here is where you go."

He got up from the couch and went into his office. His briefcase was open, the signed documents from Sam and Luciana sitting on top. He opened his desk drawer, grabbed his pistol and stuffed it into the pocket in the briefcase.

Tori scanned the area, Roger to her left. There was an odd sort of silence now, the air still and chilly, the only disruption the light hiss of steam as it filtered out the side seams of the Audi's hood.

A siren was audible in the far distance.

"Tori!" Roger whispered.

A set of headlights approached slowly from the left. She and Roger pivoted and tracked the lights as the vehicle approached. It disappeared behind the garage, and then emerged at the front. It was a crossover SUV. It pulled by the house and kept driving north along the road, having paid them no mind.

The sirens were closing now, from the south and the north. Fifteen seconds later, flashing lights flooded the road to the left and a sheriff's department Explorer arrived. Another one drew up a moment later. Both deputies recognized Tori, took one look at her Audi and immediately took protective positions, automatic rifles in their hands.

She gave it another two minutes.

"We're good," one of the deputies said, glancing back. "We got this. More are on the way."

The danger had passed. Tori closed her eyes and exhaled. Then she turned around and walked to the back of the house. Inside, she rushed down the stairs to the basement. "Quinn! Peter!"

"We're in here," Mary called out.

They were in an interior guest bedroom. Peter and Quinn were sitting with Mary on the bed. Both boys jumped up and Tori embraced them, wrapping them tightly and then taking a knee.

"Petey, no holes in you, honey?" she asked.

Peter nodded, his face ashen, eyes moist and red.

"Quinn? Heck of a week, huh?" she said, feeling her eyes starting to water, her body now shaking uncontrollably, the adrenaline wearing off.

"Are you alright?" Quinn asked.

She embraced the boys again. "I am now."

* * *

Nolan listened intently to the police radio, dreading news of casualties. She knew the incident involved Tori, and the call was to an address on the southwest side of Northern Pine Lake.

She was parked along the next street to the east of Santo's place, set in a wide gap between two houses providing an unobstructed view of the back. "What is going on tonight?" she muttered as the radio continued to crackle with urgent responses and calls. What had happened to Tori? Was Braddock with her? If not, where was he?

Santo was sitting on his couch, on his phone, college football highlights still running on the television. He talked for a minute and then stuffed the phone into his pocket and stood up. He turned off the television, walked into the kitchen and then out of sight for a minute, a light coming on in another part of the house.

Nolan scanned the house intently with her binoculars. The light that had come on went off. A moment later he was back in the kitchen. The next thing she saw was a light come on in the garage. She could see the garage door opener shaking, and then the door appeared to rise.

"Interesting you're now suddenly moving," she muttered.

She was positioned right behind his garage. She backed up just a hair and saw the rear end of his BMW. He was going south. She pulled away, her headlights off, keeping her eyes to the right, spotting the BMW between houses. When she reached the corner, she saw it going straight through the intersection. She went straight ahead herself, knowing the grid of the neighborhood, continuing to track Santo's taillights. At the next intersection, he had to turn left or right. Glancing right one more time between the last two houses, she saw his left turn signal on. She pulled to the side of the street, her headlights still off.

The radio crackled. Deputies responding to the call reported no casualties.

"Thank God," she said as she pulled her baseball hat down low.

Santo raced by.

She let him get a good block ahead, then turned on her lights and followed.

It was apparent five minutes later that this was not a quick late-night run to the convenience store. As they motored east out of Manchester Bay, Nolan stayed a half-mile behind him and debated, given all that was happening, whether to call it in.

"Let's see where you go first," she murmured to herself.

NINETEEN

"THE PICTURE IS A LOT MORE COMPLICATED"

Braddock skidded to a stop behind a department Explorer blocking the driveway. He walked up to find deputies on guard, and then he saw Tori's Audi.

"Will!"

It was Steak and Eggs, with Reese right behind them.

"It's a detectives' convention," Braddock muttered.

"What in the hell is going on?" Steak asked. "What did Tori do?"

"I don't know. Something is going on." Braddock gestured to the Q5.

"Good Lord," Eggleston blurted.

"Jeez," Reese muttered. "Everyone survived?"

Braddock nodded, hands on hips.

The entire driver's side was battered, with all the side windows gone. The front was mangled, the hood buckled and loose, the bumper dangling, the headlights shattered. A haze of steam hovered around the smashed vehicle. Steak looked underneath and saw multiple fluids dripping. "She's pretty close to totaled."

Eggleston walked the side of the Audi with her flashlight. "Black paint streaks high up on the body," she said.

"She was outsized and outpowered," Reese said. "Amazing she kept it on the road."

Braddock leaned down and peered inside. There were bullet holes in the dashboard screen and the front windshield, two in the dashboard right of the screen, and another in the far left of the passenger side door.

"Fuck me," Steak said.

"Yeah." Braddock looked down into the back seat and saw Tori's backpack. He reached inside and took it out, handing it to Eggleston. "Stick that in my Tahoe, would you?"

"They're okay, though, right?" Steak said. "Tori? The boys?"

Braddock nodded.

"Where are they?"

"Inside."

"You been in there yet?"

He shook his head. "I got here just before you did."

"Go to them. We all got this."

As he stepped inside, he heard Steak call to one of the deputies, "Hey, any sign of the assholes responsible for this?"

He walked through the entryway and past the kitchen toward the family room that spanned the front of the house. Drew and Andrea were sitting on a couch to the left, Peter between them. Tori was on a couch to the right, looking vacantly out the window, her arm around Quinn, chin resting on top of his head.

Braddock took a seat on the other side of his son. Quinn moved over and buried his head in his father's shoulder. Braddock wrapped his left arm around the boy and looked to Tori. She'd been through the wringer. He reached for her right hand, intertwining his fingers with hers. Nothing needed to be said.

The three of them sat silently for a few minutes before

Tori's phone buzzed. After a moment, she gave it a look. It was a text message from Special Agent Zagaros. He wanted to call her in five minutes with information on George Santo, with the hook: *It's interesting.* She showed Braddock the display. "Should I tell him it can wait?" she whispered hoarsely.

"No," Braddock said quickly. "We'll take that call."

She knew the tone and look. Underneath the calm veneer he was maintaining for Quinn, he was angry and was ready to take it out on someone.

She leaned over, kissed Quinn on the head and pushed herself up from the couch. She wanted father and son to have some time alone. As she walked toward the kitchen, she glanced to Drew, who mouthed *thank you* as Andrea held Peter, gently caressing his head.

In the kitchen, she fished a bottle of water out of the refrigerator. When she closed the door, Mary was standing there.

Mary stepped forward and embraced her. "Thank you."

"For what?" For the first second or two, Tori was too shocked to react, then she slowly returned Mary's hug. This was a first.

"For my grandsons."

Braddock came into the kitchen and saw the two of them embracing. Roger was right behind him and offered an approving nod.

Mary released Tori and went to Braddock, patting him on the arm before walking back into the living room.

"We'll take care of the boys here," Roger declared. "You two figure out who tried to do this to you and make damn sure they can't do it ever again. You hear me?"

Braddock looked over to Tori. "Back to it."

Steak, Eggleston, and Reese came inside the house and Braddock nodded for them to follow as Tori led them to Roger's home office.

"Someone came after you," Steak declared. "Why?"

"Clearly we did something, although what, I don't know," Tori said. "It feels like all we've done on this case so far is figure out who *isn't* responsible for Isabella's abduction." Her phone buzzed. It was Zagaros. "Maybe this will help us start getting some answers."

She answered the call. "Special Agent Zagaros, you wanted to talk. Before you do, we need to tell you about developments here." She explained the last hour, watching Steak, Eggs and Braddock's eyes widen as she described the attack. "Something has been put in motion. Do you have anything that helps us?"

"Maybe," Zagaros said. "You asked us to run the background on George Santo."

"Really?" Eggleston said, sharing a look with Steak.

"What is it?" Braddock asked them.

"Let's see what Zagaros has first," Steak said.

"Tori, when you called, you said Santo was a local businessman in Manchester Bay and owned a few restaurants."

"That's what we think we know," Tori said.

"And who told you that?"

"The Farners. Luciana Farner said Santo moved up here with his then wife. He ended up getting divorced, but has stayed here because of his businesses and because his sister and her family are here. They all seem quite close."

"That's not the whole story. The picture is a lot more complicated," Zagaros said. "Santo's portfolio is more expansive than a couple of restaurants. He has extensive financial interests in Albuquerque, New Mexico. But from what I'm looking at here, he has real problems. He is hemorrhaging cash—rapidly."

"Rapidly?" Tori asked.

"He's filed for bankruptcy in New Mexico. He's millions in the hole."

"What makes up his holdings?"

"Restaurants—the two in Manchester Bay plus seven more in Albuquerque. It looks like he tried to get a restaurant chain going down there but didn't make it. They're all closed and going through liquidation. He also owns commercial real estate, mostly strip malls in Albuquerque. They're all struggling. Lots of vacancies."

"Not a shocker. You see it in the strip malls around here," Steak noted. "Even with the new ones, there are lots of for-rent signs."

"I can't speak to the viability of strip malls there or in Albuquerque," Zagaros said. "What I can say is that George Santo is not in good financial health. His bank accounts would suggest he hasn't got nearly enough coming in. In fact, it appears he's had very little coming in in the last year. His financial hole is deep."

"Besides the restaurants and real estate, does he own anything else?"

"A house mortgaged to the hilt in Manchester Bay. He also has a ski cabin that is for sale in Taos, and he and his sister own some land maybe an hour northwest of Albuquerque, outside the small town of San Mateo. It was inherited from their parents. It's three hundred acres that looks like perhaps it was once ranchland but is now scrub brush. There is still a house and barn on the property when you look on Google Maps, although they look dilapidated from overhead. It's out in the middle of nowhere at the base of a small mountain range."

"Does he have any business partners?"

"A few. The biggest is a company called JV Enterprises. We're digging into them right now."

"What's interesting," Eggleston started, "is that Santo's name cropped up in our case." She explained what Walter Dexter had told them. "He said there was one project missing from the records. One he helped build but not install, which was unusual. He described it as a wall shelving unit with the middle section serving as a sort of hidden door."

"A hidden door?"

Eggleston nodded. "To the naked eye you wouldn't think it was a door, at least according to Dexter. But the thing is, there was no invoice or receipt showing who Weltz built that for. We started going around talking to the people who'd hired him in the last several months. One was a woman named Evelyn Goldstein."

"My dad called her Gossip Goldstein," Tori said with a little grin. "I remember her from when I was a kid. She knew everyone."

"She's the one," Steak said. "Appears to still be very much the social butterfly. She hired Weltz to build some bookshelves for her. He did a great job on a short turnaround for some big shindig she was throwing. Lots of party guests commented on how wonderful it was. She remembered that three guests specifically asked for Weltz's name and she knew they all hired him. The first two tied into receipts we reconciled. The third name was ..."

"George Santo," Tori said, and glanced at Braddock. "How much would a project like that have cost?"

"We asked," Eggleston said. "Dexter pulled out a couple of receipts for similar-sized projects. You'd be looking at around at least fifteen thousand dollars. He thought this one might cost a little more because of the door component."

"But there was no record of Santo in Weltz's records," Steak said. "And given the financial issues that Agent Zagaros just highlighted, where exactly would he have found fifteen grand for a home improvement project?"

"Good question," Braddock said.

"You were watching Santo, weren't you?" Tori asked Reese.

"I followed him from the Farners' back to his house but then left when I heard the radio go bonkers about all this."

"Then nobody's—"

Reese shook his head. "Nolan is there. We were getting ready to switch up when the radio call went out."

"It's time to confront the Farners," Tori said to Braddock.

"Damn right it is."

TWENTY

"LOVE LASTS, LUST DOESN'T"

Braddock was silent on the short drive to the Farners'. On Wednesday, when Quinn had been in danger, his hands shook, his breathing was frantic, and Tori had to drive.

Not this time.

He said not a word. Tori observed his compressed grip on the steering wheel, his clenched jaw and measured yet intense breathing. The rage was palpable.

He pulled into the Farners' cul-de-sac, looped hard around and stopped abruptly behind the Manchester Bay patrol unit parked in front of the house.

"Hey, I'm glad you both are okay," the patrol officer greeted.

"Are they inside?" Braddock growled through gritted teeth.

"Uh ... y-yes," the officer stammered.

"Anyone else in there?"

"No."

"Any visitors tonight?"

"Just Mrs. Farner's brother. He left a few hours ago."

Braddock walked purposefully up the driveway. Tori had to jog to keep up with his long strides.

"Hey, buddy, you're going in kind of hot here," she warned.

"Something is going down tonight."

"I agree, but—"

"And they know."

"Yeah, but you have to be cool."

"Fuck cool."

Oh boy, Tori thought. "But—"

"They're coming clean. No more hinting, no more cajoling," he said, and pounded on the front door.

"But you need to be in control."

He gave her a steely glare. "I am."

Sam Farner opened the door. "Uh, Will, hello—"

"We need to talk right fucking now," Braddock said, quickly invading Sam's personal space, backing him up into the house.

This didn't seem like control.

Luciana was standing at the end of the hallway, her eyes wide in sudden fear at Braddock's angry six-foot-four frame storming down the hall at her.

"You two need to sit down," he said.

"Sam ..." Luciana looked to her husband, who'd been back-pedaling the whole time.

"*Now!*"

Tori watched for the couple's reactions. Sam had initially returned a steely glare, which quickly turned to apprehension as Braddock towered over him. Luciana looked away, covering her mouth with her right hand as if knowing she'd been caught.

"You look upset," Sam said, trying to calm him, gesturing for him to take a chair. Braddock had no intention of sitting.

"Less than an hour ago, someone tried to run Tori off the road when she was driving Quinn and Peter home from Ryan Grant's house. It was no accident. It was intentional. It was an attempt to kill them, all of them."

Luciana looked to Tori and then back to Braddock in horror.

"Oh my God, are the boys okay? They weren't hurt, were they?" Her concern was genuine.

"Yeah, they're okay, but make no mistake, someone tried to take all three of them out tonight." Braddock pulled out his phone and showed them a photo. "This is what Tori's SUV looks like now." He swiped to another photo. "And those holes right there are bullet holes. And there's another one in the passenger door there, just inches from where Quinn was sitting. Where my boy was sitting!"

"But why?" Luciana asked.

"You two fucking tell me," Braddock barked.

"Hey, fuck you, Will," Sam yelled back. "You ain't shown me shit so far, pal."

"Oh really, you lying sack of shit?"

Tori stepped in front of Braddock before he could throw Sam through the picture window. "Okay, okay," she said, pressing lightly against him, feeling the stiffening of his muscles and the heaving of his chest. He was right on the edge. "Easy," she said almost in a whisper. She looked up into his eyes. "I think we have their attention now."

It was her turn to play good cop.

Keeping her hands on Braddock's chest, she turned to a terrified Luciana. "Is there any coffee in the kitchen? I could really use a cup."

"Uh ... yeah, there are single cups in the rack on the counter for the coffee maker."

Tori looked back up at Braddock, who finally exhaled a breath. He was seething. He wasn't one to lose it, but then again, the people he loved the most had almost been murdered an hour ago. At the moment, he didn't see the Farners as his friends, or even as parents who were missing a child of their own. He was looking at them as accomplices to attempted murder.

"Go on," she said calmly to him.

He exhaled a breath and turned away to the kitchen. Whether he'd intended to or not, he'd set the table for her.

She looked at the Farners. "You two sit down." She sat opposite them. Her tone was softer, but she wasn't any less direct. "You're not telling us everything."

"Now hold on—" Sam started defensively.

"You've not been forthcoming in telling us about what is going on here," she said, leaning forward, eyeing him up. "You think I'm any less angry than Will? You think I don't love Quinn too? And Peter? And I really don't like being shot at."

"And I don't like being accused—"

"Do you think this is my first rodeo?" Her eyes were locked on Sam. "For years, on too many cases to count, I've been dealing with people who don't tell the whole story, the whole truth, who leave important information out, and you know what? It always bites them in the ass." She paused for a moment. "We've sensed since last night something has changed." And now she made the intuitive leap. "The kidnappers reached out to you through George, didn't they?"

Luciana's jaw dropped ever so slightly and then she looked to Sam, whose eyes closed.

"What did they ask for?" Braddock said more calmly from the kitchen.

Sam didn't respond, looking away. Luciana, however, was done not talking, "Two million in cryptocurrency."

Tori had been wondering when she'd run into this. She'd never thought crypto as ransom would be limited to ransomware cases for computer networks. While not understanding all the ins and outs of blockchains, wallets, how to convert the currency to dollars, she'd long ago seen its potential. It was far easier to pay and avoid capture. "And do you have that much in Bitcoin or some other form of crypto?"

"No, we don't," Luciana answered. "Sam has a small amount in his experimental investment account at work, but nowhere near enough. But George has close to two million."

"Isn't that convenient," Braddock said as he handed Tori a cup of coffee. "And he showed you he had it? You saw it? You looked at an account?"

"Yeah, well ..." Sam replied, and then grimaced. "He said he had it. Why wouldn't I trust him?"

"Because he doesn't have it," Tori said.

"George is flat broke," Braddock said bluntly before taking a sip of coffee. "In fact, his hole is so deep that he's looking way, *way* up at broke. Did you know his restaurants here are for sale?"

"No," Luciana said, surprised, then turned to Sam. "Did you?"

"No," Sam said. "He hasn't said a word."

"Or that he's declared bankruptcy down in Albuquerque? His restaurant chain is closed and being liquidated. His collection of strip malls down there are all half empty. He's drowning in red ink."

Luciana's shoulders slumped and Sam closed his eyes. "You're saying he doesn't have it."

Tori shook her head. "I really doubt it. Now admittedly, we haven't seen his cryptocurrency investment portfolio. But we know he doesn't have anything in the bank."

"He's hemorrhaging money, guys," Braddock said, and then looked to his buzzing phone. "I have to take this," he said, and stepped out of the living room and into the front hallway.

"How long has this been the case?" Sam asked. "Because he hasn't said a word to us about any of it."

"As best we can tell, it's been downhill for the last three years or so," Tori said. "It looks like he's in deep with a business partner. JV Enterprises. We're still digging on who or what that is. Do you know anything about it?"

Luciana looked to Sam. "Jamie."

Sam nodded.

"Jamie? Jamie who?"

"Jamie Vaughn," Luciana said. "George got divorced seven years ago, and his ex moved back to Albuquerque with their son, Alex. For a while, George split his time between here and Albuquerque so he could see Alex when he was still in high school. While he was down there, he developed a business relationship with a woman named Jamie Vaughn, who for a time became more than just a business partner. Very pretty."

"She came up here a few times to see him," Sam said. "We had her over to dinner. George was smitten with her. Introduced her to all of us, the kids too. For a couple of years we didn't see much of him up here. He was down in New Mexico, chasing her. We thought he might move back down there permanently."

"But it didn't work out," Luciana continued, dabbing away a tear. "A couple of years ago, she broke things off. George never really talked about it with us, but we knew it had hit him hard. That was when he started spending more time up here. I figured a lot of that was about getting away from what happened with her in Albuquerque."

"He fell for the visual package, the beauty and business success. It blinded him," Sam added. "He didn't see it."

"See what?"

"She didn't love him," Luciana answered. "Sam and I realized that Jamie was all business, and from what George told me, pretty cold-blooded about it. She drove a hard bargain. He found that attractive, beauty and brains and money. And George is a handsome man, so I could understand why she'd be interested, but I could just tell that there wasn't that mutual emotional connection there. Not like you and Will obviously have. Not like Sam and I have. I said to him, George, she's never been married, never had kids. What makes you think she wants that now with you? Have you had the talk? What signs has she given that you're different from every other man she's been with?"

"She'd been with other men?"

"She was the type who probably always had a man lined up waiting for the chance. But some people aren't the type for the long haul, for marriage, kids, settling down. They're just not wired that way. That's not what they want out of life. Jamie Vaughn was one of those types."

Sam nodded. "George was just the guy at that time."

"I warned him. God, I warned him, but ... you know, he didn't listen. He was in love. She was just in lust. Love lasts, lust doesn't. When the desire was gone, she moved on." Luciana shook her head in disgust. "He hasn't been the same since. Not as ... confident and full of life. It's like he was back here hiding. But he never once said a word about how dire his financial situation had gotten. It's really that bad?"

"It's desperate," Tori said.

"And because of that, you're saying he is responsible for this?" Luciana said, her voice rising. "That he kidnapped his own niece? My God, he loves Izzy like a daughter. He'd never hurt her."

"For some people, love only goes so far, especially if they're in trouble themselves," Tori said flatly. "Self-preservation overtakes everything else."

"I don't believe it. I can't ..." Luciana wailed. "He's my brother! He wouldn't hurt her."

"We don't know that, not now," Sam said bluntly, reality setting in. "If what they're saying is true, who knows what he might do. Who knows what he's thinking."

"Or who is pressuring him," Tori said. "It's possible someone has him ... in a vulnerable position. Banks don't do things like this, but if he went to someone else to try and get out of financial trouble, or if this Jamie Vaughn is as cold-blooded as you say, that's what could be going on here."

"Oh God!" Luciana moaned, devastated. "What do we do?"

"Start by telling us the truth. You said the ransom demand was two million?"

"Yes," Sam replied.

"That fits in the sense that it would approximate to what the two of you have right now in total assets. But the problem is, two million doesn't get George out of his hole. Not even close, from what we've seen."

"Would it buy him some time?" Sam asked.

"Maybe," Tori replied, unconvinced. "If he actually had the money. How much do *you* have in crypto?"

"Around two hundred thousand in dollar value, give or take."

She sat back and folded her arms, thinking about all that had already happened, what they knew, the various threads they had pulled and how it was starting to finally form a picture of why Isabella had been abducted. "This will seem like a non sequitur, but has George done any work on his home recently?"

"What kind?"

"Woodwork? Cabinetry? A large shelving unit, perhaps."

"No," Luciana said, and looked to Sam.

"Not that I'm aware of. I mean, if he's in as much trouble as you say, why would he spend money on something like that?"

"His name came up in a murder investigation two of our detectives are working. A local carpenter named Fred Weltz. Does that ring a bell?"

Sam and Luciana both shook their heads.

"He was referred to George recently for a construction

project that may tie into all this," Tori said. "Sam, you gave George this two hundred thousand dollars in crypto?"

"I transferred it to his wallet earlier today. He told us he had to have everything ready tonight because the call was coming for the next step."

"What was the next step going to be?"

"We don't know. We assumed George would transfer the ransom and they would tell us where to pick up Izzy."

"Whatever it is, it may be going down right now," Braddock said to Tori as he came back into the room. "George is on the move. Nolan is following, but he's south of town, out in the countryside. Odd place to be going at this time of night. We need to hustle."

Tori stood up and started walking to the front door, following Braddock. She looked back. "So you gave him the two hundred thousand. Anything else?"

"Uh, well ..." Sam looked to Luciana. "There's the property."

"Property?" Tori asked. "What property?"

"Our parents' old ranchland in New Mexico," Luciana replied.

"In San Mateo?"

"It hasn't been a ranch in years. It's mostly scrub now, where animals are running wild. George has been on me for a few years to sell my half to him. He had papers drawn up, pushed me to sell it to him, but I just wasn't ready to do it. I still had some attachment to it. We grew up there and I ... Well, I just wasn't ready. I didn't want it turned into some generic real estate development of some kind. Silly really."

"When was the last time he broached this with you?"

"Tori ..." Braddock said, standing at the door.

"Hang on. Luciana, when was the last time he pushed you to sell to him?"

"Maybe six months ago. He brought the papers over. Said he'd give me a half-million for the land."

"And you said no?"

"I said I'd think about it, but I still couldn't let it go. It was Mom and Dad's place. I just didn't want to do it."

"Did he have an appraisal of the land?"

"No, not then. I mean, a couple of years ago he had one and it was worth maybe half a million at the time, so my half was two hundred and fifty thousand, but like I said—"

"And he offered you a half-million a few months ago. He doubled it. Why?"

"I don't know. I just thought he was willing to pay more for it and thought he'd make it on the back end."

"Did he tell you why he wanted it?" Tori asked.

Luciana shrugged. "He's in real estate. I think he wanted to see if he could sell it or develop it."

"Why did you sign it over now?"

"We didn't want him funding the ransom himself, so I gave him the land as part of our repayment of the two million he was paying the kidnappers."

"The two million he doesn't really have," Tori said. "Do you even know what the land is worth?"

"It's scrub brush," Luciana said.

"Yet he wanted to buy it from you. He pestered you about it —repeatedly. And offered you the full value of the appraisal recently."

Luciana looked back at her blankly.

"Come on. We have to go," Braddock urged.

"He's been playing us, hasn't he?" Sam said.

"I'm afraid so." Tori turned to run after Braddock.

Outside, Braddock took out his phone and called Steak. "You and Eggleston get on your horse. The night is not over."

Tori called Zagaros. "Two things. JV Enterprises. The JV is

likely a woman named Jamie Vaughn. She's an old girlfriend of Santo's and at one time mixed business and pleasure. Find her."

"Jamie Vaughn. Got it. You said two things."

"The land in New Mexico, northwest of Albuquerque."

"What about it?"

"It's more than an abandoned ranch." She explained what they'd just learned. "There is some hidden value there, and either Santo or someone who has his balls in a vice is after it."

TWENTY-ONE

"THE APPLE NEVER FALLS FAR FROM THE TREE"

"Uranium?" Tori repeated, looking to Braddock, eyes wide. "A uranium mine?"

"Yes," Zagaros answered. "The ranch outside of San Mateo is in an area of New Mexico where uranium deposits were recently discovered."

"And Luciana and George Santo own the land and the mineral rights?"

"Yes."

"How big are these deposits?"

"We don't know for sure. One newspaper article suggests they could be significant. If there is uranium to be mined, one imagines it could be worth many, many millions."

"Is there any confirmation of that?"

"Of the uranium deposits in the area? Yes," Zagaros said. "There is a mining company that has started operations nearby on a different parcel of land. If I had to guess, Santo and whoever he's working with know this. If you think it's about the land, I'd bet that someone has done a mineral survey and realizes it's worth mining."

"And if we're right and they've gone to these lengths to get the land, then the deposits are considerable," Tori said, finishing the thought. "Okay, do you have anything more on Jamie Vaughn?"

"Yeah, hang on." Zagaros dropped off for a moment.

"Now we know what this is all about," Braddock said.

"It would seem so," Tori agreed.

"Tori, we're still working on Vaughn, but I see the link you're making. She has a number of businesses in Albuquerque that we've found her name or JV Enterprises attached to, in addition to the ones with Santo. She's heavily into commercial real estate, restaurants, and bars."

"All legit?"

"Seem to be, but we've talked with Albuquerque PD and some Bureau people down there. As it turns out, Vaughn is a very recognizable name in Albuquerque. Jamie Vaughn doesn't have a criminal record herself, but her grandfather, father and uncles were all notorious. Theft, extortion, loan-sharking, book-making, drugs, and several suspected murders, although nothing ever stuck on those. They were canny operators, but all had files on them inches thick. They're all deceased now, but Jamie appears to have evolved from that and has perhaps kept her criminality more under wraps. The police down there know who she is. Her name pops up from time to time, but while she's been questioned on occasion, she's never been charged with anything."

"The apple never falls far from the tree."

"True that," Zagaros replied. "Vaughn is described as very smart and someone who stays well above the fray. A police sergeant down there said she probably has sources in the department to keep ahead of the police. We'll carry on digging." He dropped off the line.

They were zooming south on 25, Steak and Eggleston right behind with lights and sirens.

"Nolan, where is he now?" Braddock asked over the radio.

"Still south on 25. I'd say twenty miles out of town. Where are you?"

"We're on 25, trying to close the gap. You still have an eye on him?"

"Yeah. It's flat out here, no traffic. I can see his taillights. I'd gauge him at a quarter- to a half-mile ahead."

"Can you get in closer?" Tori asked.

"I've got nowhere to hide. It's just me and him. If he's checking his six, he'll spot me. Heck, I'm turning my headlights off from time to time and using moonlight just to give a different look."

They understood Nolan's dilemma. Highway 25 was a flat and mostly straight road. If you looked in your rearview mirror, you could see back for miles.

"Hold on a second," Nolan said. "I've got a turn signal flashing. Will, he's turning left."

"Where?"

Tori started swiping the GPS map forward.

"Hang on. Hang on," Nolan said. "We're turning onto ... County 142 southeast."

Tori kept swiping. "There. I'd say we're fifteen miles behind."

"Nolan, we know what this is all about now," Braddock said, speeding up, the speedometer approaching eighty. "Santo is leading us to the people who have Izzy. Don't lose him. We're ten minutes back, hauling ass down your way."

* * *

George angrily gripped the steering wheel as if he was trying to wring water out of it. He was well south of Manchester Bay now.

He checked the dashboard GPS system as he drove south on Highway 25, deep in the countryside. Either side of the road was marked with barbed-wire fences, with large round bales of hay visible at times. The road itself was quiet, with rarely another vehicle passing. There was little between Manchester Bay and the next town of any size, Pierz, thirty miles to the south. As he looked in the rearview mirror, he saw one distant set of headlights behind.

He pounded the steering wheel.

How did you let it get to this point?

It was a question he'd asked himself a lot the last couple of months, when she'd first threatened him, really threatened him, about his debts. That was when he'd offered Luciana a half-million for the ranch. That would have taken care of it, but she'd hemmed and hawed before declining. She just wasn't ready.

He needed more time.

"There is no more time, George," Jamie had replied. "I'm done waiting."

If he kept pressuring Luciana, she would get suspicious. She would want to know why he so desperately wanted her to sell the land. She wasn't dumb, and nor was Sam. They would start investigating things themselves. And if they found out what it was worth, what it was really worth, would she go for it?

At heart, his sister was an environmentalist. Always had been. As a child, she cried every time their father killed a chicken. It was why she didn't want the ranch turned into a golf course, resort, or housing development. She believed it should be left to the animals. It was part of the reason why she retained such an attachment to the property.

"I don't have any leverage," George had said several months back. "I can't force someone who is comfortable financially to sell the land to me. I offered her double and she said no."

"You know how you leverage someone, George? You take what matters most to them."

It had taken him a moment to understand the gravity of what was being proposed. "Are you nuts?"

"It's that or I wipe them all out so you inherit the property."

He couldn't believe what she was saying. "Kill them all?"

"Or take one for a little while."

"You know what happens to kidnappers?"

"I know what'll happen to *you* if you don't come up with the money. This is how you pay your debt. This is how you get out of the hole and eventually become very, very, wealthy. And you're going to have to play a part in it. A big one."

"You think the police won't be suspicious? You think they won't look into me at some point?"

"Not if we give them someone else to look at."

He'd spent a lot of time the past several months around Isabella. He'd asked her and Carson about school and how they got there. He'd watched as the two of them had ridden their bikes. Carson had a pack of friends in the neighborhood he always rode with. Isabella had lots of friends, but none that she rode to school with. She was more vulnerable.

"As long as we get what we want, she'll be fine, nothing will happen to her."

"And if we don't?"

"See that we do, George," Jamie had said coldly. "Figure out how you're going to coerce your sister and her husband. You'll have to hook them both."

His sister was conscientious to a fault. Maybe it was the Catholic guilt, never wanting to be in debt, to owe people anything, making sure to have all her accounts paid. As for Sam, George had discussed cryptocurrency with him in the past over lunch and drinks. Sam maintained a small position in it and was intrigued by it, knowing a little about the system but not yet enough.

That was how he could make it work.

He would offer to pay the ransom with what he told them he had. They would owe him, and he knew his sister would have difficulty with that. She would reach for whatever she had available to make him whole: the ranch.

He checked the GPS display. His next turn was half a mile ahead, a right turn. Jamie was dragging him out into the middle of nowhere.

As he slowed for the turn, he looked in his rearview mirror. It was dark. Nobody behind. He made the right turn onto a gravel road angling south again. His destination was a mile ahead on the left. As he approached, he saw a sliver of vertical light, elevated as if it were up on a small rise.

He caught the glint of a silver mailbox just ahead and noticed that the left side of the road was suddenly densely treed. Slowing, he turned left and motored up a long, narrow driveway arcing to the left through the trees and underbrush. As he emerged into a wider clearing, he realized that the sliver of bright light was from the gap between two sliding barn doors. Standing in the light was Cain, Jamie's security blanket, her muscle.

He parked and walked toward the barn with his briefcase.

"George," Cain greeted, stepping forward and patting him down. Cain's men, Lowe and Rust, were standing a little way behind him. Their guns weren't visible, but they had them, Santo was sure of that. Inside the barn, parked in the back, was a black Suburban. It was dented and scratched all along the passenger side.

"What happened to the SUV?" he asked, gesturing with his briefcase.

"A little ... activity earlier in the evening. It allowed us to spring you." Cain turned and led him inside.

Jamie was to the right, sitting casually at a large folding table, sipping Scotch.

"Jamie," George said as he sat down, putting the briefcase on the table in front of him.

She nodded before finishing her drink, then poured herself another and one for him, sliding the glass across the table. He took a sip while eyeing her.

It had been two months since they'd seen one another. She was as stunning as ever. When she was finalizing a deal, she always made herself up, even if the closing was in a corrugated steel pole barn in the middle of nowhere on a cold October Saturday night. Taking in the sight of her, his mind couldn't help but momentarily drift to thoughts of when they were together. She was curvy, with dark-toned skin, deep brown eyes, and straight black hair, which tonight was stylishly piled up. She was wearing a black leather coat, matching pants, and boots, and her white silk blouse had a plunging V-neck that provided more than a hint of what lay beneath. It was the same alluring look she'd sported the first time they'd met, five years ago at a party.

That night, she was the one who'd made the first move. He'd realized far too late that her motive for getting close was strictly financial. She liked his restaurant idea and invested. That he was on the menu too was a bonus.

He'd fallen hard, letting dreams of a future with her dull his senses. In the moments when he was truly honest with himself, he knew his obsession had fatally distracted him from the task at hand, what had drawn her to him to begin with, the restaurants. While they had all started out strong, warning signs emerged over time, small yet steady declines in business after the strong initial burst, which led to increasing problems with cash flow.

Jamie, who never took her eye off the financial ball, saw the signs, warned him of them, pressed him to focus, but he was caught up in a fog and didn't realize the hole he was slowly descending into until it was too late, until he was in a financial death spiral he couldn't pull out of.

Having more financial resources, she weathered the storm better. Her interests were more diversified and far better capitalized, but even so, she took a hefty financial hit, and she didn't suffer such things gladly. For a while, she extended him a financial lifeline, pumping money into the operation, hoping it would stave off disaster and lead to a belated return on her investment. The restaurants were in good locations and there was a market for the concept if properly executed. Unfortunately, as was often the case with restaurants, once the descent started, it proved impossible to stop.

When Jamie broke things off, he didn't take it well. He made efforts to rekindle what they'd had. That was when he saw the other side of her. When he learned for the first time that her ruthless approach to business wasn't built upon an entirely legitimate foundation. Cain paid him a visit, along with Lowe and Rust. There were to be no more phone calls or showing up unannounced at her office or home. "And one more thing."

"What?"

"You owe her a considerable amount of money."

"That's business," George had replied defiantly, offended that she'd sent someone to threaten him. "She knew the risks and signed the agreements."

"I appreciate your position," Cain said reasonably, before punching him in the stomach. His legs gave way immediately and he gasped for air. Cain held him up and walked him back to his desk chair, where he explained his new reality.

"Jamie is out a considerable amount of money. It is her view that that is because of your incompetence. She expects you to come up with a plan to make her whole. Do you understand, George?"

He explored every option available to revive the restaurants, but it was too late. A year ago, it had all come crashing down. That was when the visits from Cain became more frequent, uncomfortable reminders of his obligations. The last time, before Cain could even say a word, George said, "She and I need to talk."

"You're right, you do," Cain replied. "Because she has a proposition for you."

They met at her home. A bottle of tequila sat on the table, and she poured them each a drink and handed him a document.

"What's this?" he asked, turning the cover page.

"Just read."

It was a mineral survey of the ranchland that he and Luciana had inherited from their parents. He'd toyed with the idea of having one done. He'd talked to Jamie about it. She'd remembered.

"I know one of the owners of a company opening a mine on land adjacent to yours. The deposits on his property are significant, and they spill onto yours."

He remembered the initial euphoria of reading the report. It was short-lived.

"Here's how this goes down," Jamie said. "I can get you out of trouble. In return, I get the ranch. I'll even cut you in for a piece, a good piece, twenty percent of the profit, but you have to give me the land."

"Just give it to you?"

She simply stared back at him. Yes, he would have to give it to her.

"I've been trying to get Luciana to sell to me for years," he said. "She wants to leave the place to the damn animals."

"What was the last appraisal?"

"Half a million. I offered her half for her share, but she declined."

"Offer her the whole amount."

"I don't have half a million."

"I'll stake you."

She had set her sights on the ranch. It was how she would be made whole and then some. The potential payoff from the mine was too intoxicating. She had everything lined up; she just needed the land. There would be no stopping her. She would take it to the limit.

And now here they were. At the limit.

Jamie slid the bottle across the folding table, and he poured himself another stiff drink and took a big gulp.

"Easy with that. You weren't followed, right?"

"No."

She raised her eyes and looked past him to Cain, who was still standing outside the barn door. Cain looked back and nodded.

"Where is Izzy?" George asked.

"Business first."

He unlocked his briefcase and took out the papers. "The ranch is mine, free and clear. She signed it over tonight. Witnessed by her husband."

Jamie read through the agreement, nodding along. Finished, she reached down to a briefcase of her own and took out another sheaf of papers. "Here is *our* agreement."

"And my twenty percent?"

"Read."

* * *

Braddock turned right onto the gravel road and pulled to the side. Steak drew up behind him. He and Eggleston quickly got into the Tahoe, geared in vests. Steak handed earbuds to Tori and Braddock and they did a com check.

"Nolan is about a mile ahead," Tori said as Braddock drove, his headlights off.

"Aren't they going to see us coming?" Steak said. "Even with the lights off. When you brake, the taillights will flash."

"They haven't seen me," Nolan said over the speaker.

"Where are you?"

"Hunkered down in a ditch at the entrance to the driveway. Come up right behind my car. The trees are dense enough they should block any sight of you."

Braddock did as Nolan suggested, parking behind her. Then the four of them scrambled out of the Tahoe and jogged along the road, finding her hunched in the ditch.

"He's up there?" Braddock asked, peering up the driveway. He could make out a vertical strip of bright light.

"Yes," Nolan said. "A good fifteen, twenty minutes now."

"How many of them are there?"

"I don't know. I can't see inside from here, but I know there are others besides Santo. I snuck thirty yards up the driveway and made out a SUV that he parked next to."

Braddock looked to Tori. "I think we bring in the emergency response team."

"How long to get here?"

"Half an hour at least."

"We may not have that much time."

Braddock looked back to Steak, who radioed the call in. "Let's move in for a closer look. Nolan, you hold position here."

"What? Why?"

"No vest."

Nolan looked down at herself. "I'll concede that point."

Steak handed Braddock an earbud, which he in turn gave to Nolan. "And stay on the radio with dispatch."

The four of them made their way up the left side of the driveway, sticking close to the treeline. When they were just short of the clearing, they stopped. Braddock looked back and nodded to Steak. The expert deer hunter, always light on his feet, crept ahead to the edge of the trees, which put him about thirty yards from the barn. He lay down on his stomach in the narrow depression to the left of the driveway and scanned with his small binoculars.

After a couple of minutes, he crept his way back to them.

"I could see two men. One had his back to me. The other was standing further inside. They're both looking to the right side of the barn. What's there, I don't know. My guess is Santo and whoever he's talking to. There is also a double sliding door on the other end of the barn, just like the front. It looks to be cracked open a foot or two."

Braddock checked his watch. "Nolan, ETA on the emergency response team?"

"Twenty minutes."

He thought for a moment and then glanced to Tori. "Is Izzy here?"

Tori took a moment, thinking things through. "They wouldn't make the exchange where she could see everyone. Where she could see her uncle George making whatever deal they're making in there."

"You sure?"

"Absolutely? No, but it's logical."

Braddock stroked his beard for a moment. "That's not good enough. We need to know for sure." He looked to Steak and Eggleston. "You two cross over and work your way around the back of the barn. Tori and I will creep up to the front."

* * *

George finished reading the document. There was a line for his signature under the heading Santo Enterprises and for Jamie under the notation for JV Financial, one of her holding companies. She was true to her word: he would get twenty percent of the profit, once there was a profit. The new twist was she would take a credit against his profit until she was made whole, for having propped him up for three years.

"You take no loss, zero, on the restaurants, even though we were in them together?" George asked, shaking his head. She had all the leverage and had every intention of using it.

"I'll be funding the mine operation, and I had to do all this just to get your sister to sign this swath of scrub brush over to you. I'm taking all the risk, so damn right I get my money first."

He had no choice.

"Fine." He reached for the pen inside his briefcase and signed both copies of the agreement, then slid them back across to Jamie, who countersigned. She returned one copy to him, and he opened his briefcase to stuff it inside. He sighed in relief. The deal got him out of his financial hole. There was just one piece of business left. "Now, where is Izzy?"

"She's not here."

"You have what you want. Now where is she?"

"You can't have her back."

George looked at Jamie over the top of his opened briefcase. "That's not our deal. Izzy was leverage. It worked. I didn't even have to ask Luciana for the ranch. She just gave it up. Now I get Izzy back. That was the deal."

"Your industrious niece escaped this morning. She got out of the basement, ran down to the county road and almost got away with a delivery truck driver."

"Almost?"

"Rust shot the driver and we got Isabella back into the basement."

"You got her back. I don't see why—"

"She saw me when we chased her down. She recognized me. And she saw Cain, and Rust and Lowe."

"What are you saying?" George asked, knowing full well what was coming next.

"Now look, we'll take care of it, but she can't go back."

"And the two million I supposedly paid you?"

"That you lost trying to help your brother and sister get their daughter back?" Jamie shrugged. "We took the money and ran. We played you and them. We'll let the dust settle. I'll stake you on a soft financial landing with this restaurant fiasco, and a year from now we'll go about the process of getting that mine going and making a fortune together."

* * *

Braddock and Tori let Steak and Eggleston get out ahead of them before moving forward, keeping tight to the trees on the left side of the road. At the edge of the trees, they stopped. They were now in a direct line to the barn door, with the cars—an Escalade and Santo's BMW—halfway in between.

"I'm going to the back of the Escalade," Braddock whispered. With his gun hanging low in his right hand, he quickly covered the twenty yards through the grass to the back of the SUV, Tori right behind him.

They heard loud voices from inside the barn.

"Sounds like it's getting hot in there," Braddock said.

"I can see Santo and ... two other men," Tori replied. "There has to be at least one more person inside."

"Steak, you hear that?"

"Copy. We're nearly around the back."

* * *

"Your twenty percent will be worth a bloody fortune," Jamie urged. "You have to let this go."

"She's just a little kid."

"There is no other way," she replied coldly.

* * *

"We're at the back," Steak said. "Moving to the barn door. It sounds tense in there."

"Can you make out what they're saying?"

"No, they're talking over each other. All I know is that whatever it is, they're saying it loudly."

Braddock took a step to his left and ran to the front left corner of the barn. Tori stopped and took a quick look inside the Escalade but didn't see anyone.

She checked the barn and then ran to join Braddock. He took a step toward the opening, but Tori stopped him. She slipped in front of him, crept along the front and took a knee, then leaned forward to peer around the corner.

* * *

George closed his eyes. He wanted his last thoughts to be of his niece smiling back at him, her fun-loving favorite uncle. In his mind, he said a prayer:

Hail Mary, full of grace, the Lord is with thee. Blessed art thou among women, and blessed is the fruit of thy womb, Jesus. Holy Mary, Mother of God, pray for us sinners, now and at the hour of our death. Glory be to the Father, and to the Son, and to the Holy Spirit.

He bolted up and pulled his pistol out of his briefcase.

"That's not our deal, Jamie!"

She pointed her own weapon right back at him. He had no doubt that Cain and the other two men also had him in their sights.

"George, come on, man," Cain said. "You know there's no way out of this."

"Think," Jamie said, leaning forward. "*Think!* You're out of your mess. You knew the risk when we went down this route. This was always a possibility."

"None of this is that little girl's fault. *None of it!*"

"No, it's not, it's yours."

* * *

Tori peeked around the corner.

"Just take me to her and I can reason with her," Santo pleaded. He was holding a gun, and the woman was pointing one back at him, as were the others. "I can tell her she can't say anything. She'll listen to me, Jamie. She'll listen! Just take me to her. I can make her listen."

"She's not here," Tori whispered. "Izzy is not here."

"Are you listening to *yourself*," the woman yelled.

"Are you!" Santo yelled back. "She's twelve!"

"Oh shit," Braddock murmured as Santo's grip on the gun tightened. "*Police!*"

Santo fired.

* * *

Crack! Crack!

Boom! Boom!

George's first shot hit Jamie in the chest. Her first hit him in his left shoulder. He pulled the trigger again. *Crack!*

Boom! Boom! Boom! Boom!

He felt himself falling to the right as he was hit for a second time. As he fell, he saw Jamie's eyes wide, mouth agape, neck fountaining blood.

* * *

"*Police!*" Braddock yelled again.

Tori was still kneeling, but had edged out a little further, improving her angle.

The man nearest the woman looked right at them. One man with a gun in his left hand had his back to them. The other was standing further away, in the middle of the barn, facing them, the three men forming a loose triangle.

Steak whistled. "*Back here too!*"

* * *

Cain quickly glanced to the front of the barn. Braddock and Hunter were peeking around the corner. He checked back to see two others at the rear door. He looked down. Jamie was gone, her eyes lifeless. Santo lay on the floor, gasping, his body shuddering.

If there were more police out there, they'd have moved in by now.

It was just his three on their four.

The keys were still in the ignition of the Suburban. He looked to Rust and Lowe and shifted his eyes to the SUV. Rust was thirty feet away from the vehicle, Lowe fifteen feet from the passenger side. They too had done the math.

* * *

"Will," Tori warned, watching the eyes of the man to the left. "They think they got nothing to lose."

"Steak?"

"It's going down, boss," Steak replied. "It's going down for real."

"*Don't!*" Braddock called out.

* * *

Cain looked to Rust and then Lowe.

Lowe blurted, "Go!"

Cain fired a cover volley at Braddock and Hunter as he dashed to the Suburban. Rust fired at the back of the barn while Lowe did the same to the front, then both men turned toward the vehicle.

Boom! Boom! Boom! Boom! Boom! Boom!

* * *

Tori fired twice and ducked back, gunfire pinging off the corrugated steel of the barn door, Braddock right above her.

"They're going for the Suburban!" she yelled.

They both leaned in again and fired.

* * *

Cain jumped into the Suburban and started it. "Come on! Come on!"

Rust ran for the driver's side. He seized up, hit multiple times, and collapsed.

"Lowe! Now!"

Lowe was covering Rust. He turned for the passenger door, opened it. "Oh ..." He crumpled to the ground.

"Get up! Get up! Come on!"

He used the open passenger door to pull himself up.

"Come on!" Cain yelled, reaching with his right hand to pull him in.

Lowe was hit again and fell away.

* * *

"One of them made the Suburban," Braddock said. "It's running!"

The four of them filled the inside of the barn with fire.

Bang! Bang! Bang! Bang! Bang! Bang!

One man was down on the driver's side. The second man fell away on the passenger side. The Suburban roared ahead, coming right at them.

"*Get back! Get back!*" Braddock shouted, grabbing Tori and yanking her backward.

The SUV crashed through the barn doors, blowing them off their tracks.

"Look out!" Braddock yelled as he and Tori dove away from the collapsing doors.

The SUV sideswiped the parked Escalade before careening forward. They scrambled to their feet and fired.

Bang! Bang! Bang! Bang!

Steak and Eggleston ran out. "Holy Hannah!" Steak yelled.

"Nolan, coming your way!" Braddock said, and he and Steak sprinted down the driveway after the Suburban.

* * *

"Argh!" Cain groaned as shots hit him in his right shoulder and arm. His left hand was bleeding, but he gripped the wheel and kept on the driveway, taking on fire from behind.

* * *

Nolan watched the darkened Suburban careening down the driveway, weaving and fishtailing. Crouched, her right knee set on the ground, she eyed up the oncoming SUV, lining up the driver's side.

She exhaled and depressed the trigger.

Crack! Crack! Crack!

* * *

"Oh!" Cain gasped, snapping back at the blasts to his chest.

* * *

The Suburban zoomed straight across the road and catapulted into the air. It sailed into the farm field, landing nose first, then twisted violently to the left, rolling over and over before coming to rest on its roof.

"Holy moly," Nolan murmured.

She turned around. Braddock and Steak were running down the driveway.

"I ... I ..."

"Come on," Braddock said as he sprinted past her.

The three of them crossed the road and made their way into the field. Nolan hung back as Braddock and Steak carefully made their way to the Suburban, covering each other. Steak approached the mangled vehicle, crouched, and looked inside.

"One body," Steak said, kneeling. He reached inside and checked for a pulse, then looked back to Braddock and shook his head. "He gone."

In the far distance to the north, they saw the flashing lights of the emergency response team. "Would have been nice to have them a few minutes ago," Steak remarked.

Braddock examined the passenger side of the Suburban, noted the horizontal scratches on it. He slowly followed the scratches with the beam of his flashlight.

"What do you make of those?"

"Silver paint. Kind of like the paint of a certain Audi Q5."

* * *

Tori took a knee next to Santo lying on the barn floor. He gasped for air, his chest a bloody mess.

"Where's Izzy? Where is she?" Tori pleaded, evaluating his wounds.

"They have her ... somewhere, a ... house," he croaked. "She almost ... escaped."

"Escaped?"

"She saw all of them. They were going to ... kill her."

"Where's the house?"

He shook his head. "I don't ... know."

"Did you hire Fred Weltz to build a shelving unit with a hidden door?"

Santo's eyes went wide. "Y ... y ... yes."

"Do you know where it was installed?"

"No, Jamie sent ..." He was struggling to breathe. "You ... have to ... find ... her."

His body went still.

"George!" Tori exclaimed. "Come on, George!"

Eggs checked for a pulse. She looked to Tori and shook her head.

Santo was gone.

TWENTY-TWO

"TWELVE-YEAR-OLD GIRLS ARE NOT PAWNS TO BE SACRIFICED"

Tori and Eggleston ran to the farmhouse. Eggleston elbowed out a small pane of glass in the back door and turned over the deadbolt. They quickly made their way through the one-story ranch-style house. Isabella was not inside, nor was there any evidence anyone had been there for quite some time. This was not the location where she was being held.

"The barn was just a meeting place," Tori said. "They're holding her elsewhere."

The dead woman was Jamie Vaughn, based on the identification found in a purse in the Escalade outside. They also had identifications for the two men lying on the barn floor that would need to be run, but they had the look of hired guns.

Tori stood over one of the men, who had black wavy hair and thick stubble. "Who does he kind of remind you of?"

"Ian Pemell," Eggleston said.

"Yup."

"Was this Vaughn and Santo working together, or did she have him by the you-know-whats?"

"Maybe a little bit of both," Tori said. "If what Santo told us was true. Vaughn changed their deal on Isabella."

She called Zagaros and gave him the names of all the dead, along with a request that he dig on all of them. "This isn't over, Nick. We don't have the girl back yet."

She and Eggleston scanned the document on the table. This had been all about the ranch, a way for Santo and Vaughn to get Luciana Farner to give away her half of the property.

"All of this for that?" Eggleston said in disbelief.

"Apparently so."

"Any idea how much it was worth?"

Tori shook her head. "It had to be an awful lot to take such a risk. But then again, I'll never understand people for whom a life means so little. Twelve-year-old girls are not pawns to be sacrificed."

Braddock and Steak returned. The emergency response team had arrived and were now camped at the end of the driveway, guarding the scene. Tori brought Braddock up to speed.

"Santo told you Izzy was at a house?" he said. "But he didn't know where."

"Yes. He said she escaped and saw these guys. So once Vaughn got what she wanted," she pointed to the documents on the table, "they were going to kill her."

"And he confirmed that he hired Weltz," Eggs noted.

"Then they iced him after the install to tie off any loose ends," Steak said. "Case closed."

"This thing Weltz built is being used to secure Isabella," Tori said. "When they put her in there, when they come in to give her food or check on her, they were wearing masks. But if what Santo said was true, she got out somehow. And when they had to chase her down—"

"They weren't wearing masks."

"And Isabella recognized the dead woman because she

dated her uncle." She thought for a moment. "You know, what if there are others working for Vaughn? If these guys don't show up ..."

"We got to find her," Braddock said.

"Wherever this place is, it's not far from here."

"Why do you say that?"

"For one, if they came after me tonight, they must be somewhere nearby. And they hired Weltz, who probably didn't work ..."

"Too far from home," Braddock agreed, nodding along. "They were close to here."

"And Santo said she got out?"

"Yes. He didn't have any details beyond that, though."

"Huh. Penny Teague ... I wonder."

"Penny Teague?"

"My thing tonight. The dead woman was a delivery driver for Courier Connect. Her truck was found dumped on the north side of Little Falls. She was murdered elsewhere early this morning, most likely somewhere between her last delivery and her next scheduled spot. It's a five-mile stretch of road ten miles south of here." Braddock paused, closing his eyes. "Damn."

"What?"

"The driver was shot twice in the chest from distance and then shot in the head at close range to finish her off."

Tori understood where he was going. "She got out of the truck."

"Right. We figured she was killed to get at something in the truck. That's what the BCA was thinking anyway. But what if Isabella got out of the house and ran to the road just as Teague was driving by. Teague sees her, stops, gets out of the truck to see why this girl is waving her down out in the middle of nowhere and ..."

"Wham!" Tori finished. "One of these guys picks her off."

"Right," Braddock said, thinking it through. "Right. They were giving chase. Isabella saw them because they had to catch her and get her back into the house."

"And that changed whatever deal they had," Tori continued. "Santo comes here expecting an exchange, and instead, they tell him they have to kill Isabella."

"And for him, that was a bridge too far."

"Yeah, real standup guy," Tori said. "You can kidnap my niece so I can get out of my financial misery, but kill her? Now that goes too far."

"At least he had a line," Braddock said. "Point being ..."

"She's at a house somewhere in that area," Tori said. "That focuses our search."

They all ran out to Braddock's Tahoe, and he took out a map of the county and spread it on the hood of the truck. Steak held up a flashlight. With a pen, Braddock marked the beginning and end of Teague's route. "We have to search every house along here."

"Get everyone together at the end of the driveway," Tori said. "I can narrow this down further."

Braddock pulled to a stop at the entrance to the long driveway where Penny Teague had made her last delivery. Steak and Eggs and two Suburbans driven by the emergency response team parked up behind him. On their way to the location, Zagaros and his team had completed an online search of the properties along the stretch of road in question.

"I have thirteen properties worth a check," he reported. "Five are rentals. Eight others changed ownership in the last year."

Braddock spread the map out again on the hood. Steak and

Eggleston both had their flashlights out as the other officers gathered around. Tori put her phone on speaker and Braddock marked the properties as Zagaros called them out.

Five of the addresses were in more agricultural areas. The other eight were closer to the area of small lakes where Teague was supposed to have made her next delivery. Braddock took a head count. The ERT team had eight men. Nolan was sent back to the government center in case they needed her there. He created four search teams of three, adding an ERT officer to the Steak and Eggs grouping and one for him and Tori.

"Tor, any sense on what is more likely?" he asked.

She evaluated the map. "The five farm properties are set well back from the road. They provide privacy by their very nature, plus the kidnappers just used a farm. So those are possibilities we have to search."

Braddock pointed to the two teams of ERT men. "One team takes the first three properties, the other takes the second two. Once you've checked them, you can move east and support us."

Tori ran her finger along the route to the end. "Give this cluster of four on the north side of Sullivan Lake to Steak and Eggs. They can check them all quickly."

"On it," Steak said.

Tori circled the area west of Sullivan Lake with her index finger. "We'll take these four here along the west of Sullivan Lake."

The search teams dispersed.

Braddock reached the driveway of the first house, which was set back in the woods a quarter-mile off the road. It was 1:38 a.m. when he pulled up the driveway and parked.

"First farmhouse cleared," an ERT officer reported. "Renters are living in the house and farming the land. Husband, wife, and one teenager." The second ERT team found something similar at their first destination. "Nothing unusual to report."

Braddock approached the house and pounded on the door, with the ERT officer on the bottom step and Tori more distant, observing.

"Light just switched on in the back of the house," she said.

The porch light went on and a woman peered out the side window.

"Police, ma'am," Braddock said, pointing to his badge. "We need to speak with you."

The woman and her boyfriend were renting the house. She explained that her boyfriend was working an overnight shift at a processing plant in Little Falls. He would be home in a few hours.

"Did you happen to hear any gunshots early yesterday morning, say around seven a.m.?"

"Plenty," the woman answered. "Hunters start popping off at sunrise."

Braddock nodded. "Right. Good point."

As they walked away, he shook his head. "She's right, you know. Down in this neck of the woods, plenty of hunters are out in the morning, letting it rip. You wouldn't think twice about the sound of gunfire."

The second location was a cabin with lake access. The building was dark. Braddock and the ERT officer walked around it with their flashlights, looking through the windows, but saw no signs of recent activity. Tori checked out the detached garage.

"There's a fishing boat inside, covered. No other vehicles," she said.

"Nobody has been here for some time," Braddock said. "There are sheets covering the furniture."

"Next house, then."

The ERT teams continued to work through their properties and found nothing unusual. Steak reported the same for his and Eggleston's.

"Come our way," Braddock said. "We're en route to our third location. Meet us there."

Two minutes later, he turned left into a narrow driveway that tunneled through dense woods into a clearing. On the left was a large two-story log cabin. As he looked at the map, he saw that the land behind the detached garage to the right ran down to the lake.

"Big place," Tori said. "And a black Suburban parked in front of the garage. Maybe someone is here."

There was a long porch that ran along the front of the cabin and then around to a side door and a deck off the back. The gravel driveway made a circular loop around between the garage and the cabin. Braddock parked. The ERT officer went to check the Suburban and the garage, while Tori and Braddock made their way to the cabin.

Braddock led the way up the steps at the side of the house. He stepped to his left and around to the front. Tori peeked in the kitchen window and focused her flashlight inside. She saw plates in the sink, a dirty glass on the counter along with two empty soda cans. She looked back over to the ERT officer, who put his bare hand on the hood of the Suburban and shook his head. It was cold.

She heard Braddock knocking on the front door. She opened the screen door at the side and then leaned in to peer through the window.

The inner door swung open. She quickly stepped back and shuffled to the corner of the porch. "*Psst.*"

Braddock looked round and she waved him over.

"I leaned on the door and it opened. There are dishes in the sink. Someone either is or has been here."

Braddock stepped inside the house. The ERT officer joined him, then took the lead, moving forward with his gun and flashlight.

"Police! Anyone home?"

There was no response. The house was still and quiet.

"Let's clear it," Braddock ordered.

They quickly cleared the main and upstairs level. Tori found the door to the basement and led the way carefully down the steps. At the bottom, she flipped the light switch.

"I think this might be it."

On the far wall was a shelving unit in three sections. The bottom of the unit consisted of cabinets and the top was horizontal shelving. It was stained black and didn't necessarily fit with the style and color palette of the rest of the room.

Tori knocked on the bookcase. "Isabella! Izzy! Are you in there?" There was no reply.

She noticed two metal clamps sitting on top of one of the cabinets, then spotted two small indentations on the inside wall of the middle shelving unit. There were similar marks on the unit to the left, as if the clamps had been used to hold the two sections together. She gave the middle section a shove and felt just a little give. Shining the beam of her flashlight into the gap between the top two shelves, she caught the glint of something metallic. She ran her hand underneath the overhang of the first shelf. *There!* She pulled the latch toward her.

Ca-chunk!

The shelving section opened inward like a door. Tori stepped inside and scanned the room with her flashlight.

Empty.

TWENTY-THREE

"HE DIDN'T HAVE TO PLAY THAT CARD"

Tori stood in the middle of the hidden room with Braddock. With her flashlight beam she picked out an overhead light socket. Out in the main room she found a small reading lamp that had a light bulb. She screwed the bulb into the overhead socket and flipped the switch.

Before the shelving unit was installed, the room would have served as a storage area, given the concrete walls, cement floor and narrow glass-block window. There was a mattress in one corner. On the floor by the door was a mostly empty crayon box and a collection of crushed and cracked crayons. To the side of the mattress was a coloring book with several pages completed.

Tori lifted a balled-up blanket. "Will, she was here."

"How do you know?"

With her gloved right hand, she held up a small bracelet with an angel and two doves left on it. Two other charms were lying on the floor; one a bent angel and the other a dove with its tail snapped off.

"She escaped from here?" Braddock asked. "How?" He swung the door nearly closed and examined the back of it. "I see crayon marks back here. If she escaped using crayons, I'll be super impressed."

Tori took a knee to peer at the door. "I can't explain the marks, but it wasn't crayons that got her out. Look." She pointed to the chipped wood around the latch. "This was hacked at with something sharp."

"Those charms maybe?"

"I don't know about that. Those things are small and not real durable."

"Then how?"

"She found something else to lever this open," she speculated as she stuck her fountain pen into the gap. It wasn't strong enough to pop the latch but something of that size was used. "She popped that latch and busted out. We know she escaped once; if she got out again, she could be out there in the woods, maybe trying to find another house."

"Right. A search." Braddock ran up the stairs and out to the driveway, gathering everyone together.

Tori followed him but stopped at the back door. It had been left unlocked and partially open. Why? She swung it closed. It caught a half-inch short of fully closing. She tried again and it did the same thing. Stepping out onto the porch, she yanked at it and finally managed to close it.

Braddock ran up onto the porch. "Steak found a big patch of what he thinks is dried blood out on the shoulder of the road, thirty yards to the west." He noticed her examining the door. "What's on your mind?"

"This door. I was wondering if it was Isabella who left it unlocked."

"How could she have locked it?"

She looked at him, her eyes wide.

"What?"

Tori literally sprinted back down to the basement. She

picked up the clamps she'd spotted before, and then ran her hand over the small indentations on the shelving unit. "These clamps were used on the door to prevent it from opening."

"Yet she got out."

"Once," Tori said. "She got out once. I'm betting that after that, they used these to make sure she didn't get out again."

Braddock nodded for her to go into the room, then closed the door behind her. She could hear him tightening the clamps. She then heard him pop the latch. *Ca-chunk.*

"Give it a shot."

She tried to pull the door open, tugging on the exposed beams. It rattled but wouldn't budge.

"I can't do it."

He undid the clamps and opened the door. "If those were on that door, no way she was able to pick her way out, that's for sure."

"So where is she?"

He grimaced. "They killed her already."

"No."

"Tor ..."

"I'm just ... not ready to concede that."

"Hey, me neither," Braddock said as he exhaled a breath. "But if she's not here and wasn't at the other farm, then where is she?"

"Maybe they left someone here to guard her. When Vaughn and company didn't show up as scheduled, he took Isabella and left," she posited, but without conviction. That didn't feel right to her either.

"You might have to get your mind around the idea that they dealt with the problem *before* they met with Santo, regardless of what they told him. After Isabella escaped this morning, they killed the driver; they might have just ended it with her then as well. She was a witness to a murder and had seen her kidnappers. Why keep around a living witness. If you decided to kill her, get it over with."

Tori closed her eyes and nodded.

"The only thing I keep coming back to that gives me hope is ... what if Santo made them prove she was alive before he signed?"

"Maybe," Tori replied. "But I'm still wondering why the back door was open."

"The house settled. The door doesn't shut completely unless you really yank it."

"Fine, but the deadbolt was unlocked. Awfully sloppy, don't you think?" The question she asked was also the answer.

"They weren't sloppy," Braddock acknowledged. "You know, we went through the house quickly before. Now let's give it a thorough scrubbing."

They worked their way through each room, starting on the main level. Next, they went upstairs, taking the master bedroom first. The next bedroom had a king-sized bed, a desk, and its own bathroom. In the walk-in closet, tucked in a corner, were two backpacks.

Tori opened the first one. "I'll be damned."

"What do you have there?"

"It's all their planning for this." She handed him a photo.

"Ian Pemell," Braddock said with a wry headshake. "We thought he was set up. They, in fact, set him up."

They took the backpacks down to the first floor and emptied the contents onto the large table in the eating area. There were detailed maps and photos of the park preserve and the areas around Pemell's house and his farm, then various road and trail maps of Shepard County in general, as well as markings for the cabin they were now in and the farm where the shootout had occurred. There were route times to all the locations, and a calendar with notations of the days Pemell went to St. Cloud, almost always on Wednesdays.

"That's why they picked that day," Tori noted. "He would be in St. Cloud and then at his farmhouse. It was much less likely he could account for his time if he was down there where nobody would see him. Plus, that's where he kept the van."

There was also a thick clipped stack of paper comprising a summary of the Helena Hernandez investigation in Thief River Falls, and dozens of pictures of Pemell in various locations around Manchester Bay.

"They followed him around for weeks," Braddock murmured. "I mean, look at all these photos." He laid a bunch of them out on the table. "There must be twenty of him running, always in black. Pictures of him visiting various places around town. And all these pictures of him at the taco food truck that works the lunch rush in Manchester Bay."

"They went onto his property," Tori noted. "They went into the barn to take photos of the van. Then they went about finding an exact match." She opened a manila folder. Inside were pictures of a van the kidnappers had purchased from a seller in Louisville, Kentucky. "They were setting this up for weeks, maybe months, watching him, figuring out how to make this play out."

"They surveilled Isabella too. Plenty of pictures of her," Braddock said, laying them out on the table as well. "Here's one where she's wearing the same raincoat she was wearing on Wednesday. They planned this down to the last detail."

Tori snorted. "Which is what you might want to do rather than risk a very long prison stretch."

"I think their hope was that we'd be focused on Pemell a lot longer than we were," Braddock said. "This much planning, they probably expected us to be sweating him for days, probably with press coverage too."

"Just like in Thief River."

"Exactly. And with everyone focused on him, they could slyly run their little game on the Farners. I guess they missed him going to get that oil change in Little Falls."

"Yeah," Tori chuckled, and then froze. "Unless ..."

"Unless?"

She stood back, letting what she was looking at sink in. She glanced through to the back door, and then down at everything on the table again. *Oh my God.*

"Is that what happened here?"

"What?"

"That would explain why the back door was unlocked."

"What? What are you mumbling about?"

Her mind started racing a million miles an hour, thinking back to two days ago, when they'd had Pemell in the room. "He was sharp, intelligent."

"Who?"

"Pemell. When you think about it, really, really think about it, he was ready for us. When we searched the house, questioned him. He was ready."

"I'm not following ..." Braddock started and then paused for a moment as he started to realize where she was going. "Holy shit. He was ready, like ..."

"He knew what was coming. Not because of his whining 'every time some kid goes missing, they hassle me' routine, but because he knew they were watching him. He knew he was being set up. He knew these guys had taken Isabella, and most importantly, he knew where they had her."

Braddock closed his eyes for a moment. "Damn. He had that in his back pocket if we really were able to jam him up. If it looked like we were going to arrest and charge him, he could say *I don't have her ...*"

"*But I know who does.*" Tori nodded. "We never got there

with him. We didn't have the evidence. He didn't have to play that card. Instead, we cleared him because of the oil change on that van. Which he would have also probably used at some point if he needed to."

"And he turned it around on them."

"He came here and took her when they were gone," Tori moaned. "Dammit!"

"Why would he do it?" Braddock asked. "For what reason? What's his game?"

"Maybe for the same reason he took Helena Hernandez. The same reason he took Joey Martinez."

"Which is ... what? A seven-year-old boy? An eight-year-old girl? Now a twelve-year-old girl. How does that compute? What's he doing with them?"

"Let's find him and ask him."

Braddock reached for his radio and ordered deputies to Pemell's house. He radioed to the Morrison County sheriff's department to do the same to the farm. Five minutes later, he got the call from a deputy up in Manchester Bay.

"He's not at the house, Will. It's locked up and quiet. His SUV isn't in the garage. We have a man stationed watching the place now. We'll grab him if he shows."

Morrison County radioed five minutes later. "The farmhouse is quiet. Nobody is here. We'll station officers out along the road in case he appears."

"Is the van in the barn?"

"Affirmative."

"It's still the middle of the night," Tori said, checking her watch. It was 4:48 a.m. "If he's not home, my gut says he's got her."

Steak and Eggleston came into the cabin and she brought them up to speed.

"Pemell?" Eggleston said, gobsmacked. "How in the ..."

"That might explain why we've not found her. At least not yet."

"And Jamie Vaughn and her band of killers are dead and can't return, so we're not accomplishing anything here." Braddock looked to Tori. "The sun will be up in ninety minutes, give or take. Let's head back to Manchester Bay to figure out our next move."

TWENTY-FOUR

"WE'VE DONE BUSINESS WITH THEM BEFORE"

Ca-chunk!

Izzy bolted awake.

The door burst open, and two men rushed into the room, searching with flashlights.

One of them spotted her. He yanked the blanket off and grabbed her ankles, pulling her toward him.

"No! No!" she screamed, kicking at him. "Stay away from me!"

He batted away her kicks, grabbing both her ankles, then picked her up and flipped her over onto her stomach.

She squirmed desperately. "No, no! Stop! Stop!"

Her arms were yanked behind her back and her wrists cinched. She twisted violently, rolling onto her side.

"It does no good to fight, girl," the man growled.

The other man grabbed her ankles and held them tight.

"Get the loop around them. Get it around."

Her ankles were cinched the same way, the bindings cutting into the skin.

"No, no, n—"

Tape was slapped over her mouth. Everything went ink dark as a pillowcase was pulled over her head and then tied loosely around her neck.

"Let's go, let's go. We need to hustle."

One of them picked her up and threw her over his shoulder, his arm wrapped tightly around her legs as he carried her up the stairs.

"Get the door."

The blast of cold air shocked her system as his feet crunched rapidly across the gravel. There was the creaking of an opening door and then she was dropped hard onto a rubber floor. The door closed. She thought she must be in a van. She heard the men get in and their doors slam.

"Let's get out of here."

The wheels spun beneath her. Her body jerked hard as the vehicle pulled quickly away.

"Oof!" She felt every bump and crack in the road as they bounced along.

Were these the same men? No, probably not, otherwise why the flashlights? Who were they? And where were they taking her?

Fifty-eight ... fifty-nine ... sixty. Thirty-six minutes.

They'd been on the move longer than that. She figured it was at least ten minutes before she'd started counting. It kept her mind occupied.

One ... two ... three ...

The vehicle slowed into a turn, and then her body tipped back as they went up an incline before the ground evened out and they stopped.

The doors slammed again. She heard footsteps, and then

the door behind her opened and she felt the cool air hit the areas of exposed skin on her body.

She was thrown over the man's shoulder again. The other man walked ahead; she could hear his footsteps across gravel and then up wooden steps before a door opened. The man carrying her climbed the steps, just three of them, and she felt the warmth of indoors on her body. Then just as quickly they were going down steps again. The man took her off his shoulder and set her down on a hard floor.

The pillowcase was pulled off. A man wearing a mask ripped the tape off her mouth. The other man had a flashlight beam pointed at her face, blinding her.

"Can I ..."

"Can you what?" the man with the flashlight asked.

"Go to the bathroom? I haven't gone in a really long time."

"What do you think?" the flashlight man asked the other.

"We don't want a mess and we don't have any spare clothes for her."

"Makes sense." The masked man cut loose the restraints on her wrist and then her ankles.

"She'll be back in those soon enough," the flashlight man said. "She can have a break."

She'll be back in those soon enough.

They led her back upstairs to a bathroom. They left the door open but didn't watch. After she'd finished, she washed her hands and then asked meekly, "Can I have something to drink?"

Back in the cellar, they told her to sit by the far wall, then one of them handed her two bottles of water.

Buzz ... buzz ... buzz ...

The man who'd brought the water reached into his pocket, extracting a cell phone. "Yeah ... Where are you?" he said as he took off for the stairs, the other man following. "That far?"

The light at the top of the steps disappeared, and then there was the sound of the door locking.

Izzy opened one of the bottles and took a long drink, gulping down nearly half the water. Then, rubbing her throbbing wrists, she peered around the empty basement. It was square, with a low ceiling and the steps situated in the middle. She figured it was a storm cellar, like a friend of hers from school had at her house outside of town. They used to play hide and seek down there.

She took another long drink. Her ankles were stinging too. She rubbed them with both hands, massaging out the pain. Then, standing up, she rotated her left foot clockwise and then counterclockwise several times, and did the same with her right, loosening up the joints. She took a few minutes and did some stretches that they did at hockey for their hips and legs. There was room to roam down here. She started walking about, sipping from her water.

There was no light, but she could see. Illumination came from outside, through a narrow horizontal window at the top of the far cinder-block wall. She stood on her tiptoes and pulled herself up on the ledge to look out through the grimy glass. It was foggy outside, and the light filtering in was coming from a floodlight mounted high on a pole. In the distance, she could make out what looked like the peak of a barn roof.

The window was three separate panes of glass. Along the top of the frame there were two hinges so that the window would flip up. On the bottom was a small handle. Along each side was a slide latch that held the window in place. She tried pushing up on the latches, but they wouldn't move. As she looked closer, she saw they'd been painted over.

What was it the men had said? *She'll be back in those soon enough.* Then there was the phone call. *Where are you? That far?* Someone else was coming. No doubt for her.

The window was narrow, but she thought she could fit through. How to get it open, though. Was there anything useful down here?

Under the steps, she found two plastic tubs. The first contained old bed sheets and blankets. Inside the second were towels and some plastic picnic plates. Underneath the plates she found napkins and tucked at the bottom was a small plastic ziplock bag of white plastic cutlery. She pulled out a plastic knife and looked back at the window.

"How much longer will you be then?" Pemell asked as he walked up the steps and into the kitchen.

"At least an hour," Luis answered.

Pemell put his phone in his pocket and pulled off his mask. He wiped his face, then removed the stainless-steel teapot from the burner. Dropping a tea bag into a mug, he added hot water. He bobbed the tea bag, then blew on the piping hot liquid before taking a careful sip as he stared out of the window.

Ole's rental house was situated in a clearing fully surrounded by woods. There was an aging barn set further back on the property. Ole had told him that at one time the place had served as a hobby farm. The owners had long since retired to a warmer climate, and Ole had rented it from them for the last three years.

They were well east of Manchester Bay, in a sparsely populated section of the county. The area was low-lying, with marshes, ponds, and small lakes interspersed with dense forest. This early morning was like many at this time of year, when the cooler temperature mixed with the heavy moisture in the air, creating a light fog. He could see it starting to thicken and knew that it would end up soupy for a few hours until the sun rose high enough to burn it off.

"How long?" Ole asked.

"An hour, give or take."

Ole pulled his 9mm out of the kitchen drawer, checked the magazine, slid it back in, and chambered a round.

"You think that's really necessary?" Pemell asked.

"You never know with these guys," Ole said. "We're out in the middle of nowhere. Fog is rolling in."

"We've done business with them before."

"Better safe than sorry." He reached into the drawer again and took out another gun. "You too."

"Seriously? I hate guns. I know you have ... experience, but this is not my deal."

"They'll be carrying. We're just leveling everything out. Hold it for two hours, and once they're gone, we're in the money."

TWENTY-FIVE

"YOU SHOW ME YOURS AND I'LL SHOW YOU MINE"

Braddock turned north on Highway 25, twenty miles south of Manchester Bay. "We don't have long, do we?" he asked warily.

"No," Tori said. "If Pemell took her after all this, you can bet he has a plan, and it isn't to sit around and wait."

"He may have a plan, but he doesn't know that we suspect him—at least not yet. That's the only advantage we have."

"We have to find him, though. We can't just wait for him to show up."

"One thing is, if he has her, he probably hasn't gone too far."

"That depends when he took her," Tori said. "It's been a long night. He could be several hours ahead of us."

"Or he might not be. Whatever he's doing, he needs time for it to play out. It gives us a chance."

His optimism was something she needed to hear.

Braddock went back to making phone calls. Tori kept sifting through the photos from the backpacks, using her flashlight, taking each one out, holding it up and examining it. There were photos of Pemell around Manchester Bay, running along the paths in the park preserve, going in and out of stores. The next one she took out showed him at the Taco Truck, taking his white bag from the man in the window. She examined it intently, not so much Pemell himself as the man he was talking to.

Braddock glanced over and saw her focusing on it, then taking out another photo and holding the two side by side. She was seeing something. "What is it?"

She pursed her lips. "This picture, something about ... this guy. Pemell's always talking to him."

"Well, he's the guy who runs the taco truck. Pemell likes going there. *We* like going there. Quinn can't get enough of that stuff."

"There is another guy in that truck," she answered, showing a different photo. "But it's always *this* guy who serves Pemell. Like you said, you and I have been to that taco truck quite a few times in the past year. What color are the food bags?"

"Red. They're bright red with the taco logo on it."

"Right," she replied. "But every time, Pemell's getting a plain white bag. Why? What makes him so special?" She examined the photos again, panning back and forth between them. "And this guy at the order window, I've seen him somewhere else."

"On the case?"

"Maybe," Tori said, tapping her lips with her index finger. "If I had my case file ... I left it in the Audi at Rog and Mary's."

"It's behind your seat. I pulled it out of the Audi."

Tori undid her seat belt and reached back. She found the brown expandable file and started thumbing through it.

"Anything?" Braddock asked after a couple of minutes. They were approaching the southern outskirts of Manchester Bay.

"No," Tori said as she looked through documents and photographs from their current case and the Helena Hernandez case. The last folder was for the Joey Martinez investigation. She started flipping through the reports and photos, then suddenly stopped.

"The red hair. The bright red hair!"

"What?"

She took out a photo and held it up next to one of Pemell at the taco truck. "It's been nine years," she said, digging back into the file, speed-reading the investigative report for the Martinez disappearance. "He was a cook, a goddam cook at a Mexican restaurant."

"Who?"

"Mark Olson, the boyfriend of Joey Martinez's mother," Tori said. "Pull over. *Pull over!*"

Braddock skidded onto the shoulder. "Show me."

Tori held up the photo of Mark Olson from the Grand Forks PD file, and the clearest one she could find of the man at the taco truck.

"They sure look like a match. So Olson and Pemell are ..."

"Partners."

Braddock reached for his phone. "Pick up. Pick up, dammit," he muttered.

Nolan answered. "I just got ba—"

"Find the file on the Joey Martinez disappearance in Grand Forks nine years ago."

"Uh, boss? Why?"

"Mark Olson. He was the off-and-on boyfriend of Joey Martinez's mother. He was suspected by the police up there in the disappearance."

"Okay, but again, why?"

"Pemell's back in the game." Braddock gave her a quick recap. "He wasn't a helpful neighborly witness when Joey Martinez was abducted. He and Olson were in cahoots then, and we think they are now. I need you to find out Mark Olson's whereabouts now, and then see if he was in or around Thief River Falls six years ago when Helena Hernandez went missing. He didn't show up in that case, but that doesn't mean he wasn't there."

"Okay, okay," Nolan replied anxiously. "Give me a minute." They could hear her rustling through documents and then her fingers running over the keyboard.

"Nolan! Come on!"

"Give me a minute, would ya? This guy's name is Mark Olson. It's Norwegian–Danish Central in Minnesota and North Dakota. There are hundreds of them."

* * *

Isabella chipped away at the paint over the right window latch. Because she was having to stretch up, the force she could apply was limited, and she couldn't reach the top.

I need more height.

She grabbed one of the plastic tubs and placed it under the window. Would it hold her? Carefully she stood on the lid, but it felt like it would give way. She went to the other tub and took out several folded towels, then stuffed them in the first tub, filling it to the brim, and put the lid back on. Standing on the top now, it felt more stable. She was almost eye level with the window frame. She picked up the plastic knife and resumed her scraping.

* * *

It felt like it took Nolan hours. In fact it was just under ten minutes.

"Okay, I think I got it. He's aged ten years, longer hair now, with a beard, but he seems right," she said. "And to boot, he's living about twenty miles east of Manchester Bay."

Braddock punched the details into the computer in his Tahoe, and the current DMV photo for Mark Olson came up. Tori compared it with the one from the file. In that one, Olson had short red hair and no beard. The current photo showed longer red hair combed back and down to the shoulders, with a Fu Manchu beard. His height was still six foot, although there was an extra fifteen pounds listed.

"The eyes and nose look right." Braddock squinted at the two photos.

"And regarding his movements since Grand Forks, he moved from there to Crookston, where he was living six years ago when Helena Hernandez went missing. Crookston is fifty miles south of Thief."

"It's him," Tori said, holding a picture from the taco truck next to the computer screen. "That's him."

Braddock hit the gas and flipped on the flashing front grill lights and siren, covering the last two miles north on 25 to Highway 210 and then turning east.

"Nolan, tell us about this place Olson is living now," Braddock asked.

"I'm on a satellite map ... give me a sec," Nolan answered. "Okay, the property is heavily wooded. I can see the roof of a house, and then it looks like there is a larger outbuilding behind the house."

"How about approach?"

"The driveway is a left off Marley Road."

Tori was working the touch screen in the Tahoe, tweezing it to get a closer look at the property. She ran her finger along Marley Road, past the driveway to a left turn not much further north, a dirt road labeled Miner Avenue. "Does the property abut Miner Avenue?" she asked.

"Uh ... yes," Nolan replied.

"Is there a way onto the property off Miner?"

"What are you thinking?" Braddock asked. They were ten miles away.

"Having another way onto the property other than coming in the front door means we can see if anyone's there and what we might be up against."

"Tori, I think the driveway loops over to the dirt road. I can't tell for sure, but I can see a gravel driveway that continues past the outbuilding and on into the woods in that direction."

"That's what I'm seeing now as well," Tori said, and felt the Tahoe slowing. She looked up. "Whoa!"

"Fog," Braddock said. "It got thick in a hurry."

"It's like a blanket."

Braddock called Steak on the radio. "Where are you and Eggs at?"

"We're on County 25, twenty miles south of Manchester Bay."

"Well, get a serious move on."

* * *

Dang it!

The plastic knife broke in half in her hand. She'd chipped away at the paint on the latch and tried pushing it up, but it just wouldn't break free. It felt like it could move but it wouldn't. She needed something harder to hammer it with.

She took off her right shoe.

Using both hands, she hit up at the latch with the sole, trying to catch the razor-thin handle.

A light flashed to her right. She peered out the window. Headlights were approaching.

Come on! Come on! Come on!

She hit it again, and this time it moved. She swung the shoe once more and the latch broke free. Now for the left one.

* * *

The white delivery truck approached slowly. Pemell opened the front door and stepped out onto the stoop. The truck parked alongside the white panel van and his CRV.

Manuel got out of the truck and went to the back. Opening the door, he stepped up into the rear compartment. Luis stood at the back until Manuel emerged and pulled the door partially down. He was now carrying a backpack and the two of them approached through the fog.

"It's fucking cold up here," Manuel said by way of greeting.

"It's not even winter yet," Pemell retorted.

"It was like driving through the clouds to get here," Luis added, and then a wry smile creased his face. "What the fuck is that?" he said, pointing at the gun stuffed in the front of Pemell's jeans. "Really, Ian?"

"I've been told you can never be too careful."

"No, I guess you can't," Luis replied as he opened his coat enough so that the gun on his right hip was visible.

"Great, we all have guns. Let's just do this."

"Our package?" Manuel asked.

"Our payment?"

He snorted a laugh. "You show me yours and I'll show you mine."

"Come on." Pemell led them into the house and Ole unlocked the basement door. Manuel pulled on a full face mask as they all headed slowly down the steps. At the bottom, Pemell turned on his flashlight.

Cough! Cough!

He spun to his left. The girl was sitting on top of a plastic tub under the steps, rubbing one of her feet.

"She is older than normal," Manuel said. "Looks older too."

"She's just turned twelve," Pemell said, shining the flashlight beam on her, causing her to shield her eyes. "A little tall for her age, but her skin is certainly the right tone. And she's bilingual."

"Why are you sitting on that box?" Manuel asked the girl in Spanish.

Isabella didn't reply, squinting at the bright light.

"Why are you on that box?" he asked again.

"The floor is ... cold and ... hard," she answered haltingly but in perfect Spanish.

"I'm sure she'll do," he said.

* * *

She was still trying to loosen the other latch when she heard footsteps overhead.

Then ... *Click!*

She pushed the rest of the plastic knives down between the tub and the wall, then ran under the steps, sat down on the other tub and started rubbing her foot.

Cough! Cough!

The flashlight beam was blinding. Someone called to her in Spanish.

"Why are you on that box?"

"The floor is ... cold and ... hard," she replied fluently.

"I'm sure she'll do."

"Shall we finish then?"

The men walked back up the steps and she heard the door close with a loud click.

She ran back to the window and started hitting the latch

again, swinging harder and harder. She was painfully aware of
the noise she was making, but she had to risk it.

Come on! Come on! Please break loose.

She gripped her sneaker tight in both hands and swung up
as hard as she dared.

Crack!

The latch moved. She pushed it all the way open, then
pulled at the handle. The window still wouldn't open. The
whole thing, seam and all, was painted shut. She hopped down
and grabbed another plastic knife to scrape at the seam.

She didn't have much time.

Manuel stood at the table and opened the backpack he'd been
carrying. On the table he set out ten wrapped stacks of dollar
bills. "Hundreds, fifties, and twenties," he explained. "It's what
we agreed: three hundred thousand dollars."

Pemell looked to Ole. "We should count it."

"What? Don't you trust us?" Luis asked.

"About as much as you trust us."

TWENTY-SIX

"WHERE ARE YOUR FRIENDS?"

Braddock switched off his police lights a mile short of their destination, not that he could tell he was that close.

"I can't see but thirty or forty feet ahead," he said, leaning forward, as if it would better his vision.

Tori alternately looked at the GPS map on the police computer monitor and then to the northwest, trying to get a sense of the house, but couldn't see anything. Of course, she thought, the good news is if I can't see the house, they can't see us.

"Thoughts?"

"If she is there, the fog lets us ..."

"Get close." Braddock nodded. "Especially if we come in the back door."

He slowed past the driveway entrance for the front. They could see no more than ten to fifteen yards up the driveway. They couldn't see any structures and only what looked like the glow of maybe a yard light in the distance. He drove on and almost missed the left turn onto the gravel road that was Miner Avenue.

They turned left and drove a couple of hundred yards. Nolan was right: there was what looked to be a narrow driveway into the woods on the north side of Olson's property. Braddock turned off his headlights and inched forward into the woods, before pulling to a stop at an angle in the middle of the narrow driveway. "This way is blocked," he said. The two of them got out.

Tori pulled her Glock and walked ahead, Braddock right behind. In the woods, the fog was a touch less dense. She could at least see shapes as much as forty to fifty yards ahead.

The glow of the light they'd seen earlier came into view. It was a yard floodlight situated high on a pole. The glow let her make out a large structure just left of the driveway. The barn she'd seen on the satellite.

* * *

Isabella chipped around the bottom of the window, puncturing the paint, jamming in the plastic knife with her right hand while pulling the handle with her left.

What was it the man had said: *Shall we finish then?*

These new guys would be taking her soon.

She looked out the window again. The fog seemed thicker now, but she could see what looked like a white fence and lots of trees. If she could get out, she could disappear into the fog, then escape to another house. It was a plan. Find a hiding place and then slip away. It's what she should have done in the morning.

The window was starting to shake some now as she repeatedly jammed in the knife, puncturing the paint sealing it. She pulled the handle again, but it still wouldn't open.

Come on! Come on!

Frantically she chipped at the seam in the window.

Scrape! Scrape! Scrape!
The window opened.

* * *

As they counted, they divided the money into two equal stacks.

"Okay, I'm good here. You?" Pemell said, looking to Ole.

"Yeah, me too."

"Okay. We need to go," Manuel said. "It'll be light soon, fog or no. We want to be on the road before daybreak. Long drive ahead of us."

"Will she fight?" Luis asked, taking out a long piece of rope. "Or will I have to use this?"

"She won't go willingly," Ole said.

"She kicked him pretty hard in the melon when we sniped her from the other place," Pemell noted as he pulled his mask back on.

Ole made a show of massaging his jaw. "Caught me good," he added, before tugging on his mask. The others did the same.

"With four of us, maybe she'll see the futility of fighting," Pemell said as he opened the door and led them down the steps.

* * *

Click!

The door opened. Light filtered down the steps.

Isabella flipped up the window. She grabbed the sill and heaved herself up, then wedged her body into the gap, letting the window swing down on her upper back. She pushed with her legs and wriggled through, digging her fingers into the ground to pull herself forward.

* * *

Thump!

"What was that?" Pemell said.

Thump! Thump!

He scrambled down the last four steps, the others right behind.

He looked to the right.

* * *

Scrambling to her feet Isabella, glanced around. To her right was a big white truck and a white van, and the back door of the house.

Not that way.

* * *

"She's running to the back!" a man's voice called in the distance. "To the back! To the back!"

Tori glanced to Braddock.

"Steak, Isabella's here and she might have shaken loose of these guys," Braddock reported quietly. "Get your ass here and get us some backup."

Tori moved ahead. Through the foggy mist, she saw someone running through the yard.

* * *

She glanced back over her right shoulder and could see the silhouettes of two men coming down the house steps.

Her left foot caught. She stumbled, and her face smacked into the barn's cement apron.

"Oof!"

Scrambling to her feet, she looked back and saw at least

three men in the yard. She ran inside the barn. To her immediate right was a food truck with the word *Tacos* painted on it. Past the truck there were stalls, and the barn's back door was partially open.

She ran to the last stall and ducked to her left behind the wall.

* * *

"Where is she?" Olson hollered frantically. "Where did she go?"

"Calm down! She hasn't gotten far. Now, what's out there?" Manuel asked, squinting through the fog and the darkness, the single light on the pole to the left providing the only illumination.

"Just the barn and some fenced areas."

"Where does this driveway go?"

"To the back of the property."

"Oof!"

Manuel held his hand up. "Quiet."

They heard footsteps.

Manuel sprinted in the direction of the sound and the barn emerged in the fog. Glancing back, he saw Olson right behind him and then Luis a few steps further away, while Ian was coming out the back door.

He stopped just short of the barn and listened. There was a small fenced area to the right of the building. The driveway swung around to the left. She couldn't have gotten far yet. Not in these conditions.

He gestured with his arms for Luis and Ole to spread out.

Olson went left and walked ahead along the gravel driveway, sweeping with his flashlight. To his right, Luis did the same, although he didn't have a flashlight. Manuel went straight ahead toward the barn.

* * *

The stall had shovels, rakes, and other tools and equipment stored in it.

She peeked around the corner of the stall. The men were talking to one another, their voices getting closer. They'd find her in here. The barn's back door was twenty feet away. It was open far enough for her to slip through and get into the woods.

Run for it.

She moved. Her left foot caught something. It was a shovel, tipping away from her. She scrambled to catch it with her left hand, but missed. It fell against an old metal washtub.

* * *

Bang!

Manuel pointed inside the barn. Luis doubled back toward him, while Olson kept going around the left side and down the road.

* * *

Oh no!

She took a step to run and froze.

Just outside the back door was a small woman in a black vest. She pointed to the chest of her vest. It said *Sheriff* in block gold letters across the front. She had a gun in her hand. Isabella locked eyes with her.

I know her.

She had seen the woman at the hockey arena last week, picking up Quinn from tryouts.

The woman gestured for Isabella to stop, and then for her to sit down.

* * *

Tori looked back quickly to see Braddock on the near edge of the road, covering her right flank. She peeked around the corner into the barn. A man had stepped inside and was slowly walking toward the back stalls. Another man stood at the front entrance.

She looked back to Braddock, caught his eye, and raised two fingers.

* * *

"Come on out now, *señorita*," Manuel called calmly in Spanish, stepping forward and pointing his gun at the stall on the left. "We don't want to hurt you."

* * *

"You're not hurting anyone!" Tori said, her gun trained on the man, and then louder, "*Police!*"

The second man stepped left, ducking behind the food truck for cover. The closer man's eyes shifted to her. His hand was resting loosely on the grip of the gun in his waistband.

She saw it, the snap calculation. Were there other police out there? Was he outnumbered? Could the two of them take her even though she had the superior position?

"Where are your friends?" he said.

His right hand rotated and tightened on the gun's grip, and

there was a subtle shift of weight onto the ball of his right foot so he could make a quick spin pivot.

In one motion, he twisted right and pulled his gun.

He never got a shot off.

Boom! Boom! Boom!

Pop! Pop! Pop!

Tori ducked back as the other man fired, the shots pinging off the corrugated steel of the barn walls.

Olson walked down the driveway. He was nearly at the far end of the barn, scanning for movement in the thick mist.

"*Police!*"

The voice was to his right, at the back of the barn. He moved forward.

Boom! Boom! Boom!

He saw the woman and pivoted toward her.

* * *

Braddock crouched to the left of the road, down in a depression, covering the driveway. He heard Tori call out: "*Police!*"

There was a delay, and he saw her brace herself.

Boom! Boom! Boom!

He sensed movement to his right. A man wearing a mask and carrying a gun was coming quickly down the right side of the barn towards Tori.

"*Police!*" Braddock called out calmly.

The man turned, his gun up.

Braddock fired.

Bang! Bang! Bang!

The man collapsed to the ground.

* * *

"Manuel? Manuel?" she heard a voice whisper. Manuel must be the man lying on the barn floor, his leg twitching.

"*Police!*" Braddock hollered.

Bang! Bang! Bang!

Tori glanced right and saw him moving carefully forward, his gun trained on whoever he'd shot. There were at least three men out here and two of them were down.

She took another quick peek around the corner. "Manuel is toast. Do you want to be next, Manuel's friend?"

Pop! Pop! Pop! Pop! Pop!

The gunshots rattled off the barn door. She was steeling herself to peek inside again when she heard footsteps.

She looked quickly round the barn door. The man was running. She glanced at Braddock, who nodded, then stepped inside the barn and moved quickly to the stable wall on the left side. Izzy looked over to her with frightened eyes.

"Stay right there. Stay down."

She stepped around the stall wall and used the food truck ahead for cover as she worked carefully forward.

* * *

Braddock reached the body lying in the gravel driveway. He quickly kicked the gun out of the man's hand and yanked back the face mask. It was Mark Olson. He was gasping for air, and even in the dark, Braddock could see three gunshot wounds to his upper torso. He left Olson and jogged ahead, calling Steak on the radio. "Where are you at, because we're taking on fire here."

"Not far. Right on you."

"Call an ambulance."

"For you?"

"Them."

"Them? How many?"

"Two so far. We're chasing at least one more."

He heard an engine start.

Tori heard the engine start and sprinted ahead to the front door of the barn, looking left. A white panel van was fishtailing around to race down the driveway. Braddock came around the corner of the barn.

Pemell heard a woman's voice yell "*Police!*" and then shots fired. He heard another yell and more shooting. Luis sprinted out of the barn.

"We have to get out of here. *Now!*"

He turned on his heel and started running toward the big white truck.

"No," Pemell said. "The van."

He tossed the keys to Luis, who got in and started the van. He pulled forward and then turned hard left around the front of the delivery truck, fishtailing before pulling ahead.

Boom! Boom! Boom!

Bang! Bang! Bang!

The two of them ducked as bullets rattled around the inside of the van.

"*Go! Go!*" Pemell yelled. "Get us out of here!"

* * *

"I don't think we missed," Braddock said as he and Tori jogged after the van.

"Yeah, well, they're not stopping."

They could hear a siren. It was close.

"Steak?" Braddock called over the radio.

"We're here."

"They're coming right at you. White van."

* * *

Luis sped down the driveway only to see an SUV with police lights come to a rapid stop ahead. Another set of flashing lights was not far behind.

"Shit!" He hit the brakes, then pulled the wheel hard left and spun the van around, taking off back toward the house.

* * *

"Will—"

"Here they come!" Braddock yelled.

He and Tori set their feet.

Boom! Boom! Boom! Boom!

* * *

"Oof!" The first shot hit Luis in the upper left shoulder, the second just below. He seized up.

"*Luis!*"

The van careened hard to the left. Pemell grabbed at the wheel and tried pulling it right. It was too late.

The van ricocheted off the trunk of a massive tree, then crashed into the house, caving in the siding.

Braddock and Tori slowly approached the van, which was listing hard right.

Steak came speeding up the driveway, lights flashing, another unit following them. Once they both stopped, they could hear more sirens in the distance.

"Well, shit," Steak said, getting out of his Tahoe. "That was exciting."

"That's one word for it," Braddock deadpanned as he approached the van and peered inside. Both occupants, Pemell and a Hispanic-looking man, were bloodied. The driver wasn't moving. Pemell moaned.

"Dispatch, this is Detective Williams," Steak called. "We have the scene secured. We require multiple ambulances and fire rescue at the call location." He looked to Braddock. "Where's Tori?"

* * *

Inside the barn, Tori stepped to the body of the man she'd shot. She hit him three times in the chest. She holstered her gun and picked up the shooter's gun, which she'd kicked away earlier, stuffing it into her coat pocket.

Then she walked to the last stall on the left and looked around the corner. Isabella was sitting on the floor, sniffling, tears in her eyes. Tori took a seat next to her, pulling her legs up to match the girl's posture. Isabella was in one piece, a bleeding scrape on her face, some blood on her hands, not to mention plenty of dirt streaks on her pants, top, and shoes, the clothes she'd been wearing since Wednesday.

"I've seen you picking up Quinn at the hockey arena," Isabella said softly.

"I imagine you might have. I'm Tori, Tori Hunter."

"I'm Izzy."

"Nice to meet you, Izzy. I'm an investigator for the sheriff's department, and the reason you saw me picking up Quinn is that I live with him and his dad."

"Is Mr. Braddock your ... husband?"

"Boyfriend," Tori said, smiling. "Izzy, all the bad men are ... done. It's over. You're safe now."

Braddock came around the corner. "How we doin'?"

"We're good, I think," Tori said, looking to Isabella, who nodded.

"Hi, Mr. Braddock."

"I'm sure glad to see you, Izzy. I see you've met Tori. She's pretty cool, isn't she?"

Isabella nodded.

"We're getting to know one another a little bit," Tori said, then gestured to the blood on the girl's face and hands. "Let's go get a look at those cuts and scrapes."

They walked Isabella to Steak's Tahoe, which was parked near the farmhouse. Steak saw them and rushed over, a broad smile on his face as he pulled down the tailgate.

"Hi, Izzy. I'm Steak."

"Steak?"

"That's what they call me. A few people call me by my given name, Jake."

"What should I call you?"

"Whatever you want, kiddo." He grinned, holding out his fist for a bump, which Izzy returned.

"I like Steak. That's ... unique."

"That's one word for him," Tori muttered good-naturedly, while Braddock sat Isabella on the tailgate and fished out the first aid kit.

Eggleston made her way over, introducing herself to the girl and then pulling Steak and Braddock away for a moment. The situation was still fluid at the scene, with more officers and deputies arriving.

"It seems like a lot of people were looking for me," Isabella said.

"From the moment you were taken," Tori agreed as she evaluated the girl's bloodied hands and then the scrape on her face which looked almost like a skid mark. "How did you get this one on your cheek?"

"I fell when I was running to the barn."

"Ah," Tori said as she dabbed at it gently, keeping things light. "This is nothing bad. Just a little cut that will heal up nice. No big thing, chicken wing."

Isabella smiled.

Her right hand was scraped too, with a couple of deep cuts, though it didn't appear any stitches would be needed. She also had multiple splinters in the index finger of her right hand. One looked gettable, as the end of it was sticking out. Tori retrieved a pair of tweezers from the first aid kit. "Hold your hand still for me."

"Okay."

She pinched the end of the sliver of wood and pulled it out with the tweezers, then cleaned the wound with a wipe.

"It stings."

"Feels good, though, doesn't it, to get it out of there," Tori said. "Can I ask you a question?"

Isabella nodded.

"Did anyone harm you?"

She didn't respond.

"Honey, did they touch you?"

She shook her head.

"Nobody ever touched you? Either here at this house or the

other place they were keeping you? You can tell me. It's important that we know?"

"No," Isabella replied firmly. "I was left alone. Nobody touched me that ... way."

Tori started working on another splinter, using a wipe on the area, creating some softness in the skin. "Did they ever say anything to you?"

"Not much really," Isabella replied, watching as she poked about with the tweezers. "They did talk to me," she looked over to the house, "in the basement. A man spoke to me in Spanish."

"In Spanish?" Tori replied, looking up. "What did he say?"

"He asked why I was sitting on the plastic tub."

"Did he say anything else?"

"He said something like: 'She'll do.' And then the other man said: 'Shall we finish?'"

"She'll do. And shall we finish?" Tori repeated, confirming she'd heard it correctly.

Isabella nodded. "I don't know what they were talking about."

"Not sure I do either, but I will find out." Tori switched gears, putting on a smile. "Let's talk about something fun."

"Like what?"

"The party at our house next Saturday. Still think you're going to want to come over with your friends?"

"Yeah." Isabella nodded. "If Mom and Dad will let me."

Tori chuckled. "I can guarantee you one thing. It'll be plenty safe."

"Will you be there?"

"Of course. And Mr. Braddock too."

"And my mom and dad?"

"You bet," Tori replied. She used the flashlight from her cell phone to examine the girl's finger a little more closely, and saw two other splinters, but they looked to be in deep and would take some time. "I don't think I can get these other two out right now," she said. "But I bet I know a doctor who could help with that. I hear she's great with kids."

Isabella smiled and nodded.

Tori swiped into her contacts, then put the phone on speaker.

"Hello?"

"Luciana, it's Tori Hunter. I have someone who would like to say hello."

"Hi, Mom."

"Izzy? *Izzy!*" Luciana screamed. "Sam it's Izzy. Honey, are you okay?"

"I'm okay. I'm with Tori and Mr. Braddock."

"Izzy!" It was Sam. "Is that you, little girl?"

"Hi, Daddy!"

TWENTY-SEVEN

"I SENSE SOMETHING VERY NEFARIOUS WAS AFOOT HERE"

It was a man-made version of the Northern Lights as the kaleidoscope of blue, red, and yellow police lights filtered their way through the blanket of wispy fog and cool, dense early-morning air.

A whir of activity hummed around the crumpled cargo van and the caved-in side of the house. The front wheels were off the ground and the van dangled precariously to the right. Volunteer firemen were working to stabilize it with ropes.

Braddock caught Tori's eye and nodded.

"I'm going to talk to Mr. Braddock. I'll be right back," she said, patting Isabella on her leg.

"Has she said anything yet?" he asked.

"She says she was never touched in *that* way," Tori answered, glancing back to Isabella sitting on the tailgate of the Tahoe.

"You think she's telling you the truth on that?"

"Yes, I do. She said two men came down to see her in the basement here. One spoke to her in Spanish and then said: 'She'll do.' And the other said: 'Shall we finish?'"

"That sounds like a transaction."

"Maybe a sale," Tori agreed. "Did the other ambulance leave?"

"Yeah. Olson was unconscious, lots of blood loss, very pale."

"Thoughts and prayers," Tori replied sarcastically. "Although I'd like to ask him some questions. How about those two? Are they going to survive?"

"Pemell will. He's conscious, coherent, moaning in pain and holding his left arm, which is almost certainly broken. Once the van is stabilized, they'll get him out. The driver, like his cohort in the barn, is dead. You and I hit him multiple times. One went through his throat. I'm thoroughly devastated."

"I can tell. Those two are new players in this, though. Who are they?"

"We'll find out in time. For now, I'm wondering if we can close a case from earlier today," Braddock said.

The two of them walked back to Isabella, and Tori sat down next to her. "Izzy, we have a couple more questions."

"Okay."

"Did you get away from your captors at the cabin yesterday morning?"

"Yes," she said, nodding.

"Can you tell us what happened?"

Isabella described her escape from the house, and running out to the road.

"I got to the end of the driveway and saw this truck coming. I yelled and waved as it drove by. It passed me and then it stopped." She was speaking in almost a whisper. "The driver, she looked at me and it was like she … she …"

"Recognized you?"

Izzy nodded. "They … shot her. She went down and was looking at me. The look on her face …" Her eyes teared up and she leaned into Tori, who wrapped her arm around her. "I kept running, down the shoulder. I heard another ... gunshot."

Braddock closed his eyes, knowing that was the one that had finished Teague off.

"I was going to try to get through a barbed-wire fence and run for the woods, but one of the men caught me. He wrapped me up and threw me into the back of a black SUV. And then they put me back in that ... room. I didn't see anyone else for hours until they brought me here."

"You don't need to say any more right now," Braddock said, taking a knee in front of her. "You were very brave. And ingenious. A sink stopper?" He smiled. "Really?"

"Brilliant, Izzy," Tori added.

Isabella nodded. "Why was my uncle George's friend there?"

"Was that a woman?" Braddock asked. "Jamie? Jamie Vaughn?"

"Yes. I couldn't remember her name earlier. Jamie. That was her."

Tori and Braddock shared a quick look, and Tori shook her head. Now was not the time to talk about George Santo.

"Izzy, we're still trying to figure that all out," Braddock demurred quietly, and then turned and looked down the driveway to see a set of headlights approaching. "In the meantime, I think someone is here to pick you up."

Luciana was out of the car and running to her daughter before Sam had even stopped. "Izzy! *Izzy!*"

"*Mom!*" Isabella exclaimed, jumping off the tailgate.

Luciana wrapped her daughter in her arms, closing her eyes. Carson was there too, and gave his sister a hug. And then Sam embraced her, picking her up and squeezing her tight, kissing her on the forehead.

Tori and Braddock sat on the tailgate and took in the reunion.

After a minute, Sam Farner stepped away from his family and approached them.

"About earlier at your house, Sam," Braddock said. "I'm sorry ..."

Sam stuck his hand out. "Thank you. That's all that needs to be said here. Nothing else but thank you."

Braddock nodded and shook the man's hand.

"And tell me ..." Sam looked back to Luciana before asking quietly, "my brother-in-law?"

Braddock shook his head. "I'm sorry, Sam, he didn't make it. He was killed by the people who took your daughter."

Sam nodded. "That damn fool." He looked over to the ambulance, where Pemell was being treated. "Is that man responsible?"

"Not for your brother-in-law's death, but he was involved in all this. It's too complicated to explain right now and we don't have all the answers just yet." Braddock glanced at Luciana, who was now in doctor mode, looking over her daughter. "Do you need me to tell her?" he asked in a whisper.

Sam shook his head. "Let me. After you two left, we were both resigned to the fact that something very bad was going to happen tonight. George sealed his own fate. We have Izzy back. I'll take that." He exhaled a long sigh. "Can you tell us how it all ... happened when the time is right?"

"Yes, of course."

Sam patted Braddock on the arm and then stepped over to Tori, shaking her hand, clasping it with both of his. Luciana, still kneeling and hugging her daughter, looked to Tori and mouthed a thank you. Tori nodded back.

Once the family had left, escorted by a squad car, Steak strolled over. "Does seeing that ever get old?"

"No, my friend," Tori said, stepping in to accept a congratulatory bear hug from one of her oldest friends. "That part never, ever gets old."

Deputy Frewer approached. "Will, we have media trucks down at the end of the road now. Our local guys and two from down in the Twin Cities. Somebody should go and say something, make sure they get the story right."

"Okay, I'll handle it," Braddock said wearily.

Tori reached for his hand. "I'll go with you."

The statement made and a few questions answered, they made their way back up the driveway. Steak was waiting.

Pemell was still lying on a stretcher, his left arm stabilized in a sling, his right wrist secured to the stretcher. "He ain't going anywhere," Steak remarked. "We'll have a deputy in the ambo with him, plus an escort. But listen, I want to show you two something now that we can get in the house."

He led them behind the van, up three steps and into the house. Eggleston was standing watch.

"Well now," Braddock murmured at the sight before him.

"That's certainly a payday," Tori said.

On the table in the dining area were stacks of hundreds, fifties, and twenties. It wasn't a massive drug-bust-size collection of cash, but it was sizeable, nonetheless.

"The absence of poker chips tells me they weren't playing cards," Steak said with a grin.

"A rough count looks to me like three hundred grand," Eggleston noted. "Give or take."

"The transaction," Braddock said.

"Yeah," Tori replied, then turned and left.

"Now where is she going?" Steak said.

"Good question," Braddock replied, turning to follow. He caught her outside. "What is it?"

"The delivery truck. Look at the back of it."

The rear door was partially raised. Braddock jumped up on the bumper and pushed the door the rest of the way up. Inside the cargo area were stacks of cardboard boxes, but to the right side a rough pathway had been cleared. She peered along it. "What the ..."

"What do you see?" Braddock asked, falling in behind her.

"Something." Tori tapped on the flashlight app on her phone and followed the path. "Would you look at that."

On the back wall, a panel maybe five feet wide and three feet tall was loose and ajar. The two of them pushed it all the way up until it locked in place. Behind it was a hidden compartment.

"That's not a lot of space," Braddock said, scanning with his flashlight.

The compartment was narrow. For a full-grown adult it would be incredibly cramped. Less so for someone of Isabella's size. Inside it was a thin pad to lie on.

"There's venting in the sides for air," Braddock pointed out.

"They were going to stuff her in here," Tori observed. "I'm guessing she was going on a long journey." She lifted up the pad. "What do we have here?"

There was a handle underneath. Braddock pulled up on it, and the floor of the compartment lifted. "Hello!"

"Jackpot!" Tori said.

Now they had their drug-seizure-like money. The entire compartment was jam-packed with wrapped stacks of notes, except for a narrow section along the top.

"I bet all that money on the dining room table would fit right into this missing strip here."

"Indeed. How deep does this go?" Braddock wondered as he pulled out five money bricks. "It looks pretty deep."

"I sense something very nefarious was afoot here."

"Now why would you think that?" he quipped.

"Point being, all this money, and then they were going to stuff Izzy in here and take her. And that leads me to another thought."

Eggleston called inside. "The ambulance is getting ready to leave."

"Hold them," Tori bellowed.

She jumped down out of the truck and hurried to the ambulance, climbing inside and sitting next to Pemell on the right-hand bench.

"I just saw the compartment in the back of that delivery truck," she said in a low, biting voice. "We have you on kidnapping and human trafficking, and that's before we even count the money in the house or the millions stuffed in the hidden compartment of the truck. Did you know that federal kidnapping is a potential life sentence?"

Pemell stared straight ahead.

She leaned in. "It gets better. There are lots of dead bodies as part of all this. Did you know that if someone is killed as part of a kidnapping enterprise, under federal law, the death penalty applies?"

His eyes shifted to her.

"Now, maybe after tonight, you want to die. I could certainly understand that. Your life as you know it is over." She sat back and exhaled a breath. "But if you don't want to die, then think about what other information you have that interests me. And I'll give you a hint." She leaned in again and whispered in his ear. "Helena Hernandez. Joey Martinez. *That's* what interests me."

TWENTY-EIGHT

"TAKE THE WIN"

Braddock unlocked the back door to their house just after 8:00 a.m. They fell onto the bed fully clothed and crashed.

When Tori's eyes fluttered open, she looked to the night-stand clock. It was 1:33 in the afternoon. One wise thing she had done before she went to sleep was to completely shut off her phone. When she powered it up, she found that it had blown up with text and voicemail messages.

The story of Isabella's return had made its way to cable news, which had triggered messages from her old Bureau friends in New York City. Tracy Sheets in particular insisted on getting all the details. Tori would have to give her a call.

There were two messages from Reese. The first said simply: *Olson dead. Died in surgery.* The second reported that Pemell had been treated and placed in a hospital room to recover, under heavy police guard. That could wait.

She showered quickly and dressed in a navy-blue FBI hoodie and black yoga pants. Hungry, she opened the refrigerator and smiled. Inside were two plastic containers of Mary's homemade chicken noodle soup, along with a little sticky note: *Congratulations and well done! Love Roger and Mary.*

Tori emptied one of the containers into a saucepan. While the soup warmed, she went to the deck door and peered outside. It was a picture-postcard day, the yellow, oranges, browns, and reds of fall in full august bloom.

The soup heated, she ladled some into a large black ceramic coffee cup that had *Friends* stenciled on it, like from the TV show, grabbed the red and black plaid fleece blanket off the back of the couch and walked down to the dock, taking a seat on one of the Adirondack chairs at the end. There was a gentle refreshing breeze that made for a light roll of waves on the lake. The crisp fresh air revitalized her as she breathed it in, the blanket wrapped around her legs. She scooped up a spoonful of soup and savored the flavorful taste. The day was gorgeous, so much so that she took a few photos: the colors of the leaves, the crystal waters. She sent a photo to Tracy with a text note: *Resting and recovering. I will call you in a day or two.*

There were footsteps behind her. She looked back and smiled. It was Quinn coming down to the lake. Roger was at the top of the hill, and he gave a wave before walking back to his pickup truck.

"Hey there, buddy," Tori greeted.

Quinn sat down in the chair next to her. "You look a little tuckered out."

She smiled wanly back. "I am a little tired. I could have slept another four or five hours, but then my schedule would be all messed up." She reached over for his arm. "How are you?"

"I'm okay."

"Yeah?"

He nodded.

He sounded good, and children were often far more resilient than adults gave them credit for. Yet she knew that she and Braddock would have to keep a close eye on him. He'd had nightmares once about the abduction attack. And then there was last night. Her experience told her that that would haunt him. It was going to haunt her. "How does your body feel? The ribs?"

"Not very sore," Quinn said.

"Meaning they still hurt." She smiled. He was a typical kid, impatient when it came to having to miss out.

"They're better, though."

"You want to get back to hockey, I bet."

"Yes," he said. "I don't think Dad will let me yet, though. Unless ..."

"Unless what?" She knew what was coming.

"You convince him."

She smiled and shook her head. "Nope."

"Come on," Quinn pleaded good-naturedly, knowing his gambit had failed.

"Hockey isn't going anywhere. Just let yourself heal. You'll be back on the ice soon enough."

He nodded and looked toward the house. His dad was making his way down to the dock in jeans and a black flannel shirt, a cup of soup in his hand as well.

"Isn't Grammy's soup fire?" Quinn said. "I had some before Grampy brought me home."

"Yeah, it's ... fire," Braddock said as he tousled his son's hair and then leaned down and kissed Tori. "Sleep good?"

"Yeah. Did you check your phone?"

He nodded and sat down in one of the chairs. "It can all wait until tomorrow."

"What's on your phone?" Quinn asked.

"Case stuff, bud."

He nodded. "Why was Izzy taken?"

Braddock looked to Tori.

"Well, your dad and I, we know some of the answers," Tori replied, looking Quinn in the eye. "But not all of them. Not yet. And until we do, it's probably best we leave it at that for now. Okay? The important thing is she's home and safe and she'll be okay."

Quinn nodded.

They sat out on the dock talking for a while, until Braddock suddenly remembered that the Vikings and Packers game was on. The three of them went back inside and watched the game in front of a roaring fire, then ate a late dinner, returning to their usual routine.

Hang on! Hang on!

The dense trees stared her in the face. She turned the wheel hard into the SUV, pushing against it, careening and bumping, the left turn coming. She had to get ahead of the SUV or they were all finished.

Boom! Boom!

The shots whooshed by, shattering the dashboard touchscreen and puncturing the glovebox. Quinn's eyes were wide in fear, his look terrified.

Boom! Boom!

Tori's eyes burst open. The ceiling fan whirred above. Her body was drenched in sweat, her nightshirt clinging to her.

"*No! No!*"

Was she awake? Was this a nightmare within a nightmare?

"*Noooooooo!*"

She was awake. It was from down the hall. Quinn.

"Will, *Will!*" She flipped off the blankets.

"What?" he said sleepily. "What is it?"

"Quinn."

"*No! No!*"

His eyes burst open.

She jumped out of bed, grabbed her bathrobe and pulled it on as she rushed down the hall, Braddock right behind her. She pushed open Quinn's bedroom door and flicked on the light.

Quinn was sitting up in bed, panting hard, looking frantically around the room as if he was disoriented. She couldn't tell if he was awake or still in the nightmare, or some combination of the two.

"Hey, hey, hey," Braddock said, clasping his son's shoulder, steadying him. "Easy, you're okay, you're alright. We're right here."

Tori went to the bathroom and drew a glass a water, returning to the side of the bed and handing it to him.

Quinn took a drink, still breathing hard, his body drenched in sweat. "Dad, they were shooting at me." He turned to Tori. "They were shooting at us."

Braddock pulled a chair to the side of the bed, kicking his feet up as Quinn eventually drifted off.

"You go sleep," he said as he sprawled in the chair. "I'll be good here."

Tori opened Quinn's closet and found a light blanket, then covered Braddock, kissing him on the forehead.

Her alarm went off at 5:45 a.m. Pushing herself out of bed, she pulled on her workout clothes, then tiptoed down the hallway and looked in on Quinn, who was still sleeping. Braddock was sitting sideways in the chair, wrapped in the blanket.

She went to the basement and got on the exercise bike for a grueling forty-five-minute class, pushing herself to exhaustion, her forehead drenched in perspiration, as if she could sweat out her nightmares. That wouldn't work, of course, but at the same time, normality would be helpful. Braddock was on the same program, taking over the bike when she'd finished. At 7:30, they were both in the kitchen, showered and ready for the day, when they heard Quinn start puttering around upstairs.

"What do you think? School?" Tori asked. The middle school started at 8:30.

"Let's see what we get when he comes down."

Quinn came into the kitchen dressed in school clothes, with his backpack, looking ready to go. Normally one to say you go to school unless on your death bed, Braddock spent some time questioning and evaluating.

"I just don't want to sit at home," Quinn said after several inquiries. "If I don't feel well, I'll call and someone can pick me up."

"People are going to ask what happened. You ready for that?"

"My friends already have." He held up his phone, giving his father the "where have you been?" look. "I've been talking to them all along."

"Even about Saturday night? I mean, there was the nightmare last night. You were pretty upset."

Quinn nodded. "Pete's going in. I just want to go to school. I just want to play hockey."

Braddock looked over to Tori. "What do you think?"

What Quinn wanted was what she wanted, which was to get back to normal. Whether or not he was capable of making a conscious decision to put it all behind him, that was the desire he was voicing.

"Like he said, he can call."

"Okay, we'll give it a go," Braddock said. "Let's get this kid some breakfast. But hockey? That's going to have to wait a little longer."

"Ah, Dad, come on."

"Take the win."

Quinn exhaled a sigh. "Okay."

Braddock and Tori drove Quinn and Peter to school. There was a common area in front of the main entrance. Their group of friends were waiting and encircled them both, offering knuckles, smiles, high-fives, waves, talking with them as they walked into school together.

Tori smiled. "Those two are going to be surrounded all day by their buddies. They'll be just fine."

"It was a pretty bad nightmare," Braddock said cautiously. "And probably not the last one. But if we're limited to some nightmares and nothing else after all this ..."

"That's a win." Tori nodded, thinking of her own sleep experience.

Her phone alerted her to a text. "Zagaros wants to have a call in fifteen minutes."

"Special Agent Zagaros, top of the morning to you. What's new?" Tori greeted.

"Lots, thanks to you two. Do you go hunting for trouble, or does it just know where to find you?"

"We hunt down the people who bring the trouble."

Zagaros laughed. "This I know. The Bureau, with the assistance of Homeland Security, has now identified the individuals you hunted down. Luis Garcia and Manuel Moreno were couriers based out of Panama, although they were natives of Colombia. They were known to work with the drug cartels in northern Colombia that operate close to the Panamanian border."

"Couriering what?" Tori asked. "Clearly money, given the just over $12.5 million in their possession."

"Drugs, given the cartel connection?" Braddock asked.

"Possibly," Zagaros replied. "They each had one drug charge and did time for it, but that was fifteen years ago. No others since, and there were no signs of drugs found in that truck. However, as couriers, they could have moved a lot of things."

"Human trafficking?"

"They were never caught doing it, but obviously given what happened over the weekend and what you found in that truck, it is entirely possible. Cartels, among others, have engaged in it. They could have had a wealth of knowledge far beyond what happened to the two missing children. It's too bad one of them didn't survive. We might have learned something."

"Our sincere apologies," Braddock said sarcastically.

"They got what they deserved," Zagaros replied. "As for those two men, we're pretty sure that their real names are Garcia and Moreno, but they have several aliases and they'd been good at avoiding detection. They haven't registered on anyone's radar in a long time, perhaps as much as five or six years. However, with the identities you found on them, it is apparent that they've been operating all along."

"Operating all along, so—" Tori started.

"Yes, Tori," Zagaros replied. "Your theory may be right. INS tracked Garcia and Moreno's passports, or the entry of the Castillo and Rijo passports, back the last ten years. They were both in the country during the windows of time you asked about nine and six years ago respectively, and crossed the border south within two days of the abductions of Helena Hernandez and Joey Martinez. You took out a couple of pros here," he added. "It's important you know all that."

"Why?"

"Because the U.S. Attorney's office is taking the case against

Pemell. Pemell's lawyer called an hour ago. He wants to talk. Now, my question is, why would he be so gung-ho to do so?"

"Well, I may have jumped the gun a bit on Sunday at the farmhouse," Tori said, explaining her threat of the death penalty. "I wanted to get him thinking."

"And you think he knows where these two children are?"

"Possibly. Have we developed any new evidence for that? No, but if he did this one ..."

"He did the others," Braddock finished.

"He wants a deal," Tori said. "And he has information we need. The question is whether that information will be enough."

"Typically, we like to ... scheme things like this out a little more, but when a defendant is eager to talk, well ... you let him talk," Zagaros said.

Pemell was transported from the county jail to the government center, and he and his lawyer were placed in an interrogation room. Tori and Braddock observed him through the one-way mirror.

His left arm was slinged tightly to his body. He looked uncomfortable. His face was bruised and battered, and he had bandages on both hands. He was far from the cocksure, in-control arrestee they'd confronted less than a week ago.

Assistant U.S. Attorney Louise Cullen had driven up from Minneapolis to join them. She planned to sit in on the interrogation. "The kidnapping is your case," she stated. "But I'm curious what else he knows about these two couriers and whether he can provide us some information on that network that could be pursued."

"Latitude on a deal?"

"If he has something worthwhile, we can talk."

Braddock opened the door and Cullen stepped inside, followed by Tori. All three took seats opposite Pemell. While Tori and Braddock sat forward with their hands clasped, Cullen leaned back and crossed her legs.

"Uh, we want to talk," Pemell's lawyer started. He was a local legal aid lawyer, more than competent to handle the usual crimes and misdemeanors of Shepard County. This, however, was a whole new level. "My client could be helpful on some matters of interest."

"I'm curious as to how your client could be helpful," Cullen replied. "But regarding the kidnapping, he'll need to satisfy my two colleagues here. And their satisfaction will be necessary before I even remotely consider any sort of ... accommodation." She turned to her right and nodded at Tori and Braddock.

"You're going to sit and listen for a few minutes, Ian," Braddock declared. "And then you will have some decisions to make. You weren't the one who took Isabella Farner from that park, but even after we interviewed you, we thought you had a foul stench of guilt about you."

"And now we know why," Tori said. "Because you knew that the people responsible for taking Isabella Farner were setting you up, and you and your pal, Mark Olson, thought you could flip the script."

"And in the process make yourselves a little profit. A sweet little plan."

"Until it wasn't."

"Now you sit here a physical mess, and worse, screwed. For life."

"He's being kind," Tori said. "He's assuming you have a life left. I'm pushing U.S. Attorney Cullen here to go for the needle."

"The girl didn't die," Pemell asserted.

"But Penny Teague did," Tori warned. "And that's a big, *big* problem for you."

"Who?"

"This is what I explained to you when you were on that stretcher in the ambulance," Tori said, her hands still clasped tightly in front of her, her intense glare boring in on Pemell. "You see, Isabella escaped her captors and got out of that cabin. She ran to the county road, where she waved down a delivery truck driven by Penny Teague. Unlike yourself, Penny was a Good Samaritan. She got out of the truck to rescue Isabella, but before she could, she was shot and killed by the kidnappers."

"Two shots to her chest. Then one to her head to finish her off," Braddock said. "And my guess is that you, or Olson, or both of you witnessed it."

Pemell shifted uncomfortably in his seat.

"You did, didn't you?" Tori said.

"Wow," Cullen murmured. "That's not good."

"You knew where Isabella was all along," Tori asserted. "You stood at your home and knew where she was. You sat in this very room with us and knew where she was. But rather than tell us, you saw a financial opportunity. You held all this in your back pocket as a get-out-of-jail-free card in case we arrested and charged you. But we didn't. You let it all play out, and Penny Teague was murdered. Plus we've seen the truck, the hidden compartment. We know the two men you sold Isabella to were taking her south, no doubt over the border. Along with a lot of money. We found just over twelve and a half million dollars in that compartment. Plus, whether we can yet prove you took Joey Martinez and Helena Hernandez, they're in the hopper too. Add it all up, and that, Ian, explains why you are hosed."

"You will be charged federally, Mr. Pemell," Cullen explained. "As Tori noted, the death penalty is in play. Can I win that kind of a penalty? My office is more than willing to try. What do we have to lose?"

"How do we get it off the table?" Pemell asked.

"Tori?" Cullen asked.

"I told you what I want to know, Ian. Helena Hernandez and Joey Martinez. Fess up."

"But that still leaves life in prison. That's a death sentence in and of itself," Pemell said, looking to the floor. "I might as well take the needle. Get it all over with."

"Yeah, well, you put yourself there, sport," Braddock said.

"What would it take for less than life?"

"The recovery of Helena Hernandez and Joey Martinez, alive," Tori said.

Pemell looked up. "And if they are?"

She bolted out of her chair. "Are they alive, Ian? Are those two kids alive?"

"Hang on, hang on," the lawyer interjected. "I need to speak with my client."

Tori, Braddock and Cullen waited in the hallway. "If they are alive, what kind of deal can we offer?" Tori asked.

"If we can get these two children back somehow, I've got some flex," Cullen said. "But not too much. There are multiple abductions. Penny Teague is dead. George Santo is dead. Heck, Fred Weltz was killed too. I know that happened before the abduction, but it was still after Pemell knew Isabella Farner was going to be abducted. Pemell's sentence will remain very long even if we do get the children back."

The lawyer joined them in the hallway. "Twenty years and he'll tell you everything he knows."

"Twenty years," Tori snorted, shaking her head. "Are you high?"

"Are they alive?" Braddock asked.

"He thinks they probably are."

"Probably? That's like a wish or a hope."

"He'll have to explain it. He thinks he can get you close, ninety percent of the way. But he wants his sentence down to twenty years, federal penitentiary and not maximum security. He didn't kill anybody."

"He abducted three children," Braddock asserted.

Cullen shook her head. "The best I'll even consider right now is if his information leads to us getting those children back, then I'll consider more leniency and things might work out for your client. It won't be twenty years, but it won't be life either. We're not banking on a wish and a prayer; your client will have to be the one hoping for that."

The lawyer went back inside. It was another fifteen minutes before he came back into the hallway. "He'll tell you what he knows, knowing there are no guarantees."

Cullen looked to Tori and Braddock. "Your show."

Back in the room, Tori dove in. "Are they alive?"

"I think they may be."

"May?" she retorted angrily. "What the hell does that mean?"

"Just hear him out," the lawyer pleaded.

Pemell sat back and closed his eyes. "Ole and I took them both. We did it for pay for the people Manuel and Luis worked for. But look, they weren't trafficked, at least not in the way you're thinking. Manuel and Luis wanted them for a family."

"Explain that."

"We were paid a hundred thousand for each of them, and then you know about the price for the Farner girl."

"Why was her price higher?"

"She was older. There was more risk because of my prior exposure, plus she wasn't from a broken family. We told them we'd only do it if we were paid triple. Otherwise ..."

"You'd have told us about it," Tori said, shaking her head in disgust. "These are children. Little kids you ripped from their families."

"Those first two were living in squalor with drug-addicted parents. I'm betting their lives ended up better."

"Oh yeah, Ian, you're just a fucking saint, aren't ya? Improving kids' lives everywhere."

Sensing her rising anger, Braddock subtly dropped his left arm under the table and lightly clasped her thigh.

She sat back and took a breath.

"How did you know you were being set up?" he asked.

"I noticed a tail for a few days, especially when I drove down to the farm about six weeks ago. That's when I called Ole in. He started watching and following them. We figured their plan when they got the blue van like mine. When they took her, I knew someone would see the van and eventually you'd show up at my door."

"So you went and got the oil changed and then drove it the one time," Tori said, nodding. "Your alibi was the van, which was pretty much infallible. That, and you knew where she was. Like we said, you could play that card at any time if you had to."

"Yes."

She was seeing it completely now, Dana Bryan's analysis coming to life. The narcissistic psychopath with no empathy or emotion for his victims. There was no conscience, no regard for these children. Isabella's family life was good, but for the right price, so what. Pemell spoke as if he were trading in one car for another.

"Tell us about this family Helena and Joey went to," she said.

"Manuel and Luis were connected with a couple of Colombian cartel families. The children were for one of those families. It's why the money was so good. The requirements were that they were Hispanic or Latin American, young and bilingual, English and Spanish."

"Why bilingual?" Cullen asked.

Pemell shrugged. "Ole asked Luis about it before we took the Hernandez girl."

"And?"

"Luis said the family needed them to be able to speak English and Spanish. Why? I don't know. We found those two and they could. The Farner girl too."

"And after you delivered Joey and Helena, where did Luis and Manuel take them?"

"Panama. That's where I think the family might have been."

"You think?"

"I know they said they had to get them there, but I almost got the sense that wasn't the end of the journey. It might have been that someone connected with the family would take them on from there, maybe to Colombia."

"Were Manuel and Luis involved in the drug trade?" Braddock asked.

Pemell nodded. "That's how Ole got to know them to begin with. He worked with a drug dealer in Grand Forks. He stored the drugs and the money for this guy in the trailer he lived in with Joey Martinez's mother. Manuel and Luis picked up the money from him. I got the sense they drove around the country and collected money from other places too, then drove it south."

"Do you know which cartel family the children went to?" Tori asked.

"No. I just know Manuel and Luis had connections with a couple, and one of them wanted those kids."

"Why did they want them? For what purpose?"

He shrugged. "All I know is that we were paid to get them. This time, Ole called when we figured out I was going to be set up, and made the deal."

"That's it?" Cullen asked.

"That's all I got."

Tori sat back and folded her arms. "That ain't much, Ian. They were delivered to Panama and from there to a cartel family somewhere. You don't know which family or where, or if those kids are even still there."

Pemell's shoulders slumped. "I can only tell you what I know."

"I wouldn't get your hopes up about a downward departure from that life sentence."

Tori picked up their dinner plates and took them to the kitchen sink. Quinn excused himself. Braddock poured them each another small glass of wine.

"Pemell's lawyer was right, as it turns out," he said wistfully as he swirled his wine glass. "He got us about ninety percent of the way there."

"Ninety percent is generous," Tori replied. "All we know is they might be with some cartel family in a country the size of Texas. And we still don't know, really know, if those kids are alive."

"Maybe we never will," Braddock said.

"The only way to whittle it down is that the two couriers were thought to work with cartels in northern Colombia. That doesn't really tell us much."

He nodded. "You know what. Let's put it away for the night, start a fire, relax and find something to watch."

"That works," Tori replied, just as her phone buzzed. It was Tracy Sheets. She hit speaker and answered. "Hey."

"You don't call, you don't write," Tracy started.

"Sorry, girlfriend. My bad."

"You've had an eventful week. I want to hear all about it."

"I'm going to need a lot more wine then," Tori said as Braddock smiled and started pouring.

They spent a half-hour filling Tracy in on the case.

"You shouldn't have to buy a beer all winter with Sam Farner around," Tracy said after hearing the recap.

"I got that going for me," Braddock agreed with a laugh.

"What about these other two missing kids, though?" she asked.

"You know, funny you should ask," Tori said, looking to Braddock with raised eyebrows. "I'm wondering if you might be able to help with that. You said you were working with a drug task force, right?"

"Yeah, I am."

"Do you have access to information on the cartel families, particularly those operating in northern Colombia? I'm not so interested in their drug activities as I am in the composition of their families. I want to know about husbands, wives, children, aunts, uncles, in-laws, anyone living under their roof."

"I might be able to get you something on that."

After talking with Tracy, Tori and Braddock relaxed on the couch and caught up on episodes of *Outlander,* a new Netflix favorite they'd stumbled upon and were binge-watching. Just before 10:00 p.m. Quinn stopped down to say goodnight. After he'd gone back upstairs, Tori drained her wine glass. "Do you want to watch another episode?"

"Nah," Braddock said as he stood up and went to the kitchen. "I have a better idea." He reached down and took out a new bottle of wine from Tori's wine fridge, a Cabernet. "I've been meaning to try this one."

"Don't you have to work tomorrow?" Tori asked, twirling her empty glass.

"I'm going in later, if at all," he said. "I've worked non-stop since last Wednesday. I can cut myself some slack. Especially without a boss to report to yet." He walked over and kissed her, then took her wine glass. "Why don't you go up and start the tub while I open this and pour you a glass."

"If you insist."

"Hmm," Tori murmured. "That feels so good."

The whirlpool tub was warm and sudsy. Burning candles on the ledge beneath the window lit the room moodily. Music hummed out of the small portable speaker on the vanity. Tori was leaning forward, taking a drink from her glass of wine. Braddock sat behind her and used a small carafe to pour water on her upper back, letting it slowly cascade down while he lightly caressed her silky-smooth skin.

"Do you think Tracy will be able to help you?"

"She has contacts everywhere. I have no doubt she'll find me the information I've asked for. Whether it gets me anywhere is another story. Those kids may be alive. I feel like I ought to try and exhaust every effort to find them."

They talked about Braddock's idea to expand the house, including the small bathroom they were luxuriating in.

"Right now, you've commandeered the whole vanity with your beauty stuff, so expanded counter space, dual sinks, and lots of drawers would be helpful."

"It isn't easy maintaining all this," Tori joked, gesturing to herself.

"And the shower is small. I'd like to put in more of a walk-in, with tile. No need for a door of any kind. Lots of space, dual shower heads."

Tori looked about the bathroom and realized that with ideas like these, everything would move: tub, vanity, and shower.

"I'd double the size of our bedroom, add in a gas fireplace."

"Sounds kind of romantic."

"That's the idea."

"If you expand the bedroom and bathroom, what happens to your office?"

"I'll move it. With an extension over the garage, there'll be room for one. I don't need much space."

"And what else goes over the garage?"

"A game room, bunkhouse kind of thing for Quinn to use with his friends. If I do that, I get some of the basement back. I was thinking of adding a small bar down there."

She looked at him. "This is quite the transformation you're thinking of."

"There's three of us now. We need the space. This would allow for a big walk-in closet," he added, leaning forward and kissing her lightly on the back of her shoulder. "You need that."

She grinned. "*We* need that."

"Yes, we need it."

"It's ambitious," she said as she slid herself back between his legs, resting against his chest, letting him wrap his long arms around her and kiss her neck.

"Do you like the sound of it?"

"Yes," she said, turning and leaning up to kiss him softly. "I love it."

"Then we'll do it."

They continued to sip their wine, relaxing, talking and touching, the candles flickering, the music soft, the water warm and soothing. Braddock's hands slowly started to wander and explore, initially leading to some playful giggles and then, after a time, to murmurs and purrs of heightening approval. Tori turned to face him, leaning in to kiss him, at first lightly and then more softly and deeply as she seductively slid her right leg over so that he could draw her to him, their glistening bodies gliding sensually together. "You know what?" she whispered breathily in his ear.

"Hmm, what?" Braddock replied as he gently kissed his way down the front of her neck.

"Monday nights don't usually end this way," she said, arching her back, running her fingers through his wet tousled hair.

"I got news for you," Braddock murmured as his kisses wandered below her neckline. "The night is far from over."

TWENTY-NINE

"WE HEAR THINGS. HE HEARS THINGS. TOGETHER WE KNOW THINGS"

December 22nd

Tori pushed her way in the back door of the house just after 2:00 p.m., a shopping bag hooked over her left arm. She dropped it on the center island, then went back outside and brought in two cardboard boxes that had been left on the back stoop, items she had ordered as Christmas gifts, one for Braddock, the other for Quinn. The one on her arm was for Mary.

Christmas.

After Jessie had gone missing and her father had died when she was a freshman in college, the Christmas spirit had left her. She had no family to spend it with, and when friends graciously extended invites, it only made her think of her sister and father. When she joined the FBI, she always volunteered to work on Christmas Eve and Day so others could have time with their families.

Until last year, when she was unavoidably swept up in Christmas with the Hayes family.

Braddock was fully aware of her Christmas hesitancy. To

him, it wasn't right, not anymore. "That's going to change," he'd said.

Yet she was nervous about spending it with the Hayeses, a large, gregarious, close family. She would be meeting some of them for the first time.

"I know you're nervous, but don't be," Braddock assured her with a big smile. "Christmas Eve at Drew's will be fun. The Hayes do it up right. Do you have an ugly Christmas sweater? It's required."

"How ugly?"

"If you want to make the right impression, you will find the ugliest Christmas sweater known to man."

Whether she met that standard was open to debate, but she did find herself Christmas sweater with reindeer on the front and bells sewn on it.

"What do you think?" she asked Quinn and Braddock.

"It's hideous," Quinn said.

"It's perfect," Braddock affirmed.

When she arrived, it was clear Braddock had laid some groundwork with his extended family. Everyone made a point of making her feel welcome. Drew and Andrea, whom Tori really liked, looked after her and kept her glass consistently full.

"Drew, I'm going to be hammered if you keep me going like this."

"Good," he said, throwing his arm warmly around her. "Let's get there together."

After casual drinks and a big dinner, there was the Christmas Eve white elephant gift exchange with the whole extended family, an event she went into warily but that turned into an absolute laugh riot. Her gift ended up being a huge silver cup with handles that was bigger than her head. Andrea had found it at a garage sale. Not long after she opened it, Drew took her glass of hot buttered rum out of her hand and poured it into the silver cup, along with his. "Let's see it."

"Drew?"

"Show us what you got, Hunter. Time to prove you can hang with the Hayeses."

The whole family was looking to her.

Never one to back down from a challenge, she took a nervous breath, tipped her head back and drained the drink in one long sip, a little dribbling off to the side of her mouth, down her cheek and onto her Christmas sweater. "Ahh," she said when she pulled the cup down to laughter and camera flashes.

The party was on. Before the night was over, everyone had been well served out of the silver cup. It was the first holiday cheer she had experienced in a long, long time. This year, she was really looking forward to Christmas. Her credit card charges were evidence of that, as she'd gone overboard on gifts, especially for Braddock and Quinn.

The two of them wouldn't be home for a few hours yet. She emptied the cardboard boxes. Quinn's gift was a new Minnesota Wild jersey. She wrapped and labeled it and placed it with the burgeoning pile under the tree. Braddock's gift was a big one, a new Movado Chronograph watch. She smiled as she examined it. He had admired this very model when they'd spent some time in a shopping mall in the Twin Cities while down there for one of Quinn's hockey tournaments.

She had just finished wrapping the watch when her phone buzzed. Tracy.

"Trace, merry Christmas. What's up?"

"Pack a bag for Colombia."

"Wait? What? Are you serious?"

"Yeah. You fly out tonight. I got you a meeting with Alejandro Pinzon tomorrow."

. . .

"Can I just say again how much I don't like this idea? I mean, I really don't like this idea," Braddock insisted as Tori waited for the go-ahead to board the FBI plane on the Holman Field tarmac in St. Paul.

"I'll be fine," she replied, not at all certain she would be.

She hadn't let the case go the past two months. Between Zagaros and Tracy Sheets in the New York Office of the FBI, she'd been able to build a dossier on the families of the Colombian cartels. Given that Helena and Joey had been delivered to Panama, she focused on those cartels operating in northern Colombia, close to the Panamanian border. After reading through all that Tracy sent her, plus some of her own research, one particular family drew her interest.

The Pinzon Cartel.

The patriarch of the cartel was Alejandro Pinzon. He was now thought to be sixty-two years old, but he still cut a rather dashing figure. His handsomeness, and no doubt his immense wealth, had drawn the attention of his second wife, Daphne. Twenty years younger than her husband, she had been a struggling model from Michigan. She had met Alejandro on a photo shoot for a budget clothing line in Panama fifteen years previously. Less than a year later, she was Mrs. Pinzon and had moved to the family estate in the coastal mountain region southwest of Cartagena to live a life of luxury.

Of particular interest to Tori was Daphne's mother, Donna, who suffered from an aggressive form of multiple sclerosis and required regular and increasing levels of care. She had moved with her daughter to Colombia, and from what Tori was able to learn, neither Daphne nor Donna had spoken any Spanish at that time.

"What if," she posited over dinner one night with Braddock a month ago, "that's where Helena and Joey ended up. Daphne's mom needs care and doesn't speak Spanish. You get young bilingual kids to come and help push her wheelchair, clean up, run errands, tend to her needs."

"Why not just find a couple of Colombian kids in the hills to do that?"

"They don't speak English."

"Teach them."

"That takes time. Why do that when you could just buy the help? Maybe Daphne and Donna insisted, and Alejandro agreed to keep his young, pretty and vivacious wife and his demanding mother-in-law happy."

"You're grasping at straws here," Braddock said.

"Come on, this is possible," she insisted.

"I see your logic. But riddle me this. How do you find out? And even if you do, even if you determine they are there, how do you convince a Colombian drug lord over whom you have no leverage to let them go? What do you have to offer him in return?"

Tori sighed. "Nothing."

"Then what are we even talking about here?"

"I could just go ask him."

Braddock chuckled dismissively.

"Why not?"

Her tone told him there was a seriousness to her question. "You're literally thinking of walking up to the front door, asking to see him, and if those two kids are there, pleading for their release?"

"With some finesse, why not? What is there to lose?"

"Your life."

She shook her head. "I've been doing my homework. The Pinzon family is partially legitimate, partially cocaine, and they're getting closer to the legitimate and further from the drug business. According to Tracy, they are one of the cartels that have a reasonable relationship with the Colombian government and the DEA. I'm not saying they wouldn't resort to violence, but in general they seem to go out of their way these days to avoid trouble."

"Other than the whole cocaine thing."

"Well, yeah."

Braddock put his fork down, wiped his mouth, and shook his head. "Kids go missing every day. It's a terrible thing, but it happens. We can't find them all."

"Your point?"

"These two kids, why do they matter so much to you? Is it that Helena's mom got to you?"

"What if it was Quinn or Peter or any of the Hayes nieces and nephews? Wouldn't you want someone to care? To exhaust every effort to return your child, especially if they knew where they might be or who had them?"

Braddock nodded. "Yes, yes, I would."

"Those kids matter too. Why not try?"

"I can think of a million reasons why not in this case," Braddock answered, but he knew Tori would not be dissuaded.

Now she was going to take her shot. A local DEA agent based in Cartagena had made an inquiry through a contact that someone affiliated with the FBI would like a chance to speak with Mr. Pinzon on matters unrelated to what the U.S. Government would usually be interested in. Tori's name had been provided in advance. A week passed before, surprisingly, Mr. Pinzon agreed to meet.

"Be careful, please," Braddock pleaded on the tarmac.

"I'll be back," Tori said. "I bought you and Quinn all kinds of presents for Christmas. No way I'm going to miss seeing you open them."

. . .

Once the plane took off, Tracy called and explained who would be meeting her. "Agent Cole Lloyd is a good friend of a friend and an experienced hand down there; he's been there for years, very plugged in. I trust him so you can too."

"Trace, am I crazy for doing this?"

She laughed. "Hell yes. Now find those kids."

The flight landed in Cartagena just after sunrise. DEA Agent Cole Lloyd was waiting for her in his weathered gray Jeep Cherokee.

"We're driving to the town of Pasacaballos. It's an hour or so away. When we get there, we're to go to a café, order some breakfast and wait."

"For what?"

"Your ride to see Señor Pinzon."

An hour later, Lloyd parked along the street and the two of them went into the café and did as they were instructed.

"From here, the plan is what?" Tori asked, sipping her coffee.

"You'll be picked up by two of Pinzon's men, who'll drive you to meet the man."

"At his home?"

"That part I don't know."

"I see," Tori said nervously.

"I don't think you need to worry, Special Agent Hunter. I've worked with these guys for some time. They're very cautious, but they're also reliable. They say they're going to do a thing, they do it."

"You'd jump in a car with them?"

"Yeah, I would," Lloyd answered confidently. "I have."

"Give me your read on Pinzon."

"He's pretty legit now."

"Pretty as in totally?"

"I didn't say that. He has a couple of pharmaceutical

companies down here that are legitimate. Of course, you use some of the same chemicals to make cocaine too. So he's still in the game some, although I think more as an ... ingredient supplier than a producer."

"I get it."

"To a degree, it seems as if he made his pile of money and decided to retire and enjoy it. He's not nearly the player he once was. And to protect that wealth and his family, he's created so many layers between himself and any drug operation, you could never really get to him anyway. For that reason, he hasn't been a primary focus of ours for years."

"Then how were you able to finagle this?"

"Business. On occasion, he lets us know about certain things. Or he might reach out if a rival or an upstart has been doing something that impacts him or any of his businesses."

"If you look the other way on something else."

"Or give him a heads-up if trouble is coming his way from someone other than the DEA or the Colombian government," Lloyd agreed. "We hear things. He hears things. Together we know things."

"A nice arrangement."

"It works. It's how things are done down here."

"And does he know what I'm interested in seeing him for?"

"Per your request, all we gave him was your name. Early yesterday, his man contacted me saying he'd agreed to a visit. You can expect that he has learned who you are and what you're about." Lloyd wiped his face with a napkin. "See the man at the cash register?"

Tori turned around slowly. A man in black jeans and a gray dress shirt, with black sport coat and sunglasses, stood at the counter, ordering from a server.

"There's another man sitting behind the wheel of the Land Rover parked across the street."

She slid her eyes left. "You know these guys?"

"José is at the counter. Diego is the driver. They are security for Señor Pinzon."

José looked over to their table and tipped his head.

"That's your cue. I'll be here waiting for you."

Tori walked out after José. Diego opened the back passenger door for her and she climbed inside the Land Rover. Diego got into the front passenger seat and turned to her. "Good morning, Special Agent Hunter. Our ride will be about fifteen minutes and I will take you to meet with Señor Pinzon."

Diego drove them through the town and up into the lush hills to the north, the narrow gravel road slicing through the dense mangroves. Tori noticed the attentive way in which both men watched the road and the woods they were traversing through.

"Should we be looking for something?" she asked.

"No," José said, turning back with a relaxed smile. "Nothing in particular, but this is Colombia. One must always be ... how shall we say? Vigilant."

They emerged from the woods onto a broad expanse of lush land. Tori had never been to a plantation in the States, but this had the look and feel of one. The view from the top of the rise was panoramic, out over the valley to the northwest below, the light blue waters of the Caribbean visible in the far distance.

The Land Rover pulled past a grand expansive two-story home to a lush garden at the back. Diego parked and then got out and opened her door.

"Please come with me," José said, waving for her to follow.

They followed a winding sidewalk through the garden. Señor Pinzon may have gone more legitimate, but he was taking no chances. There was security all about, men watching intently as she followed José along the path. They weren't the only ones around either. Over on a patio she saw a blond woman sitting with another woman in a wheelchair, seemingly having breakfast. Beyond that, she saw three children playing on a large jungle gym. Those were likely Señor Pinzon's youngest children. She knew that he also had five grown children from his first wife, who had died over twenty years ago from cancer.

Servants were about, all attired in white button-down shirts and black pants. Tori tried to see faces but couldn't really get a good enough look to identify anyone. Nobody registered as either Joey or Helena.

José kept walking toward a seating area under a wide gazebo. A man was sitting in a white wicker chair with a high back, reading a sheaf of papers, a tray with a coffee pot and two cups in front of him.

Twenty feet short, José stopped. "Wait here a moment, please."

He walked up to the gazebo and spoke to the man, then turned and waved for Tori to approach.

"Señor Pinzon, this is Special Agent Tori Hunter," he said, then took his leave to let the two of them talk.

Pinzon stood up and greeted her with a warm handshake. "Special Agent Hunter, a pleasure to meet you. Make yourself comfortable. May I pour you a coffee?"

"Please," Tori said as she sat down and gazed about. "Your home and the grounds are beyond beautiful," she remarked. "Magnificent really."

"Thank you," Pinzon replied with a smile. "Sugar?"

"Please."

"And the place seems to be filled with family. I saw children over on the playground."

"Sí. Those are my children with Daphne," he replied with a smile and handed her a saucer with her coffee cup. "My whole family will be here for Christmas in two days."

"I'm pleased to hear it. The holidays are a time for family," she said, and took a sip of the coffee. It was rich and smooth with just the right amount of sweetness.

"Good, yes?" Pinzon asked.

"Sí," she said before taking another mouthful. "I'm what you'd call a coffee addict."

"Starbucks?" Pinzon said with a crinkled nose.

"I'm an American after all, but this is wonderful."

"Special Agent Hunter—"

"I should note, I'm ... retired from the Bureau."

"It is their loss, I'm sure," Pinzon said, holding up the papers he'd been reading. "I've read of your exploits. You have had a very, how shall we say, eventful and successful career. Impressive."

"Thank you."

"And let's not engage in pretense here, my dear, I'm sure my name has cropped up across law enforcement over the years, including at your former agency."

"It has, but as you say, let's not engage in pretense," Tori said agreeably. "At least not on that."

"What makes me curious is why someone of your special expertise would wish to speak with me. Your interests would not naturally seem to intersect with mine."

"Then I'll get right to it. I was hoping you might be able to help me locate some people who have gone missing. Children."

"How terrible," he replied seriously. "But that is business in which you are very well versed and I am not. How can I possibly help you?"

"Señor Pinzon, I have learned that these children I'm looking for may very well be in Colombia, in this region of the country. I was hoping you could help me find them."

"If I can help, of course."

"You see, at the time they were taken, they were very

young." She reached into her backpack and took out a photo, placing it on the table, "Joey Martinez was seven, nearly eight. He's been missing for nine years now, abducted from a trailer park just outside of Grand Forks, North Dakota." She took out another photo. "This is his mother, Juanita. When Joey was taken, she was down on her luck, living in a trailer park, having some issues with drug use. That was then. Now, she's married, has an infant child, and manages a successful Mexican restaurant in Grand Forks, but would do anything to get her son back. It would make her ... whole."

"I see."

She took out another photo. "This is Helena Hernandez. She was eight when she was taken from a road outside the northern Minnesota town of Thief River Falls. This is her mother, Rosa. When Helena disappeared, Rosa was also down on her luck, living in a dilapidated house without running water, caring for two young children. It was a struggle for her. But after Helena was taken, she got herself on a better path. She's an emergency room nurse now in Fargo, North Dakota. She would love nothing more than to reunite her son with his sister."

"That is all so incredibly unfortunate," Pinzon said.

"A few months ago, another girl, this one aged twelve, was abducted in Manchester Bay, Minnesota. We managed to get her back, though."

"I see. That's good, yes?"

"*Sí,*" Tori replied with a smile. "But she was very close to being sold. We caught one of the kidnappers. The others involved are dead." She paused for effect.

"At your hand, Special Agent Hunter?"

"In part."

Señor Pinzon nodded. "Please, continue."

"The one who lived was also responsible for the abductions

of Joey and Helena. He has testified that he sold them to two men named Luis Garcia and Manuel Moreno. Garcia and Moreno are among the dead."

She looked for a reaction, but either Señor Pinzon had the best poker face ever, or the names genuinely didn't register with him.

"The survivor, a man named Ian Pemell, sold this latest girl to them before we intervened. We recovered the cash for the transaction. In fact, in a truck driven by Garcia and Moreno, we found a little over twelve and a half million dollars. Now, Pemell told us that these two men were going to drive the girl from Minnesota to Panama, where she was to be delivered to a family in Colombia." She looked Pinzon in the eye. "The requirements were that she be Hispanic and bilingual. Spanish and English."

She saw the briefest flash of knowledge in his eyes before he said, "I see. I ... see."

"These men were known to have some contacts within the cartels down here. My career has provided me with many contacts in United States law enforcement who were able to put me in contact with people who work in Colombia. They told me that you were a reasonable man, one they have a relationship of sorts with, and that from time to time you've done business together, providing mutual forms of assistance."

"We have."

"That's why I sought you out," Tori said. "As you noted earlier, many years of my career have been dedicated to finding missing children. For a long time it was an obsession. In this case, I'm just trying to help two people who deserve a second chance to get their children back and have a life with them. To make their families whole again."

"Do you have family, Agent Hunter?"

"By blood, I don't have any family that I'm aware of, but I've been very fortunate in the last eighteen months to be taken in by one."

"A second chance?"

"Yes. Maybe. I'm not married, and I don't know if I ever will be, but I live with a wonderful man ..."

"A Detective Will Braddock, as I understand it," Pinzon said with a smile and a nod. He wanted her to know he was well informed.

"Yes, and his son, who is twelve. He's not my own child, but I love him. I worry about him. I can't imagine the feeling if he was taken from his father, from us."

Pinzon let his gaze drift over to the playground. "Children are a gift," he said quietly.

"Señor Pinzon, I was hoping you could use your considerable influence to make some inquiries for me and see if perhaps we could find Joey and Helena and somehow return them to their families."

"And your government has sent you here on this matter?"

"No. My government helped me get to this point, but I am here of my own accord. I can offer you nothing in return for your help. I don't have that authority. As you know, I'm a former special agent."

Pinzon smiled. "There are retired former special agents, Special Agent Hunter, and then there are people such as yourself. You remain special. That's what got you here this morning, no doubt."

"It doesn't really change the facts, though. I don't have the capacity to reciprocate for any assistance you provide. Of course, if you were able to help, I would report that to the people who need to know, and I'd like to think it would be noted for ... future reference, shall we say."

Pinzon sat back in his chair, taking a thoughtful sip of his coffee. "Special Agent Hunter, how long will you be in the country?"

"Not long, *señor*. I expect to fly home tomorrow. We all want to be with family at Christmas."

"Of course." Pinzon stood. Tori did as well, and they shook hands. "Please, allow me some time to think on this today. If I can help, I would be very pleased to do so."

"That is all I ask," Tori replied. "I appreciate your time, Señor Pinzon."

"Did you see Helena or Joey at this estate?" Braddock asked as they talked on the phone, Tori sitting on her bed looking out the hotel window.

"No, I don't think so," she replied. "The place was really something, though. Security everywhere. I saw his three little blond-haired kids from Daphne running about. And I saw Daphne and her mother, who was in a wheelchair."

"Do you think Helena and Joey were there?"

"I don't know." She let out a sigh. "I looked about as best I could, but I didn't see them."

"And Pinzon? What did you make of him?"

"He was cagey. I had a hard time reading him."

"The subtle, non-direct approach didn't yield results?"

"It was hard to tell. It wasn't the first time he'd played heads-up poker with someone. He didn't give away much." She took a drink of her now warmish beer. "The only time I really saw any reaction was when I mentioned the requirements for the children to be Hispanic and bilingual. It was just the briefest of flinches, but otherwise ..."

"Stone face."

"Yes."

. . .

"Any commitment that he'd call you back?" Agent Lloyd asked. The two of them were having a *cerveza* in the small bar in the hotel in Cartagena.

"No," Tori replied.

"Did you feel like you got the brush-off?"

"No. My impression is that Señor Pinzon is a man who plays things close to the vest."

"He does at that," Lloyd said, and held up two fingers to the bartender. "It was worth a shot, Tori. You saw this all the way through. We'll see if the indirect appeal worked. How long do you want to give it?"

"If I haven't heard from him by noon tomorrow, I can probably head home."

Tori woke up and looked at her phone. It was 6:50 a.m. She must have had a few too many of those heavy beers. She grabbed the large bottle of water off her nightstand and swigged from it as she shuffled to the bathroom. There she filled the sink with cold water and repeatedly submerged her face. A good coffee or two would be needed to get her going.

As she walked out of the bathroom, her phone started buzzing on the nightstand. It was an unlisted number.

"Hello?"

"Is this Special Agent Hunter?"

She recognized the voice as José from yesterday. "*Sí*. It is."

"Go to the town of Santa Ana. It's an hour from Cartagena. There is a small café on the western edge of town, Restaurante Cecilia. Lloyd knows it. Be there by ten a.m."

"And then what?"

"You wait."

She called Lloyd.

. . .

Lloyd and Tori took a table inside Restaurante Cecilia. They stayed alert while sipping coffee and chatting about their government careers and pensions.

"I figure I have about five more years," Lloyd said. "Then I can retire in some style. You?"

"I'm semi-retired now," Tori said. "I inherited a fair amount when my father passed. I was his only living relative, so between life insurance, his investments, and retirement benefits, and investing all that smartly, I've been comfortable for a long time. I'm free to pursue what interests me."

"Like risky meetings with Colombian drug lords?"

She smiled. "Exactly."

"Sounds nice."

"These days, it really is."

His eyes slid left. "Tori, the front door."

She turned to see a thin boy with black hair, dressed in a white button-down shirt, black pants and black tennis shoes and carrying a small backpack. Right behind him was a shorter girl with long black hair in a ponytail, wearing a similar outfit. They both sat down on the bench inside the front door, their hands clasped on their laps. She did not recall seeing either of them yesterday, but they were wearing the same attire as the estate servants.

She gave it a minute before she stood up and walked over to them, kneeling in front of them and smiling. "Hello. My name is Tori." She showed them her Shepard County sheriff's department identification. She looked to the boy. "Would you by any chance be Joey? Joey Martinez?"

"*Sí*, yes."

"What is your mother's name?" She was sure it was him but wanted some confirmation.

"Juanita."

"And are you Helena? Helena Hernandez?"

The girl nodded. "Yes. My mom's name is Rosa."

Tori smiled. "I can't tell you how happy I am to meet you both. Would you like to go home?"

When they reached the airport, they immediately put Helena and Joey on the plane. The engines were humming to life and the door was closed. Tori made a quick FaceTime call to Braddock.

"Hey there."

"We got them."

"Wait? What? You did?"

"Yeah. They're sitting on the plane with me, drinking ice-cold Cokes and eating sandwiches." She turned her phone around and the two of them smiled and waved.

"My ... God."

She turned the phone back. "They're healthy. They look like they were treated well. They worked at the estate, served Daphne and Donna, but I'm reasonably sure Señor Pinzon didn't know the specific circumstances of how they came to be there."

"The indirect approach must have worked, though. That or you charmed the man."

"Or I gave him a graceful way out. Whatever it was, we have them back. The plane is taking off shortly. We're going to get out of here."

Braddock put his phone down for a moment.

"Will? Will, are you still there?"

"Yeah," he said, and she thought she heard a sniffle.

"Are you okay?" Hearing his emotion finally had her starting to feel it as well. "Will?"

"I'm good," he said, raising the phone back up so she could see him. He wiped at his eyes with the back of his hand. "I'm ...

just thinking about what a Christmas present this is for their mothers."

"Then make the calls for me. To Juanita and Rosa. To the police in Thief River Falls and Grand Forks. To Cullen and Zagaros. Steak and Eggs. Call everyone."

It was just after midnight when they landed back at Holman Field. The plane taxied to a stop. A small gathering of people waited on the tarmac near the hangar.

The plane door opened. Tori stepped out and then looked back inside. "Come on out. It's going to be a little cold."

Joey ventured out first. He reached back inside for Helena's hand and held it as they walked down the steps behind Tori. When they reached the bottom, Juanita and Rosa ran forward and embraced their long-lost children.

Tori watched as the joyous families reunited. After a minute, she made her way through the crowd, accepting thanks along the way. When she reached the other side, she was given a reason for tears of her own.

Braddock and Quinn were waiting for her.

She fast-walked right into Braddock, who wrapped his arms around her. "Look at what you did," he said softly, watching the Martinez and Hernandez families celebrate.

Tori glanced up and kissed him. "Why aren't you two back home celebrating Christmas Eve?"

"You're kidding, right?" Braddock said. "I had to be here for this."

"Besides, Grammy and Grampy cancelled tonight," Quinn said, sliding in for a sideways squeeze from Tori, at eye level with her now even though he was only twelve. After a moment, she decided sideways wasn't good enough. She wrapped both arms around him, holding him tight, her eyes closed.

"I feel bad that they felt they had to do that."

"Mary said it wouldn't have been right to have it without you. Not when you're ..." Braddock looked to the Martinez and Hernandez families, "Responsible for all this. Plus Drew said the white elephant exchange wouldn't have been the same after last year. He wants an encore. So we're doing it tomorrow night instead. I'm guessing you're going to be in a celebratory mood."

"Ya think," she replied with a big grin. She turned to look back at the reuniting families one more time, soaking it in for as long as possible. "Let's go home."

As the three of them turned to leave, Braddock wrapped his right arm around her, pulling her close, "I love you," he murmured in her ear.

Tori looked up and kissed him. "Merry Christmas."

A LETTER FROM ROGER

I'm grateful that you've taken the time to read *Missing Angel*. The kick I get out of writing is shaping a world for my characters. Whether it's Tori learning to let go of the past and live in the present, Braddock's navigation of her hang-ups and quirks, or Steak's various and sometimes ill-timed quips, I get to put myself in all their shoes and give them strengths, vulnerabilities, weaknesses, foibles, and uniqueness. Each time I write, I get to build on those and then expand on the canvas that is Manchester Bay, northern Minnesota, and the lakes country I've grown to love over my lifetime. I wake up each and every day thinking about that world, and I hope you enjoy reading the adventures of Tori and Braddock and the gang every bit as much as I do writing them.

If you did enjoy it and want to keep up to date with all my latest releases, just sign up at the following link. Your email address will never be shared, and you can unsubscribe at any time.

www.bookouture.com/roger-stelljes

One of the best parts of writing is seeing the reaction from readers, both those who have read all my books and those new to the scene. My goal every time I write is to give you, the reader, what I always look for in a book myself. A story that excites you, puts you on edge, makes you think, pulls at the heartstrings on occasion, and always make you want to read just one more page, one more chapter because you just couldn't put it down.

If you enjoyed the story, I would greatly appreciate it if you could leave a short review. Receiving feedback from readers is important to me in developing and writing my stories, but is also vital in helping to persuade others to pick up one of my books for the first time.

If you enjoyed *Missing Angel*, Tori, Braddock, and their friends can also be found in *Silenced Girls*, *The Winter Girls*, and *The Hidden Girl*, and in more stories to come.

All the best,

Roger

www.RogerStelljes.com

 facebook.com/rogerstelljesbooks

twitter.com/RogerStelljes

instagram.com/rogerstelljes